BLAZE OF PASSION

Jean LeClair hurried up the wide staircase of his Telegraph Hill mansion. There was much to do tonight. As leader of the Barons, Jean had to regroup them and stop the ravaging, burning and killing of the Rangers, who'd already set half the Barbary Coast afire.

But first, he thought, there was Amoreena. She brought out a side of him that he didn't know existed—a tenderness as well as a passion.

She had just finished her bath and was wrapped in a fluffy white towel. She was bending over, drying her long hair as Jean entered, exposing her slender legs and giving him just a glimpse of her firm derrière.

As she turned around, she did not seem startled to see him standing there. Pehaps she was still numb from the shock of her brutal rape at the hands of the Reverend Drummond, he thought, as she moved to sit on the edge of the bed.

"You smell as fresh as a spring rose," LeClair said. "I trust you are feeling better?"

"Much better, thank you," she said. "If it weren't for you, that horrible man would have killed me. As it is he . . ." She shook her head sadly. "I was saving myself for Beau, but now I have nothing to offer him or any man."

Jean moved toward her. "Wrong," he said. "Any man would be lucky to have you just as you are. I know I would."

She blushed, as their eyes met. Slowly, LeClair kissed her and she responded with passionate sighs as his lips moved down toward the most secret places of her body . . .

THE
BARBARY
COASTERS

Lee Davis Willoughby

A Dell/Emerald release
from James A. Bryans Books

Published by
Dell Publishing Co., Inc.
1 Dag Hammarskjold Plaza
New York, New York, 10027

Dell TM 681510, Dell Publishing Co., Inc.

ISBN: 0-440-00457-8

Printed in the United States of America

First printing—April 1983

1

SOUNDS FROM a honky-tonk piano echoed in Jean LeClair's ears as he approached the dark Montgomery Street alleyway that led to a flight of wooden steps descending from street level to the Pirates' Nest, a concert-saloon in the cellar.

LeClair knew the entrance well, even though it was nearly hidden in the littered alleyway, for he had built this and other dives along with several and varied enterprises since he had arrived in San Francisco thirteen years earlier. As he walked down the steps, he had to smile to himself. The man at the piano actually had talent. He played with an amazingly light touch and his voice was pleasant as well. It was worth paying a little more to get the best, he reasoned.

As LeClair opened the heavy planked door and looked inside the smoky room, he saw that in just one day the new pianist had substantially increased business, and that

5

was good. Profit without pain. That was his motto. Do whatever you must to make money, but keep a coin in the pockets of those who work for you—as well as your own. Jean LeClair was a hard man, but he treated his employees evenly and it had helped to make him respected by the denizens of the Barbary Coast, as well as feared, for he punished cruelly those who betrayed him.

Now as the tall, dark-haired man took a seat at a table in the saloon, his blue eyes scanned the rectangular room until he found what he was seeking. The room was large and low-ceilinged with a bar along one side, space for dancing on a polished hardwood oval at the center of the room, and a platform where the musicians played. Recently, the Pirates' Nest had acquired not only new pianist, but a fiddler, a trombonist and a clarinet man as well.

LeClair's eyes swept past them and the numerous patrons until they rested on a beautiful red-haired girl sitting alongside the wall. She was one of the many pretty "waitresses" who worked there, women aged from sixteen to forty, whose jobs were unique. They were an integral part of the system of the Coast's dives in that it was up to them to see that the male patrons of the saloons parted freely with their money. What they did to accomplish this might be construed to genteel folk as barbarous, but this was, after all, the Barbary Coast—and it earned its reputation as well as its name. Nowhere in the United States was there a place as corrupt, as sinful, as filled with vice.

LeClair as a young boy would have found the Coast fearsome, but not the grownup LeClair. The smile he had worn at seeing the girl faded at the thought. He was only what society had made him. What his *brother* had made him!

If evil in a man's heart could be placed on a scale and weighed, perhaps the least corrupt of the Barbary Coast's crime barons would be Jean LeClair. He was one of the few leaders still possessed with a "measure" of conscience. And that was surprising, considering his background.

Born Jean Louis LeClair thirty-four years ago, the younger half of a pair of identical twins, he met fate's cruel hand at an early age. The memory of what his twin brother Armand had done to him still rankled, and whenever he felt his conscience bother him, he'd simply focus on that horrible day twenty years earlier to explain his actions. It justified who he was and what he did. Not only justified, but fed and nourished his need for power. And revenge.

One of the pretty waitresses approached Jean. "A drink, mister?" she said.

"Bourbon," he said, and watched as she strode to the bar. She had a nice derrière, he mused, and wondered if she was new to the Nest. He saw rather than heard her order his drink and then nodded as the bartender saluted him. Jean scowled, noticing that the barman wore his hair in a new style—parted in the middle—the way Armand used to comb his.

He hadn't seen his brother Armand in twenty years and that pleased him, for he had sworn he'd kill Armand with his bare hands if he should ever meet him again. His scowl grew darker now as he recalled the gleam in Armand's eyes when he had convinced the British "bobbies" that Jean had done the murder Armand had committed. Armand had lied to the authorities, punctuating his report of what had occurred with tears and a convincing case of hysteria.

Jean had been to a fair in London earlier that day with Armand. Sons of an English mother and French father, poor commoners eking out a meager existence in the streets of Chelsea, the two boys grew up wanting—always with empty stomachs and heads full of schemes. But only Armand put into practice those schemes.

One of them, to lure tourists to a trick exhibition at the

London Fair, then rob them, ended in violence and murder. Jean had learned what his brother was doing, tried to stop him, but was too late. When Jean entered the exhibition booth where Armand had operated he found the body of a man lying in a pool of blood—stabbed in the back. Armand was nowhere to be seen.

Jean was about to leave to seek the police when he spotted Armand's pocket watch on the ground next to the body. It was an expensive watch their father had given Armand on his fourteenth birthday three weeks before, and Jean guessed it must have broken off Armand's watch chain. He had admired that watch on a number of occasions and admitted to himself that he was jealous his father had given it to Armand, though Jean understood why. Armand was the favorite of the two boys in the elder LeClair's eyes, because he gave part of the money he stole from merchants of Chelsea to his father. Jean wanted no part in the thievery and was, therefore, considered weak by his father.

Jean remembered all too well the shock and bitterness he felt when he opened his own birthday gift and found a watch chain—but no watch. "You'll have to steal the watch," they told him. Jean had wanted to take that chain and throw it at his brother and father to make them stop laughing, but instead he had done nothing. He'd hated himself each day thereafter for not taking action.

So on the day of the murder, with the watch gleaming in the day's last light, he made up his mind he'd possess that watch. He stooped down to pick it up. Just then the police broke in, with Armand LeClair in their custody.

"That's him!" Armand had cried. "That's me bloody brother, he is, and a thief and murderer, too! I saw him knife that man and now he's stealing the bloke's watch!"

There were four bobbies carrying nightsticks and their gaze fell upon the watch in Jean's hand. "Aye," one had said. "He surely has the watch. The lad's proven his guilt in me eyes."

Jean had protested his innocence, but it did little good. Armand had witnesses on his side—people he'd paid off with the money he had stolen—to swear he was with them during the time of the crime. Others testified at the trial a few months later that the boy they'd seen entering the booth was Jean LeClair.

Jean had been convicted by the English Courts and sent for life to a penal institution in Sydney, Australia. But when, after seven years of hard labor, the opportunity arose to break out of jail and steal aboard a ship bound for California, he did not tarry. He was determined to get revenge on the world, on his brother, his father, everyone or anything that stood in his way. He was embittered and hurt, and he fit in nicely with the lowlife swarming about the wharves and streets of the quarter of San Francisco then known as Sydney-town.

Now as the unpleasant memory of his past filled his mind, Jean closed his eyes and forced it from his thoughts. He had been nothing but a young hoodlum then. The years had smartened him, taught him not to "expect" anything out of life, rather to reach out and take it. He had, and now had an empire to prove it.

When he again opened his eyes, they were focused on a red-haired serving girl. She had been staring at him, and when their eyes met, hers were bold, saucy, and enticing. And well they should be, for she was his property. His private harlot. All the pretty waitresses were his, but this one was special. Although she had at first tried to hide her accent, Jean had recognized that she was, like him, an English exile. She, too, had buried her British past, but for reasons still unknown to him. On several occasions he had tried to get her to confide in him, but to no avail. She pleased him in bed, but would offer nothing of her mind or heart to him. He enjoyed her, though he did not love her, and after a while gave up trying to know her and contented himself with the pleasures she gave him. He didn't even know her real name, for she would never reveal it. She had come to him in rags two years earlier, hungry, frightened, and looking for work. On the grimy collar of her gown she had pinned a rose, pilfered, but fresh, and so he had dubbed her 'Rose'. He had fed and clothed her, and set her to work in his employ. She had proven one of the finest of his girls and he'd never regretted taking her in.

Now as the other waitress placed Jean's bourbon on the table before him, he noticed a man approach Rose. She stood up. Her short red skirt enticed Jean's eyes to travel down the length of her long legs clad in dark silk stockings. A filmy black blouse hinted boldly at her charms, and Jean suspected that the man who approached her was drooling, for it was hard not to. Although she was only eighteen, Rose possessed the full, ripe body of a woman twice her age and the face of a goddess. A goddess in heat, Jean thought, with a chuckle.

It was customary that if a patron wished to see more of the pretty waitress of his choice, he'd pay fifty cents for the privilege, whereby the girl would let him see all of her. The stranger handed Rose the coins and she led him to a closed booth at the rear of the hall and began to undress. Jean could not see what was taking place, but knew well what the stranger was witnessing. Rose was tall, her breasts full, her hips slender. Her hair fell in length to the middle of her back and there was a birthmark on her thigh. He sipped his bourbon, his thoughts lost in the remembrance of the first time he had seen her naked.

Since Rose had arrived for work at the Pirates' Nest an hour ago, she had shown her body to six different men, but it didn't bother her. Seeing was, as she had told Jean, not touching, and few men had touched her intimately since she had become LeClair's personal property. She was smart, and used her brains as well as her body and made her money without giving herself to the men who paid her. She knew that not far away in Chinatown the prettiest of the harlots had men waiting outside her door—as many as eighty to one hundred a night! They stood in lines with their money ready in their left hand, their hat in their right. It was a hop-on, hop-off proposition and Rose marveled that the men could pay for "sloppy seconds" and not mind the high risk of disease.

Two minutes later she was dressed again and back at her post by the rear wall. There she would wait for the "catch" of the evening—sodden seamen eager to spend money and too drunk to make love.

Now Jean picked his way through the crowd toward her. Although he owned the Pirates' Nest, hardly anyone, including his own help, knew him. A few trusted assistants did all the hiring, while LeClair spent most of his time running his varied operations from the mansion he had built high on Telegraph Hill.

As he reached Rose, his eyes fell upon the top button of her blouse which she had forgotten to fasten. He could see the creamy swell of her breasts, and he thought of the coupling they would enjoy in a few hours. "Come to the Hill later," he told her, as he pulled her up and whisked her into a dance. The "Hill" was what he called his mansion. "Around nine. Tonight's special. We're celebrating two years ago today, when you showed up at my doorstep."

"But I work till dawn," she protested, "and the sailors'll be coming. I hear the *Falcon's* due in sometime tonight. It's only six o'clock, Jean. There will be a lot of money waiting for the taking."

"Faye will have to make do without you," he said.

Faye Langlois, ex-prostitute, and now madam, in her early forties, managed part of LeClair's empire—the bagnios—and was in a sense Rose's boss. LeClair owned several large parlor houses and cowyards (four-story buildings divided into cubicles called cribs housing nearly 300 prostitutes under one roof) on Pacific and Montgomery Streets as well as in Chinatown. Faye had given birth to a daughter thirteen years ago; the father, one of the many "Ducks"—escapees from the penal colony in Sydney— who frequented the Coast's dives. Faye could never be certain who the child's father was. She had lain with six men, one of them Jean LeClair, a striking lad of twenty-one. She had enjoyed this union to the point of experiencing her first climax with a man. It was he, she believed, who had fathered her child. Although she never voiced her suspicion, LeClair knew there was a possibility he was the father of Faye's child and for years contributed generously toward young Monique's education at fancy boarding schools in New York.

But now he noticed the uncertain look on Rose's face and wondered that she could wish to stay at the Nest rather than celebrate at the "Hill" with him. "The worst Faye could do is fire you," he teased, "and she'd first need my approval. But if you'd feel more comfortable, I'll speak to Faye myself." Faye ruled her girls with an iron hand and Jean figured that must be part of what was troubling Rose.

Rose hesitated, her eyes on the men who had just entered the saloon. They were half drunk, stumbling into tables and chairs—easy prey. She'd have to work fast to separate those men from their money. "All right," she said to Jean. "I'll see you later."

He watched as she sauntered over to the newcomers and positioned herself on a man's lap, then shrugged and went to find Faye.

*   *   *

Out of the corner of her eye, Rose watched LeClair disappear into the hallway leading to the dens upstairs where Faye Langlois had an office. The dens were tiny rooms each containing a cot where the girls would bring men from the saloon. The men would pay Faye one dollar before engaging the girl of his choice.

Rose had brought men up there on a number of occasions, but cleverly avoided physical contact with them. It was because of her cunning and her ability to get money without giving of herself that Jean let her stay on at the Pirates' Nest. The usual wage for a pretty waitress was anywhere from fifteen to twenty-five dollars a week plus a commission on liquor sold, half the proceeds of her own prostitution, and half the fifty cent fee for a dance. Rose was paid differently. She kept all of what she earned from stripping and dancing, half from the sale of liquor, plus a weekly salary of fifty dollars. Any additional monies she managed to wangle out of the pockets of her prey was hers to keep. Some weeks she'd earn as much as four hundred dollars. She owed her good fortune to Jean LeClair and would do nothing to ruin it, even if it meant sleeping with him occasionally—a privilege she found only tolerable. Not that he wasn't desirable, for he had to be the handsomest, most intelligent man in San Francisco, a catch for any woman. It was just that she simply disliked the act of making love, and well she might, after what had happened to her back in England. Even to this day she could not think of it without nearly going to pieces.

Prostitution was a job to Rose, that and nothing more. She prided herself on her ability to keep her men at arm's length and made it a game each day to think of new ways to make them believe they had gotten what they paid for. On the rare occasions when she had no choice but to lie with a man, she'd wash herself thoroughly with hot water

and scrub her skin until it was red—then force herself to
forget the coupling as quickly as she could.

Suddenly she felt tears in her eyes and quickly dismissed the thoughts of her former life. She threw her arms
around the stranger's neck and bussed him lightly on the
lips. The taste of salty sweat made her reel, but she
managed a tight smile.

"I'll bet you got a big one," she said. "What's your
name, stranger? You from around here? A sailor perhaps?"

The man was heavy-set and balding. Three blackened
front teeth made his breath stink like the docks at low tide,
but Rose kept up her false smile. It's only an act, she told
herself. She could do or say anything as long as it was
simply an act.

"The name's McSween," he said. "Heck, I ain't no
sailor, but I sure wish I were. Hear tell they get to see lots
of pretty ladies in those foreign ports."

Rose lowered her hands to his jacket pocket, pretending
to caress his broad chest. "You're so strong," she said.
Her fingers found the bulge of a wallet and from past
experience knew by its size that it contained a lot of
money. "Want to dance?" she asked. The band was playing
a slow number.

"Can't," he said.

She smelled spirits on his clothes and guessed he had
been drinking at another saloon before entering the Nest.
"How about a drink then?" she said. "I'd sure love one
myself." He didn't answer, just stared lasciviously at her
breasts. She frowned. If he didn't dance and didn't want a
drink, what was he doing in a dance hall? Was he simply
after bedsport? Then he should have gone to one of Jean's
brothels. Well, if he wanted her only for *that*, he'd have to
wait a long time, for she wasn't about to give him bedsport
and she wouldn't turn him over to another girl so that the

other girl could get his money. "You just stay here," she said sweetly, "until I return."

She left the table and went to the bar. The bartender had been a pugilist until he got mad and killed an opponent in the ring. He was subsequently barred from the profession and came to work for LeClair as a bartender and bouncer. He was well known to the regulars who frequented the Pirates' Nest, and because of him there were fewer brawls and murders in LeClair's establishments than in any other dive along the Coast.

Now Rose bent over the bartop and whispered to him, "Let me have a beer and whiskey with the works."

Hank, the bartender, nodded. He never smiled and he didn't now as he began to prepare the drinks Rose had ordered. He drew beer from the tap then laced it with a pinch or two of snuff. He poured two fingers worth of whiskey into a medium-sized glass and added an equal amount of the juice of plug tobacco to the whiskey. The nicotine in the tobacco would have a calming, euphoric effect, making McSween not only want more, but because of its addictive tendency, need it.

Hank set the "loaded" drinks aside, then took a bottle of cold tea and poured some into an amber colored goblet. As a rule, the girls of the establishment drank ordinary tea, which was charged to the male patron at the price of a mixed drink. Hank said nothing as he handed the tray laden with drinks to Rose, who took them back to McSween's table.

She knew the amber goblet contained her tea, so she placed the other two drinks before the stranger. It would either make him so high he didn't know what he was doing, or make him dreadfully sick. If the former occurred, he'd be putty in her hands. If he got sick, he'd no doubt be willing to pay for a soft bunk to lie down on. Either way, it was only a matter of time before he surrendered all his money to Rose.

"The drinks are on the house," she said to McSween. No one ever refused free liquor and McSween didn't now. His eyes glistened as he raised the whiskey to his lips, drained the glass, then followed it down with the entire contents of the glass of beer. He licked his lips approvingly as he sat back in his chair. A moment later a silly grin spread across his beefy face and he blinked several times to clear his blurred vision.

"Mighty good stuff you serve here," he declared. "Real potent. Think I want another. How much it cost?"

"One bit—twelve and a half cents—for the beer, two bits for the whiskey."

"What's that stuff you're drinking, honey?" he asked.

"A mixed drink. Like some?"

He shook his head. "Do you want another one, too?" he asked her.

She grinned. "Sure. Another bit ought to do it."

McSween reached into his coat pocket and pulled out five bits and placed them in her palm. "Keep the rest for yourself," he said.

Rose returned to the bar, ordered the same, this time with a double dose of "extras". Five minutes later McSween had finished his drinks and was having trouble holding up his head. "More," he said.

"Your money, please?"

"Huh? Oh, yeah, How much did you say, honey?"

The drinks had had their desired effect. Already his mind was going. She could say or do anything and he'd go along. "One dollar for the beer, and three for the whiskey," she declared.

He felt so good, he didn't notice the discrepancy in price. He fished into his pocket, pulled out his wallet, and placed five dollars on the table. She took it and went to the bar. A half hour later McSween was under his table, singing, calling out between choruses for more drinks.

"Five dollars for the beer and ten for the whiskey," Rose said boldly, for she knew he had the money to cover it but not the sense to know he was being taken.

McSween fumbled for his wallet again, pulled it clumsily from his coat and leafed through the remaining bills. He cursed, shrugged, then tossed the wallet over to Rose. "Bring me as many of them damned good drinks as it'll buy," he roared.

He was so sodden with drink and drug, he did not recognize that his last beer and whiskey were just that and nothing more. There was no further need to "load" his drinks. Rose paid Hank for the beverages and stuffed the remainder of McSween's money in her skirt pocket. Without a glance at the babbling man, she moved past him to another table and new prey.

In her upstairs office, Faye Langlois was pondering over a letter she'd received earlier that day when she looked up and saw Jean LeClair walking across the hallway. She stood quickly and crossed to the open doorway to meet him. There was a frown on her heavily-painted face as she said, "What brings you here, Jean? The only time I see you anymore is when something bad has happened."

"You exaggerate, Faye," LeClair answered, seating himself on an upholstered chair across from her pine desk. "You manage my girls so well there's no need for me to interfere."

"Thanks," she said, then changed the subject. She was not the kind of woman who liked flattery. She knew when she was doing her best and when she wasn't, and pushed herself until she, herself, was satisfied. Jean knew her well enough that he didn't dwell on compliments. "I've been wanting to talk to you," she said. "One of the girls has latched onto a man and is leaving us to marry. I wouldn't burden you with such trivia except that she's our *virgin*."

The professional virgin was a young girl who acted each night for a select, paying audience, as if she were chaste and being taken against her will for the first time. It was, of course, a sham, but it drew much business. Many patrons returned night after night to view through peepholes in the wall the same girl performing the act of losing her maidenhead. Although the job was exclusively hers, the male partner changed every couple of nights. The men who paid to watch her lose her virginity either didn't look at her face, what with all her charms so temptingly arrayed, or didn't care that it was simply a farce. "We're going to have trouble replacing Violet," Faye said. "The girl's a natural for the part. She's only fourteen and has an angelic face. Perhaps you know of someone . . ."

Jean shook his head. "You'll find another girl," he said confidently.

"That reminds me. Aren't we due for another shipment of Cantonese girls?"

"The ship's been delayed in China. A storm at sea wrecked her sails and they had to be repaired before the ship could get under way."

"How did you learn that?" Faye asked.

"Lance Morgan's shipment came in yesterday and one of his sailors told me." Lance Morgan was a one-time friend of LeClair's. They had broken out of jail together, but were now engaged in competition in the China slave trade.

"This is the first time his ship has beaten our *China Queen*," she said. "Bet the old bastard's gloating over it. How were his girls?"

"Better than his last group. He's hired a new man in Canton to do his buying. He's good. I might take him on myself to help Ti Wang." LeClair and Morgan each had agents in Canton to find girls to work for their masters in the Barbary Coast cribs and cowyards. Neither LeClair,

Morgan, nor any other slave trader felt immoral in purchasing these girls, for the plight of a Chinese girl was sad at best. Sons of the Celestials were prized but daughters were considered nearly worthless to their parents. Their only value was that they could be sold for a handsome price to eager American traders. LeClair had authorized his agent in Canton to pay the highest prices for his girls, thus assuring him the youngest, and the prettiest. Whenever he received a girl he considered too young for prostitution—under age fourteen—he'd send her to a special school he had started with his own funds and staffed with hand-picked teachers.

When the girl was educated to the degree that she could speak English, read and write, he'd sell her to a wealthy politician as a servant. Most of the Chinese girls ended up bedding their masters, but to bed one man as opposed to the never-ending chain of strangers who patronized the cribs and cowyards of Chinatown was not such a bad deal.

Morgan cared little for the underaged girls and put them to work immediately on Jackson Street, in the lowest dives where the life expectancy of a young prostitute was not more than six years. Hardly any survived past the age of twenty.

"Jean, there's something else," Faye said, wringing her hands in the folds of her green silk skirt. She furrowed her brows as she stared at the letter she had been reading earlier.

"What's wrong, Faye? I can't remember when I've seen you so upset."

"It's . . . it's Monique," she said. "I received a letter from New York today. It seems she's being dismissed from school."

"They're throwing her out!" Jean declared. "Why? I thought she was getting good grades."

"She was. It's . . . they say she's been in some sort of

trouble. They wouldn't tell me what, Jean, but from what they intimated, I'm afraid I can guess. She's thirteen now and . . . That's why I sent her away, so she wouldn't end up like me!''

"Calm down, Faye. You're imagining the worse. It could be something quite innocent. Is she coming here?''

Faye sighed. "At the time the letter was written, she was boarding a packet boat bound for San Francisco. She should be arriving here in about a week. Oh, Jean, what am I going to do? I'm no fit mother. Hell, I don't even know what to do with a girl her age! The only girls I know are bawds.''

Jean wanted to smile but held it back. "I'm sure Monique is as unsure of how to deal with a mother as you are of how to handle her. Give it time and a little patience. I'll help in any way I can. Rose is only a few years older than Monique. I'm sure they could become friends.''

"That's just it!'' Faye cried. "I don't want Monique associating with people like Rose. I've tried to give her a chance in life.''

"She'll get it. There are schools here. Good schools. In fact, the school I started would be excellent for her. She'd be with other girls her own age learning the fundamentals and you'd be able to keep an eye on her.''

"I . . . don't know. Give me some time to think it over.''

"Take as long as you need.'' He stood to go, then remembered why he had come. "By the way, Rose will be leaving early tonight. Just thought I'd let you know.''

Jean LeClair owned several chaises and had a coachman waiting to drive him anywhere at anytime, yet he preferred to walk, more for the exercise than for any other reason. He enjoyed a brisk stroll the first thing each morning and would usually pick his course along the wharves and docks of the harbor, making mental notes of the commercial ships in port and those that were expected shortly. Many a time his diligence and early start earned him the edge over a competitor and thus, he was able to purchase the cargoes of newly-arrived ships and re-sell at top prices through a network of stores he owned throughout the quarter.

It was dark as LeClair made his way on foot from his tour of his "Nest" establishments (the Pirates' Nest, a concert-saloon on Montgomery Street; the Rat's Nest, a dance-hall on Kearney Street; and the Crow's Nest, a dive on the corner of Washington and Dupont) up Montgomery Street in the area of Pacific Street, which was notorious for its dangers. Gamblers, thieves, murderers, whores, and drunken sailors prowled two or three blocks and made it virtually impossible for a decent citizen to pass through without being molested. Jean had walked this way often when checking on the operations at his "nest" establishments on his way home northward on Montgomery Street at Telegraph Hill, and had managed to escape being "selected" for attack by the lowest crime element of the Coast—the *Rangers*. The reason for this was that the Rangers all knew him, and feared the kind of retribution that LeClair could and would bring down on the heads of any who had the temerity to assault him.

Tonight, however, after leaving the last of his dives on his tour and setting up his evening with Rose, being molested was the last thing on Jean's mind. He was unaware of a new crime element on the Coast, a band of young teenaged toughs without a formal leader, itching for trouble, and ignorant of the unwritten rules concerning LeClair.

It had rained most of the day and now a layer of fog spun the city in a close, damp web. Jean proceeded mostly by instinct, for in some places the fog was so thick it was impossible to distinguish the footpaths from the street.

Suddenly he heard the sound of leather scraping dirt behind him. His heartbeat quickened and his eyes widened, alert for trouble. He still carried in his coat pocket, as a token of the early years when he prowled the streets, a set of brass knuckles. Recently he had taken to wearing a deringer strapped inside a shoulder holster, more because he liked the feel of it against his ribs than for protection. He had never used it and doubted he ever would.

Now, seemingly from out of nowhere, three tall youths appeared. One blocked Jean's path while the other two flanked him. They wore lopsided grins as they stood legs apart, hands looped in the corners of their pants pockets. Jean's own hand was busy slipping into the brass knuckles.

"Well, lookee here," said the thug blocking Jean's way. He was a tall red-haired youth with wire-rimmed glasses. "We got ourselves a prize, gents—a real fancy one at that. The name's Luke, dude," he said to Jean. "Remember that when they fish you out of the Bay."

"Hey," said one of the others, "Why are you all dressed up, mister? You going to a wedding?"

Jean smiled slowly, his perfect white teeth gleaming like a beacon in the dismal fog. His eyes remained on the tough in front of him as he said, "Not a wedding, friend. A funeral."

"That so?" asked Luke. "How'd ya know you'd be meetin' your maker tonight?"

"The funeral is yours, my foolish friend, unless you abandon this insane idea. Have you not heard the name LeClair?"

The young tough frowned. "LeClair?" he parroted. "LeClair who?"

"Jean LeClair." Suddenly Jean swung out with his right hand, the one encased in the brass knuckles, striking Luke square in the jaw. The sound of crunching teeth and splintered glass from his spectacles filled the stillness of the night as he crumpled in a heap to the dirt street. The other two young toughs sprang upon LeClair. The first grabbed Jean from behind and locked his arms through LeClair's, pinning him, while the other wielded a knife. The fog had lifted somewhat and the silver metal of the blade glistened in the light of a quarter moon. The look on the tough's face was crazed as he held the knife upright before him, laughed once, then sprang at LeClair, teasing, slicing the air before Jean's face with the knife, taunting him. LeClair lashed out with his legs, kicking the one with the knife in the groin, doubling him over in pain. The knife fell out of his hands to the ground. Then Jean, with a mighty heave, lifted the one holding him up over his head and sent the youth flying through the air. The thug hit the ground, tumbled once, then lay still. But now the one LeClair had kicked in the groin was recovering, his eyes upon the knife he had dropped a few feet away. He reached for it, but LeClair saw the move and brought a heavy boot crunching down on the tough's hand. The boy screamed with pain as LeClair bent and picked up the knife, then stuffed it in his belt.

"When your friends wake up," Jean said, "tell them to stay out of Jean LeClair's path or you'll all find yourselves on a ship bound for China."

It was no idle threat.

By the time Rose appeared at his mansion that night for their celebration, Jean had all but forgotten the incident with the young toughs. He and Rose were in the parlor, a breathtaking room with floor to ceiling windows on three sides, overlooking the Bay.

Rose stood looking out, a crystal snifter of brandy in her hand. Her nose pressed up against the windowpane left a small patch of condensation on the glass, temporarily blocking her view of the golden Gate. She pulled back and frowned. In the moonlit distance came the ghostly sight of white sails against a black sky. "The *Falcon*'s coming in," she said to Jean, who sat in a tufted rocker not far from her, watching her.

"The *Falcon* is a whaler," he declared. "Why should it interest you?"

"She carries a sizeable crew of thirsty sailors."

"Thirsty? Or hungry?" he asked.

She turned to him. "I don't understand."

"It's obvious you'd rather be down at the "Nest" tonight," he said irritatedly. "Is it the money, Rose? If it is, *I'll* give you what you'd be making at the saloon. Or is it their hunger for a woman that compels you?"

She shook her head vehemently. "The thought of bedding any of those dirty . . ." Her hands began to shake and she used her left to brace the other hand holding the drink.

He took her in his arms. "I don't understand you, Rose. Dammit, who are you? What is there in your past that's so terrible you can't bring yourself to talk about it?"

She backed out of his arms, took a long pull of brandy. "My past?" she questioned, her eyes dark and wide. "Why, there's nothing to tell. I've led an incredibly dull life. As for who I am . . . I can be anybody you wish, from the lowest guttersnipe to a direct descendant of British royalty! In my mind, though, I'm simply Rose, the girl who owes you everything." Now she smiled, placed her glass on the table, and moved against him once more, seeking and finding his lips. She kissed him long and hard and a moment later was lifted off the floor and carried into a bedchamber upstairs.

As always their lovemaking was frenzied. Rose had become adept at faking pleasure and fooling Jean. She said and did the right things at the right times, even sighed and groaned when the pace of his thrusts increased substantially, signaling his climax. The only things she didn't need to fake were the sighs of genuine pleasure when it was nearly over, which Jean mistook as cries of ecstacy.

Afterward, Jean kissed the tip of her nose and placed a small package wrapped in bright yellow paper next to her on the pillow. Then he left her for the comforts of the parlor, another glass of brandy, and a cigar.

After he had gone, Rose shivered with revulsion. She yanked the sheet off the bed and wiped herself with it, then rolled it up into a tight ball and flung it angrily across the room. It hit the wall and fell to the floor. Then she saw Maude, the grey-haired maid who stood in the open doorway, watching.

"Excuse me, ma'am," Maude said, "shall I fetch the usual?"

"Yes, quickly." Rose felt dirty, soiled and used. She would not feel right again until after she'd rid herself of all trace of Jean. It was not that she disliked him—only what he'd done to her.

Maude returned a few minutes later with a jug of hot water, a basin, syringe, and a short length of rubber tubing.

Rose impatiently yanked the articles out of the maid's hands. "You can go now," she said, turning away. She was in such a hurry to cleanse herself that she didn't notice the maid's continued presence. Maude backed into a dark corner of the bedroom and watched as Rose lay down on the bed, placed the basin beneath her, filled the syringe with water, then set about her task, wincing as the hot water scorched her tender flesh.

A moment later Rose stood, dried herself with a towel, then wrapped it around her. Still unaware of Maude lurking in the corner of the dimly-lit room, she noticed the box on her pillow. In her haste she had forgotten about it. Now she ripped the paper off, lifted the lid and squealed with delight at the contents. It was a strikingly beautiful pearl and ruby pendant on a gold chain! The ruby was her birthstone and she had once told Jean she admired pearls and wished she could own them. He had remembered and she was pleased.

Just then Maude stepped out of the shadows. "May I see it too, ma'am?" she asked. Startled, Rose dropped the necklace. Maude picked it up and stared admiringly at it. "I'd give my eye teeth for such a beautiful piece," she said. "Yessir, my eye teeth."

Rose snatched it back. "You may prepare my bath now."

But Maude ignored her. "I've been mister LeClair's maid for almost two years and he never gave me no gift half as nice. But maybe that's because I'm only the maid and not his . . ."

"Stop babbling," Rose broke in, "and fetch my water."

"I wonder what the master would say if I was to tell him how quick you are with the syringe after he leaves you."

Rose's face pinked with anger. "You would tell him?" she snapped.

"I sure wouldn't do that, ma'am," Maude said, "not at least if *I* were to own this here necklace."

Rose couldn't believe her ears. The maid was trying to blackmail her! The necklace for her silence! She grabbed the old woman by the arm and pulled her up close. "It'll be a cold day in hell before you wear *my* necklace. As for telling Jean, go ahead! In fact, I'll tell him myself! And you can be sure I'll add what a thief he has for a maid."

"He wouldn't believe *you*," Maude said, pulling away from Rose's grasp. "I've been a good servant. He wouldn't take the word of a . . . a whore . . . over mine!"

Stung, Rose slapped Maude with the back of her hand, causing her to stumble and fall onto the bed. Like a lion springing on its prey, Rose jumped on the woman, pinning her to the mattress. She slipped the necklace around Maude's neck, then pulled the ends of the chain tight to bring terror to the woman's eyes.

"Stop!" Maude screamed. "You'll kill me!"

Rose laughed. "It would be so easy," she said. "All I'd have to do is . . ." She gave another pull on the ends of the chain, wrenching a gasp from Maude's lips. "If I ever hear another word from your mouth other than 'Yes, ma'am, right away, ma'am,' I'll finish what I started. Do you understand?"

Maude nodded feebly. "I promise, ma'am, I won't say nothing. Just let me go."

Rose relaxed her grip, then frowned, wondering whether she had indeed taught the maid a lesson. Deciding that she had, Rose backed off and got to her feet. Maude jumped up and ran out the door.

Now Rose stood staring at the ruby and pearl necklace in her hand with mixed feelings. It was a symbol of LeClair's ownership of her, and that disturbed her. She belonged to no one. She never had and never would!

Could she wear this necklace?

The necklace itself was pretty, but what it represented was unpalatable and only served to remind her of what she had become—and how far she had sunk.

But there was little she could do to change her past, or even her future, so she slipped the gem around her throat and looked at her reflection in the gilded mirror above the bed. If she were to spend the rest of her days as a tramp, she thought, at least she'd do it in style.

2

Summer, 1862

AN EERIE stillness permeated the harbor at Norfolk, Virginia as residents of tall, narrow frame houses near the waterfront waited for the dark skies to break open in a downpour. Beau Ashton was one of them. He stood looking out from the Ashton's second floor library window to a pier a block away, remembering how frightened he was, as a boy, of hurricanes. Tonight, Beau knew, judging by the absence of a breath of wind, the storm was going to be mean. Even though storms didn't frighten him any more, he was glad he was indoors. It was a good thing, too, that Doctor Barnes had arrived earlier that day from New York.

The thought of the medical man reminded him of something he would have liked to forget. He lowered his gaze to the crutch beneath his right armpit, which was supporting the weight that should have been on his leg. His nearly useless leg! His love of the sea and ships and a misguided notion that joining the Confederate Navy would provide excitement and adventure had cost him the use of his right leg.

He cursed now as he always did whenever he thought of that worthless mission. He had been first officer on a Confederate ship during a scouting expedition in northern waters when his ship had been attacked by a Union gunboat. In the ensuing cannon fire, one-third of Beau's crew had died and a piece of shrapnel had lodged itself in Beau's right thigh. It all had been for nothing, he recalled, since they had not even reached their destination—Washington—and had, therefore, learned nothing of the enemy's fortifications. Fortunately, the ship was faster than the Union gunboat and they had managed to outrun her and return safely to home port. Beau spent the next two months in an army hospital only to have the doctors agree that it was impossible to remove the piece of metal in his leg without leaving it paralyzed.

And so he had shunned surgery, learned to get around on a crutch, and hobbled out of the hospital to his father's home to nurse a bitter resentment of the war and the gross injustice that he should have to spend the rest of his life as a partial cripple.

It was only through the firm and loyal support and loving ministrations of Amoreena Welles, his fiancée, that Beau was able to come to grips with his handicap.

But he soon found he had another problem to contend with. He had not been home for a month when Monte Ashton suffered a mild seizure. Beau's father had been strong and healthy for most of his sixty-five years and didn't want to see a doctor. Beau finally persuaded him, however, and he made an appointment with the local physician, a crusty oldtimer named Cobb. After a quick examination, Dr. Cobb said what Monte had suffered was a gas pain. "Nothing the matter but a little trapped gas," he said.

Monte Ashton experienced several more "gas pains" in the days following Cobb's visit, but did not mention them to Beau. Then, less than a week later, he suffered such severe pains he was confined to bed.

Beau called Dr. Cobb again, who prescribed laudanum and bed rest, but insisted Monte would recover "quickly".

Instead Monte grew worse each day, then slipped into a coma-like sleep.

It was Amoreena who finally convinced her fiance that Cobb was unable to help and that Beau should contact his mentor in New York City, the good Dr. John Barnes. If anyone could help Monte, she said, it was the headmaster and chief physician of the highly respected New York Medical College Hospital.

Amoreena was not only beautiful but smart, too, and Beau knew he was lucky to be betrothed to her. She was right about John Barnes. If anyone could help the elder Ashton, it was he. So Beau wrote him a letter.

Born and raised in Virginia, Beau had spent the three years in New York studying medicine under Dr. Barnes and the two had become close. Despite good grades, however, Beau found the lure of the Atlantic irresistible and debated deserting medical school for the life of a sailor. He spent hours discussing it with Dr. Barnes, and the man had proven not only wise, but a true friend. He had told Beau that "the ability to realize one's dreams lay in the heart" and that although he'd miss him, Beau should follow his inner promptings. And so Beau left New York.

The attack on Fort Sumter in April of 1861 put an end to his dreams before they could begin. In spite of being a southerner, Beau was not a dyed-in-the-wool Confederate. His father was a businessman who had never owned slaves, and he and his family had lived for a time in the North and Beau had liked it. His speech was clear and precise, more northern than southern. He found the seceding states' claims for a separate government questionable and disagreed with the need for war.

Yet, by Spring of '61, the only ships allowed in or out of Norfolk Bay were warships and the only way he could sail was in a naval vessel. So Beau enlisted in the newly-formed Confederate Navy. His term, however, was a short one. It was less than a year before the tragedy that crippled him. The Navy declared him unfit for further service and sent him home. And now, in the summer of 1862, he stared longingly at the sea. A little older. A bit wiser. And bitter.

A knock on the library door brought him back to the present. A moment later an elderly man in a frayed suit entered. His gray hair was mussed, sweat beaded his forehead and upper lip, and he carried a small black bag in his left hand. He looked exactly as Beau had remembered, and for a moment Beau wanted to run to him, embrace him fondly, then blurt out the agony he felt over his father's illness, his game leg, and the mess his life had become. But he held himself back, shifted the weight from his bad leg to the other, and managed a composed, "I'm glad you're here, doctor. When I received your reply to my letter saying you'd come, I was pleased yet concerned, too, with the fighting and reports of trains ambushed. I wasn't sure you'd be able to get through."

"It wasn't as bad as it could've been, Beau, though there was some fighting north of here and we had to stay clear of the cities, which took us out of our way a bit. I had to leave the train sixty miles north and come the rest of the way on horseback. It would have been impossible to enter the city had Norfolk not been in the hands of the

Federals. As it was, all I had to prove was that I was a northerner.''

"I'm just thankful you were able to come at all. I know it wasn't easy for you to leave your post at the school. . . . and I'm grateful. I hope you can help Father.''

"I've just come from seeing him. He was heavily sedated.''

"I'm sorry I wasn't here to welcome you earlier when you arrived," Beau said. "I was with my fiancée in her parents' home across town. As soon as I returned, Dobbs told me you were with Father and I didn't wish to disturb you then.''

Dr. Barnes' gaze dropped from the fair-haired young man's face to the crutch under his arm. "What happened?" he asked, concern on his lined face.

Beau shrugged. "Took a nasty piece of shrapnel in my thigh, doctor. It's still in there and I'm told there's nothing that can be done for it. Forget me. What about my father?''

The doctor shook his head. "That's too bad, my boy.'' Then he took a chair by the fireplace and motioned for the younger man to join him. When Beau was seated, Barnes was sober-faced and serious as he said, "In all the time you've known me, Beau, have I ever lied or withheld the truth?''

Beau shook his head.

"I haven't, Beau, and I won't begin now. This so-called doctor who's been treating your father . . . what's his name, Cobb?''

"Yes.''

"Well, Cobb's fit to doctor a horse's ass! He's given your father massive doses of laudanum and a new-fangled drug they've tried out on only the wildest of inmates in an institution! He must think he's dealing with a crazy man rather than a heart patient. I hate to tell you this, Beau, but your father is a very sick man.''

"Deep in my heart I already knew that. I didn't want to call in another doctor after Cobb because . . . well, frankly, I was afraid of what he might tell me. I wanted to believe Cobb because he said what I wanted to hear. Amoreena convinced me that Father needed help from a good doctor . . . and that I had to know the truth about Father. I think I'm ready now to hear whatever it is you have to say."

The doctor lowered his eyes. "It is difficult to be the bearer of bad news, but your father is dying. He may not last the night."

Beau blinked. He stared dumbly at the doctor. He had half-expected this, yet . . . no one was *truly* prepared for the death of a loved one. There was always the hope that he might have been wrong. Could Barnes be mistaken? Even as the thought was born, the doctor shook his head.

"No, Beau," he said, as if reading Beau's thoughts. "I'm certain of my diagnosis. I wish I weren't. I'm sure he'd like to see you now. He's off the sedative and can talk a bit. Don't overtire him, though. If he's kept quiet, it'll stretch his time somewhat."

"I understand," Beau said. "There's a lot of things I want to tell him." His voice was almost a whisper, and the doctor placed a sympathetic hand on his shoulder.

"God give you the strength, son."

By the time Beau reached his father's room, the storm had arrived. Ear-splitting thunder shattered the calm, followed by pellets of rain so large they rattled the window glass. Beau shivered, not because of the storm, but because the weather seemed so damnedably appropriate. It would be infinitely more difficult to lose his father while the sun shone and the birds sang.

Dobbs, an old family retainer and the only servant the elder Ashton employed, was sitting beside the bed watching his master sleep. When he saw Beau, he stood up and whispered, "He hasn't said a word. I've been hoping . . ."

"Thank you, Dobbs. You may leave us now. If he needs you, I'll call."

The servant looked sadly at Beau, then again at his beloved master before leaving. Beau approached the bed. It was a large canopied affair and his father, once so healthy and robust, looked small and frail lying in the midst of it.

"Father?" he said softly. Monte Ashton didn't stir. Beau took his father's hand. It was cold—cold as death. For a moment panic seized him, but then he saw his father's nightclothes flutter ever so slightly over his chest and Beau relaxed. He stared at the hand in his. The skin was paper-like, the veins prominent. A few weeks ago his father had been laughing and full of life, now he was little more than a skeleton. Hard to believe? It was impossible!

"Father?" he said again, squeezing gently on Monte's hand. This time the man's eyes opened and a trace of a smile spread across his pale face.

"Beau! Wha . . . what time is it? I feel like I've been asleep for days!"

"You have, Father. How do you feel?" It was a stupid question, Beau knew, but he found himself unable to say what he wanted to—*had* to—before his father died.

"I'm not feeling at all, Beau. What I am is . . . sort of numb all over. Must be the medicine."

"Father, I . . . hell, I just want to tell you that I love you. It's been too long since I said it last."

The man's eyes misted. "You're a fine son. Always were."

Beau swallowed hard. "Can I get you anything?" The old man shook his head slowly. Beau let go of his father's hand, pulled up a chair beside the bed, and sat down. "I've called in Dr. Barnes, my teacher from the New York College. Well, he's also the most gifted medical man I know, so I wanted him to have a look at you."

Monte said nothing, his eyes unnaturally bright as he waited for his son to continue.

"He's here now. He examined you while you were sleeping." Now Beau stopped. How could he tell his father that he was dying!

But Monte seemed to sense it. "He discovered I've got more wrong with me than gas pains, right?" Beau nodded slowly. "I haven't much time, have I, Beau?" he asked softly.

Beau struggled within himself. He wanted to blurt out, "You'll be fine, Father," but knew it was not only a lie but that his father would see right through it. So he lowered his eyes to the carpet and said, "You have a bad heart, Father."

"I'm dying then . . . how long have I got?"

"Only God knows that. But if you rest and obey Dr. Barnes' orders, you'll . . ."

"Stop treating me like a baby, Beau. I'm sick, not feeble-brained!"

"I'm sorry."

"Just answer my question, son. Tell me straight."

Beau sighed deeply. "Dr. Barnes says . . . you can die . . . anytime." There, it was said. He braced himself for his father's reaction. Monte took it surprisingly well. Beau wondered if *he* could have handled it with such calm if the situation were reversed.

"I'm glad you told me the truth, son, for there are things you should know. It hurts to talk, so listen carefully."

Beau pulled his chair closer.

"When I'm gone," Monte said, "everything I own dies with me. The house is heavily mortgaged, and I'm broke. We've been existing on the small sum your dear mother left in trust for you when she died. I'm sorry, son, for using your money, but we would've lost the house, everything, without it."

"I understand, Father."

"The war—already the Yankees have taken our city. Soon all the South will fall. Brother fighting brother is an evil thing and no good can come of it. I want to know now that you'll not be here when the South falls and turns into a barbarous living hell. Get out of Virginia. Take that lovely young lady of yours and go west." His speech exhausted him and he closed his eyes for a moment.

"West?" Beau asked. "How far west?"

"All the way . . . to California!"

"But California is a northern state. They're supplying gold for the Yankee treasury, I hear. I don't belong there."

"Yes you do. You're a northern property holder, Beau. Back in '49, when you were just a lad, I prospected in California for a year. I had a partner, a fellow named Larry Barre. We found a large vein in the hills outside Yerba Buena, which they now call San Francisco. I don't know what Larry did with his share of the money. He disappeared soon after we staked our claim. I took my money and invested it in San Francisco coastal property. I still own it. The deed's in my safe. When I die, it'll be yours. A lot on the east corner of Montgomery and Washington Streets. There was nothing but adobe huts and mud then, but I hear the area has been built up quite a bit. That piece of property could be worth a fortune now." As lightning filled the dismal room, Monte took a deep breath. "Go there, son. Locate your land. Sell to the highest bidder and build a home for yourself and Amoreena. It's the only thing I can leave you besides my love."

"Father . . ." Beau's voice cracked with emotion. "I don't know what to say. Of course I'll go to California. I'll build the biggest, most beautiful house for Amoreena and we'll raise lots of children. We'll name the first boy Monte, after you."

Monte managed a smile. "That'll be nice," he said. Then he closed his eyes and fell asleep.

Beau dropped to his knees beside the bed and buried his head against the mattress. Then the tears came.

Just after midnight the storm turned into a hurricane and Monte Ashton died peacefully in his sleep.

The *Sea Lion,* a square-rigged, 1,300 ton wooden clipper ship with a hold full of cargo destined for California and a deck crammed with nearly fifty passengers, sailed out of Pier 20 in New York City's East River bound for a 15,000 mile voyage down around South America's Cape Horn to San Francisco. With luck and good weather, the *Sea Lion* would complete her trip in about three months.

There were many reasons why the passengers, at three-hundred dollars a ticket, boarded this clipper—the only one sailing to California during these turbulent times. Some were leaving because of the oppression of the war, others for the excitement of points unknown. But one of the passengers, thirteen-year-old Monique Langlois, had her own reason for sailing to San Francisco. She had no choice. The private school she had been attending had thrown her out and were sending her back to a mother she had no recollection of.

Now the pretty, raven-haired girl frowned as she leaned against the *Sea Lion's* side rail watching white-capped waves roll to and from the hull. Her mother. All Monique had to prove she had a mother was a faded picture of her. Monique had been raised by a maiden aunt who died when Monique was five. She vaguely remembered the tall, heavily-painted woman who came to the funeral, then took Monique by ship to New York to leave her there for the next eight years. That woman, she now knew, had been her mother.

Other than the picture she kept in a locket she sometimes wore around her neck, Monique had known nothing

of the woman who was her mother. Nothing, at least, until
she had met Randy. Randy was a nickname for Lucille
Randolph, a precocious girl who had transferred to Miss
Montvale's School for Girls six months ago when her
parents had moved to New York from San Francisco.
Randy knew a lot about the Coast in San Francisco and its
abundance of low women and drunken sailors.

"One of the worst of the whores," Randy had told
Monique during a conversation, "is a lady named Faye
Langlois. I know because my pa says so. He even met her
once and said she was real bad. It's funny that she should
have the same last name as you!"

Randy had thought it an interesting coincidence, but it
had made Monique curious; and that night after the school's
headmistress retired, Monique broke into the records office
and rummaged through the files. She found, incredibly,
that her mother's first name was Faye.

So, she thought now, her mother was a whore. Well, so
be it. There were, after all, worse things she could be.
There was nothing wrong with bedding a man—Monique
had done it, and enjoyed it. If you could get paid for doing
something enjoyable, then why not?

Monique's own initiation to the pleasures of the flesh
began quite innocently one afternoon nearly a year earlier
on a field hike with her class. She had tarried too long
over her inspection of a frog she'd found and was left
behind. At first she had panicked, but then she saw she
was not alone. From a nearby town a brawny young man
had been watching, and stepped out from behind a tree to
confront her.

She grinned now as her gaze fell upon a handsome
young man directly across the deck from her, standing
beside a girl only a little older than Monique, looking out
at the Narrows. He was blonde, just like the boy who had
taken her maidenhead that fateful afternoon in the forest.

Her eyes dropped to the crutch he was leaning on and she wondered how he had been wounded. The war? It would seem logical since he looked quite young. She wondered idly how a man with a game leg performed in bed, then decided he was probably a terrible lover. It might be interesting to find out, but she would not waste time on him when there were so many other handsome men aboard. She then stared at another—a dark-haired crew member— the second mate. Wouldn't it be fun, she mused, to sleep with each of the mates and work her way up to the captain! Perhaps they'd even fight over her favors. That would be . . . fantastic! She edged her way through the crowd of sight-seers to be closer to the lad and saw that he was tall and slender, and his cheeks dimpled as he smiled.

Monique, too, was tall for her thirteen years and had the body of a woman. Her breasts were full and firm and larger than those of her teachers at the school. She had discovered it was simple to lure any man she wanted into bed with her. All it took was a look, a touch, and men were putty in her hands. The crew of this ship would be no different. She would simply flutter her green eyes—she enhanced their natural almond shape with charcoal and pinked her lips with salve—and bare the tops of her breasts. Before boarding the ship at New York, she had pawned all her sedately-styled clothes and used the money to buy sensual, low-bodiced, tight-fitting gowns. She wore one now, with a thin crocheted shawl around her shoulders to protect her from the cool winds whipping off the Atlantic.

As she was deciding what she'd say to the young mate, the woman companion of the man with the crutch turned around and stared in Monique's direction. She did not seem to notice Monique, but Monique drank in every inch of her. She had never seen a lady so pretty.

Monique was instantly jealous. Probably some rich man's daughter with a head full of air. So what if the girl's hair was long and curly, her complexion soft and delicate. She couldn't be much of a prize if she was being squired around by a cripple!

She forced her mind off the girl and started across the deck to where the second mate was conversing with a passenger.

Beau Ashton ran a hand through his wavy hair. There was so much open space at sea, he thought. Thousands of miles between Virginia and California. Since he and Amoreena Welles had boarded the train with Dr. Barnes en route to New York after his father's funeral, he had asked himself over and over if he were doing the right thing in uprooting Amoreena and whisking her off to San Francisco. He had no answer then and he had none now.

He turned and looked at the woman beside him. She was beautiful. In the strong afternoon sun, the pale blue of her gown against the gentle golden color of her hair made her look doll-like, untouchable. And untouchable she was, for in all the years he had known and loved her, he had never taken her to bed. Not, of course, that he hadn't wanted to, but she was a proper southern lady and would have died of shame if he had taken her as he longed to. They were engaged to marry and soon he would have all of her. But this was no time to think such thoughts, he told himself, for their future was hanging on their journey west. "I hope we'll never regret this trip," he said to her.

She turned large blue eyes to him. "How can we? The sea is lovely. I've never been out of Virginia before and the train trip we took north to New York was fascinating. I'm enjoying myself immensely."

"But we don't know what we'll find when we reach California," he said.

"Yes we do. We'll find a valuable piece of property. Your father would not have told us to go there if the land in San Francisco wasn't rich and well worth the trip. We'll sell it and start anew, just the two of us.''

He shook his head. "You amaze me, Amoreena. You've just left your family and friends for God knows what, yet you remain calm and unperturbed. How do you do it?''

She laughed. "I don't allow myself to think about bad things," she said. "I wasn't always that way. There were times when you left to go to medical school and then to sea, that I despaired of ever seeing you again. If I had given in to my grief then, there's no telling if I'd be here at all.''

"I wish I could be optimistic about the land," Beau said. "It's been almost fourteen years since father bought it. A lot can happen in that length of time.''

"Good things can happen in time, too, darling.''

"I suppose so." Now he took her in his arms and bussed her cheek. His mood was lighter as he said, "Tell me, how long has it been since we became betrothed?''

She giggled. "Too long. You first asked me to marry you when you were thirteen and I was eight. I said yes then and I'm still saying it. And I'm still not Mrs. Ashton!''

He smiled, a wide, happy smile. "I promise you we'll be married right after I sell the land. No more delays. Nothing will keep us apart anymore.''

"Excuse me," Monique said sweetly to the second mate, who eyed her with interest, having rid himself of a less attractive passenger a moment earlier. "I seem to be having difficulty with my cabin door," she said. "It simply refuses to open!''

"Well, now," the young mate said, "we'll have to do something about that. The name's Ross, miss. Georgie Ross. Glad to help in any way I can.''

"You can be of *great* service to me, Georgie," she said, smiling prettily.

Just then a piercing scream sounded high above them.
They looked upward as the man with the crutch yelled,
"Up on the mainmast!"

Near the top of the 200 ft. high mainmast, an apprentice
"tuning" the rigging had lost his balance and fell. His fall
had been broken by the heavy canvas topgallant sail and
now he hung precariously upside down, spread-eagled in a
tangle of rope and sail.

"We've got to get him down!" Beau Ashton yelled to
Georgie, the nearest crew member.

Georgie's mouth dropped open. He stared dumbly up at
the sailor, then at the young man with the crutch who was
eyeing him expectantly. If he sent sailors up there, the
swaying of the ropes might trigger the lad's fall. But he
wasn't sure. Why, in times like this, was he always unsure?
It was, he knew, because he was incompetent—at times
downright stupid. If it weren't for his widowed mother
being the captain's brother, he would never have been
made second mate. He was determined to prove his worth
someday, but now was not the time. He made up his mind
quickly. "I'll get the captain," Georgie said, rushing off
to find Captain Grover.

"That poor man!" Amoreena exclaimed, squinting up
at the dangling figure.

"Damn this leg!" Beau cried. "I could get him down.
I've seen these things happen before. If it weren't for this
leg, I could help instead of just standing here!"

The captain appeared soon after along with Jones, the
first mate. Captain Grover removed from between his teeth
the corn-cob pipe he habitually smoked and took one look
at the trapped youth. "That's Miller," he said. "He's only
an apprentice. What's he doing up there?"

"My fault, sir," Jones said. "I gave him the duty."
But Jones grinned at the sight of the upside-down young
crewman.

"One of these days you're going to learn that even apprentices' lives are worth something," the captain declared. "Sending a raw recruit up there's like signing his death warrant."

The first mate shrugged and watched as the captain sent two bare-chested sailors scampering up the rope ladders to free the snarled seaman. Beau was at Georgie's elbow as the sailors scrambled onto the yard arm nearest the apprentice.

"The captain's a good man," Georgie said to Beau. "I've sailed with him for almost a year now. He's fair with the swabs and there ain't nothing he can't handle. Not like me. I just do the best I can, and most of the time that ain't good enough."

Beau studied Georgie, who was shorter than him by about an inch. "You have high regard for your captain, and that's good. I, too, respected my commanding officer, but he was killed during an attack on our ship by a Federal gunboat."

"You're a *rebel?*" Georgie asked. "I wouldn't have figured it."

"I'm neither rebel nor Yankee. When I lost the use of my leg, I lost my zeal for war as well."

"I can understand why," Georgie said. "I couldn't decide which side was worth fighting for, so I signed aboard this ship. I've learned a lot, but there's still a bunch to know. Someday I'd like to be good enough to be a ship's master."

"That was always my dream, too," Beau said. "I hope you realize yours."

The passengers watching the rescue attempt yelled encouragement then applauded as the rescuers freed the white-faced apprentice and carried him safely down to the deck.

A girlish voice behind Georgie startled him and made him turn on his heel. "My cabin door?" Monique asked.

He grinned, then glanced at Beau. "Let's us talk more later. We've got something in common, I think, and I'd like to hear about your experiences in the rebel navy. But for now, I have to help the lady." He winked.

Beau nodded and smiled. Judging by the low-cut blouse of the lady, Beau thought, Georgie would be gone for a while. He liked the mate and looked forward to seeing him again. "I'll be here," he shouted just before the second mate and the girl disappeared below deck.

3

A FULL moon shone high over Telegraph Hill as Jean LeClair stirred fitfully in his bed. Earlier he had found sleep difficult, but now, just past three a.m., he was wide awake and staring at the stream of moonlight filtering through the voile curtains. Too many thoughts plagued him. His latest shipment of girls hadn't arrived from Canton and was long overdue. And there was talk that the Rangers—the lowest of the Coast's thieves, cut-throats, and murderers—were forming up to declare war on the organized crime leaders such as LeClair, who were known as the Barons.

For years, the Rangers had kept to their own streets and back alleys along the eastern and northeastern fringes of the Barbary Coast where they preyed on innocent night-walkers, but never interfered with the workings of the dives, brothels, or boarding houses owned by the former Sydney-town "Ducks". Some of the other Barons used Rangers to do their "dirty work" but paid them handsomely for it. The two crime elements had co-existed nicely until now. Jean had learned through his informers that the Rangers had acquired new leadership in the form of a stranger who had just arrived in San Francisco a few days ago. Who he was, no one seemed to know. None of the crime Barons had as yet seen him, so there was skepticism about his existence.

Jean's thoughts were interrupted now by the clip-clop of horse's hooves on his cobblestone drive. He jumped out of bed, wrapped a robe around him and padded down the hall stairway to the front door. A young boy dismounted his horse and raced up the flight of steps to Jean's front porch.

"You Mr. LeClair?" the boy inquired.

Jean nodded. The boy handed him a folded sheet of writing paper and without waiting for a reply, jumped upon his horse and galloped away.

Jean frowned at the familiar scent he detected on the paper. Then he went inside the parlor, lit a candle, sat down in an easy chair and unfolded the sheet. He frowned again at the large, scribbled handwriting which suggested it had been written in haste. He muttered an oath when he had read the note and seen the signature. Something was wrong at the Pirates' Nest!

"Jean," the note said simply, "Trouble. Come quickly. Faye."

Hays, Jean's servant, had also been awakened by the messenger and now stood in the doorway with Jean's pants and coat folded neatly over one arm, a hat in the other. He said nothing as Jean grabbed his clothes and dressed quickly.

"Thank you, Hays," Jean said as he rushed out of the house. He saddled a horse and was at the Pirates' Nest within a few minutes, but he was unprepared for what greeted him inside. All the patrons had been cleared out, and the girls were huddled together in a corner by the bar, weeping and frightened. The liquor bottles and mirror behind the bar and crystal chandelier overhead had been shot to pieces! Bullet holes lined the walls and lying in the center of the dancefloor were two lifeless bodies, a man and a woman. Their blood ran in jagged rivulets across the polished mahogany floor. The girl, face downward, was frozen in a fetal position clutching her stomach.

Jean reeled as he recognized the dead man as Hank, the bartender. The woman was one of his girls. Faye Langlois was with the girls huddled in the corner. "What happened?" he asked her.

The girls wailed louder at his question, and Faye gave up trying to comfort them. "A half hour or so ago a gang of black-coated thugs came in and started roughhousin'. They demanded free drinks for everybody and Hank told them to beat it. One of the thugs threatened Hank with a knife and that's when all hell broke loose, Jean. There were at least ten of them—all of them armed—against only Hank and the three bouncers. A wild shot wounded the pianist, and the other musicians and the customers ran for the door. The girls and I dove for cover. Sarah wasn't so lucky. She caught a bullet in the gut."

Suddenly Jean remembered that Rose was supposed to be working. "Rose!" he cried. "Where is she?"

"Easy, Jean, she's with the doctor. She'll be o.k."

Jean raced into the adjoining room where a local doctor—a patron of the Nest—was bandaging Rose's upper arm. Jean dropped to his knee beside her and gently stroked her bruised cheek. Her face was damp; she had been crying. "Are you all right?" he asked.

She smiled. "I'll live. The doctor says I've bruises, but no broken bones."

"How did you get involved?"

"Hank was my friend. I tried to help him."

"Damn! Who were the bastards, Rose? Who did this to you?"

Rose frowned. "I don't know the others, but the one who shot Sarah and Hank and then hit me was Billy Hagan."

"Hagan!" LeClair scowled. Hagan was a *Ranger*. If it *was* the Rangers who were responsible for this, the rumors about them were true. He stood up, a cold anger growing within him. "He'll pay for this," Jean declared. "They all will."

The respectable citizens of San Francisco were at times horrified by the lack of law and order in the Coast, but could do little about it. Once, eleven years earlier, an aroused citizenry took action against Sydney-town's vicious and lawless "Ducks". They for a time took the law into their own hands and administered it through what was known as the Vigilance Committee. The vigilantes hanged a number of the "Ducks", and finally succeeded in terrorizing the terrorists and restoring law and order.

Most of the "Ducks" left San Francisco for points East, but Jean, himself a "Duck", spent the next several months at sea on a merchant ship. A bright and ambitious man, he capitalized on a mutiny aboard ship to take it over and become it's master. Eventually he sold the ship and its cargo and used the proceeds to buy two others, now employed in transporting Chinese girls from Canton, and silks and tea from the Orient.

Many of the "Ducks" returned a few years later and crime once again filled the streets. The Vigilance Committee was reorganized and sprang into action. This time the vigilantes based their operations at a small square near the waterfront—in buildings where they constructed cells, courtrooms, a guard-room and meeting room. They called it Fort Gunnybags, and a fort it was, armed with guns and cannon and manned day and night. It took less than a year to rid the Coast of its crime and then Fort Gunnybags was shut down.

But it was now almost impossible for the honest citizens of San Francisco to start up a third Vigilance Committee, for the leaders of the movement in the fifties were now in league with, or owned by, the very crime barons they opposed. Graft was rampant; officials looked the other way rather than lose the bribes supplied them by LeClair and his contemporaries.

But now something was going wrong with the system. The lowly Rangers were rising up against the Barons and that was unpardonable! It was, the Barons felt, like a son turning against his father.

The next morning Jean called a meeting of the Coast's crime Barons—some of whom he liked, some he only tolerated. They all agreed the Rangers were getting out of hand and might well be forming up for a war, especially if they were unifying under a single leader as rumored. If a war was what they wanted, the Barons agreed, they would get it.

Now Jean decided to pay a visit to Reverend Cornelius Drummond of the First Church of San Francisco. The rotund minister was one of the original members of the vigilantes' executive committee. Jean despised the minister as a hypocrite who preached against the evils of greed and corruption each Sunday, then went home to his large house on Rincon Hill and his pretty Chinese concubine. The girl—a fresh one each year—was a part of the price LeClair paid Reverend Drummond to discourage the community fervor for vigilante action against the Coast and its crime leaders.

The pretty Celestial now answered Jean's knock and ushered him into an ornate drawing room. Jean recognized the girl, but she did not speak to him, keeping her eyes on the red carpeting beneath her dainty satin-clad feet. She

had finished her studies at Jean's private school several
weeks earlier, just before Jean turned her over to Drummond.

"Lotus?" he said. "Do you remember me?"

She nodded but did not look up.

"How is the Reverend treating you?"

Lotus Blossom's large eyes lifted and for a moment a
look of terror spread across her young face, but she lowered her eyes quickly and her face once more became a
mask. "Master Cornelius treats me well," she said in
perfect English. "I will tell him you are here." Her gait
was so light, it was as if she floated across the room.

The minister, dressed all in black, appeared at the door.
"Jean!" he said, "how good of you to drop by." There
was a crystal goblet of white wine in his hand, but he did
not offer any to his guest. "Sit down. We haven't had a
chat in months."

"This is not a social call, Cornelius," Jean said. "You've
probably heard by now about the murders at the Pirates'
Nest last night."

Drummond nodded. "It seems several other dives were
looted as well, and Arnstein's place was burned to the
ground."

"The Rangers did it. They want war, Cornelius."

"What's this to do with me?"

"There's going to be some killing, for the Rangers are a
bad lot. We'll shanghai and ship to the Orient as many as
we can. I speak for the Barons when I ask that you head
off citizen involvement. If left alone, we'll make short
work in ending the Ranger menace. You've got to make
them see that. When the newspapers' headlines read "Crime
has gone rampant in the Coast", and the citizens are fired
up and ready to reactivate Fort Gunnybags, we expect you
and your friends on the executive committee to calm them
down and keep them out of the way. We don't want
innocent people being killed."

"You think your war is the answer to the Ranger problem?" the minister asked, a sanctimonious look on his face. "You ought to come to church and hear the word of God."

"I'll come when you bring Lotus there and stand beside her at the pulpit," LeClair said. "When you tell your community how you've just traded another Chinese girl for her—and how you'll trade Lotus, too, when you've tired of her!

"And speaking of Lotus," Jean continued, "what have you done to frighten her?"

Drummond ignored the question, calmly sipping wine until he had finished the contents of his goblet, then placing it on a silver tray. "That's fine wine. You really ought to try some."

"I asked you a question," Jean declared.

"Oh? Yes, of course. Lotus. She's a good servant and I'm pleased with her. I treat her well enough. If she seemed frightened to you, I'd say it must be your imagination. She has nothing to be frightened of."

"I hope you're right," Jean said.

"Put your fears to rest, my friend."

Jean rose to his feet. "You *will* remember to pass our request along to the other committee members."

The minister got up, walked across the room to the wall facing them and straightened a huge oil painting which was hanging there. He stared at the painting for a moment, then turned to face LeClair. "Art is one of God's gifts to man. It enriches. I'd love some enrichment in my bed-chamber. Do you think one of your . . . er . . . associates might arrange it?"

"Is that what it takes to insure your help?" Jean asked. "An oil painting?"

"Not just any oil, Jean, a masterpiece."

Jean was tempted to say, "Then ask God for it," but merely shook his head and left.

The next afternoon a new Renoir hung over Reverend Drummond's brass four-poster bed.

Twenty-four hours after his attack on LeClair's dive Ranger Billy Hagan stood alone on the top floor of a warehouse near the waterfront. It was only seven o'clock, yet it was dark. The beginning of October had brought an early dampness to the air, and the absence of windows or artificial light in the long, wide building made the warehouse pitch black.

Hagan had been celebrating the success of his raids on the Barbary Coast dives in a saloon near the water when a fellow Ranger approached him and slipped him a note. The note said that the "chief" wished to meet Billy right away. Never having met the "chief", Billy all but flew off his barstool and raced the three blocks to the address given in the note.

He at first wondered if he had the right place, but as he entered the dilapidated warehouse and climbed up the two flights of rickety stairs, he realized it was a logical place to meet. Obviously "Mr. Big" didn't want his identity known to anyone, least of all the Coast's dive or lodginghouse operators who were members of the ruling barony. So what better place to meet than a dark, remote building?

But now as he stood alone among large crates, Billy felt fear. Why, he wondered, did the chief want to see *him*? Hagan had not been one of the twelve members of the Ranger Committee who had voted to unite the separate factions into one organized group, and find a leader who could spark a successful revolt against the Barons who owned the Barbary Coast and gleaned all the profits earned by the Coasters—using the Rangers to do their dirty work.

Hagan had not been important enough to land a spot on

this important committee, so he had taken it upon himself and a few of his closest Ranger friends to lead the first revolt against the Barons, hoping to show the Committeemen that they had made a mistake in not including Billy Hagan in their group. Had it worked? Was his summons to meet with "Mr. Big" because of his spurious attacks yesterday?

At that moment he allowed another thought to enter his mind that had first occurred to him when he stepped inside the warehouse but dismissed as being ridiculous—that maybe he was being set up by his own people to be killed. Unsure of what to think, perspiration ran freely down his underarms to his elbows and he considered making a dash for the stairs.

Before he could do anything, however, he was paralyzed with fear by the sound of metal clinking. The hair on the back of his neck stood on end. A gun being cocked? No, he decided, it was the noise a swivel chair might make when a heavy person heaved his bulk off it.

There was someone else here! Even though Billy could not see him, he felt the other's presence.

"Hagan?"

The voice was low and deep and sounded as if it came from across the floor no more than twenty feet away. "Yeah, that's my name," Billy said. "Where are you? *Who* are you?"

"Light a match, Hagan, I want to see your face."

Billy's eyes had adjusted somewhat to the darkness and he could barely make out the outline of a tall, heavy-set man. There was a musical quality about his voice—the way he rolled his r's, like a foreigner would do. He must be French, Billy thought, since the only information he had on the mysterious new leader was that the man had slipped into the country from Vancouver.

Hagan pulled a match packet from his trousers and

struck a match, holding it up before him. "I can't see *you*," he said.

"You don't have to see me. There's something I must do before I make my identity publically known."

"Why did you call me here?" Billy asked.

"You led a group of Rangers yesterday in an attack upon several Barbary Coast dives, one of them the Pirates' Nest."

Billy swallowed hard. Would his actions yesterday bring praise from the man or a sentence of death? "What do you want from me?"

"The Pirates' Nest . . . I've heard it's owned by a man named LeClair. Is this true?"

"Yeah. He owns lots of other places, too."

The silence that followed was so loud Billy could hear the blood rushing through his head.

"You've done well, Hagan, and because of it, I want you to watch LeClair, follow him wherever he goes, and report back to me. I'll be in touch as to where we'll meet. If you'll turn around now and reach inside that empty crate, you'll find fifty dollars. If you perform well, Hagan, there'll be more."

Billy turned quickly and reached into the crate behind him. Immediately his fingers struck something and he pulled it out. Even without light he could tell by the feel and smell of it that it was indeed a wad of money. "Thanks," he said. "I'll watch LeClair real good."

"One more thing, Hagan," the chief said. "From now on no more attacks without *my* order. We'll strike where and when I say so. Do you understand?"

"Yessir!"

"Go then, and tell no one of this meeting."

Elated by his encounter with the chief and the man's obvious trust in him, Billy Hagan decided to spend the fifty dollars the man had given him in a night of celebration.

Surely the chief wouldn't expect him to begin his surveillance of LeClair tonight. There would be plenty of time to watch his movements come morning.

So Billy made his way to Spider Joe's Hideaway, the worst of the Ranger-infested deadfalls and the place Billy went whenever he had a few dollars to bet on pit fights between dogs and rodents. He made a slight detour near the wharves and sauntered down a flight of slippery stone steps leading to a bulkhead where several skiffs were moored. No one was there, so he waited.

He was not disappointed. Soon a pair of scraggly-looking boys followed him down, tugging an oversized canvas sack between them. "Ahoy!" Billy said. "What've you got there?"

The boys knew Billy. He was one of several Rangers who bought from them on a fairly regular basis. Tonight they had caught a rat twice the normal size. "Feast your eyes on this one, Billy," one of the boys said.

They opened the sack and Billy peered inside. Squirming to free itself was the biggest, ugliest gray rat Billy had ever seen. His heartbeat quickened. He pulled his knife from his back pocket and shoved the tip down into the sack. The rat snatched at it with such fury that Billy feared the beast would bite off his finger and drew back quickly.

He had tested many rats with his knife before, but none had been so aggressive. Billy knew this one was a winner. He had no idea what dogs would be fighting tonight, but this rat could easily rip any of them to shreds—even the toughest dog on the coast, a terrier named Satan.

"How much?" he asked.

The taller of the two boys said, "He's mean, Billy, meaner than any we've caught all summer. Gotta ask more for him. How's thirty-five cents sound?"

"I'll give you thirty."

"Sold."

Spider Joe's Hideaway on Pacific Street, between Drum and Davis Streets, was a three-story frame structure housing boarding rooms on the top floor; a saloon on the middle floor; and on the first floor, which was lower than street level due to the slope of the ground, a large dirt pit. Beneath the building, tidewater flowed, and during a storm the pit would flood with sea water.

But tonight as Billy entered the saloon, there was not a cloud in the sky. Not far from Spider Joe's establishment, a large clipper ship was getting ready to sail, but otherwise there was little activity in the area.

Spider Joe was a Ranger and a fanatic in his love for spiders of all colors and sizes. No killing of spiders or destroying of webs were allowed on the premises and webs draped from the ceiling to the walls, across the lighting fixtures, and around liquor bottles. They practically obliterated the pictures of nudes hanging on the walls. The only people who frequented Spider Joe's were the local Rangers, and they were so used to the webs, it was to them a part of the furnishings. They insisted, however, that the bar, tables and chairs, as well as the glasses from which they drank remain clean or they'd take their business elsewhere. Spider Joe gave in grudgingly.

Spider Joe's was not the real name of the establishment, rather it was the Boar and Grizzly, but the Rangers had called it Spider Joe's in honor of the proprietor's obsession.

As Billy took a seat at the bar and ordered a beer, he noticed that the dive was packed. Across the dimly-lit, smoke-filled room a sexual exhibition, which featured a boar thrusting furiously at a jaded prostitute was taking place, but it was usual fare and most of the customers paid little attention. He wondered why the place was so crowded. "Why's business so good tonight, Joe?" he asked the bartender-owner.

Joe was a short, ugly man with thinning white hair and a

perpetual lop-sided grin. He grinned now as he trapped a fly and slipped it between the bars of a cage he kept on the bartop, in which he housed his pet tarantula. "Ain't you heard?" he said. "Tonight's the grand fight. Slimy Lewis brought his killer terrier. That's why we're packed."

Billy's eyes sparkled. Slimy Lewis was the man who owned Satan! He'd had no idea when he bought the rat earlier that he'd be placing the rodent against the best. It pleased him greatly, for he had no doubts that the beast in the bag at his foot could beat Slimy's dog.

"I got me a fat rat in this bag," Billy said, lifting and opening it a crack for the man to see. Joe peeked in, stared open-mouthed for a moment, then shook his head.

"It looks mean," he said, "but . . ."

"I got me fifty dollars," Billy interrupted, "and I'm so sure of this here rat that I'm gonna bet it all. Before I leave tonight I'm gonna double and maybe even triple it!"

"I dunno. Heard Slimy's dog ain't no ordinary mutt. Wins every time."

Hagan laughed. "That's only 'cause he's never fought *my* rat. When's the first fight begin?"

"Right after the bear."

Billy drained his glass and ordered another, leaned back against the bar and made himself comfortable for the bear show, which he had seen at least a dozen times before. The boar and the prostitute, he thought, were more interesting than the grizzly and the man. The first time he had seen the depraved act between the man and the bear, he had heaved up his supper, but not now. It had become commonplace, and he could watch the man sodomize the bear without batting an eye.

Halfway through the exhibition, Billy grew bored. He didn't notice two mean-looking strangers enter the saloon and take a seat near the bar. When the show was over and everyone, including Billy, took their drinks below to the

pit, the two strangers approached Joe with a billfold stuffed
with money. They exchanged words, then Joe nodded and
took the money.

Below, in the damp arena, the first fight had begun.
Slimy Lewis' killer terrier was stalking a large brown and
white rat, having hurt the rat badly in the opening moments of the life or death fight by catching its neck in
vice-like jaws and slamming it against the planked side of
the pit in which they fought.

"Don't play with 'im . . . get that *mouse* outa there!"
shouted a man who had bet on the dog.

"Kill 'im, Satan," Slimy ordered his dog.

Immediately the dog sprang and all but tore the rat apart
with a vicious assault. When the rat was dead, the dog
strutted around the ring, its tail wagging in victory. After
another challenge accepted by Slimy's dog—and won—the
crowd began to break up. Billy had not yet produced the
contents of his bag, but knew it was time to make his
move.

"I've got fifty dollars here that says my rat can eat
Slimy's mutt for lunch. Who wants to cover me?"

Several Rangers, who had been halfway up the stairs,
stopped and returned to the pit. "Let's see your rat," a
big, bewhiskered man with curly eyebrows growled.

Billy shook his head. "Not until I see the color of your
money," he said.

"They ain't made the rat what can stay with Satan for
long!" declared Slimy, looking over at Billy interestedly.

"We'll just see about that," retorted Billy, "after somebody covers my fifty—at 2-1 odds, since your dog's been
beatin' all comers."

"I'll cover your money," Slimy said. "Now show your
loser."

"Loser? You'll soon enough see he ain't!" Billy picked

up the sack after opening its drawstrings to let Slimy look into the bag's interior.

"Hmmmm," said Slimy, "mean-looking old boy, ain't he? Almost as big as Satan, too." His eyes opened wide as he saw that the rat had chewed a hole through the side of the canvas sack and its sharp teeth were visible through the shredded fabric.

"I'll bet twenty dollars on the rat!" declared the bewhiskered Ranger.

"I'll bet ten," said another.

"Will you cover them, too?" Billy asked Slimy.

"Will runners bring in sailors? If you want to toss your money away, Billy-boy, let's get at it before you change your mind."

Moments later, all bets covered and the pit surrounded with half-drunk Rangers, the two animals faced each other in the six-foot square dirt pit. At first the rat retreated, then scurried around the sides of the pit—seeking to escape—to the delight of Slimy.

"You sure got some brave rat there," Slimy declared.

"Yeah? Well, just wait, Slimy. Soon as he realizes he can't go nowhere, he'll stand and fight. And he'll give your damned Satan a goin' over, he will."

In a moment, as Billy had predicted, the rat found it could go nowhere and stopped in one corner to glare at Satan, who now, at Slimy's urging, moved in to attack.

"Get 'im, Satan, old boy. Now!"

But as the dog leaped at the rat with open jaws, the rodent dove beneath it, winding up on the other side. Then, as Satan flipped around to find his prey, the rat sprang at its neck and drew blood. The dog howled in pain and backed off. Slimy scowled.

"Kill him, Satan!" he roared. "Now!"

The dog tried. Ignoring his bleeding neck, Satan circled

the rat rapidly, twice in succession, then leaped for the rat's head.

But the rat was again ready, moving aside to meet the dog's thrust with a quick one of its own, and clamp its razor-sharp teeth on Satan's front leg.

Satan's yelps of pain were greeted by cheers from the Rangers and a groan from Slimy. The dog was limping on three legs now but still managed to respond to Slimy's order. "Kill 'im, Satan. You can do it! Now!"

But the dog's three-legged jump was met by the vicious rat, who burrowed into the other side of the dog's furry neck, to draw blood a second time—and hang on while Satan howled and thrashed about on the ground in pain, alternately trying to counter-attack and free itself from the rat's iron grip.

Then Satan's cries stopped and so did his thrashing as the life began to ebb from his body. The dog's eyes were glazed as they met Slimy's. The man turned his back on the animal, cursing angrily.

The Rangers cheered and Billy was ecstatic. He had won! "Drinks for everybody!" he shouted, and all except Slimy scrambled upstairs to the bar. When everyone had gone, Slimy stepped over the lifeless dog into the pit, where the rat was still trying to escape. He had gnawed a hole through the wooden side of the pit by the time Slimy reached him. Quickly Slimy threw the canvas sack over the rat, then drew the drawstrings tightly together. He grinned as he flung the sack containing Satan's replacement over his shoulder. Slimy Lewis always owned a winner, and he cared not that the winner was a rat instead of a dog. He scurried up the stairs and out a back door before Billy could come back for the rat.

Upstairs Billy was downing a brew and looking for the stranger who had backed his rat heavily just before the fight began. He found him, with another man Billy did not

know, seated at the bar talking to Joe. When he approached the man, their conversation ended abruptly.
the man, their conversation ended abruptly.

"The name's Hagan," Billy said, offering his hand. The stranger ignored it. "Just wanted to say you were wise to bet on my rat."

The man grinned. "I always bet on a sure thing," he said. "Joe, give the kid a beer—on me."

"You don't have to do that," Billy returned. "I'm buying."

"Not this one, friend. This drink's on me."

Behind the bar Spider Joe drew beer from the tap, then turned his back as he spiced it with knock-out drops. He put it down in front of Billy. The stranger raised his own glass and drank deeply, then wiped his mouth on his sleeve. "Drink up, my friend," he said, "for tomorrow we die."

Billy chuckled. Not tomorrow, he thought, as he drank most of the brew without stopping. He was still young, so it would be a day more than that. "What's your name, friend?" he asked.

"I haven't seen you around here . . . before." Suddenly the room seemed to swim before him. "Hey!" he said, shaking his head to try to clear it, "I've got to . . ." Then he slumped forward on the bar and his forehead banged down upon it.

The stranger reached into Billy's pocket, removed the money he'd won, and stashed it into his own pocket, then slid a small envelope into a pocket in Billy's jacket.

Joe pushed a tiny button under the barcounter and the floor beneath Billy's chair dropped away. Billy plunged through the trapdoor some fifteen feet into a waiting rowboat beneath the building. The man in the boat rowed the unconscious Billy Hagan to a big ship nearby, which had finished loading and was ready to sail. Two mates hauled

Billy aboard, and the man in the boat rowed away. Billy Hagan was still asleep as he was thrown into the cold, damp, dark ship's hold.

Just past midnight the clipper "*China Sea*" sailed for open waters on the beginning of what would be a two year voyage to the Orient, Africa, and South America. Twenty-four hours later Billy awoke in the ship's hold with a fierce headache and total confusion. He blinked, looked around in dismay. When he realized what had happened, he stood and shouted, "Help! I've been shanghaied! I gotta get outa here!"

No one answered. He tried the door; it was locked. Suddenly he remembered the money he'd won. Perhaps he could offer it to the captain for his safe return home. He fished into his pockets and a look of helpless hatred spread across his face. Where the money should have been was nothing but a folded note.

He stared at it blankly for a minute before he opened it. Somehow he knew that his fate depended on what he'd find inside. He took a deep breath and unfolded it.

> "*Billy Hagan!*
> *I trust you'll enjoy your reward for sending my people to theirs. I've instructed my friend, your captain, to see that you aren't disturbed during your long voyage so you can meditate long and hard on the seriousness of murder.*
> *If you grow lonely, there are sure to be a few of the rats you love so much in the hold to keep you company. Perhaps you can kill one for food. If so, you might even be fortunate enough to shorten your voyage, for I'm told ship's rats are active carriers of deadly disease.*
> *Au revoir.*
>
> *J.L.*"

J.L.? Jean LeClair? Billy cursed and kicked at the wall of the hold. The strangers had been hired thugs! *LeClair's* hired thugs! He had been a fool! Damn, he thought, it was over for him now! And just when everything had been picking up.

He re-read the note and his heart sank for it was obvious he was not destined to see the Barbary Coast again.

4

THE SIXTIETH day of the *Sea Lion's* voyage from New York to San Francisco was one of strong breezes and good weather. That was surprising, for the ship was sailing through the Strait of Le Maire, between the granite cliffs of Cape San Diego and Staten Island at the southernmost tip of South America, where many a ship was lost to treacherous squalls and storms. Soon the *Sea Lion* would be approaching Cape Horn, a group of rocky islands which jutted eastward from under the continent, then out into the wide open Pacific.

The passengers, some of them excited and fascinated, and others—especially the women who had been apprehensive at the start of the journey—had become sea-sick at first, then bored with the sameness of the slate-gray seascape. By the time the *Sea Lion* had reached the equator some twenty days out of port, not a passenger other than Beau Ashton and Amoreena Welles desired to come up on deck, choosing instead to remain in the

relative comfort of their cabins playing cards or otherwise entertaining themselves.

Monique Langlois had her own idea of entertainment.
She had succeeded in getting the second mate, Georgie
Ross, into bed with her on several occasions, but had since
grown tired of him. He was a fair lover, but it seemed to
Monique every time she wanted him to visit her in her
cabin he was either on duty or busy talking with the
crippled man, whom she had learned was a southerner
named Beau Ashton. Georgie's lack of attention irritated
her and she decided it was time she moved on to bigger
and better game.

She left her cabin and headed up the companionway to
the main deck. The sky was a pastel blue streaked with
fluffy white clouds and the air was brisk. She wrapped her
cape tightly around her and buttoned up her collar. The
weather was strange, she thought, either cold or hot. No
in-betweens. The first mate, Jones, was in the wheelhouse
checking on the helmsman when Monique approached him.

"Mr. Jones, is it?" she asked.

"That's my name, miss," he said, looking interestedly
at the thick dark curls pushing out from under a fur bonnet
and framing her pretty face. "What can I do for you?"

She did not answer, instead turning to stare at the view
from the top of the ship—at the endless miles of sea all
around and at how the sun seemed to sprinkle a blanket of
diamonds upon the waves. "My, but the view is breathtaking out here," she said.

"That it is, miss," he said, frowning. "Now get on
with it. I'm a busy man."

"You can call me Monique," she said, smiling her
prettiest smile. "I've been watching you, Jones, the way
you stand so proud and seem to know so much about
everything. I thought if you had some time, maybe you
could tell me all about the operations of a ship like this."

"Yeah?" he said, beaming. "I can make time."

"That's what I thought," she said. "You're important, not at all like that nasty Georgie Ross."

"Ross? He's not only nasty, Monique, but a bloomin' coward as well. If I'd anythin' to say about it, I'd drop him off into the bloody sea. Trouble is, his uncle's the captain."

She laughed. "So that's how he made second mate!"

"I don't mind tellin' you that I don't like him much. If he ever bothers you, let me know."

"Well," she said, batting her eyes demurely, "you see, he *has* been bothering me. Almost every night he comes to my cabin and tries to get me to . . ." Now she brought a lace handkerchief to her eyes and dabbed at them.

She did not have to spell it out. He knew well enough what she was trying to say. "That no-account bastard!" he roared. "I'll see that he'll not bother you again!"

"Oh, will you?" She touched his hand. "That would be wonderful. Perhaps I can repay your kindness later—when you get off duty."

A knowing leer appeared on his rugged face. "Your cabin or mine?" he asked.

"Whichever has a softer bunk," she replied, flashing him a smile as she departed.

Beau Ashton and Georgie Ross were in the galley amidships eating a plate of stew the cook had given them when Jones stormed in, followed by two armed guards.

"Take him!" Jones barked and the two soldiers grabbed an astonished Georgie. Each took an arm and pinned it behind Georgie's back.

"Stop!" Georgie cried. "What's this all about?"

There was a sneer on Jones' face. "You'll know soon enough."

"What's the meaning of this?" Beau demanded, following as they pulled Georgie towards the captain's stateroom at the bow of the ship.

"Get out of here, cripple," Jones snarled. "This is none of your business."

"It *is* my business. Georgie's my friend."

"Your friend," Jones said, "has been harrassing one of our passengers and that's a major offense at sea, mister. He's going to pay."

Georgie's mouth dropped open. "Who have I been harrassing?" he asked.

"Miss Monique," Jones said. "She told me all about how you tried to rape her!"

"Rape her?" Georgie said. "That's ridiculous! I didn't have to rape her—she was all too willing!"

An evil look crossed Jones' face and Beau feared he would reach for the pistol stuffed in his belt, but the mate did not, instead grabbing Georgie by the collar.

"You're not only a fool and a coward, Ross, but a real pig of a man to try to ruin a lady's reputation. I've been waiting for something like this so I could get rid of you. Now I have it."

"Why do you hate me?" Georgie asked.

"You're an idiot, Ross. You don't belong on a sailing ship. You want *my* job, and that damned uncle of yours will probably give it to you eventually—if you stay around long enough. Then I'll be nowhere! I'm not about to let a little nothin' like you get away with that."

"That's no reason to believe what that girl claims," Beau spoke up, "*if*, in fact, that's what she said!"

Jones let go of Georgie and took a step toward Beau. The mate's hands balled into fists and his temple twitched with fury. "You callin' me a liar?" he asked.

Beau shrugged. "If the shoe fits . . ."

Jones raised a burly arm to lash out at Beau, but his arm

was stayed in mid air by the harsh voice of the pipe-smoking captain.

"What the devil's going on here?" Captain Grover asked.

Jones swiveled to face his superior. "Mr. Ross has been accused of assaulting one of our female passengers, sir. I was bringing him to you."

"And along the way you were assaulting one of our *male* passengers?" the captain declared.

"He tried to stop me," Jones said.

The captain stared at Beau, then at his nephew. His expression was hard, his eyes cold. "Well, Georgie, what have you to say for yourself?"

"I didn't assault nobody, sir," Georgie declared.

"I believe him, Captain," Beau added. "I know of the girl in question. She . . . she had the gall to approach *me* in my cabin one night . . . with my fiancée only a cabin away!" Beau saw the confused look on Georgie's face. "Georgie doesn't even know about this, sir," Beau said. "He seemed smitten with the girl and I thought it best not to tell him. The truth, Captain, is that the girl's a slut. What your first mate claims is preposterous. You must see that."

Grover nodded, then turned to face Jones. "I've no question that what this young man says is correct. I, myself, have know such women and the poison they can inflict on men. If it were only that you've been poisoned by this girl, Jones, I'd let this matter rest. Unfortunately, I've had nothing but trouble with you ever since I signed you on as first mate. I'll have no more. This is your last voyage with me. You're relieved of your duties. You'll be confined to quarters for the remainder of the voyage."

"But, captain . . ." Jones protested.

"Silence!" Grover exclaimed. He turned in disgust from the sulking Jones to his nephew. "And you, Georgie, shall fill the newly-opened position of my next-in-command. What you lack in knowledge and experience, you make up for in honesty and a willingness to learn. With a little help, you'll do fine."

"Thank you, sir!" Georgie said happily.

"You sonofabitch!" Jones snarled, glaring at the captain and his nephew.

Grover signalled the two guards who had been holding Georgie. "Escort him to his cabin," he ordered.

One of the guards reached for Jones' arm, but Jones shoved him away, cursed, then stormed off toward his stateroom with the guards right behind.

That night a knock on his cabin door awoke Jones from a deep sleep and immediately angered him. It had taken him hours to clear his mind of anger and humiliation so as to find sleep—only to have someone awaken him in what seemed like barely moments after he had drifted into a peaceful, dreamless state. "Who's there?" he croaked out.

"It's me," a soft female voice replied. "Monique."

"You! I'm all screwed up because of you! Go away."

She knocked harder. "We have a 'date' tonight, remember? If you don't let me in, I'll wake the ship."

"Go ahead. I'm not afraid of what the captain might do. Not any more. I'm already dirt on his list."

"I know. That's why I need to see you."

He frowned. She knew? How? Did Ross tell her—gloating over how he'd gotten the upper hand? Jones jumped off the bunk and opened the door. "You have one minute," he said. "Then I'm going to sleep . . . alone."

She stepped inside the small room and looked around. It was square in shape with a bunk, foot locker, and mess gear. "I'm sorry," she said, turning to face him. "I heard about what happened and came to see if there was anything I could do."

"You could jump overboard," he said bitterly.

She stiffened. "Come now, Jones. You can't blame me for what happened. You couldn't have believed what I told you about Georgie Ross. I even winked when I said it. You knew all I wanted was you. I never told you to make an ass out of yourself. You did that on your own."

"If it weren't for you havin' hot pants, I wouldn't have made an 'ass' outa myself!"

"I guess I was wrong about you. Georgie's more of a man than you'll ever be."

Jones flew into a red-faced rage and grabbed her, his fingers digging painfully into her arms. She tried to pull away, but he only drew her closer, his lips bruising hers as he forced a kiss. "You're nothing but a whore. Don't fight me," he said, but in answer, she bit his hand.

For a moment it looked as if he'd throttle her, and she recoiled, but he merely laughed.

"Not a whore," he said, "a she-wolf! And I ain't never met a she-wolf I couldn't tame."

She broke away and ran for the door. He caught her, scooped her into his arms, and threw her down on the bunk. Quickly he tied her wrists together with twine, then stuffed a scarf in her mouth when she threatened to scream. She squirmed on the bunk, kicking out with her legs, but he held her in place with two powerful arms, then mounted her. With one hand he loosed the buttons of the fly of his long underwear, then raised her gown, pulling aside petticoats and tugging down lacy underthings. Without preliminary, he plunged his erect organ deep inside her.

Five minutes later it was over and he rolled off her. It took a few moments to catch his breath, and during that time he stared at her. She was still bound, her legs spread in the position he had left her, but it was her eyes which caught and held him. They seemed strange, as if they were laughing at him. Suddenly he realized why. He had done exactly what she wanted him to do! He shook his head. "You've made me the fool twice today," he said. He undid the ties and removed the scarf from her mouth. "I was wrong about you. You're no she-wolf. You're the devil himself!"

She rubbed her wrists, then looked up at him teasingly. "You might say that. I wanted you to take me that way. Why not? Is it so wrong to want variety?"

He sighed. "I don't know," he said wearily. "Now get the hell outa here, Monique. I'm tired."

"You're more than just tired, love," she said. "You're finished. Any man who allows another to humiliate him the way you let Grover has got to be either a coward or an idiot. Which are you, Jones. My guess is both."

He brought his arm up to strike her, then stopped. He stormed over to the door and yanked it open. "Get out!" he roared. "While you still can *walk* out!"

"You wouldn't *dare* touch me," she said, "but I'm leaving anyway. The stench of you is making me sick." She laughed as she sashayed past him through the open doorway out into the passageway.

He slammed the door behind her. Monique was a bitch, he knew, but she was gone and he'd have nothing more to do with her. But Grover was another story. The man could pass the word through channels that he was a troublemaker and keep him from finding a job on another ship. Jones' anger got the better of him and he slammed his fists against the wall. He didn't want any other job—he wanted to be captain of *this* ship! And no pipe-smoking, gray-haired old man was going to ruin it!

His blood boiled. He hadn't been able to get to sleep before because of the murderous thoughts he'd entertained, and now they flooded his mind again. Many times in the past he had wished he could make the captain walk the plank the way the pirates of old used to do, and now the idea made him break out into a cold sweat. If Grover were dead, *he* could have command of the *Sea Lion*. It would be a simple matter to get rid of Georgie Ross. Ross was incompetent and everyone knew it. The only man qualified to sail the clipper was Jones.

A wide grin spread across his face as he realized what he had to do. Grover's death would be no loss, he reasoned. The man was nearing sixty and would probably die soon anyway. He would simply hasten it a bit.

Jones dressed, then rummaged through his foot locker for a knife and slipped it into his belt. There was not a star in the sky as he made his way quietly up the companion-way to the main deck. The wind had died and now the ship lay idly amidst a black sea, waiting for a breeze. Some-where in the distant sky came a low rumble of thunder. Judging by the calm and the heavy sky, it would storm soon. The deck would be humming with activity to prepare the ship to ride the storm, so Jones knew he'd have to hurry.

The captain usually took a walk around the ship before retiring to his quarters for the night. The last thing he'd do before leaving was have a chat with the helmsman, so Jones headed in the direction of the bow. It was almost midnight and he hoped the captain hadn't already turned in. Jones kept to the shadows of the sails and jibsheets as he crept past the mainmast and foremast toward the great concave bow. A moment later he spotted the captain and sighed with relief.

Grover was standing on port side, out of the helmsman's field of vision, puffing on his pipe while he stared up at the blackening sky. Other than one of the four crew members assigned watch at various stations on the ship, no sailors were in sight. The closest seaman on watch stood about thirty feet from where Grover stood, a lantern at his side. In the yellowish beam cast by the lantern, Jones saw that the sailor on watch was leaning to one side against the mast as if dozing. If Jones kept away from the narrow field of the lantern's light, he'd encounter no difficulty reaching Grover.

He felt for the knife in his belt, slipped it out and clenched it firmly in the palm of his hand as he stole out from under cover and crept cat-like across the deck to the rail. Grover was easy prey. The captain stood perfectly still, his back to Jones, unaware of his danger. Suddenly Jones sprang. With one fierce plunge he buried the blade of the knife between the captain's shoulder blades. Grover grunted softly, then slumped over the rail. Jones looked to the seaman on watch to see if his actions had been spotted, then saw that the sailor had not moved, apparently unaware of what had happened. Quickly Jones grabbed the captain's legs and heaved the man over the side. Even before the dead captain hit the water, Jones had dived for cover. He held his breath and waited.

The man on watch, awakened by the splash, raced across deck. With his lantern held out in front of him, he peered down into the inky sea. A moment later he shouted at the top of his lungs, "Man overboard!"

Almost immediately the deck was filled with excited people dressed in nightclothes, passengers as well as sailors, among them Ross and the southerner Ashton. Jones scowled. He didn't fear Ross, but the crippled one was another matter; he was no fool. Jones realized he had to get rid of Ashton, too, if he were to make his takeover of the ship a reality. But now, with the crew as well as the passengers watching, was the wrong time. He had to get out of there and fast. Already several sailors were lowering the longboat in search of the man overboard. In the dark, and with a storm approaching, chances were they would not find the body. Jones fled from the center of activity toward the booby hatch, where he made a hasty retreat to his quarters below.

He had no sooner bunked down in his cabin when the wind picked up. The *Sea Lion's* masts creaked as she took the wind on her quarter and picked up speed. The winds blew harder and seemed to change direction even before the ship could be brought about and set back on course. Once she'd be riding before the wind, and then behind it.

Georgie and Beau went back to their cabins to change into dayclothes then returned to the deck. The lifeboat had been out in the water nearly ten minutes, and because of the change in wind velocity and the course of the *Sea Lion,* it was being carried further away from the mother ship. Even if the man who had fallen overboard had managed to survive the fall, Beau thought, the water was too cold to sustain life. And *they* couldn't even be *sure* a man had gone over the side. If those sailors on the lifeboat didn't come back now, there was a chance they wouldn't be able to. Someone had to order them back. "Where's the captain?" he asked Georgie. "We've got to call those men back."

Georgie scowled. "Grover ought to be up here, but I ain't seen him. I can't imagine him letting a cry of 'man overboard' go unanswered. I'd better see if anything's wrong."

"Send one of the seamen to find Grover," Beau said. "Right now you've got to get those sailors back. You're first mate now. *You* give the orders."

"Christ, you're right," he said. "I *am* first mate." He looked none too happy about it. Nevertheless he went to the starboard rail, picked up a megaphone, and shouted for the sailors to cease their search and return to ship. Ten minutes later a half-dozen windswept, sea-drenched seamen clambered back on board. They had found nothing in the water. The passengers, relishing the excitement, were disappointed and headed back to the comforts of their quarters.

Georgie had sent one of the apprentices in search of the captain, and he returned a few minutes later to report that the captain was not in his stateroom. Georgie ordered him and several other sailors to scour the ship in search of Grover. He then initiated a head count of all sailors, apprentices, and passengers, to find out who might have gone overboard. The helmsman, informed of the search, told Georgie he'd spoken briefly to the captain only moments before the guard shouted for help. But the sailors involved in the headcount returned to report all passengers and crew were accounted for—except the captain!

Neither Georgie nor Beau spoke for a moment, each with the same thought—that the man overboard and the captain were one and the same!

"Are you thinking what I'm thinking?" Georgie asked.

Beau nodded. "I'm sorry, Georgie, but I'm afraid I am. It must have been Grover."

"But how could it have happened? He's too able a seaman to have fallen overboard!"

"Could he have jumped?"

"He had no reason to do that. He loved this ship and was happy with his life."

"Then I'd say *if* the man down there is the captain, he was probably pushed over the side."

"Murder? But why? Who would do such a thing? Who would want to?"

"There's only one person on this ship who might've thought he had reason to kill Grover," Beau said. "And that's Jones."

"But if it was, we can't prove it. So what'll we do?"

"Nothing for the moment," Beau declared. "You've a ship to keep on course and a nasty storm about to break any minute."

Georgie stood beside Beau at the wheel on the bow. The winds were gaining in strength. His eyes focused on the streaks of flashing light in the sky many miles to the north and a shiver racked his slender frame. "I've a confession to make," Georgie said. "I'm scared. Especially now that my uncle may be . . . I don't know how to handle this ship in a storm. I never had to. It looks like I'm going to have to bring Jones up here to save us."

Beau kept his eyes pinned to the white-capped waves, remembering all too well the years he had been terrified of storms. He was glad he had outgrown that fear. The sea was like a series of hills that marched down on the clipper, lifting her stern and rocking her. Salt spray stung Beau's eyes as he fought the urge to shout the orders himself— something he'd been qualified for, but had never had the chance to do. "If you bring Jones up here now," he said, "You'll be making a big mistake. *I* know how to handle a ship in a storm. We weathered a few in the navy. I'll tell you what to do, and you can give the orders. No one will know."

"You think it'll work?"

Beau nodded. Then, as they made their way to the shelter of the wheelhouse behind them, he gave the first order which Georgie issued—to furl the royals, topgallants and skysails, and double-reef the topsails, lessening their exposed area by a third. With the winds growing in intensity, it was necessary to cut down the sails or the ship would be battered and blown all over the sea.

Then Beau saw out of the corner of his eye a woman clad in a heavy woolen robe and slippers walking unsteadily across the swaying deck toward them. "Amoreena!" he cried. "Go back. This is no place for a woman!"

"The passengers below want to know what's going on, and I volunteered to find out."

"We're going to ride out the storm," Georgie said.

"Tell the passengers everything's going to be all right and to stay below."

"Will you be all right up here?" she asked, her worried eyes on Beau. When he nodded, she said, "Well, to be sure, as soon as I've reported to the passengers, I'm coming back."

"No! You've no idea what it'll be like up here when we get the full force of the gale," Beau said. "Men get swept all over the deck. Some even go over the side. If you think for one minute that I'd let you stay . . ."

"And you, Beau? A man with only one good leg? *You* won't get swept overboard?"

Her words stung, but served to remind him of something he'd almost forgotten—that he wasn't the man he once was. "I guess you're right," he conceded. "I suppose a woman with two good legs is equal to a man with only one. You can stay, but only if you understand you're to do whatever you're told."

She agreed, then started back across the deck just as the rains began. It poured so heavily, and the wind-driven raindrops were so large and cold, Amoreena had trouble reaching the hatch, so she turned and raced back to the cover of the wheelhouse where Beau and Georgie stood.

Beau didn't have time to send her away, however, as he suggested to Georgie to have the helmsman ease the ship off the wind, then order the topsails shortened to the last rows of reef points. Georgie did, and a minute or two later, all the ship carried were close-reefed topsails and staysails, which were intended to help steady the *Sea Lion* as she ran before the storm. The ship lurched and heaved as she rose and fell with the mountainous waves.

Now Beau turned to Amoreena and asked Georgie to take her below. "Better get all hands at their places on deck," he added. "Looks like we're sure going to need them."

Amoreena protested, but one stern look from Beau warned her she'd better do as told. She went grudgingly with Georgie, but they got only as far as the apprentice's bunkhouse amidships. Every time they took a step forward, the wind would blow them back two. Georgie told Amoreena to stay inside the bunkhouse, where it was safe enough, and where she could see through the windows what was happening on deck, then went back to the wheelhouse.

Her eyes were large when she saw gale-driven waves smashing over the bulwarks and sweeping sailors off their feet, knocking them around as if weightless. She shrieked as Georgie, making his way back to Beau, lost his footing and tripped, to be swept backwards several feet by a wave. But he scrambled to his feet and managed to run the rest of the way to Beau.

Beau, Georgie, and the helmsman lashed themselves in place with rope. Suddenly the winds whipped the main-topgallant, royal and skysail masts—the three highest on the mainmast—and with a crackle of splintering wood, the topgallant crashed to the deck in a tangle of shrouds. As it fell, it severed the rigging of the mizzenmast behind it, and with its support gone, the mizzen-topgallant tore away and fell into the wreckage.

Only moments before the masts fell, Jones had arrived on deck. His eyes swept the sea-washed bow and focused on Ross and Ashton. They were giving orders! The *Sea Lion* was *his* ship and *he* should be issuing orders! Jones pushed through the sodden sailors and fought his way up the heaving ship toward the steerage. He would take charge! With the captain gone, it was his ship, not Ross'. But Jones never made it to the wheelhouse. The last thing he saw was the main-topsail yard, one of the ship's longest spars, break loose and come plunging down on him.

Amoreena, from her window in the bunkhouse, saw Jones being crushed under the spar's great weight. Beau had not told her about the unpleasant encounter earlier that day between Georgie, Grover and Jones, so she had no idea who he was and what he'd done, as she dashed out into the pouring rain and ran to him. She called out for help to free Jones, but her cry went unheard in the howling of the wind, the drumming of the rain, and the frantic thunder of the wild sea.

She felt for Jones' heartbeat and found none. He was dead! Terror now gripped her and she half-ran, half-slid the rest of the way forward to where Beau stood at the wheel. The helmsman had been injured in the wreckage and dragged into the captain's quarters.

Amoreena was only a few feet behind Beau when a giant wave broke over the hull, tossing the ship to one side, sending several screaming seamen sliding across the deck. Amoreena grabbed for a post and missed it, then screamed as she went tumbling the width of the ship to strike her head against a rail. She was barely conscious for several moments, but reached for and caught the rail at the starboard side of the ship to keep from going over into the boiling sea.

Georgie saw what had happened to Amoreena. Before Beau could free himself from the ropes holding him in place at the wheel, Georgie had raced across the deck to help her, heedless of the danger to himself. Just as he reached for her, however, another wave struck the *Sea Lion* and he lost his balance and went flying off the deck, over the rail and into the murky void beyond.

Beau saw the mate go over the side, then hit the water. Amoreena was alive and safe for the moment, so Beau raised himself up over the rail and jumped over the side into the water—taking the end of a guy rope with him. The water was frigid and he had barely touched it when his body shook with the cold.

"Georgie!" he shouted, clinging to the rope. He could

see nothing. "Georgie!" he shouted again, straining to stay up above the crests of the waves. For a moment he was blinded by spray, but then he caught a glimpse of Georgie's red jacket. Just then the sailor returned his call. Georgie had a grip on a piece of one of the ship's broken masts, the tip of which was partly dragging in the water.

Beau released the rope. They could climb up the mast—if Georgie had strength enough. A wave broke over him just as Beau tossed the rope away and set out to swim to Georgie. Immediately he found himself carried away from the ship and the man he was trying to save. He stroked as strongly and rapidly as he could, but made little headway against the wind-whipped waves. Then the ship suddenly veered and was aimed straight at him, riding high on a wave.

Now he was propelled close enough to the ship to see Georgie again, and grab for the mast himself. He did, but missed. He began swimming toward it again, and on his second try, managed to grab it.

"Beau!" called out Georgie, who had by now raised himself out of the water. "We've got to get back on board."

"Are you hurt?" returned Beau.

"I don't know. My left arm hurts a bit, but . . . I'll make it."

Beau reached up and grabbed a spar and pulled himself even with Georgie's position. "Come on," he said, "I'll help you."

Up on deck Amoreena held the side rail in a death grip as she watched Beau and Georgie climbing slowly, painfully to the deck up the broken mast. She held her breath when the ship was swept upward again by a huge wave—and dropped back to the surface of the sea so hard she was certain Beau and Georgie would be dashed to pieces. Miraculously, they were not.

She saw a rope ladder tied to the side of the ship and was wondering if it would help when Beau and Georgie reached the side rail and fell to the deck, drained of strength and gasping for air.

When he was again able to move, Beau dragged himself to his feet. "The wheel!" he yelled above the clamor of the storm. "It's torn free of its lashings. I've got to get to it."

"You're hurt!" Amoreena said.

But he shook his head. "I'm all right. Tend to Georgie, though. He's hurt his arm, I think."

Then Beau was gone, racing as fast as he could across the deck toward the wheelhouse. Amoreena gasped at the realization that his crutch was nowhere in evidence—yet Beau seemed not to be hindered or even remember that he needed one!

Her eyes left Beau only when he'd reached the wheel. Then she helped Georgie to his feet and the two of them made it to the captain's cabin behind the wheelhouse, where Georgie retrieved his strength while Amoreena returned to Beau's side.

The seas were still rough, but the rain had lessened considerably and so had the wind. The storm was passing!

Beau, drenched and shivering, held the wheel firmly between his two hands. "How's Georgie?" he asked.

"He'll be fine," she replied. "It's you I'm worried about."

"I'll be all right."

"I'm proud of you, Beau," she said. "In more ways than one."

"You mean because I tried to save Georgie?" he asked. "Hell, I didn't think. He tried to help you the same way—without thinking. Someone had to go after him, and I was the only one available. Maybe if I'd had time to consider that I might be risking my neck, I'd have stayed on deck."

"I don't think so," she said, "but there's something else, Beau. You've just proved that you don't really need your crutch. You may always limp a little, but you can get along fine without a crutch."

His eyes widened as he remembered using his bad leg first in the water, then in walking across the deck. Now he looked around for his crutch. When he didn't see it, he stared down at his right leg and felt his thigh, then lifted the leg up and flexed it. The muscles were sore, but Amoreena was right, he *was* standing straight and had walked without the crutch! Pleased? He was ecstatic! His eyes were warm as he tried the wheel, then pulled Amoreena into his arms.

"Now we'll really have a new life in California," she said.

Georgie came up behind, swathed in blankets and trailed by two sailors. "Thanks," he said to Amoreena and Beau. "I owe you for helping me, Beau. I'm afraid I can never repay you."

"Just get this ship to San Francisco in one piece. That'll be payment enough."

"I'll sure try, Beau. You know, I *think* I can."

"I know you can, Georgie," Beau declared.

5

IN THE weeks that followed the storm off Cape Horn, Amoreena noticed a change in Beau, a warm, infectious glow that reflected his new-found confidence, which was in sharp contrast to his earlier pessimism. He limped happily about on deck during the daylight hours helping Georgie Ross, pitching in wherever he could, then spent the evenings with his fiancée, joining in the activities the passengers devised to entertain themselves. The bitterness he'd held inside since receiving his leg wound seemed to have disappeared along with his crutch, and Amoreena couldn't have been more pleased.

Aside from a healthy mental attitude, he had acquired a deep golden tan from the clear, hot skies they had been enjoying since the ship, her sails, masts and other storm damages repaired, had sailed around the Cape and propelled by brisk winds, headed north up the coast of South America. His normally dark blonde hair had been bleached by the sun many shades lighter, and Amoreena noticed that as his hair lightened, his skin darkened, making him far more handsome than the man she had set out with from New York.

In spite of the equatorial heat. Amoreena chose to remain below deck most of the time, sewing in her cabin, to avoid the burning and drying effects of a sun reflected by a glistening sea and brisk, salty northeast trade winds. Thus, by the time they passed the equator and headed up the Mexican coastline, she had a dozen new skirts and blouses to wear when they reached San Francisco. She had even sewn a pair of frilly curtains to hang in the bedroom of their new home.

Sewing, however, was not all Amoreena did during the long, hot days. She had become friends with several of the women passengers and they often spent the afternoons playing cards and chatting. A frequent topic of conversation was the bold Monique Langlois, who the women feared was after their menfolk. Monique kept her distance from the women, but was often seen, scantily dressed, talking and giggling with the male passengers as well as the crew. Amoreena had wanted to sympathize with the girl, who was traveling alone and was obviously very young, but found she could not, for Monique was frivolous and uncaring. When Amoreena caught Monique for a second time flaunting her charms at Beau, she backed the girl up against the portside rail and warned her to stay away from him "or swim the rest of the way to California."

Monique Langlois stayed away from Beau after that, but she was angered by the turn of events since the night of the storm. The crewmen thought Jones had thrown Captain Grover overboard and she figured it was true, for she knew she had made Jones furious.

And now, as a result, Georgie Ross had become captain. If she hadn't lied to Jones about Georgie, causing Jones to try to have Georgie stripped of his duties and thus angering the captain enough to dismiss Jones from command, both Jones and Grover would doubtless be alive and Georgie would not be captain.

And Georgie had shunned her when she had tried to win back his attentions! "You're a rotten little tramp!" he had snapped. "I want nothing more to do with the likes of you."

Nothing had worked out right. The trip was long and tedious, becoming more boring by the minute. In the beginning when she had set her sights on Jones and the captain, she had envisioned lavish, sumptuous dinners at the captain's table as well as a fat purse from Jones and Grover in appreciation of her bed-time ministrations. Instead, she ate slop from the galley and wound up gaining the attentions of only common sailors. None of them offered her a penny, and she would not ask for it, for she was not a whore like her mother.

So Monique chose to spend the sweltering days alone in her quarters, reading the books she had taken from the school's library, or sleeping.

Amoreena longed to take Beau as a lover, but they had agreed earlier that they would wait, as convention ruled, until their wedding night. There were evenings when Amoreena would lie awake for hours, wondering how it would feel to have Beau's body beside her, his hands upon her. Always she told herself it would not be long before she found out.

Soon she heard from a deckhand that the Farallon Islands were ahead and that meant the Golden Gate and San Francisco could not be far. It would not be long before she'd enjoy the pleasures of bedding a man. She had wanted Georgie—who had such power as the ship's captain—to marry them, but Beau said no. They would wait and be married in the city where they would build their home.

The next day, some forty days after the storm at the Horn, the weatherworn *Sea Lion* sailed past the Farallon Islands and into the narrow entrance to San Francisco Bay called the Golden Gate. The sails were full as she glided proudly past the tiny island of Alcatraz, then came around and set a direct course for the anchorage off North Beach at the foot of Telegraph Hill.

Beau was with Georgie at the helm when they entered the Bay. Beau gave an excited shout, and Amoreena, who had been taking an early morning stroll on deck, ran to his side.

"Look," Georgie said, "over there!" He handed her a spyglass.

"Is it San Francisco?" she asked, lowering the glass to stare hopefully at him.

Georgie nodded. "And a pretty sight it is. I've seen it before."

Beau gathered his fiancée into his arms and they watched in silence as the clipper skimmed through the white-capped waves toward the wharves. Beyond the several long wharves were the sun-bathed roofs of countless dwellings, stores, and businesses dotting the waterfront.

"It's so much bigger than I thought!" Amoreena declared, as Georgie called out orders to his sailors to slow the ship by reefing sail.

As he stared across the water at the city, Beau was deep in thought. He had not expected San Francisco to be so heavily developed. It seemed as if every piece of available land near the water must certainly have been built upon and he wondered about his own land. Would he find his father's property untouched?

He and Georgie had spoken much during the voyage about their childhoods and their dreams, but they had not before now discussed California. A feeling of dread tightened the muscles in his stomach as he asked Georgie, "What's San Francisco like?"

Georgie laughed. "It's a big, wicked city and full of wicked people. There's a lot of Chinese who live in Chinatown. The rich folk are on Nob Hill, Rincon Hill, and Telegraph Hill. When San Francisco was first settled, I'm told, Telegraph Hill was where the prostitutes lived. The Chilenos once owned the city—but then came the big gold strike and the rough, tough 49ers and Sydney-town "Ducks". Some of the "Ducks" got rich in San Francisco. They're now called the Barons. The lowlife call themselves the Rangers. You'll want to stay out of their lairs."

Amoreena shivered. "Where's that?"

"It's called the Barbary Coast, Amoreena, and it's a quarter on the seacoast crawling with pickpockets, murderers, sex perverts, saloons, and bordellos. It runs from Broadway in the north to the waterfront, over to Chinatown, then south a couple of blocks. It's quiet by day, but a deathtrap by night, especially for people who don't know how dangerous it is. The Rangers feast on people like you. I know, because I found out the hard way. They rolled me in a Barbary Coast alley. I was out cold before I knew what happened and when I woke up, they'd turned my pockets inside out and all my money was gone."

"Where's Montgomery Street?" Beau asked apprehensively. He feared he already knew the answer.

Georgie furrowed his dark eyebrows. "Right smack in the heart of the Barbary Coast. You know it?"

Amoreena and Beau exchanged worried glances. "That's why we've come to San Francisco," Beau explained. "My father died and left me a piece of land on the East corner of Montgomery and Washington."

Georgie looked at them sadly. "I'm afraid you're in for trouble then," he said after a moment's thought.

"Trouble?" Beau echoed.

''That's Jean LeClair's roost,'' Georgie said.

''Who's LeClair?'' Amoreena asked.

''Around San Francisco, he's sort of a god. Owns half the Barbary Coast, he does. Don't tangle with him.''

Reverend Cornelius Drummond looked the perfect minister when he stood at the pulpit Sunday mornings, attacking the evils of lust. His speeches were always fiery, moral, indignant—demanding contriteness, quilt, and often tears from his audience. He believed himself to be what he seemed, no matter what he was privately.

Only Drummond's manservant knew Lotus' true functions in his house. Jean LeClair thought her merely a bed companion. The truth was a little more involved, for the 260—pound reverend had appetites far more sadistic than sexual, and Lotus was the current outlet for them.

At the heart of his sadism was his hatred for his mother, for Felice Drummond had been a shrew who complained constantly, nagged her husband almost to death, and beat her son simply for the pleasure of it. She had dubbed her fat son ''Corny'', and he had hated the name almost as much as he hated her. Only one man had called Drummond by that name in his adult life, and he was promptly sorry, for Drummond had broken his nose with a beefy fist.

Whenever he felt a twinge of guilt over beating Lotus, he told himself it was his mother's fault—that he wouldn't need to beat women had his mother not ingrained it into him. She had humiliated Cornelius' father often and eventually caused him to choke her to death. Cornelius was hardly sorry his mother was gone. But when his father was sent to prison for life, the boy was placed in an orphanage. He had grown up hating his mother and all women because they reminded him of her.

At the age of thirteen Cornelius Drummond realized he

found a strange sort of passion whenever he read of a woman who'd been robbed, beaten or sexually abused in the Coast's dark alleyways. He had taken to stealing out of the San Francisco orphanage at night to loiter in the trash-lined passages of the Coast, hoping to see such an attack, praying for it. When he actually witnessed one, the result was always the same—a wet spot in the front of his trousers.

Eventaully he grew up and became a minister, and could no longer haunt the alleyways seeking thrills. Instead he allied himself with the Vigilance Committees during the early fifties. It had been the best thing he could have done, giving him the chance to watch as harlots were stripped and flogged for their immoral activities. And now, LeClair and the others offered him bribes in the form of Celestial slave girls to keep other vigilance committees from being formed.

Now he dug into the locked top drawer of his bedroom bureau rummaging under a pile of underwear until he found the instrument of his passion—a many-tailed leather whip. The very feel of the straps as he ran them through his fingers excited him. The thought of the tails striking Lotus brought a lump to his trousers and he walked around the room impatiently waiting for her.

A moment later the girl arrived, her slanted eyes downcast as she quivered in fear of what was to come. She wore a robe and Drummond knew nothing was beneath it, for Lotus knew arousing his anger could make her ordeal far worse.

"Your robe," he said.

Without hesitation she undid the fastenings of her blue silk robe and dropped it to the floor. Then she covered her breasts with one arm, her furry black triangle with the other hand as he had taught her to, her head still bowed.

Drummond licked his dry lips. "Across the bed," he ordered. She fell backward onto her scarred back, still covering her genitals. Since she had become his property, he had beat her on two occasions, the last more than a week ago—too long ago!

He shook with desire as his eyes caressed her flesh. Then he brought the whip back and snapped it forward. Lotus flinched as the leather nipped at her breast beneath her arm, but did not cry out.

With a quick snap of his wrist, he again brought the leather tongs down upon her tender flesh. Again no cry. Again and again the whip snapped. Finally a tiny cry escaped her lips.

Each time he tore at her skin, leaving a trickle of blood in the whip's wake, he felt himself coming closer to his own gratification. When she could no longer stand his abuse and her arms and hands fell limply away, he threw his head back and cried out. Ecstasy was upon his face, a telltale wet spot on the front of his pants.

Afterward, Lotus crawled back to her room to clean and dress her wounds while Drummond shuffled off to his study. After Sunday services, there was the matter of donations to be counted and recorded in his ledger. He trusted no one but himself to do it. Also, if he did it himself, he could pocket half the proceeds. The congregation never questioned the use of their contributions and Drummond had managed to stash away a tidy sum.

He had barely finished counting the money when his manservant's knock startled him. "There's a gentleman here to see you, Reverend. He says it's urgent."

"Who is he?" the minister asked.

"He wouldn't leave his name. Shall I send him away?"

Drummond frowned. If it were one of the Barons or even a Ranger, the man would give his name. It meant that the stranger had to be a sinner looking for spiritual guidance. "Why didn't he come to church service this morning?" Drummond grumbled. Wasn't it enough that he went through the same ritual every Sunday? Did he have to give his free time as well? He sighed. "Very well, send him in."

A tall, heavy-set man with dark hair and a beard entered. He stood with his hands in his coat pockets, a blank expression on his face. He did not move from the rear of the room.

Drummond's mouth slowly dropped open. Those eyes . . . He had seen their intensity before, yet he didn't know this man. "Have we met?" he asked. "You seem familiar."

The man shook his head. He still did not come closer.

"What can I do for you?" Drummond asked, slightly unnerved by the stranger's manner.

"Reverend Drummond?" he said.

"That's right." That voice . . . it held an accent. Spanish? French, perhaps? Drummond had lived in Canada as a young child and remembered the French-Canadians spoke with such an accent. "How can I help you, sir? You are in need of spiritual guidance?"

"I daresay if I were, I might find a better source than you," he said mildly.

Drummond grit his teeth at the insult. "Who are you then . . . and why *are* you here?" He felt a chill of fear as his visitor's eyes seemed to strip away his mask of respectability. There were and always had been some frightening people on the Barbary Coast, but none who rivalled the man before him. Drummond had the feeling this one would personally carve out the heart of anyone who crossed him.

"Sit down, Reverend," the man said now, suddenly cold and businesslike. "We will talk."

Drummond sat, but the man remained on his feet, towering over the minister, his eyes now accusing as they bored into those of the Reverend. "You will take no more orders from the Barons," the man said, his voice a leathery whip in the stillness of the room.

Immediately Drummond tried to rise. "I take no orders from anyone!" he sputtered.

But before he could stand, the other man shoved him down with the palm of one hand. "You have," he told Drummond, "you do, but you shall not any longer do Jean LeClair's bidding. Is that clear?"

Drummond quaked with fear, but gathered himself together enough to continue to protest his innocence. "Really, Mister . . . what did you say your name was? I don't know what you're talking about. I'm a minister and take orders only from God. As for the Barons—or LeClair—I know them only by reputation. I hardly think . . ."

"Would you like me to show the bruised flesh of your Celestial to your congregation, Reverend?" the other man asked. "Would you like them to know of your secret passion? Of how you must whip a woman to achieve your sexual gratification?"

Drummond's face turned the color of the purple carpet beneath his feet. "Why, that's a . . . confounded blasphemy! A lie! It's . . ." But a look at the expression on the other man's face stopped him in mid-sentence.

Now the other smiled. "You needn't fear, Reverend. I'll not announce to the world what a satanic creature you are in your black soul. I don't have to, for you're more valuable to me with your reputation intact than you would be if I shattered it. Now, let us discard your pretenses and get to business. You heard what I've told you? You'll not do the Barons' bidding any more. Understand?"

Drummond, sick to his core, could easily have retched. But he did not—merely nodding his agreement. For what choice had he? How, he wondered, had this man come to know of his needs. He must find out. And would, somehow!

"LeClair's single demand upon you is to keep the Vigilance Committee from a rebirth like your Christ, am I correct?"

Drummond nodded. Did the man know everything? "What do *you* want of me?" he asked.

"Nothing more than control of your loyalties . . . for the moment. Then we will see what is necessary."

"Are you . . . the one LeClair spoke of? The one who has been brought in by the Rangers?"

A flicker of anger passed over the other's face, but it was quickly replaced by a look of amusement. "So," he said, "Jean knows of my presence, does he? Well, all the better!" He laughed.

"You are the one, then?" Drummond asked.

"I am who and what I am!" his guest declared ominously. "You will do well to know neither. Now, one more thing—you will say nothing of my visit to LeClair or the others. A word from you will bring about an early reunion of you and your God. Do you understand?"

Drummond gulped, his throat dry. "What of my . . . remuneration? Mine is a poor church and I've needs that the Barons have looked after."

"Needs?" The other man laughed uproariously. "Yes," he said at last, "I suppose you do, you wretched parson. You may continue to accept what Jean and the other Barons offer and if you prove yourself to me—by reporting to me the next time you receive a visit from the Barons—I will arrange something for your other needs. A pretty white virgin, perhaps?"

Drummond's knees were suddenly weak and his senses spun. A white virgin?

"I know the objects of your affection have always been Chinese, Drummond," the other man said, "but surely it is only because of the difficulty in obtaining and keeping subservient white flesh. So we will see if you serve me as you have Jean."

When the man was gone, the Reverend poured himself a tall glass of wine and tried to calm his jangling nerves. His visitor, he thought, was a man to be reckoned with. What he wanted was a mystery—unless what he was trying to head off was a Baron-ordered Vigilance Committee! Yes, he thought, that was it! As long as the Barons paid bribes to prevent a Vigilance committee, there would be none. But what if the Barons found themselves in an all-out war with the Rangers? Then LeClair and the others might well ask for a Vigilance Committee to check the destruction caused by their own pawns! And the Vigilance Committee would still be comprised of Baron-supporters, so they could take care that Baron-owned enterprises would be preserved and protected.

The minister shivered as he thought of the man's promise to find him a pretty white virgin.

His hands shook at the thought of having a beautiful white body splayed obscenely on *his* bed. She would, he thought, not be as obedient as the celestials, but he could overcome that. He would bind her and gag her first. And then . . .

Later that afternoon, Beau was in his cabin preparing to disembark when he heard Georgie Ross shouting through the megaphone, "All hands on deck." Was there fear in his voice? Beau wondered, as he stopped packing and limped up on deck, making his way forward to be met by Georgie's angry scowl.

"Out there!" he said, pointing towards the distant shoreline. Heading toward them at a fast clip was a small fleet of skiffs.

"They're Whitehall boats," Beau observed, his eyes appraising the sails headed their way. The Whitehall boat, he knew, was a type owned and operated by professional boatmen who ran a ferry service from shore to incoming ships. It was a Whitehall boat which had brought their pilot less than an hour ago. "Are they coming to transport the *Sea Lion*'s passengers ashore?" he asked.

The mate shook his head. "Not those boats, Beau. They're carrying runners. A bad lot, those runners. Unscrupulous procurers of men, working for the waterfront boardinghouse masters. Around the Barbary Coast the masters are called crimps, but I call them bastards. They're tricky, tough shanghaiers, and in league with some of the thieving ship's captains. The runners are paid money for every sailor they shanghai and bring to the crimp, and the crimp makes money selling the sailors back as crew to some ship's captain. It's a bad business. We've got to keep those runners away from the *Sea Lion*'s crew, and it won't be easy. They're tough as nails and dirty as sin."

"You've been to San Francisco before," Beau said. "How did you keep the runners away the other time?"

"Grover handled it. I suppose he bribed them, but I can't be sure. He went down into one of their skiffs and spoke with them. The boats turned right around and left. I wish he were here now."

"Well, he isn't, Georgie, so *we're* going to have to do something and quickly. Those boats are going to be here damn quick."

"If they can't get aboard," Georgie said, "they can't do any harm. I guess that's our only hope—to keep them from boarding." Georgie issued orders to pull in any ladders, rigging, or other ropes a runner might use to climb up the side of the ship. Then he told the crew to arm themselves. "Prepare to repel boarders, men," he roared in as firm a voice as he could muster. "If not, you'll soon find yourselves shanghaied on another ship!"

Soon the Whitehall boats had closed to within shouting distance, surrounding the *Sea Lion* and keeping pace with her. "Ahoy, there, *Sea Lion*," one of the runners called out from the first row of boats. "Let us come aboard."

"Permission denied," Georgie called back defiantly.

A moment of silence followed. "Who the hell are you? Where's Grover?" the runner bellowed.

"Lost at sea. *I'm* the captain here."

The runner, a big, burly man, laughed uproariously. "Since when are they makin' captains outa snot-nosed kids?"

"Turn your boats around and head back to shore," Georgie roared. "You'll not trick any of *my* crew into going with you."

"I've got plenty of free whiskey here for all, so why not let your men decide?"

"They've already decided. Now get out of our way."

"We'll leave, *captain*," the runner declared, "when we get paid insurance money."

"Insurance?" Georgie echoed. So that was what they were up to.

"Against us taking over your ship!"

"You'll get no money from me!" Georgie shouted. The fact was he had none to give them. He did not know about the contents of the captain's strongbox in the captain's cabin.

"You're not being wise, lad," the runner responded, brandishing a sword menacingly. "Now Grover, *he* was plenty wise. He paid insurance money. And you'd better come across, too. Five hundred dollars ought to do it."

Georgie turned to Beau. "My uncle *did* pay them, Beau. What should I do?"

"Pay them nothing. When we reach shore, we'll get the law and . . ."

"There's not much law on the Barbary Coast," Georgie said sadly.

"What kind of a hellhole is this place?" Beau declared. Georgie just shurgged.

"What's it gonna be, mates?" the runner yelled.

"We're not going to give you bastards one cent," Beau shouted. "Now get the hell out of here!"

But his words were barely out when, without warning, runners from a half-dozen boats tossed grappling hooks over the ship's sides, then began climbing the ropes up the *Sea Lion's* hull.

"Repel boarders!" Georgie screamed. He drew his cutlass and went to the rail. The ship's crew, some fifty strong, armed with pistols and cutlasses were ready for the runners' efforts to get on board. Wielding their blades, they cut every rope and laughed as the runners toppled backwards into the icy cold Bay. Then they stood, pistols in hand, and watched the runners climb back into their Whitehalls.

Georgie, spotting the spokesman for the runners still in his boat, took aim and fired at the mast beside him. The runner jumped away, then cowered on deck. "I think *you* need the insurance, lad," Georgie called out.

"You're crazy!" the runner returned, but already the boat had come about and headed back toward shore. The other boats soon followed, to the cheers of the *Sea Lion's* sailors.

Georgie was ecstatic. "We showed them, didn't we!" he declared.

There was a grin on Beau's face, even though in his heart he was beginning to dread setting foot on what obviously was a rough, tough Barbary Coast. "Captain Grover couldn't have handled it better, Captain Ross," he said.

Although Georgie had assumed command of the ship after Grover's death, no one before this had called him captain. They called him "sir" and "Mister Ross", but never captain. "*Captain* Ross?" he said now, his eyes bright. "Say, that's bloody all right, Beau! I'm beginning to even feel like a captain!"

"You should, Georgie," Beau said.

The new captain, his crew, and the passengers were elated over the events and their arrival on the California coast, but there was one of the last who was not. Not far away stood Monique Langlois, who was irked that Georgie should benefit from the events which she had set in motion. Well, she would get even when they were in port. If her mother was anything like she had heard, arranging for Georgie Ross' comeuppance would be simple! Monique was aglow with anticipation as the ship, directed by it's pilot, moved into port.

Jean and Faye had just finished their monthly business dinner in the LeClair mansion's formal dining room. The conversation during the entree of flounder stuffed with crabmeat and dessert of lemon pie had been mainly on the monthly profit picture of LeClair's bagnios. As always, prostitution was a money-making business and LeClair was reaping the rewards.

Now, as they sipped sherry in the parlor, the sun's rays filled the room with a subdued glow, and the conversation turned to the last shipment of Cantonese girls. They had arrived late, but safe, yesterday morning.

"We've got a good group," he told Faye. "One or two are actually beautiful. I'm saving them for our Chinatown parlor house. The others are pretty and healthy and should command a high price at the auction the day after tomorrow."

"How do they compare to Lance Morgan's shipment?" she asked.

"No comparison. Ti Wang's still the best agent around."

Faye swished the amber fluid in her glass, her mind already on another subject. "You know, Jean," she said, "the girls at the Pirates' Nest still haven't gotten over the killings the other night. They keep expecting Hagan and the others to come back. I don't know what to tell them."

"Hagan's gone," Jean said. "I've had him shanghaied. As for the Rangers . . . there will most likely be a war, but things have been quiet lately. They're planning something, and we've got our informers out there seeing what they can learn. Tell the girls not to be scared, Faye. The Rangers won't hit the same place twice. It's the Rat's Nest and Crow's Nest they'd go after, so I've posted extra guards there. If it'll make you feel better, I'll send some more men over to the Pirates' Nest as well."

She nodded, and for a while they both sipped their drinks in silence. The sun had just set and Jean went to the panoramic windows of his parlor to stare out at the orange-red sea. Just then a flurry of sail appeared on the horizon. Was it the *Sea Lion*—the ship Monique was coming in on? It was due any time now. He called Faye to the window.

Her gaze fell upon the slowly approaching ship. Jean handed her a pair of field glasses and she brought them to her eyes and waited until she could read the large red letters painted on the ship's hull. "That's the *Sea Lion*," she said, "Monique's ship." There was no joy in her voice. She lowered the glasses and looked sadly up at Jean. "I hate to admit it, but I've been half hoping that ship might get lost at sea."

"She's just a child, Faye," he said. "Since when have you been afraid of children?"

She smiled bravely. "I ain't afraid of anybody!" she declared, then drank the rest of her sherry in one gulp.

Jean patted her gently on the back. "That's the tough bird I know. For a moment I thought you'd gone soft." His eyes were warm and teasing.

"Will you . . . come with me? To the docks?" she asked. There was a pleading tone in her voice that Jean had never before heard.

"You're really frightened, aren't you?" he observed. She nodded. "Well, all right. I'll come."

The year-round temperatures in San Francisco were pleasant and mild, but the nights could and often did turn cool. Tonight it was chilly and would be even more so at the docks. Jean helped Faye into a light wrapper, then donned his own black coat. It was just beginning to get dark, so they rode to the water's edge in Jean's chaise. The docks were alive with milling people, some with horses, others with carriages. Some waited for the passengers, others for stevedores to unload the cases of merchandise in the ship's hold. The *Sea Lion* was to take on the wares and produce of local San Franciscan merchants on her return trip to New York scheduled in about two weeks.

The giant clipper had dropped anchor as Jean's chaise pulled up at the wharf. "I'm not even sure how Monique will look, Jean." Faye said. "Do you think she'll be pretty?"

"With a mother as gorgeous as you?" he said with a chuckle, "how can she not be?"

"You don't have to butter me up, Jean. I'm gettin' old and not so pretty . . . and I know it. I hope for her sake she's turned out as ugly as Spider Joe. On the Barbary Coast, beauty is more of a curse than anything else."

"You fear for her too much. You've got to give the girl some room, Faye."

"Speaking of room, I've got to find a new place. My place over the Pirates' Nest is only one large room and not big enough for both of us. A growing girl should have some privacy."

"I'll check with my associates, Faye. I'm sure we'll find something right for you and Monique. Maybe even a house."

It was the perfect solution, but Faye's reaction was strange. She stared at the hands folded tightly in her lap and said, "I appreciate that, Jean, but that's not what I had in mind. I like living where I am—close to my girls. I like *my* freedom. Know what I mean? How could I entertain *my* friends with a teenaged girl around?"

Jean frowned. Now he understood what had been bothering her all along. She was afraid Monique would hamper her lifestyle. And no doubt she was right. Faye's lovers were hardly something she could conceal for long, and not easy for a girl of thirteen to understand. "So you don't want Monique to stay with you," he said. "That's going to pose a problem."

"Not if . . . *you* were to take her in," Faye said eagerly. "You've plenty of room in that house of yours. You wouldn't even have to see her if you didn't want to. I'll come by often enough and take her here and there." She stopped and stared at the unenthusiastic expression Jean wore. "It's only fair," she added. "After all, Monique may be your daughter, too."

He had wondered how long it would take before she threw that in his face. "Or she might be Lance Morgan's," he observed, "or Otis', or . . . shall I go on?" He didn't wait for her reply. "I paid for Monique's schooling at Miss Montvale's. What have the others done, Faye?"

She cursed. "I'm sorry I asked. Forget it."

Jean studied her profile. Faye was forty-three, a hard-bitten madam whose passions were money, drink and young men. She was a good worker who got along well with her girls because she knew intimately their trials and joys. But as a mother, Faye had already failed. Living with such a woman could do Monique little good. Jean had no idea where the girl should go. For the moment, at least, she had to stay with either her mother or him. He supposed he could offer her lodging—temporarily. "She can stay with me, Faye, but only for a little while. Then we'll have to make other, more permanent arrangements."

Faye grinned. "I knew you'd come around," she declared.

The first of the passengers began to walk unsteadily down the gang plank. Jean and Faye left their chaise and stood among the waiting crowd. Night had fallen and overhead gas lights illuminated the docks. A tall blonde girl stood at the top of the gangplank, her back to them. Jean spotted her and wondered if she might be Monique. "Is Monique short or tall?" he asked Faye.

She shrugged. "I've no idea."

"What color is her hair?"

"Brown. No . . . black. Hell, I don't know!"

LeClair sighed. "We can't walk up to every dark-haired girl and ask if she's Monique. I'll get the captain. He should be able to point her out." Leaving Faye at the docks, he made his way up the gangplank.

6

FALL, 1862

SAN FRANCISCO! They were really there! Amoreena was exultant as she finished packing while the clipper ship docked. Moments later, a stuffed carpetbag in each hand and a satchel tucked under her arm, she made her way to the gangplank through the opening in the bulwark of the *Sea Lion*. Beau, himself loaded with bags containing not only clothes, but all the meager possessions they had managed to pack for their new home, was right behind her until one of the passengers—a fat old dowager by the name of Brumyster, pushed her way past him. The woman was three times the size of Beau, and had her spindly grandson with her. She and the young boy fell in directly behind Amoreena as she set foot on the top of the gangplank.

Amoreena found the Barbary Coast awe-inspiring when she got her first close-up view of it. There were so many people! It was night, but the scene before her was brightly lit. Beneath the multitude of gas lights lining the wharves

were regal carriages of the rich as well as worn conveyances of the poor workers. She saw the seemingly endless
row of docks, heard the creaks and groans of wooden
clippers rocking at anchor nearby, and smelled the savory
scent of fish frying in distant restaurants. Square lamp-
lights illuminated the fronts of boardinghouses along the
waterfront, and carried along by the brisk breeze was the
jingle of piano music. It was like a giant carnival!

Just then fat Mrs. Brumyster, spotting her daughter
waiting amongst the crowd on the pier, barreled through
the people on the top of the gangway, thrust Amoreena
aside and waddled down the plank, her grandson tugging
on her coatsleeve. The force of the woman's shove sent
Amoreena flying forward, to trip on her skirt hem and fall
flat on her face. Her bags went toppling down the wooden
inclined gangplank straight into a man who had been
coming up.

Amoreena, her face bruised and cut, scrambled to her
feet, dusted her gown and tried to re-arrange her mussed
hair. She hoped no one had witnessed what happened, yet
knew instinctively the man at whose feet the bags lay had
seen everything. She glanced behind her and saw that
Beau had not yet emerged from the ship onto the gangway.
When she turned back, the stranger had picked up her bags
and was making his way toward her. Her cheeks burned
with embarrassment as he arrived and stood smiling before
her. Disheveled and mortified at having been seen at such
an inopportune time, she could only smile back at him
rather sickly.

He put the bags down and removed a white linen handkerchief embroidered with the initial "J" from an inside
coat pocket. Before she could protest, he dabbed gently at
the cut on her cheek, cleansing the wound of dirt and
blood. She allowed him to continue, noticing how tall he

was, and well dressed. He wore light gray trousers beneath an elegant black coat. On his head was a black hat, beneath it hair of ebony black. He wore sideburns long and thick, and his tanned face and dark attire made him look strangely attractive, yet menacing.

"The fat old hag deserves to be thrown in the Bay," he said, sounding more than a little serious. He finished cleaning her cut, then handed Amoreena the handkerchief.

"Thank you," she said, ignoring the comment even though she could not disagree.

Despite a tear in the skirt she had made during the voyage, and several golden strands of hair which had come loose, she was a pretty sight and the stranger looked at her approvingly. "You'll be fine now," he said. "If I can be of further assistance . . ."

"Thank you, but no thank you," she said. "My fiancée is aboard." Just then Beau appeared through the bulwark and stepped onto the gangplank. "Here he comes now," she said, pointing.

Beau saw her and hurried down to the middle of the plank to join her. His eyes widened at the sight of her face and the strange man talking to her. The man glanced in his direction, bowed to Amoreena, then continued up the plank to disappear into the ship.

Beau frowned. "Who was that?" he asked, "and what happened to your face?"

"I have no idea who he was," Amoreena said. "I tripped and he . . . caught my bags." Suddenly she realized she still had the man's handkerchief. She started to say something about it to Beau, then checked herself and stuffed it in her purse.

"From the cut of his fancy clothes, I'd say he's probably one of those rich men Georgie told us about—the ones who live up on the hills."

Amoreena didn't reply, just shrugged and followed Beau down to the pier.

"Yes, sir," Georgie said to the tall man in the elegant black coat in answer to his questions, "I'm the captain. Miss Langlois? Yes, she's aboard. She's still on board the ship, too, 'cause I just came by her cabin and heard her packing. You her father?"

"Where are her quarters?" Jean LeClair asked, ignoring the question.

"Down the stairs and to the left. Third cabin on the left."

"Thanks." Jean went below, found Monique's cabin and knocked once. The door was opened by a tall, slender girl with long, dark hair.

A wide smile lit her face and her eyes glistened at the sight of him. "If all San Franciscans look like you, Mister," she said, "I think I'm going to like it here."

Jean grinned. "You must be Monique," he said.

"That's right. And who are you?"

One of a group of passengers who appeared just then heading for the stairs accidentally shoved the corner of her hatbox into Jean's ribs and, although Jean shrugged it off, Monique grimaced. "Stupid clown!" she declared. Then she said sweetly to Jean, "Please come inside where it's more pleasant."

He stepped into a tiny, but neat, cabin. "I'm Jean LeClair," he said. "A friend of your mother."

"Friend? Hah! You must be the one who's been paying to keep me at that horrid Miss Montvale's."

LeClair frowned. Faye had told only one person—Miss Montvale—of his financial help. "Who told you that?" he demanded.

"I . . ." She was about to lie, but a look into LeClair's

fierce eyes changed her mind. "I read through my files at the school, Mr. LeClair. I also learned that my mother is a whore."

"*Was* a whore," he corrected. "She's now a madam. She shepherds *my* whores. But tell me, what does a child of thirteen know of whores?"

"I'm not a child, Jean." She moved closer to him and he was aware of the sweet fragrance of her perfume. He was surprised at the large breasts straining against the blue velvet material of Monique's bodice. Her nipples were hard and erect and stuck out like small buttons, and he had the discomfiting urge to touch them. He had to remind himself that Monique was thirteen—and might be his own flesh and blood—to keep from seizing her and accepting her undisguised invitation.

"I know of whores, and a lot of *other* things, too," she said. She pushed her body against his and her arms snaked around his neck. She closed her eyes and parted her lips, moistening them provocatively with her tongue.

She was tempting and it took some will power to ignore Monique's mouth. He laughed inwardly that he should find such a young girl inviting. "I'm flattered, Monique," he said, gently removing her arms from his neck, "but . . . ."

"But what?" she asked. Her eyes flipped open and she stared disappointedly at him.

"But I might well be your father," he said.

His revelation startled her, but only for a second. "I should have guessed," she declared. "Why else would *you* pay for *my* schooling." She stepped back, her pretty face drawn into lines of anger. "Are you still bedding my mother. Do I have brothers and sisters I know nothing of?"

"Your mother and I were together only once," LeClair snapped. "Now, your mother is waiting on the pier to see you. Are you ready?"

She shrugged, turned away, shut the catch of the last of her bags, and pulled it off the bunk. "Let's go," she said sarcastically. "I can't wait to meet my mother the whore."

Jean had a feeling there would be fireworks when she did.

"Well, what do you think of San Francisco?" Beau asked Amoreena as they rode in the rear of a carriage they had hired, which was now winding its way through the waterfront to a two-storied green building on Pacific Street called the Pacific Inn.

"There's so many saloons!" she declared, "and aren't those dancehalls?" She pointed to several buildings with gaudy signs featuring scantily-clad women. "Why do those rows of houses over there have red lights above the front doors?"

"They're houses of ill repute," Beau said, "bawdy houses."

Amoreena was not shocked by their nature, only their number. "But so many? Are the men of the Barbary Coast so hot-blooded?"

Beau chuckled. "I hope not. I'll have to fight them off to keep them away from you."

Now, as they pulled up before the brightly-lit hotel, Amoreena's brows furrowed. "Aren't we going to seek out our property tonight?" she asked.

"I thought it best that we wait until first light. It'll be easier to find. Everything looks different in the dark of night."

"Why? The main streets are lit. Only the alleys and side streets are in darkness. Surely after all these weeks at sea, wondering . . ."

"I want to wait until morning," Beau cut in. When he saw that his tone had hurt her, he apologized. "I have a feeling we may not like what we see, darling,'' he explained. ''I'd rather face it in daylight after a refreshing night's sleep. Please try to understand.''

She nodded. ''I think I do,'' she said. She took his hand in hers and kissed it. ''Tomorrow then, after breakfast.''

He helped her out of the carriage, paid the fare, then walked arm in arm with Amoreena up the hotel's flight of stairs. The clerk was a smallish man, friendly, and he smiled a welcome.

''We'd like two rooms, please,'' Beau said, and the clerk nodded and opened a leather-bound register, showed Beau where to sign.

But now Amoreena pulled Beau away from the desk. ''Could we get just *one* room?'' she whispered. ''It would be cheaper, and . . .'' The scandalized look on his face stopped her. ''I'm . . . this is all so new, Beau. I'd feel . . . safer . . . if we were together tonight. You could have the bed, Beau. I could sleep on a cot.''

''No, Amoreena,'' he said. ''I'll not allow you to do something you'll regret later. We've waited long for our marriage night, and I've respected your strict upbringing. I won't start our new life here in San Francisco on the wrong foot. Surely you agree.''

She didn't, but this was not the time to argue with him. There would be plenty of nights together after they exchanged vows. ''All right,'' she said. ''Separate rooms. But, Beau, try to get them adjoining each other if you please.''

Late that night Beau was startled when Georgie knocked at his door. ''I'm staying at Mrs. Dupree's lodginghouse a few blocks down toward the water,'' Georgie explained, ''until the *Sea Lion* goes back to sea in a couple of weeks.'' Then his face sobered. ''The reason I'm here is . . . well, I was drinking up near Montgomery Street, Beau. You're not going to like this, but as I suspected, there's a concert-saloon on your land. It's called the Pirates' Nest, and it's owned by the biggest and most powerful of the Barons—Jean LeClair!''

"No!" Beau cried. "Dammit, are you sure?"

"I wish I weren't. Checked it out by askln' around the dives in the neighborhood."

"LeClair," Beau said slowly, as if it were a dirty word, "He's the one you warned me about on the ship. He . . . the bastard *stole* my land!''

"He did, Beau, but there's little you can do about it. He's a Baron, and he didn't get to be one by playin' fair.''

"I don't care if he *is* a Baron! He's a damned thief and I'm going to get my land back!''

"Don't be stupid," Georgie said. "You don't just walk up to someone like LeClair and call him a bloody thief!''

"What am I supposed to do, Georgie? Go over there and thank him for stealing what's mine?''

It took Georgie nearly an hour to calm Beau and convince him to "at least think about it overnight." Beau, still fuming, agreed reluctantly.

Then Georgie left, saying he'd meet Beau tomorrow night at the Pirates' Nest for a drink and a look around. Then together they'd discuss what to do about getting back what was rightfully Beau's.

Alone again, Beau climbed into his bed and tried to sleep. But instead his mind was filled with thoughts. LeClair *had* stolen his land! Even back in Virginia when his father, on his deathbed, told him of the property, Beau had been uneasy about it—had feared something like this. What should he do? Confront LeClair? Accuse him directly? If what Georgie said about the man was true, and Beau suspected it was, such a foolhardly act would probably get

his head bashed in. So what was his alternative? Like a
dog with his tail between his legs, should he run away and
give up his claim on the land? The idea was repulsive and
he quickly put it out of his mind. There was only one thing
he could do. He might have a game leg, but he was still a
man and had to act like one. He had to face LeClair. Yet
even as the thought was born, he knew it was foolish and
agonized over it.

The grandfather clock in the hotel's hallway chimed
twelve times—the midnight hour. It was time Beau stopped
feeling sorry for himself and for the bad luck that had
befallen him and Amoreena. But now, suddenly, his uncer-
tainty was replaced with intense anger. No one had ever
pushed Monte Ashton around, and no one would step on
Beau Ashton either! He stared up at the dark ceiling and
muttered, "Don't worry, Father, I'll get our land back—
complete with LeClair's saloon! I have your deed, signed
by you, and that's all I'll need to prove to this Baron
bastard that he must give it up! I swear that no matter what
I have to do and how long it takes, I'll get our property
back!"

He was sure his father, wherever he might be, was
pleased. Beau was too. With that oath on his lips, he fell
into a sound sleep.

On Telegraph Hill, Monique sat with her mother and
Jean in the study of Jean's home answering questions
about school, the voyage, and her first impressions of the
Barbary Coast. All were "boring". But she was as disappointed in her mother as she was bored. She had expected
a beautiful, vibrant, lady-of-the-evening, and instead found
a hard-spoken, fading woman.

Jean had escorted Monique down the gangplank to the
waiting Faye an hour earlier and the two women had stared

at each other for long, awkward moments, saying nothing. Finally Jean had interceded and introduced them.

"Your nose and mouth resemble mine," Monique had said bluntly, "but you're a lot older and less attractive than I'd expected."

Jean had seen Faye's rising anger and headed it off by suggesting that they get inside the carriage and proceed to the "Hill". Conversation during the ride to LeClair's mansion was light, mostly about the myriad sights and sounds of the Coast's nightlife. Monique seemed to glow when Jean spoke of the crime and how important it was "that you never walk alone at night" in these parts.

Now, after a cup of piping hot rum—which Monique had insisted she be served despite her age—she stretched in the winged chair and said, "I have a favor I'd like you to do for me, mother."

Faye had felt uneasy all evening. After her monthly business dinner with Jean, she was supposed to have met Charles Latimer for an evening together. Of Faye's several lovers, Latimer was her favorite, and the most difficult to pin down. Charles and she had finally succeeded in arranging a "date", only to have Monique's ship arrive and spoil their plans.

Faye's first impressions of her daughter were mixed. She was pleased that Monique had turned out so pretty, but was in a strange way jealous of her.

Now Faye sat bolt upright, hoping the night would soon end so she could go home and forget her ruined plans and the strange girl who was her daughter. At least put it out of her mind until tomorrow. But what was this about a favor? she wondered. Monique had just arrived and they didn't even know each other. What favor could she possibly ask?

"What kind of favor?"

Monique opened a button at the base of her throat to

expose only the barest hint of white breasts below. She glanced in Jean's direction momentarily then turned back to her mother. "The way I figure it, Mother, you must feel pretty guilty for keeping me in that prison of a school all this time. And even now, after thirteen years, you push me off on Jean here. Not that I won't like staying with him. I think I'm going to *love* it." She threw him a seductive look, which Fay didn't fail to notice. "The fact is that you've been a lousy mother and you gotta feel rotten right now. So, I'm gonna give you a chance to redeem yourself."

Faye did feel rotten. Many times over the years she had chided herself for not writing to Monique or taking a trip to New York to visit her. She knew she was a bad mother, but resented being told so. There was fire in her eyes as she rose and stood before the girl. "So you're going to give me a chance to redeem myself," Faye said sarcastically. "How nice of you! Redeem myself? For what? I sent you to the finest of schools . . ."

"With Jean's money," Monique cut in, unperturbed by Faye's sudden change of tone. "If he hadn't been rich, where would I have been? Rotting in some gutter? Prostituting myself?"

Faye fumed, but she had no answer. She could have kissed Jean when he stepped in to support her.

"There's no need to mince words, Monique," he said. "You were a mistake. Your mother tried to rectify that mistake by giving you the best home she could provide. Hell, she knew she'd not be able to care for you, and that's the only reason she sent you away."

"You can stuff it!" the girl snapped. "I don't care why things happened back then—all I care about is now!" She turned to Faye. "Are you going to be a mother to me now and help me, or are you going to turn your back on me again?"

Faye wanted to tell her to go to hell but swallowed hard and calmed herself. This snippy little brat *was* her daughter. In a way Faye had failed in her obligations to the child, and she knew she was lucky to be having a second chance. Perhaps with a little attention, Monique could yet turn out all right. But the first thing Faye had to do was establish authority or the girl would step on her every chance she got. "Look, Monique," she said, "I'll meet you halfway, but you must do the same. If I do you a favor, you'll do one for me in return. Do we understand each other?"

Monique made a show of studying her red-painted fingernails. Then she sighed and said, "All right. Now will you listen?"

Faye nodded.

"I need your help. I have no one else to turn to. I . . . I was *raped* aboard ship."

"Raped!" Faye gasped. "Why didn't you say so before?" Her face turned crimson with rage. "Who?" she demanded. "Who was the bastard who did it to you?"

Jean shook his head at the exchange, but neither the woman nor the girl paid attention to him now. He knew it was time he left—before he said the wrong thing. Monique had all but tried to seduce him aboard the *Sea Lion*! Raped? He doubted anyone had to rape her, but he said nothing. This was a matter between mother and daughter. He had given of his time just to go with Faye to pick Monique up at the docks, then offered the girl the hospitality of his home. What more could he do? What more did he *want* to do! He stood up and excused himself.

After Jean left, Monique began to cry. They were fake tears, but nonetheless aroused her mother's sympathy. She knew she had Faye right where she wanted her. "It was awful," Monique sobbed, then jumped up to throw herself into her mother's arms. "He made me do all kinds of horrible, disgusting things."

The close contact with Monique awakened Faye's long dormant maternal instincts. "Who is he, child?" she demanded. "I swear I'll make him pay for hurting you."

Monique pulled away and stared teary-eyed into her mother's eyes. "Would you? I'd really be grateful. His name is Georgie Ross and he's the captain of the *Sea Lion*."

Faye set her jaw. So the man was a sailor. All the better. She'd had a few sailors shanghaied over the years. Give them a few drinks, a little drug and sex, and it was easy to send them to where they'd never been seen or heard from again. "He'll bother you no more," she said.

Monique squeezed her mother, planted a kiss on her cheek. "Now, what can *I* do for you in return?"

Monique seemed eager to show her appreciation, and Faye found herself beginning to like the girl. Maybe in a while, when they grew to really know and understand each other, respect—and even love—might follow. "For now," Faye said, "just be happy here in your new home."

Monique grinned. "I already am."

In his bed a short time later, Jean heard the thud of the front door closing as Faye left, the clatter of her horses' hooves on the cinders outside, and the creak of stairs as someone came up the main staircase. He supposed it must be Monique, for it was late and the servants had gone to bed.

The footsteps stopped just outside his door and a knock sounded. What did Monique want at this hour? he wondered, then scowled. He had a feeling he knew. Even if she *was* his daughter, she was a hot little wench. So hot, in fact, she was fire and he never played with fire.

He shook his head with the insanity of it all. Monique was pretty, admittedly not a virgin, and openly desirous of him. There was only a single chance in six that she might be his child, so why should he sleep alone in a cold bed tonight?

"Jean?" she called softly. "Are you there?"

He was sorely tempted to let her in, but a nagging voice at the back of his mind warned him not to. He said nothing.

"Please, Jean, I know this is your room. I have to . . . talk to you."

Talk? Huh! He stared at the empty spot beside him in bed, groaned, then flopped over on his stomach. A moment later he heard a sigh, then the soft scuff of her bootheels as she strode down the hallway to her suite.

Armand LeClair had his headquarters in Dupont Street on the fringe between Chinatown and the Barbary Coast—one small, dingy room inside a twelve by fourteen foot wooden "crib". A crib was a one-story shack, divided into two rooms by heavy, coarse drapes, and in it Chinese prostitutes catered to white, black, and Chinese men. Young boys aged from ten to sixteen were given a special price of fifteen cents.

This crib was owned by an ambitious Ranger named Blackjack Pete. It was Blackjack, as he was called by his compatriots, who had single-handedly pulled together a band of Rangers to seek a capable leader to unite them in their revolt against the Barons. And it was he who learned of the availability of the notorious Armand "Lee," who had just fled Canada where he was wanted for extortion and murder. It was Blackjack who arranged to bring Armand to the Barbary Coast, then convinced his fellow Rangers that Armand had the strength to achieve their goals.

At first Armand had laughed at Blackjack. "Why me?" he had asked. "And why should I help *you*?"

"You're one of the lowest, most conniving bastards around," Blackjack had responded, "and I know you could do the job. There would be a fat bonus in return."

"Money?" Armand had said contemptuously. "I have plenty of money."

"Not money. *Power*!"

The word had a magical effect on Armand. His face was animated as Blackjack told him about Jean LeClair and the empire the man had built. "So that's the real reason you want *me* for your savior," Armand said. "You know my real name's LeClair and that there's no love lost between me and my brother. You figure I'd do my damnest to bring Jean down and steal his throne." He laughed uproariously. "You're damned right, m'boy! That I would! I'll help you with your war, not because I give a damn about you or your Rangers, but for the sheer fun of it!"

Now Armand and Blackjack Pete, his lieutenant, sat across from each other at a small wooden table, smoking cigars and discussing developments. From the other side of the heavy burlap curtains one could hear squeaks from the iron bedstead and the grunts of a young boy who was being initiated into manhood by an equally young, but entirely experienced black-haired Chinese girl.

"So you say Hagan has disappeared," Armand said.

"Sure looks that way. After your meeting with him at the warehouse the night before last, he went to Spider Joe's where he teamed up a rat with Slimy Lewis' dog. No one's seen him since."

Armand grit his teeth. He and his brother were both blessed with strong, perfect teeth. "My brother works fast," he observed.

"He must've found out Hagan led that attack on his Nest and had the poor bastard trailed and killed. There's any number of places to stash a body around here,"

Blackjack said. "It's my guess his body's feedin' the fishes in the Bay."

Armand studied the lit end of his fat cigar reflectively. "Keep on it, Blackjack. If it was Jean's doing, I want to know. I want to know everything he does, everyone he meets with—his whole routine." Blackjack nodded. "No one but you knows who I am?"

"No one but me. I told the others you were Armand Lee. Figured you'll have an easier time of it if your brother didn't get word of you until you want him to."

"Good. The time to surprise dear Jean has come."

"You're going to see him?"

"Of course," Armand said. "If one is to kill a lion, one must eventually visit his den. We will soon know if Jean would rather engage in war with me than share his empire with us."

Armand left the crib, hailed a horse-drawn streetcar, and proceeded to the lodginghouse at the waterfront where he was staying. The lodginghouse, an old converted ship which had been abandoned by a gold-crazed crew back in '49 and was now permanently moored at the Pacific Street wharf, was owned by an attractive widow who had been warming Armand's bed for the past week. Although Armand enjoyed her body, he felt nothing for her. He had never been in love with a woman, mainly because he found them all too eager to fall into bed with him. And didn't trust them anyway. Armand LeClair trusted no one, a fact which had, he was sure, saved his life on a number of occasions.

The thought of a woman's charms, however, brought a frown to his dark features as a new thought was born. Did Jean have a woman? A mistress, or perhaps even a wife? Jean no doubt had both. And they would be beautiful, Armand was sure, for he knew the Jean he remembered from years before was pleasing to the feminine eye and quite desirable.

Would Jean's woman find his twin desirable? Armand wondered. The streetcar rounded a busy corner near the docks and pulled up before a line of ships rocking at anchor, one of which was Mrs. Hunt's lodginghouse. His spirits were light as he made his way to the black and red ship. Perhaps he would not only steal Jean's empire, but the love of his woman as well!

7

BRIGHT AND early the next morning Beau and Amoreena left their hotel and walked the half dozen blocks to their property. The sun was warm on their faces as they left the Pacific Inn and proceeded west on Pacific Street, the first street cut through the sand hills behind Yerba Buena Cove in the days of the gold rush. It was an important thoroughfare to Portsmouth Square and the western end of town.

Even in the early morning hours the street was alive and brimming with activity. There were scores of people on their way to work in the neighboring stores, offices, markets, and warehouses or simply on their way to shop in the cheap John clothing emporiums dotting this section of Pacific Street. They crowded Beau and Amoreena off the narrow sidewalk into the street, which was littered with fly-covered dung left by the horses pulling wagons and other conveyances. Various articles of clothing dangled from brightly-painted poles above the doorways of the stores, indicating their wares, while the sidewalks were cluttered with tables exhibiting used sailors' clothing, trinkets, and junk.

Beau, half anticipating, half fearful at what he'd find on his property, noticed few of the sights they passed, but Amoreena found them fascinating. When they approached a large building that had no windows or doors but was completely open to the street along its front, Amoreena stopped and stared, then tugged on Beau's arm.

"Please, Beau, let's go inside," she said.

He gave it a glance, then made a face. "We have far more important matters to attend to this morning," he said.

But Amoreena was undeterred by Beau's disdain, for she liked to shop. Back home in Virginia she and her mother would take a week or more to ride into Richmond and then spend leisurely hours browsing in city stores which sold clothes and household items. She had filled the boring hours at sea sewing, and had thus extended her wardrobe, but it was not the same as acquiring a new store-made article. "Oh, please, Beau," she pleaded. "Just for a minute?"

Beau was anxious to get to his property, but he realized Amoreena had been a dear, never having complained during those long weeks at sea, so he shrugged and said, "Take as long as you like. I'll wait out here."

Above the entrance was a huge canvas sign twenty-five feet long. On it was painted the picture of the steamship *Great Eastern* driving before a gale, and the words GREAT EASTERN AUCTION MART. Amoreena went inside and was impressed greatly by the endless rows of shelves rising from floor to ceiling. They were stacked with clothes in demand by shore-going sailors, denim trousers and jackets, jewelry, and other miscellaneous items. Amoreena found a colorful ladies' bonnet embroidered with flowers, bought and paid for it.

Outside Beau was watching a man on the sidewalk attending a large, odd-shaped machine he called a lung-tester. The man was middle-aged and had a voice powerful enough to call from ship to shore without the aid of a megaphone. Beau looked on in awe as the man, who called himself "Professor" Terry Shiner, shouted at the passersby that he would, for five cents, blow into the machine—which registered the strength of the blow in pounds—and make the needle "go crazy." The professor succeeded in drawing a crowd, collected several nickels, then took a deep breath and blew into the machine's mouthpiece, making the needle flip back and forth, spin wildly and set off hidden bells and lights from the machine. Beau was wondering idly how far *he* could make the needle jump when Amoreena came out of the auction mart and joined him. He grunted as she removed her pretty straw hat and replaced it with a garish blue affair she'd just bought.

"You ought to buy something," she said, giggling. "I'm sure they have men's hats too."

"I'll pass," Beau said, and they walked down the street.

They had covered only two blocks when the shopping district ended and changed into dance-halls, wine and beer dens, and saloons that by day looked respectable and hardly fearsome, yet were pits of hell after sunset. Now they reached Montgomery Street and were faced with a huge two-story wooden building fronted by a sign depicting the head of a pirate with a black patch over his left eye and bearing the words THE PIRATES' NEST. It stood on the corner of Montgomery and Washington Streets. It was Beau's property!

Beau's face turned crimson with rage at the sight of the imposing structure on land which ought to be vacant. So this was what had become of his father's precious land— the land he'd bought with the gold he'd panned upriver!

Beau was glad his father wasn't alive to see it. Not only
had someone—this infamous LeClair—stolen his land but
he had defiled it by using it for a saloon-whorehouse! Beau
could barely contain his rage. He spat at the low sign and
hit his target—the pirate's eye!

Amoreena, too, felt anger. This land had held the key to
their future—was supposed to provide them with funds for
a home. Now what? Would Beau postone their wedding
again? She loved him, but couldn't wait forever. In her
disappointment she did not speak, but her expression
matched Beau's and conveyed her thoughts.

A young man, who had been pushing his way through
the carts lining the street, found a place to stop and rest for
a minute on the top stair of the flight leading down to the
entrance to the Pirates' Nest. He plopped his skinny frame
down on the step and wiped sweat from his forehead. He
seemed unconcerned that Beau and Amoreena stood close
by on the sidewalk staring at the building behind him as he
reached into his pocket and pulled out a glass medicine
dropper with a pointed end. The device was filled with
clear fluid. He rolled up the sleeve of his plaid shirt, then
with a force that wrenched a gasp from Amoreena's lips,
plunged the point of the dropper deep into a vein in his
arm, drawing blood which he dabbed away with the tail of
his shirt.

The sound of her gasp made the "hoppie" look up and
smile. The fluid drained from the dropper into his arm,
then he stuffed the dropper back inside his pocket and
placed an old iron pan on the stair beside him. "For fifteen
cents, lady," he said, his eyes on the pan already containing a few coins, "I'll let you see close up the holes in my
arms."

Amoreena, repulsed, could only shake her head and
mutter, "No . . ."

Beau grabbed her and led her away. He was cursing

under his breath as they made their way back toward the hotel. "I'm going to confront LeClair," he announced when they reached it, "before Georgie can talk me out of it." When she started to protest, he added, "It's dangerous and I don't want you to get hurt. You'll have to stay at the hotel until I get back."

"I want to go with you," she said.

"No. You can't, Amoreena. You must do as I say."

"Someone has to go with you, Beau, to prevent you from doing something foolish and getting hurt. So, I'm coming."

"Amoreena!" he growled. "Why must you be so stubborn!"

"Stubborn?" she repeated. "You're the one who's stubborn . . . and foolish. For that's what it is to see LeClair now, while you're mad enough to boil him in oil, and before you've had a chance to plan your move. Don't be foolish, Beau. Think. You fought in the war. Did your officers act first and think later? Or did they plan their attack?" She waited a moment to let the effect of her words sink in. "Either I come with you now, or you go with Georgie later. Which will it be?"

Amidst young and old alike brushing by them on the sidewalk, she stood facing Beau, her hands on her waist, a determined look on her face. Beau knew she meant every word—and she *did* have a point. If he went now to see LeClair in a rage, he would simply accuse the man of being a thief. True or not, such an accusation would get him nowhere. He needed to calm down and think over what and how to say it. He had tried last night. Tried and failed. This was not the time to approach LeClair, he knew that now. He could meet Georgie Ross tonight in the Pirates' Nest and talk it over with him.

"You win," he said. "I'll not do anything until after I've discussed it with Georgie."

*   *   *

After dinner that evening Beau left Amoreena in the hotel at work on her sewing while he took a streetcar to the Pirates' Nest. He was prepared to hate the place but found to his surprise upon his entrance that he could not. It was neat and clean, with fresh sawdust on the floor. The air smelled of tobacco, spirits, and perfume, and the serving girls were really pretty. He felt a perverse sort of pride that the saloon on *his* land should be first class.

One of the pretty waitresses, a tall redhead, spotted him and threaded her way among the tables of the busy saloon toward him. She was attractive, he noted, in a short black skirt and thin red blouse, which more than hinted at her ample breasts beneath. He scolded himself for his disloyalty to Amoreena as he admired the girl—and wondered what she looked like beneath her clothes.

"I'm Rose," the girl said. "What's your pleasure? A drink? A dance? Sex?"

Even though the sun had just set and the hour was still early, there were several couples moving around on the dancefloor to a bouncy piano tune and other girls drinking with men at little square tables scattered about the smoky room.

"I'm to meet a friend," Beau said, "for a drink." He quickly looked around and concluded that Georgie had either not shown yet or was engaged with one of the girls.

Rose looked around also. The only single people she saw was an older man and a woman. "Is your friend a man or a woman?" she asked.

"Does it matter?"

"Suite yourself."

"My friend is a man," he said. "The captain of the newly arrived *Sea Lion.*"

At the mention of the ship, a look of interest appeared on her pretty face. "Well now, we don't get many captains around here. I'd sure like to meet this one when he shows."

"Be my guest. I'm sure Georgie would like to meet *you*."

Rose showed Beau to a table near the piano, went to the bar for a beer for him and a plain tea for herself, then sat down beside him. "You new to the Coast?" she asked. He nodded noncommittally. "Bet you just came in on the *Sea Lion*. You look strong, like a sailor, all tanned up and all. Are you sure you're not in the mood for a little bedsport?"

"No, thanks."

She shrugged. "Every sailor I ever met had the hots so bad after he pulled into port, he seized the first girl he laid eyes on. You sure you're a sailor?"

"I used to be one," he said, "until . . . I got hurt in the war."

She frowned. "Hurt where?"

"On a ship—in battle. Off the coast of Washington."

"That's not what I meant."

"Oh. I hurt my leg," he said.

"That's all? From the way you act, I thought you might've hurt something else!"

Vulgar, he thought. But what else could he expect from a whore? "*That*, my dear, is quite well," he snapped.

"I don't believe you."

"What?"

"I said I don't believe you. Two dollars says you can't get it up."

Beau scowled. "Are you daft, girl?"

"Hardly. I usually win my bets."

"No wonder they call this place the Barbary Coast," he said sourly. "With people like you, the runners, crimps, hoodlums, procurers, and land-thieves, how could it have been named anything else?"

"And which are you?" she asked nonchalantly.

He paled. "Why, a southern gentleman, of course."

She laughed. "And I'm an English lady of quality," she declared.

Now *he* laughed.

"Well, mister southern gentleman," she said, placing her hand firmly over the fly of his pants, "do we have a bet?"

Beau was shocked. Never had he met a woman so bold, so brazen. He pushed her hand away. He was spared an answer, however, as just then a man walked into the Nest and approached their table. It was Georgie.

"You came at the right time," Beau said. Rose turned and faced the young sea captain. "Have a seat. The Coast's answer to English aristocracy here is dying to meet you."

Georgie flushed as he took a seat at their table. "My pleasure, ma'am," he said.

"Rose," she answered.

"Rose is an expert on male potency," Beau declared. "She was just about to check mine out when you appeared."

Georgie looked as if he didn't know whether to believe Beau or not. He said nothing.

"A drink, captain?" Rose asked.

"That sounds good. A gin'll do."

A moment later she brought Georgie his gin and another tea for herself which she added at whiskey prices to Beau's check. After she had placed the drinks on the table, she started to sit down, but Beau grabbed her wrist and held it in a vice-like grip. She met his eyes in angry defiance.

"Just the drink," Beau said. "We'd prefer to be alone, if you don't mind."

"Queer!" she spat, but left them alone.

"Weren't you a little rough on her?" Georgie asked, after she'd gone.

"Are you serious? She's just a whore!"

"Whores have feelings, too," he said.

Beau, irritated, wrinkled his bushy eyebrows. "Maybe I should leave so that you and Miss Society could go upstairs or wherever it is these whores take their tricks."

"You're . . . different tonight. Not the same Beau I met aboard the *Sea Lion*."

"I'm sorry, Georgie, it's just . . . hell, wouldn't you be bitter if you were me? Look around you—this saloon—it's on my *father*'s land!"

"I know. Listen, Beau, I did some checking this afternoon. This LeClair fellow, he lives up on Telegraph Hill in a big white mansion. They say he's pretty fair in his business dealings and is about as honest as any crook around. That's not much, but it's something. If you showed him your father's deed to this place, maybe he'd work something out with you."

"You really believe that?" Beau asked incredulously.

"I do, and you should too. You haven't much else."

'I suppose you're right. I was planning on showing the bastard the deed, but I figure he'll laugh in my face."

"Would you like me to go with you?"

Beau shook his head. "This is something I have to do alone. Thanks anyway." He pushed his chair back and began to rise.

"Where you going?" Georgie asked.

"To see LeClair."

"Now?"

"Why not?"

"Not now, Beau. First there are things you should know about the Coast, and there are places you must see. I'll show you tonight. Tomorrow, when you're a great deal wiser, you can confront LeClair. Now, do you carry a gun?"

After learning of Georgie Ross' presence in the Pirates' Nest, Rose scurried upstairs to Faye Langlois' office. "That rapist bum you're after,'' she said, ''the one who messed up your kid—he's here in the Nest. Name's Georgie, right?''

''That's him!'' Faye exclaimed, jumping up from the seat behind her desk. ''Is everything set?''

Rose nodded. ''I already alerted Jake and Ned. Before the sun rises again, the bastard will be on his way to China!'' She didn't say it, but she thought it anyway—the sea captain didn't look to her the way she always thought a rapist would. But then, neither did her father.

Rose left Faye's office and went to the bar, told the new bartender Faye had hired after Hank's murder to lace a beer with a double dose of morphine. She delivered the beer to the table of Georgie and his friend. She had never learned Beau's name and she didn't care. Queer or not, he was a cocksure bastard and the drink she was about to give him was well deserved.

''This one's on the house,'' she said to Beau, placing the beer in front of him. ''Consider it an apology.'' She had to grit her teeth to say it. His expression softened, and she thought he'd actually believed her. Perhaps if things hadn't happened in London, she could have stayed and become a famous actress. She would have liked that.

''Well now, that's good of you, Rose,'' the man said. ''I must have looked thirsty,'' he said to Georgie.

Although he had finished the beer she'd brought him earlier, he made no move to touch the ''loaded'' drink. ''Drink up,'' she urged.

The blonde man shook his head and pushed the glass aside. The young captain's face bore a smirk as if he and his friend were enjoying a secret joke.

''Rose, honey,'' Beau said, ''I seem to have suddenly lost my thirst, so you can have this.'' He opened her hand and placed the glass squarely in her palm, then stood up and threw four coins on the tabletop.

It could only mean, Rose thought, that they must have figured out that the drink was drugged! She felt her cheeks warm as the men headed for the door.

"Drink up, Rose!" the blonde man called out, as he and the sea captain stopped before leaving and waved. She could hear them burst into laughter as they went outside.

Rose stared at the door which closed behind them for a moment before turning away. They thought they were smart, but they weren't, as they'd soon find out. This round hadn't ended yet! Still holding the mug of drugged beer, she nodded to a pair of burly men who stood near the door awaiting her signal.

Immediately they left on the heels of Beau and Georgie. Vaguely Rose hoped the arrogant blonde man would be with the captain when her men took the rapist prisoner. It would serve him right.

While Beau met with Georgie at the Pirates' Nest, Amoreena tried to mend the gown she had torn while leaving the ship. But she was taut and tense worrying about Beau and what he might do and soon she put the dress aside. She wished she could do something constructive—something to help Beau.

She crossed the floor of the carpeted room to a west-facing window and looked down the street. In the light from a full moon, the white of a nearby church steeple shone like a beacon. The church! That was it! If she were home now, she'd go to church. A little prayer never hurt, her mother always said.

On their way to the hotel that afternoon, she and Beau had passed a large white church—the First Church of San Francisco—she recalled. It was only two blocks away, sandwiched between the auction mart and the first of the long row of saloons. Beau had cautioned her to stay in the hotel where it was safe, but she was sure she could walk the short distance to the church in safety.

So she threw a cloak around her shoulders, took a deep breath to quiet her nerves, then left the stuffy room. The cool night air stung her face, but the moon's light illuminated the two block area she would have to walk, and it gave her the courage to go on.

Several youths loitered along store fronts across the dirt street, drinking beer and giggling like school children. She hoped they'd not notice her, or accost her. As she walked briskly by on the opposite side of the street, however, one of them called out to her in a loud voice:

"Hey there, lady-fair, I like your hair. The name's Luke and that ain't no fluke!"

The others thought Luke's rhyming words funny and fell over with laughter, but Amoreena ignored them all and kept walking. No one followed her, and soon she had reached the church and was ascending the steps leading to its front doors. She was glad to find them open, for she had feared the doors might already be locked in such a place as the Barbary Coast.

The interior was spacious and warm, with stained-glass windows and cushioned pews. On the altar was a pot of fragrant gardenias. The church was empty so she took a seat on a pew at the rear of the church and bowed her head to pray, unaware of the eyes watching her from a cloak room near the entrance.

Dear God, she prayed, *please let Beau return safely and give him the courage and strength to face LeClair. I ask not for myself . . . although I could use a little strength, too, to live in this strange land . . . but for Beau and his father.* She thought of one more thing. *And please, God, let Beau get his land back quickly so that we can marry. Thank you.*

When her prayers were finished, she looked around at

the altar, the windows and mahogany paneling, mentally comparing it to the churches she had attended back home, and drew a conclusion that despite its location in such a barbaric land, it was nicer and cozier than the Virginia churches. She could almost hear the resounding strains of an organ, accompanied by voices from a choir.

Suddenly a man's voice shattered her reverie. "It's nine o'clock, miss, and I have to lock up now."

She turned and saw a black-garbed man standing near the candles at the front of the church near the entrance.

He saw her eyes on him and smiled pleasantly. "I don't recall *your* face," he said, starting up the center aisle toward her. "I know all my congregation by their faces, if not their names." He stopped and stood at the end of her pew. "I'm Reverend Drummond."

"My name is Amoreena Welles," she said. He seemed nice, she thought, and she was glad he was a minister and not a ruffian like that Luke. She couldn't help noticing, though, how fat he was. Pleasantly fat, she thought, for what was there to fear about a fat man?

"Are you new to San Francisco?" he asked.

"I just arrived by ship from New York." Then she realized he referred to the Barbary Coast as San Francisco. "You're the first person I've met who called this area San Francisco and not the Barbary Coast."

"Then, my dear, you have met the wrong people. God-fearing citizens refuse to think of their beautiful city as anything but San Francisco. Only the Barons and Rangers feel differently. If it weren't for the likes of them, the streets around here would be safe at night and I wouldn't have to lock the church so early." He heaved his bulk next to her on the bench of her pew. "Tell me, where are you staying?"

She wondered why he wanted to know, then figured he was only trying to be sociable. "At the Pacific Inn," she said.

"Fine choice. I hear they serve excellent shrimp in their dining room. You must try some before you leave our fair city."

"I'm not leaving," she said. "I plan to live here."

He clapped his hands delightedly. "That *is* good news. San Francisco needs more young people—decent ones— like yourself, my dear. I hope you'll join my congregation."

"I'd like that, Reverend."

He stood up and offered a hand to assist her to her feet. "Any time you need a friendly ear, just come see me." He escorted her to the front doors to let her out. "Remember, Miss Welles, if you need a friend, I'm always available."

"I'll remember. And thank you."

Cornelius Drummond's eyes were again on the young girl as she walked down the church steps and departed. He wished she had not kept her red cloak wrapped around her inside the church as well as out, for he had always derived satisfaction from seeing how the charms of his young women parishioners strained against their clothes. And no less so now than ever, for lately he had been beset with a pleasant, but unsettling, daydream. Ever since his visit from the new leader of the Rangers, the minister's head had become increasingly haunted by beautiful visions of white flesh displayed inspirationally before him while he . . .

He closed his eyes and felt a rising heat in his loins as the girl he had been imagining suddenly had yellow hair and the beautiful face of Amoreena Welles.

The image was staggering and he stood at the doors of his church and swayed for long moments before he could, with a massive effort, force it from his mind. He backed inside the church, to close and latch the heavy doors at the main entrance, and then leaned back against them—his eyes closed again. This time a new vision was in his

mind—of the Welles girl cowering before him as he ordered her to take off her cloak.

"No, please, Reverend," she would cry.

"Remove it, my dear, or I shall tear it off!"

"But I've nothing on beneath it."

"All the better, Amoreena. You must not be afraid to
show your all to me, for God is with me."

But now Drummond's vision ended, just as the girl took
off the cloak. He opened his eyes. She's the one, he
thought. She is the one I want—the one I must have. I
must know the sweet, white, virginal flesh her cloak hides.

Then he frowned. Was Amoreena alone in San Francisco?
Or was she with someone? A mother? A sister? A man?

He shook his head. No, she was alone, he decided,
otherwise she'd have spoken of whom she was with. Alone
at the Pacific Inn only a few blocks from here.

He must have her! She was perfect!! Her face—so
pretty! The eyes were innocent and trusting. He would put
fear into them. Then they would be filled with such beauty
as he had never seen!

Would the leader of the Rangers deliver her to him? He
must find out, and soon, for there was no telling how long
she would remain at the Pacific Inn.

Moments later he left the church, returned to his house
and study to write a note to the Ranger leader.

It was one o'clock in the morning when Beau returned
to his hotel room. Before retiring he knocked on Amoreena's
door. "Amoreena?" he called. "Are you awake?" He
kept his voice low, not wishing to disturb her should she be
asleep.

The door to their adjoining rooms flew open and she
stood before him, wide-eyed and very much awake. She
wore only a thin, white gauze nightgown and from behind
her in her room, moonlight drifted through her window,

making her gown appear almost transparent and revealing the sensual curves of her breasts and hips, the shaded secrets between her thighs.

He didn't want to stare, but he had never seen so much of her, nor realized from the modest clothes she usually wore how enticing was her figure. Her breasts were neither too small nor too large and disturbed him greatly. Her hips and thighs were slim. He allowed his gaze to travel to the juncture of her thighs, where an enticing darkish shadow lay beneath the fabric of her gown.

"I'm so glad you're safe," she said, throwing herself into his arms.

Her hair was free of its pins and hung to her waist. He felt it tickle his hands as for a moment the vision of a scantily-clad Rose flashed across his mind. He quickly shook the thought away. How could he hold his fiancée in his arms, yet think of a common whore! But the memory of the bold hand Rose had placed upon the front of his trousers that afternoon warmed his blood. He pulled Amoreena closer, flattening her breasts against his chest, then sought and found her lips in a crushing kiss. As his tongue forced its way between her teeth and dove into her mouth with feverish intensity, he lifted a hand to her breast. Immediately she pulled away from him, looking bewildered.

"What's gotten into you, Beau?" she exclaimed. "You're gone one evening . . . and you return an . . . an animal!"

At her words his ardor vanished, and was replaced by anger. "You were the one who always wanted to be kissed like a whore, Amoreena! Now you call me an animal! Who was it who only a few hours ago wanted to sleep in the same hotel room?"

"Oh, Beau, you don't understand. I've been worrying about you. I even went to a church and prayed for your safety. And now you come back hours later than I'd expected . . . and you're ready to make love to me! Why?"

Her words struck home and now Beau slumped into a chair beside the bed. "I'm sorry, Amoreena. I have behaved badly. I guess I'm just tired. I've been touring the Coast with Georgie. We've been down cellars, climbing hills, exploring hidden alleyways, drinking in saloons and visiting dance halls, Mexican fandango houses. Georgie even showed me an opium den in Chinatown. Then we had to run for our lives to escape young toughs who wanted to use our heads for slingshot practice." He saw a question in her eyes. "No, there was no need to visit the bagnios. Georgie wanted to show me what went on around the Coast so I could stand up to LeClair tomorrow, and he surely did! You wouldn't believe what I've learned about the crime here, and the corruption! And the city's inept police force which does little more than draw pay! Whatever we do about getting our land back, we'll get no help there. So we're on our own."

She sat down on his lap and put her arms around him. "I'm sorry I called you an animal, Beau. I'm sorry, too, that your tour only proved how futile our situation is. If you want to kiss me again . . ."

He wanted to do more than just kiss her, but the walking he and Georgie had done all night had tired him more than he realized. He drew her to him, kissed her softly, then abruptly released her. "Go to bed, my love," he said. "We both need rest."

"Do you love me, Beau?" she replied, her eyes soft as she looked at him.

"Of course I do."

"Then when can we marry? I've found a minister who'll . . ."

"My God!" he cried. "We're in the middle of a confounded crisis and you go hunting for a minister?"

"I was hardly hunting for him," she said, stung again by his tone.

"I've told you we'll marry when I have a home to offer you and not before. You didn't ask this minister to marry us, did you?"

"No. I didn't mention you at all, knowing how you are. But Beau, I'd be satisfied living here, in this hotel, if I could be your wife."

"Nonsense. You're a lady of values and before long you'd hate it . . . and me. I won't take that chance and ruin our happiness. Trust me, Amoreena. I know what's best."

She sighed. "I do trust you. I'm just edgy, I guess."

But she wished Beau could understand that it was him she wanted—that home would be wherever they'd be together.

Georgie Ross left Beau at the front of Beau's hotel, and keeping to the brightly-lit main thoroughfares, soon arrived at his lodginghouse near the waterfront. All in all, he thought, it had been a good day. He had showed Beau as much as he could of the Barbary Coast and how to exist there. Ironically, he had emphasized that Beau had to be wary and careful, yet neither he nor the southerner noticed the two shadowy figures following them as they toured the city's nightspots.

Now, as Georgie climbed the creaky dark flight of steps to the second floor landing, his thoughts were of a hot, soothing bath. However, when he walked down the long hall to the door of his room—which was a dark brown affair with chips of paint flaking off even as he slid his key in the lock and turned the knob—he wanted only to rest.

He had been lucky finding this room. Several ships had put into port during the last week, he had learned, and all available rooms near the waterfront had been taken by the ships' crews. Even though the building was in need of repair, the rooms small and sparsely furnished, his bed was comfortable and the rate fair.

He opened the door and walked in, then struck a match to light the oil lamp that sat on a table near the door. As light filled the room, he gasped. Directly ahead, sprawled comfortably on the bed and waiting for him, was a man with a Colt .44. The gun was pointed directly at Georgie!

The man smiled. "Congratulations, Georgie-boy. You gave us a run for our money. Ain't too many sailors come here who know as much about staying alive on the Coast as you do. You don't make too many mistakes. Only one, I know of. Too bad you gotta pay for it by taking a sudden, unexpected trip."

Unexpected trip? Shanghai? Was he about to be shanghaied? Fear so strong he could taste it shook him, and he felt his knees knocking. "Why?" he sputtered. "What've I done?"

"You messed with LeClair's property, Georgie-boy."

"How?"

"You tumbled the wrong wench, friend."

"Who? I've not had a woman since . . ." Suddenly he remembered the voyage and the conniving Monique. Could she be LeClair's mistress? Oh, God, he thought, he'd done it now! "Listen," he said, "I didn't know . . ."

He never finished his sentence, as just then he heard the creak of a floorboard behind him. The man holding the gun nodded to someone behind Georgie and Georgie turned quickly—but not in time to see another man bring a length of lead pipe crashing down on his skull! Georgie felt a huge pain, then blackness engulfed him and his legs buckled. He dropped to the floor.

8

A HOT sun shone down on the auction platform in Portsmouth Square where Jean LeClair's latest shipment of Cantonese girls stood basking in the warmth of an uncommonly warm October day. The sun's rays highlighted the luster of their blue-black hair, rendering them more than appealing to the group of nattily-dressed businessmen who sought to purchase them.

The bidding was brisk and the proceeds more than satisfactory to Faye Langlois, who was overseeing the auction. It was one of her many duties and one she did with relish. The auction was over well before noon, and Faye was pleased with the price the girls brought. The men who bought them were Barons who ran clean, high-class bagnios, and a few private citizens—some members of the city's government. The latter would use their Celestials as servants and concubines, but would not harm them or treat them unkindly.

While Faye was at the auction, Jean was busy compiling

figures on his latest transactions when the butler Hays interrupted him.

"There's a gentleman here to see you, sir," Hays said.

"Isn't it a bit early for visitors?" Jean asked.

"It's nine o'clock, sir."

Jean had been up working since seven that morning and the time seemed to have slipped by. "Who is he?" he asked.

"He wouldn't give his name. When I told him you were busy, he said he'd wait, that you'll be surprised to see him."

Surprised? LeClair did not like surprises of any sort, especially early in the morning. The butler should not have admitted the stranger at all. No one with legitimate business would refuse to identify himself.

Jean, irritated, went directly to the large parlor where he received guests. The morning sun had filled the room with a warm glow admitted by the large floor to ceiling windows. A man stood with his back to Jean, looking outside. His hands were clasped loosely together behind his back. He was tall and dark, and from what Jean could see, well dressed.

"Good morning," Jean said, "I'm Jean LeClair. You wanted to see me?"

The man turned. A grin covered the lower half of a bearded face, above it a pair of familiar cold blue eyes. Jean gaped at the man. He knew those eyes. It had been years but he would know them anywhere. They were the mirror image of his own! And belonged to the only man in the world he truly hated—his brother Armand!

And yet . . . Jean stared at the other man. If it was Armand, the years had changed him, added weight to his frame, thinned his hair. He and Jean no longer looked identical, as they had when Armand arranged for his sudden deportation.

"Armand," Jean said, disliking the taste of the word almost as much as his brother's presence. "You have the cheek—the unmitigated gall—to come here?"

Armand LeClair seemed unperturbed, his grin undiminished. "Is that any way to greet your brother?" he replied.

"No, I suppose not," Jean said coldly. "It's much too civil."

Armand laughed, then pointed a ring-bejeweled finger to a pair of green velvet chairs nearby. "Come," he commanded, "sit down with me. We've much catching up to do."

Catching up? Jean felt a murderous rage building within him. He remained standing, and said tightly, "You have five minutes, Armand, to say whatever you have to say. Then I'll throw you out!"

"The years have sharpened your tongue, Jean. All right, five minutes. *Now* will you sit down?"

Jean shook his head. "Five minutes," he repeated, glowering at his brother. "Now how did you find me?"

"It's a long story. It would take longer than five minutes to tell. Let's just say Providence shone down on me and led me to your door."

"How long have you been on the Coast?"

"Long enough to learn of your good fortune and vast holdings, Jean, m'boy. I must admit I was surprised. Last I heard, you were rotting in an Australian jail."

"Thanks to you, brother. Yet it's turned out well. If it weren't for your framing me back in London, I wouldn't have come to San Francisco and become who and what I am." A look of irritation crossed Armand's face, but the look passed quickly and Jean could derive only brief pleasure from it.

"Nice place you have here. Have you married?"

"Your time is nearly gone," Jean said.

Ignoring Jean, Armand now lifted a Ming vase from the table beside his chair and inspected the markings underneath. "Mmmm," he said, "excellent. But then you've the means to have good taste."

"What do you want?" Jean now demanded. "Quickly, brother, for I'm at the end of my patience!"

Armand placed the vase back on the table and met his brother's eyes squarely. "I've heard you're having your troubles these days, Jean. The Rangers are not pleased with you. They've a new leader who'll see that they not only win a war they plan against you and your Barons, but chase you all out of San Francisco as well."

"I'm not losing any sleep over the Rangers."

"You should, Jean. Their new leader has the power to make or break you. He can start a war—or stop it. The best thing you could do right now is make a deal with him."

Suddenly Jean knew why Armand was here. His presence on the Barbary Coast and the Rangers' sudden revolt coincided. It was obvious that Armand was their new leader! "Since when have you become a mercenary?" Jean asked. "A pawn for others? I thought murder was your game."

The old look of arrogance that Jean remembered flicked across Armand's face. "I want to propose a deal, brother. A deal that can profit us both."

Any deal Armand had to offer, he was sure, would benefit only his brother. "I make no deals with you or the Rangers," he said.

"Put your pride aside for a minute, Jean, and listen to me. The Rangers are powerful and getting more so each day. They're angry and out for blood. With my help they'll not only wipe out you and the Barons but half the Coast as well! They don't much care who gets hurt as long as they get what they want. I, and I alone, have the power to stop them, and I'll do it, Jean, for a price. I want half your empire.''

"Is that all? Just half?'' Jean asked acidly, his face a mask. Half for now, he thought. Armand would steal the rest later!

"Just half,'' Armand said.

Jean stood and walked to the window where a ship far below was sailing slowly toward port. He watched as the white-capped waves tossed it about, pushing it out of view, but saw nothing but a red veil of anger. His hands balled into fists and he stuffed them inside his pockets. He wanted to strangle the son of a bitch!

Now he spun on his heels, a gleaming deringer in his hand. "It took me twenty years to get here. You believe you can get it for the asking? Never, Armand! You can have my empire over my dead body!''

Armand jumped to his feet, his face black with anger. "That, my brother, can be arranged!''

"Your five minutes is up. Get out!'' Jean snapped, fingering the trigger of his pistol.

"I'll leave, but this is only the beginning, Jean. You'll live to regret your refusal.'' He turned and left, a smile on his face. The interview had gone exactly as expected.

Amoreena awoke at eight o'clock the following morning to the sound of snoring coming from the other side of the door dividing their rooms. She had not fallen asleep until after three a.m., worrying over the confrontation Beau would have with Jean LeClair today, but even though she slept for only five hours, she felt refreshed. Beau had not found sleep easy either, she knew, for he had not yet begun to snore when she drifted to sleep. Only when she had decided that *she* must pave the way for Beau's meeting with the powerful Barbary Coast Baron had her mind been set at ease and let sleep overcome her.

She was a woman, she reasoned again, as she rose and quickly prepared to carry out her decision, and women could manipulate men the way a man could not. A look, a smile, a flash of the calf beneath her shirts—all could serve her purposes with Jean LeClair. She chose her prettiest gown—a sky-blue velvet and satin affair—dressed, and tiptoed out of her hotel room. Judging by the deep sleep Beau was enjoying, however, it would be at least another hour before he awoke. By that time, she would have seen LeClair and returned to the hotel. He would never know she had gone.

It was a bright, clear morning, and Amoreena wondered why the women on ship had called San Francisco a foggy city. Since she'd arrived, it had not rained nor had she seen any fog. Perhaps it was just coincidental, she thought, but it could also be an omen—that life was going to be full of sunshine for her and Beau.

Outside the hotel she found a carriage, its driver looking for a customer. She hired him to take her to Telegraph Hill. She did not know which of the Hill's mansions was LeClair's, but figured a native such as the driver of a carriage for hire would know of LeClair. Her reasoning was correct.

"That white Georgian place back there," said the driver, a friendly light-haired man, as they approached the drive of a wooded estate on the side of the hill. "It's Jean LeClair's. You can't see it for all the trees."

A moment later the vehicle turned from the dirt street onto a narrow cobblestone drive winding upward. Amoreena looked out the carriage windows at the rolling green lawns, fir trees, and well-trimmed hedge. It was neat and smelled pleasantly of pine. About two hundred feet above the road loomed a huge white, two-story building with columns fronting a wide porch. Overhead a balcony ran along the entire front of the house.

"It's beautiful," she said. "It's so different here from the waterfront . . . like two separate worlds!"

"The rich always live like this," the driver said sourly. "No matter what the city, they always have the best. The likes of LeClair fills the town with vice then moves up here, away from it. If I had money, I'd move up here too—just so's I could bring some sin to *their* neighborhood!"

Amoreena chuckled. They were nearing the front entrance, and she noticed another vehicle parked a few yards from the two massive front doors. "Pull up behind that carriage," she told the driver.

As he followed her instruction, he asked, "Shall I wait, miss?"

She had no idea how long she'd be or even if Jean LeClair was home. Since it was only nine-thirty she supposed she'd catch him at breakfast, but couldn't be sure. If she sent the carriage away, she'd be alone and at the mercy of LeClair. The thought frightened her. "Yes," she said, "please stay." She then opened the door and stepped out onto a thick expanse of lawn.

No sooner had she done so than the ornate front doors of the mansion opened and a tall man dressed in fancy clothes appeared and strode toward the other carriage. It must be LeClair! she thought, turning toward him. "Wait!" she cried. The man looked to his left, saw her, and stopped short of his carriage, a bemused look on his face.

"I'm Amoreena Welles," she said. "Are you Mr. LeClair?"

The man frowned, then started to speak, but did not. Instead he glanced back over his shoulder in the direction he'd just come. When he again looked at her, a smile was blooming across his face. "LeClair's my name," he said. "What can I do for you?"

"I'm glad I caught you before you left. There's something very important I have to discuss with you."

"That sounds urgent. Come with me in my carriage and we'll talk while we ride."

"Well . . ." She looked back to the carriage she had hired. "I suppose that will be all right," she said. "But first I must tell my driver I'll no longer need him."

She paid and thanked the driver then joined LeClair, who was already inside. Sitting beside him in the narrow carriage made her slightly uneasy. She had an odd feeling she'd seen LeClair before. Yet she couldn't have. "Where are we going?" she asked.

"To the waterfront. Afterward my driver will take you wherever you wish to go."

She wondered what business he had at the sleazy waterfront but did not ask, for it was none of her concern. She had interrupted LeClair's schedule and was lucky he was taking the time to talk to her. "I'll try to make this brief," she said.

"Whatever you have to say can wait a moment, love. First you must tell me why I haven't seen you around here before. Surely the Barbary Coast is not so large that such a lovely creature could have remained hidden from me!" He thought his words clever, and he chuckled.

"I've only just arrived," she said. "My fiancé owns land here. That's what I must discuss with you."

The man seemed disinterested in her words, but not in her. He picked up her hand and made a show of studying it. "Business before pleasure is bad for one's health, love," he said, "so tell me about yourself."

She pulled her hand away. "Really, Mr. LeClair, you must listen to me. Beau, my fiancé, and I have just found out that his land was stolen and built upon."

"That is unfortunate. The thief should be shot."

"I'm glad you feel that way," she said. "It'll make it easier for me to . . ."

He raised a hand to caress her curly hair. "Your hair is

lovely, like fine silk from the Orient. Would you spend the day with me? We can work something out for the night later.''

"Mr. LeClair!" she exclaimed, "I'm betrothed!"

"A simple betrothal is nothing. Even marriage, when two people are mad for each other, is no obstacle. And, my dear Amoreena, I'm mad for you!"

"I'm beginning to get mad *at* you," she snapped.

He laughed delighted. "What can I do for you?"

"You can give up all claim to the Pirates' Nest. It happens to be on Beau's land, and you've no right to it!" She braced herself for the explosion her words were bound to cause, her eyes upon him. To her surprise there was none.

Instead LeClair roared with laughter. "M'love," he said, "Is the Pirates' Nest all you want?"

"Why . . . yes." She could not understand his laughter and was at a loss for words.

"You must become my woman, my dear. Then I'll give you much more than just a saloon. You'll have half the LeClair empire!"

"I don't want half your empire, and I don't want your attentions either. Just the land that is rightfully Beau's."

He shook his head sadly. "Can't give it to him, love."

"Why not?"

"Because I don't own it."

She stared at him. Was he joking? There was no trace of humor in his eyes now, however. "I thought . . . I'd heard that Jean LeClair owns the Pirates' Nest," she said.

"He does. For now."

"Then . . ." She frowned. "You *are* Mr. LeClair, aren't you?"

He nodded.

"Then I'm not sure I understand."

A look of amusement now spread across his face. "You

never said which Mr. LeClair you wanted, so I hoped I'd do.''

"You're *not* Jean LeClair?"

"The thought repulses me," he declared. "The scoundrel who stole your land is my brother. My name is Armand."

"Oh!" She felt her cheeks begin to burn. "I had no idea . . .''

Armand put a finger to her lip to silence her. "Now," he asked, "how shall we spend our day?"

When a few minutes later Amoreena finally convinced Armand LeClair that she had no intention of spending that day or any other day with him, his driver took her back to the hotel. There she met an angry Beau in the lobby. He had been questioning the clerk to see if the man knew where Amoreena had gone.

When she walked in and he saw her, he left the clerk and stormed across the lobby toward her. "Where have you been?" he demanded in a loud voice.

They were standing in the center of the busy lobby, and more than one person stopped and stared at them. "We're attracting attention, Beau," she whispered. "Let's go to my room."

"Not until you answer my question."

"I've been . . . for a walk," she said lamely. "It's such a lovely morning and . . .'' She stopped at the look of fury on Beau's face.

"You're lying, Amoreena. I know you too well. Now look me in the eye and tell me again that you were taking a walk."

She drew him to a corner, beside a large potted elm, where their voices wouldn't attract so many curious glances. Angry now herself, she stared at him as she said, "Are you accusing me of meeting a lover?"

Her words startled him. "Of course not. I was just

worried about you. I told you never to go out alone, and twice you disobeyed."

"I'm not a child, Beau Ashton!" she raged. "This was quite different. It's broad daylight and the area is busy and safe."

"Still, all sorts of things could happen, Amoreena. The Coast is filled with evil men who would accost you in daylight. I don't want you going anywhere alone. If you want to venture outside, I'll go with you. You must promise you'll not leave the hotel again without me."

If he was confining her to the hotel now, she thought, what would he do when they had built a house and moved permanently into this city of sin? Would she forever be under lock and key? Even if it was solely for her own protection, she was not sure she could live like that. But for now she felt it would be best to agree with Beau, or he'd keep questioning her, and she might slip and tell him about her meeting with Armand LeClair. That would be terrible. She felt utterly foolish, and didn't want Beau ever to find out what a stupid mistake she'd made. He would either laugh at her or scold her, and she wasn't sure which would hurt her more.

"I promise I'll let you know wherever I decide to go," she said.

After Armand left the "Hill", Jean stewed for over an hour. First he paced the floor, then he sat down at his desk and tried to work, but no thoughts other than murderous ones flowed from his head to the paper in front of him. He hadn't been so furious since before his arrival in San Francisco back in '49. So his despised brother was running the Rangers? What could be worse? A battle with the rebellious bastards was bad enough, but if they were to be led by the scum of the earth . . . It had taken Jean twenty years to get where *he* had what Armand wanted, and not the reverse. It seemed Armand was the one who always possessed such things as the watch, their father's affection— everything Jean wanted. Now Armand had his eyes on Jean's empire, and Jean knew as sure as he knew his own name that he'd blow it all to bits before seeing it fall into Armand's hands.

Now he glanced at his pocket watch and frowned. It was nearly noon. He had to see Faye over at the Pirates' Nest and find out how the auction went, then call an emergency meeting of the Barons to inform them of Armand's presence and the likelihood of a war with the Rangers. And to top it off, he had promised to take Monique shopping! He wished he hadn't made that promise.

Jean headed for the front door. He stopped in his tracks just as the butler was opening the door to let someone in. He watched as a young man and woman entered. The man was limping and obviously had an injury of some sort. He handed Hays his coat, then his eyes fell directly on Jean, who stood at the end of the hall not more than fifteen feet away.

The young man's face looked familiar but Jean could not place it. The girl had long blonde hair, but he couldn't see her face yet as she was removing a red cloak and offering it to Hays. Now she turned and her mouth parted slightly in an ''O'' when she saw him.

Suddenly Jean remembered. She was the girl who had tripped and fallen on the *Sea Lion*'s gangplank, and he had wiped the blood from her cheek. It had been a pleasant interlude in an otherwise unappetizing evening. The man with her now was her fiancé. But what did they want with him?

''Jean LeClair?'' the man said, stepping forward. ''I'm Beau Ashton and this is Miss Amoreena Welles of Norfolk, Virginia. If I may have a word with you . . .''

''I'm a busy man, Mr. Ashton. What is this about?''

"Could we talk privately?"

Jean scowled. The girl he could make time for, but this man? He was a little curious, however, as to what they wanted, so even though he had been on his way out the door, he supposed his business could wait a little longer. "Very well," he said. "Follow me."

He did not take Beau and Amoreena to the parlor. Only a little while ago the room had been polluted by Armand's presence and he did not want to go there. Instead he led his guests to a large study on the second floor. He motioned for them to be seated, then sat on a swivel chair behind a massive antique rosewood desk.

"Mr. LeClair," Beau said, fidgeting nervously in his chair, "I know you're busy so I'll try to get right to the point. My father prospected a short ways north of here back in '49, struck a vein, and bought a good-sized piece of land on the Coast, figuring it was a good investment. It's on the east corner of Montgomery and Washington Streets. San Francisco was nothing but shacks and lanes of mud at that time. Well, he died a few months back, and now the land has passed to me. That's why I'm here—I've come to claim it."

Jean, who had been watching the girl out of the corner of his eyes, was brought up short by Beau's bold statement. Montgomery and Washington Streets? He knew the location well, for that was where his Pirates' Nest was located!

Jean cleared his throat and scowled as he regarded Ashton. "So you've come to me because my saloon is on what you believe is your property?" he said mildly. "You are mistaken, my young friend. I own the Pirates' Nest and the land on which it stands. I and no one else."

Ashton's eyebrows arched upward. "It is *my* land!" he declared. "Your saloon sits on the exact location set forth in the deed my father gave me—which I have in my possession."

"It happens, Mr. Ashton, that I, too, have a deed, properly executed and made out to me. So you must be mistaken." He stood up. "I think you must leave now, for I have much to do."

Blood rushed to Beau's face and he, too, stood to glare at his host. "Listen, LeClair, you can't get rid of me that easily. I've been around. I know who you are and how you got where you are. You've no deed to my land. You couldn't have, for you *stole* my land!"

"Beau!" Amoreena gasped.

Beau ignored her. "So what are you going to do about it, LeClair?" he demanded.

"Please, Mr. LeClair," the girl interceded, "Beau didn't mean to call you a thief. He's very upset and . . ."

"I'm not upset!" Beau protested.

"Enough!" Jean declared. His eyes were cold as they bored into Ashton's. "I may be a number of things, Mr. Ashton, but a thief I'm not. You would do well to remember that. Men have been sorry for calling me less than that. As for the land, I told you once and I'll tell you no more—the land is mine. I bought and paid for it. My deed is, I assure you, quite legal. The matter is now closed."

"Not just yet!" Beau snapped, producing a rolled sheet of paper and handing it to LeClair. "Look at it," he said. "You'll see that the deed is in my father's name. Monte Ashton."

LeClair sighed, but he took the sheet and examined it. It was a deed, and it was made out to Monte Ashton. *Monte Ashton*? Suddenly he recalled that name as he searched the recesses of his memory—then frowned, as recognition dawned. The old man who had sold him the land was named Monte Ashton!

Laying Beau's deed down on the desk, Jean crossed the room and opened a cabinet. Inside was a small safe. He opened it and dug among papers until he found a scroll tied with thin red ribbon. He pulled it out, closed the safe, and returned to the desk.

The others were watching him carefully as he unfolded the deed and read through it, then placed it on the desk for Beau to see. "Your father sold me this land, Mr. Ashton, back in 1849 when I first came to the Coast. It says so right here on this deed. It's even signed by your father."

"Impossible!" Beau said, but he grabbed the paper and forced himself to read through the legal jargon to the signature. The girl looked over his shoulder, herself reading the deed.

Jean sat back in his chair watching them. It was apparent to him Monte Ashton never told his son of the sale. A shame, really. To have come all the way from Virginia across two seas only to find . . .

"This is a bloody forgery!" Beau now exclaimed angrily. "A damned lie! This is not my father's signature. Who sold you the land, LeClair? Describe him!"

"The deed is legal, Ashton!"

"That's not what I asked, dammit! What did the man look like?"

Jean was losing his patience. "An old man, in his sixties. He was going home to Canada and wanted to sell his property. He was short and bald, as I recall. Two front teeth were missing."

Ashton shook his head disbelievingly. "The man you described is Larry Barre, my father's one-time mining partner. He disappeared shortly after he and Father sold their claim, and Father never knew what happened to him. He must have bribed a land official to issue a second deed in Father's name, then sold our property to you, signing Monte Ashton's signature. He took the money, along with his cut of the gold, and left the country. He swindled you, but that means nothing to me. The important thing is you did not buy the land from my father, therefore, the land is still mine!"

LeClair's eyebrows arched skyward. "What you say may be true, but you're forgetting something. Possession is nine-tenths of the law. *I* possess the land and, whatever you say, a valid deed. With your father dead, who is there to prove or disprove his signature? I'm sorry if the deed I have may have been a fraud, but I've invested a lot of money and time in the Pirates' Nest, and I'm not about to hand it over to you or anyone else. I don't think you would either, if you were in my shoes."

Beau's face paled. The energy seemed to drain from him and he was quiet for a moment. The girl stared at LeClair's deed as if it were a spectre.

"This is not over yet, LeClair," Beau said. "My father, and he alone, had the right to sell the land. I'm going to do everything I can to get it back."

"You're wasting your time," LeClair declared. His anger was rising, but at the same time he could understand and even, in a strange sort of way, sympathize with the Virginian. Jean could not retreat from the position that his deed was legal, but what Ashton said had the ring of truth to it. Jean had lived long enough to learn that where there was life there was greed, and greedy men were not adverse to forging deeds. But Jean had bought the property in good faith, with hard-earned cash—and he wasn't about to give it over to the first person who contested his right of ownership, no matter that Beau's claim seemed valid.

"I'll tell you what, Ashton," he said, surprising himself even as he said it, "I'll give you $5,000 for your claim to the property. It's a good deal more than your father could have paid for the land back in 1849."

"That's very generous of you, Mr. LeClair," Amoreena said.

"It's robbery," Beau snapped. "He knows the land's

easily worth ten times that much." He turned to Jean. "No deal," he said, standing up. "Come, Amoreena, our business is over. We have other resources and Mr. LeClair will soon learn what they are."

She stood slowly, her eyes wide and pleading. "Beau," she said, "perhaps we should consider Mr. LeClair's offer. With $5,000 we could buy another tract of land somewhere else and build a house."

Ashton, furious, turned on his heels and stormed out of the room. The door banged shut behind him.

The girl stood looking after him, expecting him to return, then turned to Jean. He could see the beginnings of tears in her eyes, but she quickly blinked them back. "I don't know what to say, Mr. LeClair. Beau's upset and rightfully so. But you were kind, I think, and I want to thank you. Please keep your offer open. Perhaps I can convince him to accept it."

"I doubt it," he said, "but I will keep it open for your sake. You are a charming and wise young lady."

Suddenly her face lit up and her hand dove into her purse. "You forgot this," she said, handing his handkerchief back to him. As he took if from her, his fingers brushed hers and it affected Amoreena strangely. She seemed to almost shudder at his touch. Their eyes met and held, then shaking, she drew back and headed for the door.

"Amoreena," he said, impulsively, "where are you staying?"

"At the Pacific Inn," she replied, then turned and fled.

He sat down and made a tent with his fingers. She was a beautiful woman, but there was something other than beauty that attracted him. Was it her loyalty? Loyalty to the Virginian? Jean had never met a woman like her. Ashton didn't realize it, but *he* had something even more important than ownership of the Pirates' Nest—he had Amoreena Welles!

*   *   *

Monique had been listening at the door to Jean's study while he and his two visitors quarreled over ownership of the Pirates' Nest. The voices of Jean's guests were somehow familiar to her, so she peeped through the oversized keyhole to get a glance. She was surprised when she saw that the voices belonged to Beau Ashton of the *Sea Lion*—the man with the game leg—and Amoreena Welles. It was a small world! At least it was a small Barbary Coast!

After hearing some of the conversation, Monique was not in the least disturbed by Beau's accusations that Jean had stolen his land. Whether or not Jean was guilty mattered little to Monique. She knew Jean LeClair would not suffer from the loss of the Pirates' Nest, but knew it would never come to that. No one could fight Jean LeClair and hope to win.

The one thing that did bother her, however, was the light she thought she saw in Jean's eye whenever he looked at Amoreena. Was she mistaken, or was it lust? Monique, in the short time she had known Jean, found him fascinating, and had made up her mind that, father or not, she would have him for a bed partner. She wanted to find out first-hand what her mother had experienced with Jean thirteen years earlier. He had not as yet succumbed to her, but it only made her desire him more. She didn't need competition from Ashton's whore! She wondered with a chuckle if her mother would consent to having Amoreena Welles shanghaied. Yet she knew she would not ask it, for to demand too many favors at the outset would be detrimental. She might need a really big favor later and she did not want to push too hard now.

Did it bother Monique that Jean might be her father? Not at all. Why should she deprive herself of a rich, attractive man, she reasoned, simply because there was a small chance he might have sired her? There was, after all, no way to tell for sure and she had an intuitive feeling Jean was not her father. That was good enough for her.

Suddenly her thoughts were shattered when she heard Beau say, "Come, Amoreena, our business is over." They were leaving! She raced down the hall to a tall wooden coat stand, hid behind it, and watched as Beau limped out of the room, paused for a moment staring at the closed door, then slammed his fist against it in disgust and continued down the main staircase to the front doors.

Then Monique frowned. The Welles woman remained behind in Jean's closed study! What was she doing in there? Monique wanted desperately to sneak back and listen at the door, but she didn't want to chance getting caught. She bit her lip and waited for what seemed like an hour but was only a minute. At last the door opened.

Amoreena, unlike Beau, was smiling as she left, and it made Monique boil with anger. If only she had heard what transpired between the two.

When Amoreena reached the stairs and started down, Monique stepped out from her hiding place and went to Jean's study. Jean was alone now, sitting behind his desk, his fingers fiddling absently with a glass paperweight, his eyes on an oil painting on the wall opposite the door.

She sauntered inside and stood before him. When he seemed not to notice her, she snapped her fingers and said, "Hello!"

He dropped the paperweight and it made a loud thud on the top of his rosewood desk. "You startled me, Monique," he said. "Is something wrong?"

"Do you know what time it is?"

He raised an eyebrow. "Just before noon I'd say."

"No, silly. Have you forgotten? You promised to take me shopping this afternoon."

He scowled. "I'm sorry, Monique, but I'm going to have to cancel. Today has not been the best of days and

it's far from over. I have several things I must attend to.
We'll go shopping another time.''

Was his business a blonde bitch by the name of Amoreena
Welles? Had he promised to meet her somewhere? "I was
looking forward to this afternoon,'' she pouted. "Can't
your business wait?''

"I'm afraid not.'' He stood and gathered some papers
together in a satchel.

"I could wait for you,'' she said. "How long will you
be?''

"I have no idea. You go on along without me.''

She wanted to tell him she knew where he was going—
who he was going to see. She held her tongue only because in doing so she'd be admitting she was eavesdropping.
"Very well,'' she snapped, "I'll go by myself. But if I get
accosted, it'll be on your conscience!'' She raised her
skirts slightly and marched out of his study.

Monique found the streets of San Francisco not only
steep and hilly, but thrilling to ride over in a horse-drawn
streetcar. The streets looked like ribbons leading straight to
the sky. At the top, there was a breathtaking and immediate drop, often with an enchanting view of Alcatraz Island
out in the bay. Always there was a thrilling sort of fear
that if the horses were spooked and got out of control, the
streetcar would fly off the ground into the sky—or the bay.

She arrived at the stores a little after noon, bought a
lavender promenade gown in Finckle's Emporium on Pow-
ell Street near Jackson, then ate a chicken sandwich in a
small Jackson Street restaurant. While sitting at the counter,
she noticed through the restaurant window a streetcar filled
with passengers stop to let an oversized wagon loaded with
vegetables pass by. More than half the passengers were
Chinese men, and she thought them odd-looking with
funny wide pantaloons and long hair braided in the back

like young girls. She almost choked on her sandwich as she wondered what would happen if someone sat on a Chinaman's hair, or queue, as it was called, and the Chinaman had to stand up quickly or miss his stop. That would hurt, she thought, and it would no doubt serve him right, for Chinese people, after all, were inferior creatures classed even lower than those black skinned Negroes who caused the war in the East, and those Indian savages running wild in the plains states.

Back at school Lucille Randolph had mentioned to Monique that on the Barbary Coast pranksters would throw red pepper in the Celestials' eyes simply because the Chinese were considered socially inferior and despised by the Occidentals. Monique had never known a Chinese person and had no reason to hate the race—other than their strange appearance—but she found that was enough.

She finished her sandwich just as the streetcar she had been watching began its climb up the hill and disappeared from view. Since it was a lovely day, she decided to walk home. She headed east on Jackson Street toward Chinatown, where her attention was caught by a small group of rough-looking young boys loitering on the corner across the street. She noticed a few other pedestrians cross in the middle of the block to avoid the boys, who were yelling profanities at them.

Monique was not afraid of them. The youths were just having fun. She stepped into the street and headed in their direction. One of the boys reminded her of the lad who had taken her maidenhead back in New York, and she wanted to get a closer look.

The smallest of the lot jabbed a red-haired youth in the ribs and said loudly, "Look what's coming our way, Luke."

The one called Luke turned brown eyes on Monique,

cocked his head, and whistled. "Hey, hey, that *is* my day; look what a doll is headin' my way!"

As she got closer, she noticed that the one called Luke did look a lot like her lover back East. She also thought his rhyme cute. She quickened her pace and crossed the street, stopped and stood directly before Luke. He was only a half inch taller than her, and he looked at her expectantly through horn-rimmed glasses.

"A doll I am, but neither weak nor meek; pleased to meet you, the name's Monique," she said.

A roar of laughter swept through the group. "You're pretty good," Luke declared. "Ain't never met a girl who could rhyme half decent. This here's my gang; Ralph, Fred, Hernando and Pete."

She nodded a hello to each. "You live around here?" she asked Luke.

"Yeah, my pa owns a saloon east of here on the bayfront. Ever hear of Spider Joe?"

"Can't say I have. I'm new here."

"Where you stayin'?"

"Up on Telegraph Hill."

"That's fancyville," said Ralph. "We don't mess with fancy folk too much."

Luke frowned. "Once we tried to rob a Telegraph Hiller, a hot-shot named LeClair. I never heard of this dude until after we messed him up, and my old man was ravin' mad—told me I was dumb. How was I supposed to know he was the big cheese?"

"You attacked Jean LeClair?" she asked, amazed.

"I busted his goddamn nose," bragged Ralph.

"That ain't all," added Hernando. "I busted his fat ass!"

"I scared the shit outa the bastard," Pete said. "He'll never walk alone at night again."

What a pack of lies, Monique thought. Jean LeClair

could blow them over with one breath. They were nothing but kids trying to be tough. "How about you, Luke?" she said. "What did *you* do to LeClair?"

"Me?" he said. He shuffled his feet uncomfortably. "Hell, I . . . Aw, shit! You look to me like you're too smart to fall for a dumb lie. The fact is we're lucky to be alive! LeClair could've chopped us up or blew a hole in our brains with that shooting iron he was carryin'. Afterward his thugs coulda put us on a ship bound for China. We were damn lucky."

At least Luke was honest, she thought. "So now all you do is stand on street corners and toss dumb insults at people?"

"Naw. What do you think we are, a bunch of yellow crumbs? We roll a sailor here and there and set fires in old warehouses and such."

She had an idea. If Jean didn't have time for her this afternoon, she'd find her own entertainment. "Tell you what," she said, "if you're interested, I'll show you how to have fun without getting in trouble."

Luke's eyes widened. "You do that, baby, and I'll make you a special member of our club."

"Hey!" protested Ralph, "we can't have no skirts hangin' round with us!"

"This ain't no ordinary skirt, Ralphie. This doll's special, so let's give her a chance, huh?"

The others grumbled for a while, then reluctantly agreed.

Monique took them to Dupont Street, in the heart of Chinatown, where she told them they'd wait for a streetcar filled with Chinese men. The boys looked at her as if she had four breasts, but the determination on her face kept them quiet and expectant. She then told them her plan.

"The idea is," she said, "to tie the Chinamen's queues together, one to the other and so on, until they're nothing but one large circle of tail! The car won't stay here too long, so you'll have to work fast before the slant-eyes realize what's happening.''

Luke's eyes glistened with excitement. ''Say, that's great! Why didn't I think of that?''

''One more thing. Do you carry a knife?'' she asked.

Luke nodded and dug into his pocket for it.

''After you and the boys have tied their hair together, cut off whatever ends you can. Later we'll make something out of it.'' A thought struck her. ''How would you like a new hair belt?''

''You're as nutty as those redskins out in the Dakota Territory,'' Luke said. ''I love it!''

Now a half-empty streetcar stopped at their corner to pick up and discharge passengers. Huddled in the back of the car was a half dozen Chinamen with their long queues hanging out through the barred sides of the car so as not to sit on them. Monique gave the signal and Luke and the others raced into the street toward the streetcar. There were only four passengers left to board, so they had to work fast. They kept low and scrambled up to the side of the car, then quickly caught and tied the unsuspecting Chinamen's hair together. When they were finished a brief moment later, the queues formed a hair rope around the outside of the streetcar. A couple of quick snips with the knife and they scurried off with their prize.

Monique joined them as they raced down the block the streetcar would be turning onto. They hid, giggling as they did, and waited for the car to pass by. From their spot in an alleyway, they could watch the fiasco that was sure to follow.

The streetcar stopped half-way down the block. Two of the Chinamen tried to stand in order to get off, but the pull of their tied queues brought them stumbling back to their seats. Their voices rang loud and frenzied as they shouted at each other in Chinese.

Monique doubled over with laughter and so did Luke, who grabbed and hugged her. "You're one of us now, Monique," he said, still laughing at the sight of the frantic Celestials trapped in the streetcar. The others cheered.

"Do you have a headquarters, Luke?" she asked. "A place where you and the others meet?"

Luke looked befuddled. "No, not exactly. Do we need one?"

"All clubs have houses. We'll need a place to plan things. Like more fun with the Chinese, for starters. Maybe we could do something with their laundries."

"I know of a place where we can meet," he said. "There's a decayin' shack next to my old man's saloon. Nobody goes there anymore 'cept an occasional street whore."

"Then we'll use it!" Monique declared. "I've got to go now, Luke, but we'll all meet there after supper tomorrow night."

Luke left the others to walk her down the block. "I like you," he said, when they were out of earshot of the others.

"I like you, too."

Monique waited for him to ask her the inevitable—if she'd tumble with him. But he surprised her. He kept his eyes ahead as they walked, and said nothing. She turned to him. His cheeks were red.

"Did you ever bed a girl, Luke?" she asked, knowing by his manner that he had not.

"Sure," he lied.

"I'll bet."

"I bedded lots. Ask the gang, they'll tell you."

"I wouldn't believe them. And I don't believe you either. But it doesn't matter that you've never had a girl. I'll be happy to teach you what to do—if you're interested."

"Are you kidding?" he said. "Sure I'm interested. When?"

"That depends," she said, her thoughts on the handsome Jean LeClair at home. If she succeeded in getting him to her bed tonight, she'd hardly be able to steal out to meet Luke. "Soon," she promised.

Jean LeClair had had a hectic day. He had spent the entire afternoon and a good part of the evening in meetings with the Barons, Faye Langlois, and lastly, Abe Thompson, a young Barbary Coast lawyer friend he had backed financially.

Jean had sought Abe's legal opinion on Beau Ashton's chances of suing for and winning the Pirates' Nest. "It would cost him a heck of a lot of money, Jean, and time," Thompson had said.

"But has he a chance?"

"There's always a chance of anything happening, Jean. San Francisco could break away from the mainland and sink into the ocean tomorrow. But in this particular case, I'd have to say that Ashton's chance of winning is slim, almost non-existent. He has no evidence to support his theory. You hold all the cards. No judge or jury I know of would rule in his favor."

Jean was in slightly better spirits but tired from his busy day, so when he left the lawyer's office he went straight home without stopping at one of his Nests for a drink. It was just past nine o'clock when he stepped into a dark and quiet house. Where were the servants? he wondered. It was too early for them to have retired.

"Hays?" he called. No answer. "Hilda?" Hilda was the cook, and he went to the kitchen in search of her, only to find dirty pots and dishes laying about on the table as well as in the huge brick fireplace. There was no food and no sign of Hilda.

He went to the servants' quarters and found their suite of rooms empty. Had everyone deserted him? What other surprises were in store for him today?

Then he remembered Monique. She had to be home from her shopping by now and could explain what had happened. He went to her bedroom and found it empty.

Furious, he stormed into his own dark room and tore off his coat, flinging it haphazardly onto the bed. A muffled cry caught his ear and he quickly lit an oil lamp in time to see Monique yank the woolen coat off her face.

"Is that any way to greet a guest?" she exclaimed, giggling.

Jean gaped, for she wore no clothes. Only a thin coverlet hid her from the waist down. Despite his surprise, he couldn't help but stare at her large, upturned breasts.

She took her breasts in her hands and cupped them, offering them to him. She fingered erect nipples invitingly, then patted the mattress. "Come," she said, "I've been waiting for you."

She was appealing, but also appalling—and a sneaky little temptress. Jean needed her like he needed a war with the Rangers. Now the servants' absence made sense. "What've you done with the servants?" he asked.

She beamed. "I gave them the night off. Told them you wanted them to have free drinks and enjoy themselves at the Pirates' Nest. They didn't stay around long enough to ask questions!"

Jean checked the impulse to take this saucy, bitchy, child over his knee for a fierce canning. "Sending them away was unnecessary, Monique," he said. "It won't get me into bed with you. You've the breasts of a woman and the morals of a whore, but need I remind you that I may be your father?"

"I don't care about that and neither should you." she declared.

"Well I do care, Monique, and you're going to have to leave. Now!"

"Not on your life, Jean LeClair!" she said with a smile, and threw back the coverlet to reveal the rest of her. Her legs were long and lean, her stomach flat, beneath it a small patch of dark hair. She spread her legs invitingly. "I need you, Jean," she said, her voice thick with lust. "Don't you like what you see?"

Jean had to admire her gall—as well as her body. It had been nearly two weeks since he'd had a woman. "Get up, Monique," he said. "I see naked girls often—prettier ones than you as well as more mature. Your body does not arouse me."

His words did not deter her. She jumped off the bed and hurled herself at him, flattening her flesh against him. She gave him no time to protest, pulling his head down and planting her mouth on his.

Before he could stop her, she tried to work her tongue between his teeth and into his mouth, but he shoved her away in disgust. With a man boldness was expected, but Monique was like a bitch in heat!

After he broke free of her mouth, he had to hold her at arms length as she tried to move back against him. "Stop this now, Monique," he said. "Can't you see that I don't want to make love to you?"

"But I don't care that you may be my father, Jean," she declared.

"It's not that, Monique. I wouldn't take you even if I knew for sure that you weren't my daughter!"

"Why not? You think me ugly?" She looked like a little girl about to cry—exactly what she was.

"I've had many girls," he said, "but they had one thing in common—they were all past sixteen and grown up. You're a child, Monique, and I don't need a child as a bed partner."

The hurt look disappeared, in its place pure rage. "So I'm a child, am I?" she declared. "Georgie Ross didn't think so, nor did any of the others. But I'm not old enough to suit you, am I? Hah! Well, I wanted you, Jean, but I don't need you! There are plenty of others who desire me. But I won't forget how you spurned me. I swear I'll find a way to make you sorry!"

"I didn't ask you here, Monique, but now I'm asking you to leave."

"I'm going! I'll not only leave your room, but your house as well!"

She grabbed her clothes and rushed off toward the door. He caught her by the wrist and spun her around. "Where are you going?"

She pulled free and glared at him. "I don't have to report to you. And I don't have to stay here. I'm moving out."

"You mother will want to know where you've gone."

"She doesn't give a damn about me."

"You're wrong. She cares very much."

"You think so? Well, if she cares so much, then I'll move in with her and see how she likes it!"

Monique packed her bags and stormed out of the huge white mansion. It was foggy now, but she hurried along, not caring who or what she bumped into as she half-walked, half-stumbled down the sloping street toward the bay. Tears stung her eyes. Only her anger prompted her on, and with each step she cursed LeClair and swore revenge.

She had gone little more than two blocks when the last of the nightly streetcars came by. She boarded it, and as she rode to the docks, she tried to think of something she could do to hurt him, and the thought reminded her of the time she'd spent with Luke that afternoon. Luke. Would

he be at the shack at this hour? She hoped so. If Jean
didn't want her, at least Luke did.

She went to the deserted shack near Spider Joe's saloon
and was delighted to see Luke there.

9

"YOU'VE BEEN sulking here in this stuffy hotel room for the last two days," Amoreena said, staring at Beau, who lay on his back on the bed, his eyes open but unseeing. "It's not like you. You haven't eaten much, and you barely sleep. I know you're angry and hurting, but you've got to stop torturing yourself."

"What would you have me do?" he asked. "Kill LeClair?"

"You told him that we have other recourses open to us. What are they, Beau, and why aren't you following one?"

He sighed. "I said that to throw a scare into LeClair. I guess it didn't work. Sure we have recourses. So does he. I can sue him; he can have me shanghaied!"

"Really, Beau, I doubt he'd do that. Are you afraid of him? I never knew you to be afraid of anyone."

"Stop nagging, Amoreena. I'm not afraid. I'm just not sure how to fight him."

"Maybe someone else could help us."

"Who?"

"Does San Francisco have a mayor? Councilmen? Judges?"

"LeClair no doubt owns them, Amoreena, or so I've heard."

"LeClair can't own all the officials in this city. There's got to be at least one man who's too decent to be bought."

"I suppose so. I wonder . . ."

"What?" she asked.

"I wonder if the land official that Larry Barre bribed is still around. He could prove useful in a law suit."

A short time later, at the urging of Amoreena, Beau left the hotel and walked three blocks to the county hall of records, where he asked the registrar if the man who handled deed transfers in '49 was still in San Francisco.

"No, sir, he died several years back. But we've got a copy of all deeds here on record."

"Can I see a transfer of property between Ashton and LeClair," he said.

The clerk went to a large wooden cabinet, pulled out a cluttered drawer and dug through countless files until he found it. "Here it is," he declared. "As filed, sir, Monte Ashton to Jean LeClair."

Beau looked it over, then told the clerk that he believed the deed to be false, and explained why. The clerk was sympathetic, but said there was little he could do. As far as the city was concerned, the deed on file was legal and binding.

"You might sue," the registrar suggested. "Try the courthouse first. They'd know more there."

Beau found the clerk at the courthouse equally sympathetic and wondered if LeClair really did own the city officials.

"Sure, you can sue Jean LeClair," the clerk said, "but

it'll take money. And he'll fight you every step of the way."

"I have money," Beau said. Not a whole lot, but enough, he thought, to get a suit started.

"I don't know you, son, but I know LeClair. He's got more money than you could dream of earning in a lifetime."

"How do I go about filing suit?" Beau asked.

"First you got to get yourself a lawyer. There'll be legal fees, filing fees, court fees, a great deal of paperwork, and who knows what else. Your lawyer can tell you more."

"Since I'm new here, could you recommend a lawyer?"

The clerk scratched his head. "Well, there's a mighty bright young fellow who has an office in the Russian Hill area, on Vallejo Street. He handles Barbary Coast cases. His name's Thompson—Abe Thompson."

It was almost suppertime when Beau arrived at Thompson's law office. He was kept waiting for a half hour, but then Abe Thompson's secretary led him into a plushly carpeted office. The young lawyer was tall and well dressed, with exceptionally long fingers. His handshake was firm, his voice low and without emotion.

Beau explained in detail about his father's mining partner, the forged deed, his father's recent death, and his confrontation with LeClair. "I believe I have legal recourse, Mr. Thompson. Your name was suggested to me. Will you represent me?"

The big man had sat quietly behind his desk, his eyes on the collection of hand-carved statuettes on a shelf opposite the desk. Now he looked Beau squarely in the eye. "Anyone can sue anyone else, Mr. Ashton. All it takes is money and time. You haven't much in your favor, however, as you cannot prove the deed Mr. LeClair has as false. Nor can you produce this Mr. Barre or the land officer who was supposed to have issued a fraudulent deed. Mr. LeClair, on the other hand, can produce a valid deed and has the money to appeal any ruling in your favor you might receive from the lower courts and take it all the way to the Supreme Court.''

A look of despair crept over Beau's face, but he shook the feeling off. ''Are you saying you won't represent me?'' he asked.

''I want you to think about your suit a little longer. Twenty-four hours. Consider the large fees, the months, perhaps years, it would take to settle. Consider also the hopes that might be dashed, the test of nerves you'll be forced to undergo. If you still feel, after careful consideration, that you wish to sue Mr. LeClair, then come back and see me. We'll talk more then.'' He stood up.

''Thank you for your time, Mr. Thompson. I'll be seeing you again tomorrow.''

When Abe Thompson was alone, he wrote a brief note to Jean LeClair telling of his visitor and dispatched it by messenger up to Telegraph Hill.

Beau didn't go back to the hotel. He wanted time alone to think before he told Amoreena what he'd learned. He felt the need for a drink, so he stopped at the Pirates' Nest, which was nearby. It was on his property, so was as close to ''home'' as anything in the Barbary Coast.

Even though it had just begun to grow dark and a light mist was settling around the buildings, already the saloon was brimming with customers. Beau suspected it never cleared out enough to see from one end of the room to the other. LeClair was doing all right, he thought. If the Nest became his, could he keep it prospering? What did he know about running a saloon and whorehouse? Beau frowned. He knew nothing and wasn't sure he wanted to. If Monte could see him now, he'd turn over in his grave.

Suddenly Beau wished Georgie were there to confide in. He could talk to Amoreena, but that wasn't always as easy as it should be. He was a sort of god in Amoreena's eyes. He had to uphold that image around her, and it wasn't easy. He wasn't a god, and whenever he felt disheartened and let it show, she'd make him feel small—as though he had let her down. She meant well, and surely she had gotten him out of many a bad mood, but now he needed someone who wasn't as close as Amoreena—someone who could listen objectively and let him weep over his beer if he damned well pleased.

Where was Georgie? He hadn't heard from the young sea captain since their whirlwind tour of the Coast two nights earlier. What was the name of the lodginghouse where Georgie was staying? Try as he might, Beau could not remember.

Now as he sat at a small table in the rear of the Pirates' Nest drinking a beer, he noticed a familiar face. Rose, the pretty waitress he had met the last time he and Georgie had been here, was weaving her way through the tables toward him.

Rose was surprised to see the blonde man who had been with Georgie the other night, back in the Pirates' Nest. She had heard from Faye that the shanghai of Ross had been successful, and Rose half hoped Ross' arrogant friend might have been taken by Faye's thugs as well.

She scowled now as she remembered the nickel tip he had left her. She had made little money on him that night, and it always angered her whenever she spent time on a man without seeing monetary results. She made up her mind that the blonde man was going to line her pockets heavily tonight no matter what she had to do to get it.

She pushed her way through the crowd to him. She noticed his eyes upon her, the grim smile he wore as she reached his table. "Well," she said sarcastically, "if it isn't the last of the big tippers!"

"I knew I left too much," he replied with a shrug, his

grin widening at her irritation. "Once you leave a big tip, they'll always expect it."

"I'm an old-fashioned girl, mister. I might get spoiled by such riches. So . . ." She threw a nickel on the table in front of him. "Take it," she said. "You need it more than I do."

He scooped it up, turned it over in his palm, then pocketed it. "You just may be right," he said. Then he laughed. "Sit down, Rose, and talk to me and I'll give you a real good tip. Okay?"

She hesitated for a moment, then smiled and sat on a chair opposite him.

"I'm Beau Ashton from Virginia," he said.

"Well, Beau Ashton from Virginia, can you dance with that game leg?"

He would have said no, but for the challenge in her words. It had been a long time since he'd held a woman on a dance floor. A sign on the wall opposite their table read, DANCE WITH A PRETTY GIRL—ONLY 25¢. He took her hand and placed a shiny quarter in her palm.

"No," she said, handing it back. "This one's on me." Let him think she was not after his money, she thought.

He led her onto the dance floor. The pianist was playing a slow song and Beau pulled Rose close.

She was aware of his smell—masculine and sweaty—but found it pleasant compared with the Coasters she frequently had to dance with. Beau Ashton was clean and well groomed, and his sweat was not offensive. He had had only one beer, so his breath was slightly scented with alcohol and not reeking of it like a drunken sailor. She wondered what he'd look and smell like after she'd finished with him later tonight.

"You know, Rose," he said, "I've never said this to a girl before, but . . ." He hesitated.

She pulled back and looked into his eyes. What was he about to tell her?

". . . but I think you're a damn good dancer."

A good dancer? "I'm an even better bed partner," she said, hoping to shock him. If she did, however, his expression didn't show it.

He just smiled. "I'll bet you are," he said without rancor. "You must get a lot of practice working here."

"Not as much as you might think. *I* choose *my* partners and not the reverse."

"Oh? What is it you look for in a partner?"

"Good looks, strength, masculinity, kindness. Generosity. Shall I go on?"

"Sounds like you're describing me," he said with a chuckle, his breath hot upon her ear.

"That's odd. I didn't notice any similarity."

The dance ended and they went back to their table.

"Rose, honey," Beau said, "you needn't worry. I'm not after your favors."

Why not? she wondered. Nearly every man she met fawned over her. Why was this one special? "It's my job to see that everyone has a good time," she said tightly. "Mooning over a beer is not my idea of fun. How about going in the back with me to get a peek at what's beneath my clothes? Only cost you fifty cents."

"Sorry, Rose. I don't feel much like peeking tonight. Besides, if I want that sort of a good time, I can get it free from my fiancée back at the hotel."

So he was betrothed! Rose thought. Was that why he didn't want her? She wondered idly how much he could love his fiancée if he already went places like the Pirates' Nest without her. Knowing he was spoken for, however, only made him more of a challenge for her. Not that she really wanted him sexually—she could do nicely without that—but as another conquest to jot down in her little red book of "impossible men". These were men who either disliked women or refused to spend money for one. These were the ones she'd flatter, tease, then bring them to their knees, begging for her affections. All it took was a few lies—and a little cantharides in their drinks.

Since Beau Ashton was betrothed and showed no interest in spending money or taking her to bed, he was well qualified as an "impossible."

"I'll tell you what," she said. "You need someone to talk to, so let me bring you another beer and sit here for awhile. You can get whatever you want off your chest."

"There's really no need to . . ." He stopped short, for she had already gotten up and was on her way across the room to the bar. He kept his eyes pinned to her slim form until she returned a moment later with a beer and a whiskey.

"I hope you don't mind," she said, "but I was thirsty too. Since you didn't offer to buy me a drink, I simply went ahead and ordered one for myself." She didn't tell him she charged it to his bill at twice what it was worth.

"Be my guest," he said with a shrug.

"Now, tell me what's troubling you." She took a sip of whiskey. Normally she drank tea in order to stay sober throughout the long evening and night and because of the countless men she'd have to entertain, but now she felt a need for something stronger. She didn't have time to wonder why.

"Nothing's troubling me, Rose. Why do you ask?" He drained the remainder of his first beer.

Rose eyed the second expectantly. "You look kind of sad, like you lost your best friend."

"Try my best *property*," he said softly. He brought the new glass of beer to his lips, but stopped and grinned before he could take a sip. "You didn't drug this, did you?" he asked.

"Of course not."

"Well, then, suppose you take a little sip of my beer first."

"It won't mix with my drink," she said.

"Sure it will. Come on, a little sip."

She fumed. If he didn't drink the beer . . . She hoped one little sip wouldn't hurt her—or affect her. She took the glass and drank a little from it, forcing a smile as she swallowed it. "See, Beau? It's fine."

He looked doubtful, but finally sighed and took a long pull. "Tastes normal," he declared then. "Can't be too sure of anything here on the Coast. You know, in a way I'm glad you're here, Rose. I do have a problem." He took another mouthful. "It has to do with some property my father left me when he died." There was unhappiness in his eyes now as he thought of his situation.

"Go on," she urged, "I'm listening."

"Someone stole my land. Someone you know. Everyone knows him. I . . ." A strange expression flicked across his face and his eyes took on a new light. They were at once wild and daring, yet soft and vulnerable.

Rose had seen men affected differently by drugs, but mostly they'd want to claw at her, rip the clothes off her body—become a part of it. Ashton seemed mildly affected.

"Drink more," she said, then added, "it'll make you relax and let the words flow easier."

He stared at the glass, then drank the golden fluid down in one last drag. "You're right. Already I feel so much lighter . . ." He stared at her as if seeing her for the first time. "You know, Rose, honey, you're a damned good looking woman."

Now for a lie. "I think you're kind of nice yourself. Why don't we go upstairs?"

He blinked and his hand stole down to a suddenly super-heated groin. A grin spread across his tanned face. "I shouldn't, but . . . sounds good. Lead the way."

He followed her to a small, dark cubicle upstairs, forty feet down the hall from where Faye had her office. Normally Rose would take her customers to the largest of the rooms—the one next to Faye's office and private quarters—but late last night Monique Langlois had sauntered into the Nest and informed a startled Faye of her intent to live with her. She then moved into and took over Rose's cubicle. Rose intended to speak to Jean about it the first chance she got.

Now she lit a candle. There was only a small chest of drawers and a cot in the tiny cubicle. She motioned for Beau to lie down, but instead an aroused Beau swept her into his arms and kissed her.

The pressure on her lips was brutal and demanding, and she yielded to it. Then he edged her backward toward the cot. Rose knew the drug was at work. It would not be long before he threw her down on the cot and took his pleasure, so she withdrew from his arms and said, "First I must remove my clothes."

"I'll do it for you."

"No. Lie down and relax. Close your eyes. I want to prolong the pleasure . . . make you enjoy me that much more."

He seemed to think about it, then lay down and closed his eyes.

Rose worked fast. Inside the bureau drawer was a small bottle of clear fluid and a white handkerchief. With a skill borne of much practice, she poured a drop or two of the powerful chloroform onto the handkerchief and dropped to the floor beside the cot.

Sweet dreams, she thought, as she quickly brought up her arm and pressed the cloth over Beau's nose and mouth. He resisted, reaching up to grab her hand and wrench it away, but she pressed harder and the chloroform did its work. In seconds his arms fell limply at his sides and she pulled the handkerchief away.

"Beau?" she asked, though knowing he was unconscious. He did not stir and she got to her feet, satisfied.

So, she thought, now she had him where she wanted him. The last of the big tippers, indeed! She peeled back his coat and dove a hand into his pockets. There she found a wallet. In it was a piece of paper—a discharge document from the Confederate Navy—stating Beau's name and Virginia address. In a separate compartment of the wallet were several greenbacks, thirty dollars worth!

She took the money and stuffed it all into a special satin purse she had sewn and wore beneath her gown, pinned securely to her chemise. The wallet she threw into a container that would be dumped as garbage into the alley.

Rose stepped back and stared down at him. He looked at ease, much more so than when he had come into the Nest. Perhaps she had done him a good turn. Tomorrow he might even thank her for a restful night's sleep, despite the fact that he'd wake up thirty dollars poorer.

But in spite of her good fortune, something disturbed her. That one sip of Beau's beer was beginning to take effect on her. She felt an all-consuming heat between her thighs and sweat broke out upon her forehead. She moved a hand across her breasts, closing her eyes as she did so. The ache between her legs was growing stronger and she opened her eyes and stared at the unconscious man upon the cot. Once more she dropped to her knees beside him, this time her object was the still rock-hard member between his legs. She touched it, timidly at first, then found that stroking it excited her even further. She actually *liked* what she was doing! She, who had never touched a man of her own free will! She who hated physical contact! It shocked and frightened her and she stood up quickly, drew back.

The drug couldn't have affected her to this extent, she thought, so it had to be Ashton. He had a strange, evil effect on her.

She dashed out of the room and headed for Faye's office. "I've some trash I have to dispose of," she told the Madame. "Send two bouncers to my den," she said.

Faye was not surprised. There was always trouble of one sort or another around. Monique was hers.

Five minutes later Beau Ashton was unceremoniously dumped from the Pirates' Nest into a filthy, dark alleyway.

The Virginian was lucky he was unconscious. He would have cringed at the putrid stink of rotting trash, the rats which scurried across his huddled form to feast upon the garbage nearby. A fog had rolled in an hour ago and now hung heavy over the city, but Beau didn't know it. He could neither hear nor see and thus was spared the horror of his predicament. He was still unconscious and didn't budge when, less than an hour later, three burly runners from a nearby Ranger-owned boardinghouse found him, searched his pockets for money, then, realizing he had none, hoisted him up and carried him off down the mist-laded alley.

10

WHEN BEAU didn't come back to the hotel by six o'clock that night, Amoreena was concerned. When he didn't show by nine o'clock, she went from simple concern to worry. At eleven o'clock, she was wringing her hands and biting her nails. At one-thirty in the morning, Amoreena was crawling the walls with fear. There was no logical excuse for his being gone this late, she knew, unless he was hurt. If he were all right, he would have gotten word to her that he planned to stay out past a reasonable hour. Since she had received no message from him, she could only suspect the worst.

Her eyes were red and swollen from crying and she washed her face with cool water from a pitcher atop her bureau. She tried to get herself together to do something constructive about her fears.

The streets at night were dangerous but she had to try to find him. Mixed with her own misgivings of venturing out alone was the horrible feeling that Beau wasn't coming home—tonight or ever. The thought sent chills down her spine, and she was grateful for the heavy woolen coat she had just slipped on.

Heart hammering, she started for the door, but stopped as her hand touched the cool glass of the knob. Where would she seek him? The Barbary Coast might be a small quarter of a growing San Francisco, but it was a never-ending maze of streets and dark, forbidding alleyways. Beau could be anywhere. Finding him would be nearly impossible.

As she stepped out of the hotel and stood for a moment at the top of the steps leading down a small hill to the street, the ghostliness of a fog-shrouded night seemed to slap her in the face. She shivered. She had expected darkness, but from her warm, cozy hotel room, she had been unaware of the fog that had rolled in off the sea. It was frightening enough to have to walk the streets alone in the dark, but in fog as thick as pea soup?

The urge to retreat to her room was great, but so was her determination, and, squaring her shoulders, she forced herself to step down the stairs and go on. Beau needed her—she was sure of it. Beau might scold her for being out alone on such a horrible night, but she knew that if he were alive and well and she could see him again, she'd gladly accept his rebuke.

Where should she head first? Beau had been bound for the county hall of records that afternoon, but it was closed at this hour and anyway, she had no idea where it was.

Who did she know here in the Coast? Beau, of course, and Georgie . . . and Jean LeClair. She did not know Georgie's whereabouts or even if he still was on the Coast, so that left LeClair. But would LeClair help her? He was opposing Beau's claim to the Pirates' Nest property, yet he knew the area well and if anyone could help her find

Beau, it was he. She decided she'd give him a try, for she had nothing to lose by doing so.

Wishing it was earlier so she could have hired a carriage for the trip to LeClair's, she hurried down the steps and made her way slowly, carefully, along the stone sidewalks of Pacific Street to where she bore right and headed up Dupont Street toward Telegraph Hill. The fog in places was so thick she had to proceed like a blind woman, reaching out before her to feel her way around what seemed like uncharted wilderness. She bumped into corners of buildings and sharp edges of store front signs. Once she tripped and fell in a puddle of mud, and nearly cried from frustration. Her hands and gown were smeared with mud, but she scrambled to her feet and headed on.

Then she heard raucous voices nearby—men's laughter! Drunken men's laughter! Were they ahead of or behind her? Her senses were jumbled in the sheer isolation of the fog. She hoped they couldn't see her and quickened her pace, less cautious now about where she stepped. Soon she had left the voices in the distance.

Ahead were the dim glow of red gas lights. They were to her right and high off the street, so she guessed they must be hanging over doorways or in windows.

Suddenly she heard the clip-clop of horses' hooves on the cobblestone street. She stared into the dense, swirling fog, trying vainly to figure out where the sound was coming from. She edged toward her right away from the street at the left—not realizing she had wandered blindly into the middle of the street.

She froze as the clatter of a carriage drew closer still. She could even smell the sweating horses now.

"Who's there?" she called out.

A horse neighed, and then out of the fog appeared a large coach! "Get off the bloody street!" the driver shouted, reining in the team.

The *street*? She jumped to the side and reached the safety of a building to her right as the coach rolled by. The fog seemed even thicker now and she again had to reach out ahead of her to feel her way. She had gone a few blocks when her fingers encountered something warm and wet, which seemed almost alive. She shrieked and drew back instantly, and a moment later found out it *was* alive.

A lilting voice broke the stillness. "China girl nice! You come inside, please?"

Amoreena could not see the owner of the voice, but now could guess what she had touched—the mouth of a Chinese prostitute leaning out the window of her crib looking for customers. This was Chinatown!

"Your father," the prostitute added, "he just go out!"

She thought Amoreena a Chinese man—and a potential customer! It was considered an honor for a Chinese man to bed the same woman his father had bedded before him. Chinatown prostitutes often used the lie to attract customers.

Amoreena plodded on. Her footsteps outside their windows triggered more of the same solicitations from other prostitutes, and although Amoreena ignored what they said, she was glad at least to know there was life nearby and she wasn't alone in this murky world.

It took almost two hours for her to walk from the hotel to LeClair's home, a distance of roughly a dozen or so blocks. She almost collapsed from exhaustion on his front porch. Incredibly she had not been waylaid by the ruffians she had heard so much about since arriving in the Barbary Coast. It must have been due to the fog, she thought. Even the pickpockets and murderers didn't want to be out on a night like this!

She mustered the last of her strength and knocked upon the heavy doors. The thud of her knock came back at her in the fog, and she hoped someone inside could hear. It was well after three o'clock, and everyone would be asleep.

Had she done the right thing in coming here? she wondered, as she waited for the doors to open. She hoped so. For the first time she considered that the fog might be the reason Beau hadn't come back to the hotel. Perhaps he was unsure of the way home and decided to stay where he was until morning?

She was suddenly puzzled and disheartened. Had she come all this way, taking her life in her hands, for nothing? The more she thought about it, however, the more firmly she believed she had done the only thing she could. If Beau was staying somewhere until the fog lifted, he would have managed to get word of it to her. Therefore, since he had not, it only meant Beau was beyond sending messages.

She knocked again, louder, more persistent. Please, she thought, let someone answer my knock! She was cold, tired and shaking with doubt.

A moment later a sleepy-eyed Jean LeClair partially opened the door. He was dressed in a black and white silk robe and his face bore a look of irritation at having been disturbed. When he saw her and the mud on her dress, however, his eyes softened and he opened the door wide. "Miss Welles!" he declared. "What brings you here at this hour? Please, come in."

She stepped into a warm hall and could have cried with relief. Her trek was over and she'd made it safely. Her eyes were clouded with tears of fear and relief as she said breathlessly, "It's Beau, Mr. LeClair. You're probably the last person who would care about him, but he's gone— disappeared. I've no idea where to look for him and I didn't know where else to turn."

He studied her for a minute, then cleared his throat. "Step into the parlor and we'll talk."

The parlor was huge and elegantly furnished. Though

she would have loved to sit down, she didn't want to stain the chairs with dried mud from her clothes, so she remained standing.

Jean LeClair poured two drinks and handed a sherry to her.

"Thank you," she said. She took the glass and stood before the fireplace. In it were the ashes of a fire begun hours ago. "I'm sorry I awoke you, Mr. LeClair," she said.

"Jean," he corrected, "and please do sit down."

"My gown is filthy," she said.

"No matter. My servants will clean up later. You must be tired."

"I'm afraid I am. Thank you." She sat upon a velvet settee facing him. "I was waiting for Beau to come back to our hotel. He had been gone all afternoon and I expected him back before it got dark. He didn't return. You're the only one I could think of to come to, so I came here."

"You walked all the way here in the fog?" he asked, amazed. He knew there were no streetcars or carriages for hire at this time of night.

"I did more falling than walking," she said, "as you can see from the dirt on my gown."

"That was foolish. Any number of things could have happened to you on the way. Then not only would Beau be missing, but perhaps you as well."

"I gave my safety little thought, Mr . . . Jean. I had to see you, to beg you to help me find Beau."

He drank the entire gobletful of sherry in one gulp. "You're a fine young woman, who obviously cares for her man very much. I admire that, but your Mr. Ashton and I are on separate sides of the fence. To put it bluntly, he's about to sue me, so why should I go out of my way to find him?"

"Sue?" she said. "He's been thinking about it, but hasn't made up his mind."

"On the contrary. At least that's what he told Abe Thompson."

"Who's Abe Thompson?" she asked.

"A lawyer."

How did Jean LeClair know that Beau went to see a lawyer? *She* didn't even know that! Suddenly a horrible thought entered her mind. If LeClair knew Beau had been to a lawyer, then he had to have had men following him! When LeClair learned of Beau's intentions to sue, he could have ordered his men to dispose of Beau! How could she have been so blind! "My God!" she cried, jumping to her feet, "It's you! You had reason to get rid of Beau— you and only you. We know no one else in San Francisco!"

"Calm yourself, Amoreena. I've done nothing to him, I swear it. I haven't even seen him since he left here."

"You're lying! I shouldn't have come here. I've been a fool. Whatever made me think that you, of all people, would help me!"

"Amoreena," he said, "please sit down. I swear on my love for the Pirates' Nest and all my establishments that I don't know what happened to Beau or where he is. If you leave now, you'll only be lost in a different kind of fog. I know the Coast and can help you find Beau. I shouldn't, but I will."

She stared at him. He looked and sounded sincere, but could she trust him? Yet did she have any choice? She sat down. "Will you search for him yourself?" she asked.

"I'll check with my sources. If anything has happened to Beau, we'll know in a few hours."

"By then he might be . . ." She found it difficult to think, let alone say, what she feared. "He might be . . . dead," she choked out.

"Don't think such thoughts, my dear. Chances are he's

had a few drinks too many and is sleeping it off somewhere. I'll check the Pirates' Nest first to see if he's been there."

"Oh, please!" she said. "Could you do it now?"

Jean was tired, but nodded. "First you must get some rest. You may use a guest room upstairs. I'd have Hays show you to it, but alas, my servants seem to have deserted me tonight."

"Thank you for offering, but I couldn't accept."

"Why not?"

That was a good question, she thought. She couldn't accept because Jean LeClair was alone in the house and social convention ruled against such accommodations. But more than that, she knew deep down in her heart that she didn't want to be alone with Jean LeClair, but would not ask herself why. "It's improper," she said lamely.

"This is hardly the time to worry about being proper, Amoreena," he said. "I assure you I will keep my distance, and not disturb you unless I hear some news of your fiancé."

A soft bed would feel good, she thought, and she did want to be close so she could learn quickly of Beau's whereabouts, yet suppose Beau returned to the hotel in her absence and found *her* gone? That would be tragic! "I really can't stay," she said, and told him the last.

"Very well. I'll drive you back to the hotel. We can stop at the Pirates' Nest on the way." He stood up and the fabric of his robe parted to expose a strong chest matted with thick dark hair.

She stared admiringly at him, then averted her eyes when she felt his gaze on her. "I really do appreciate your help," she said.

A short while later he had changed into traveling clothes and they were riding in his carriage to the Pirates' Nest. The fog had begun to lift. Only the first floor of the Pirates' Nest was visible and it looked eerie to Amoreena.

"Stay here," Jean said, as he jumped down from the driver's seat. "It's probably safer out here now than it is inside."

"No. I want to go with you." Before he could protest, she had climbed down from the vehicle and was following him down the stairs leading to the saloon.

Inside, the Nest was wrapped in a fog of its own—the result of the tobacco and opium smoking of a hundred customers. Amoreena coughed.

"There's a lot of lowlife here at this hour," he said, "so stay close to me."

She nodded and followed like a puppy as he shoved his way through the crowd toward the rear of the saloon. A dark-haired, middle-aged woman saw and approached him.

"Jean!" she said, "this is a little late for you, isn't it?"

Amoreena had been behind Jean and now she stepped to his side in full view of the woman.

"Ah!" she said. "You have a new friend!"

Jean frowned. Amoreena was not her concern. "Faye," he said, "I'm looking for a man. He's tall and blonde, and walks with a limp. His name's Ashton. Beau Ashton. Has he been here tonight?"

Faye arched pencil-thin eyebrows. "Don't recall anyone like that, but I wasn't down here all night."

"Who was on the floor who might've noticed this man?"

She scratched the tip of her straight nose. "Let's see . . . there was Mary, but she left an hour ago. Wilma and Rose were here, too. They both worked before midnight."

"Good. Get Rose and Wilma for me right now."

"Can't, Jean. Rose is with a customer upstairs and Wilma went home about a half hour ago."

"Which room is Rose in?" he inquired.

"The little one at the end of the hall, but . . ." Faye gaped as Jean pushed past her and took the stairs two at a time. Amoreena followed, though more slowly.

Jean strode down the hall to the room Rose was occupying, with Amoreena right behind. Now he turned to her and said, "You'd better stay in the hall. What's going on inside is hardly what you'd consider proper."

"All right," she said.

"Open the door, Rose, it's Jean," he called out. "I need to talk to you."

A moment later the door opened a crack and a disheveled red-haired girl peeked out. "What do you want?" she asked, her displeasure obvious.

"Did you see a man here tonight . . . a blonde man with a limp who goes by the name of Beau Ashton?"

Rose's look was immediately petulant. "Who's that with you?" she asked, her eyes on Amoreena.

"She's Ashton's fiancée," he said. "Well?"

"There were a lot of blondes here tonight," she said evasively. "This guy you're looking for might've been one of 'em. Why do you ask?"

"He's missing," Amoreena said from behind LeClair, "and I'm terribly worried something bad has happened to him."

"Wish I could help you, honey," Rose said, "but like I said, there was a lot of men who fit that description here. As far as the limp, I wouldn't know, 'cause they were all sittin' down. If your Beau was one of them, he's sure as hell gone by now." She turned large eyes to Jean. "I got a live one in here, Jean, so are you finished with me?"

He nodded. "Can you . . . handle him?" Jean asked, nodding toward the inside of the room.

A sly grin appeared on her face. "Sure. You ought to know better than to ask that."

She quickly closed the door, and Jean sighed. "No luck," he said, as they went back down the stairs, "but I'll check again in the morning."

He took her back to her hotel, then left. She got a key

from the night clerk and let herself inside Beau's room to see if he had returned during her absence, but his bed was empty and there was no evidence of him having been there.

She went to her room and sat dejectedly on the bed. The room was dark and lonely, but she did not light a lamp. The darkness was soothing now, and she fell exhausted to the pillow.

Amoreena slept badly the remainder of the night. When she could sleep no more at seven o'clock in the morning, she visited Beau's room again. He was not there. She was sure now that he wasn't coming back.

She dressed and caught a ride on an early-morning streetcar. It let her off three blocks from LeClair's mansion, so she walked the remainder of the way. This time she was greeted by the butler.

"Mr. LeClair is still asleep, miss," Hays said. "I cannot disturb him. Perhaps if you were to come back later . . ."

"This is very important," she said, "and he's expecting me. I'll wait."

Hays shrugged, showed her into the parlor. He left her to go about his business, and Amoreena settled herself on the same settee she had occupied only a few hours ago. A short time later a maid brought a tray laden with coffee and pound cake. Amoreena devoured it gratefully.

At eight o'clock, however, she grew restless waiting for LeClair to wake up. Every minute she waited for him was a minute less she could be hunting for Beau. She called out for Hays. When the butler answered the call, she would ask him to awaken Mr. LeClair.

But Hays, busy in the rear of the large house did not hear her. She got to her feet and went down the hallway outside the parlor door. "Hello!" she called out, "is anyone there?"

When no servant answered, she took matters into her own hands and proceeded up the main staircase to the second floor. LeClair's bedroom had to be there somewhere.

As she walked down the red-carpeted second floor hallway she saw on the left two elegant doors enameled in white and decorated in gold leaf pattern. This must be his room, she thought.

"Mr. LeClair?" she called. "Jean? Are you awake?"

If this was his room, he was apparently a sound sleeper, for unlike Beau, no sounds of snoring came from inside the room. Hesitantly she tried the doorknob. She gave it a turn and the door opened soundlessly into a large bedroom colored in red and gold. A dying fire still crackled in a marble-topped fireplace near a huge, four-poster brass bedstead, and on it lay a sprawled and sleeping Jean LeClair. A naked Jean LeClair! Sometime during the night the fire must have gotten too hot for him and he had thrown back his covers!

She felt her face warm at the sight of him, but she could not, as her conscience demanded, look away. She had never seen a man without clothes, and found now that it fascinated her. Often she'd wondered what Beau looked like in the nude, but she had never let her curiosity be known.

Now she closed the door behind her and stepped into the room. She tiptoed across the gold carpet in order to get a closer look without waking him. He was on his back with his head facing the fireplace. She looked with a feverish interest at his broad shoulders, and narrow waist, then his flat stomach. Her gaze lingered on the thatch of dark, curly hair and the sleeping, yet formidable flesh protruding from it. She longed to touch it, feel it grow in her palm—as she knew it must before it could be used in loveplay.

Then disaster struck as Jean turned and opened his eyes. "Oh!" she declared, stepping back quickly.

A half-smile creased his tanned face. "You seem to be popping up at all hours," he said.

"I . . . I'm sorry," she stammered lamely, "for . . . for being in your room like this . . . but I was . . . afraid Beau might be . . . lying hurt somewhere . . . and you were still sleeping and . . ."

He looked down at his legs. His half smile bloomed into a full one and he lazily pulled the covers back over him, then sat up in bed. "I haven't forgotten about your Beau," he said. "After I left you at your hotel, I spent some time investigating." He looked at the clock on the nightstand, then frowned. "Hell, I've only been asleep for two hours!"

"I haven't slept much either," she said. "What did you learn?"

"The word at six o'clock this morning was that a man had been picked up late last night who matched Beau's description. Don't get your hopes up, though. The man was unconscious, without money or identification."

"What happened to him?" she asked.

"He may not have been Beau at all," Jean cautioned.

"And it may have been! Answer me, Jean. Please!"

"Several Rangers found the man in an alleyway near the Pirates' Nest and carried him away with them."

"Where?" she demanded. "Where did they take him?"

"My sources weren't certain, but they, as well as I, can guess."

"Yes?" she asked, practically pulling the words from him. "Where?"

"The men who carried your Beau, or whoever he was, off were runners working for a crimp who owns a boarding-house near the docks. I hate to say it, Amoreena, but the man could be anywhere by now."

"Anywhere? What do you mean?"

"I'm afraid he might have been shanghaied."

"My God!" she cried. "How could something like that happen to Beau?"

"It happens frequently on the Barbary Coast," he explained. It could happen to anyone. The runners aren't particular about their victims. They'd shanghai me if they could get their hands on me."

"Isn't there something we can do?" Her stomach was in knots and she sat down on a chair near the bed lest she faint from the sudden racing of blood.

"I'll see," he said. "Every day ships enter and leave San Francisco. Beau may be on a ship right now preparing to sail, or he may already be out to sea. Then again, the man who was carried off by the runners might not be Beau at all."

"I have a horrible feeling he is, Jean. Only something terrible could keep him from getting word to me."

"He's a lucky man to have someone care about him the way you do."

She blushed, then looked from him to the framed picture of a red-haired girl that stood with several other pictures on his mantle. The girl was pretty and looked familiar. Suddenly Amoreena recognized her—she was a clean and neatly dressed Rose, the prostitute she'd met last night. "Is *she* the one *you* care about?" Amoreena asked incredulously.

He followed her gaze to the picture. "Rose holds a special place in my heart, but she is not my lady."

Suddenly Amoreena was reminded of her situation—in a strange man's bedroom, talking to him as though he were a close friend, while she was betrothed to another man who was in terrible jeopardy and might even now be drifting farther away from her every minute in the hold of a ship bound for God knows where. She should leave now, and quickly.

As if he could read her thoughts, he got up, and heed-less of his nude state, stood before her. His eyes were soft as he reached out a hand to caress her cheek, then tenderly brush aside a lock of wayward hair. She noticed with a start that the lifeless member at his groin was suddenly alive.

"I . . . should go . . ." she muttered. His touch, his nearness, confused her, made her knees weak. She wanted to back away, yet her legs felt as if they weighed a ton. "Please . . ." she pleaded, "I . . . must . . . go . . ."

He took his hand away, but his dark eyes remained on her face. "You're free to go, Amoreena," he said. But his eyes said something different.

She swallowed hard, tried to force her mind off the naked, handsome man before her, off the evidence of his desire for her. "Please, Jean," she said, "help me find Beau before it's too late."

"I will try, *ma cherie*," he murmured.

Amoreena waited downstairs while Jean dressed and downed a quick cup of coffee. They then rode together to the waterfront. It was a gray morning, but the fog which had made her journey to LeClair's last night nearly impos-sible was gone. Jean didn't speak to her during the ride, and she noticed that his expression seemed as though he were far away. Soon their coach pulled up at the Broadway Wharf before a tall ship. Across from the ship was a small building badly in need of paint, bearing the sign, "Harbor-master".

"I'm going to see the Harbormaster," Jean said. "While I'm questioning him, talk to one of those sailors loading crates onto the barque and see what you can learn. Be careful. They don't know how to act around a beautiful, well-bred lady."

She noticed his compliment, and the smile that spread

across her face conveyed her pleasure better than words
could have.

Jean went to the harbormaster's office and she walked
apprehensively toward the rough, crude-looking sailors who
were hauling crates up onto the gangplank of the *Singapore
Queen*. She noticed across the way a tall man in a striped
shirt who had a kind face and she walked straight up to
him. Some of the others stopped and whistled, but the man
she approached didn't look up from his work until she
said, "Can you help me?"

He turned then, and she had to stifle a gasp at the sight
of the hands he held before him. They were red as lobster!
The left side of his face matched his hands, and she
realized he had once been badly burned.

He grinned a toothy smile. "Thinkin' of takin' a cruise
on this here ship?" he asked, chuckling. The *Queen* carried cargo, but seldom passengers.

"Not at the moment," she said. She made a valiant
effort to look past his burns, but her eyes seemed glued to
the very places she tried to avoid.

"Then what can an 'ol swab do for something as purty
as you?"

"I'd like some information," she said.

The man moved closer and she could smell the sour
stench of an unwashed body.

"What kinda information?" he asked.

"I'm looking for a man who may have been shanghaied."

He scowled and Amoreena backed away. "I dunno
nothin' about that." He turned away and picked up a
crate.

"Do you know anyone I can ask?" she said.

"Go away, miss. It ain't healthy snoopin' around."

Just then another sailor confronted her. The one with the
scarred hands shook his head and walked away. "The

name's Lassity," the sailor said. "I heard what you asked 'ol Seamus. I think I can help you out."

"Good. The man I'm looking for is . . ."

"Why don't we go next door and talk about it," he said, taking her by the hand. Next door was a lodginghouse.

"Next door?" she repeated, pulling her hand away from his clutching fingers.

"It's more comfortable in a bedroom, if you get my meanin'!"

She glared at him. "I do get your meaning, sir, and I resent it. I'm looking for information, nothing else!"

He grabbed her and pulled her up against him. "Listen here, sister! No one refuses Lassity. You're comin' with me or else I'll . . ."

"Is this man bothering you, Miss Welles?" came a firm voice from behind.

They both turned to see a man clad in solid black, except for a riding crop he held in his right hand. Amoreena was surprised to see that it was the minister she'd met a few days ago. She had forgotten about him.

"Mind your own business, pastor," Lassity growled, "or I'll put you out to pasture." He managed a single laugh at his words before the minister's riding crop slashed the side of his face to the bone. The sailor released Amoreena and backed away as the minister struck him repeatedly. "Hey now! Don't . . . Leave me be, dammit!"

"You're a debauched sinner," the minister snarled, "and deserve all I'm giving you and more."

Lassity turned and fled to the gangway of his ship and disappeared inside. Amoreena stifled a gasp. She was at the same time grateful for the minister's intervention—and shocked by it. What manner of holy man was he that he could act with such violence?

"There, Miss Welles," the reverend said now, "he'll

not be bothering you any more." He laughed. "I'd say he'll think twice before he bothers anyone anymore!"

"I should think," Amoreena murmured. "But was it necessary to be so . . . harsh on him? You really hurt him."

"I meant to, my dear. He is scum and scum deserves no better. If ever someone needed church it is such as he—but no church would admit the likes of him. Certainly not mine! A young lady is never safe on the docks. You should not be alone."

"I'm not alone. I'm with Jean LeClair."

"Oh?"

Just then a dour-looking Jean left the harbormaster's office and came up behind them. His expression was made even more grim by the presence of the reverend. "Cornelius," he said, "are you trying to convert the heathen sailors?"

"The only heathen I know is you, my friend. I'm here on business. I wasn't aware that you and Miss Welles were acquainted."

"I wasn't aware *you* knew Miss Welles, Cornelius."

"There are things even *you* don't know about, Jean," he said. Then he bowed to Amoreena. "It was a pleasure seeing you again, Miss Welles. I'm looking forward to your joining my congregation. For now I have business I must attend to. My best to you."

After the minister crossed the street and headed toward a long row of boardinghouses, Amoreena said, "He's a strange man. He told me when I met him that he wanted to be my friend and I could always turn to him. Yet last night I didn't think to go to him."

"You did the right thing in coming to me, Amoreena. Stay away from Cornelius Drummond. He's not what he seems to be."

She could agree with that. There was an odd air about

the reverend she had sensed even before his recent display of violence. She was more than a little frightened of him. But she dismissed her fear now, anxious to hear what Jean had learned in the harbormaster's office. "What did the harbormaster say?" she asked.

"He knows nothing, or is saying nothing. I'll have to have my men check all the ships starting with this one and question the captains and some of the crew. It'll take time. It might be best if you went back to my house to wait."

She lowered her eyes. "I can't," she said. "You've been terribly nice and I do appreciate it, but if Beau managed to return while I was gone and discovered that I was with you, he'd be furious. You're his enemy, Jean."

"To hell with that!" he exploded. "I'm going out of my way for him and . . ."

"For him?" she interrupted, "or for me?"

He grit his teeth. "There isn't a hell of a lot of difference, is there?" He turned away. "Go back to the hotel. I'll get word to you when I've learned something."

After his unexpected but pleasant exchange with Amoreena Welles, Cornelius Drummond met with the leader of the Rangers in the Olde Seafood Cafe, a small nautically-furnished and decorated restaurant near the water.

It was Armand LeClair who had summoned the minister, and now the tall man took a bite of his shrimp salad sandwich, chewed and swallowed it. He dabbed the edge of a spotless white table napkin to his lips, then said, "About your note requesting one Amoreena Welles for your uh . . . pleasure, Drummond, I've met the girl and I must say you've excellent taste. I've considered your request, and if the information you're about to give me pleases me, you shall have what you want."

Drummond nearly choked on his salmon. "You'll not be sorry, Armand," he said.

LeClair looked at him sharply. "You called me Armand?" he said. "Why?"

A cunning look appeared on the minister's face. "It's your name, isn't it?" He didn't wait for an acknowledgment. "I've learned many things in the last several days. The thought of Miss Welles in my bedroom spurs me to great heights, Mr. LeClair."

Armand sat back, his face a mask. "Tell me what you've learned."

Drummond took a final bite of his salmon before he said, "Jean has called a meeting with the Barons. He informed them of your identity. I must admit *I* was surprised to learn that you and he are brothers . . . twins, no less. There appears to be an age difference between you, but I'll not elaborate. It was decided at the meeting that at the first sign of Ranger-incited trouble, Jean and the others would come down hard on you."

"Is that right?" Armand said, amused. "We'll see about that. Is that all you've learned?"

"There's more. Jean is having troubles of a different sort. Some young man—I haven't learned his name—is contesting Jean's ownership of the Pirates' Nest and the land on which it sits. Claims he has a deed that proves Jean stole his land. Jean's been to Abe Thompson about it."

"I already knew about the man but not that it's progressed so far as to involve a lawyer. That's good. With Jean involved in court action, he'll be less prepared for any attacks the Rangers might make. Go on."

"A young girl moved in with Jean, then left his home in anger. Her name's Monique and she may be the bastard daughter of Jean and his madam. She's quite a hellion, I hear, and the last report is that she's been seen pulling pranks in Chinatown with Spider Joe's kid."

"What has that to do with me?" Armand said.

"She's mad at Jean and has moved in with Faye Langlois at the Pirates' Nest."

Armand began to see the point. "Interesting," he said, his mind several steps ahead. If the girl was angry enough at Jean to leave such a comfortable mansion, he thought, she'd want revenge and that Armand could use to his advantage. "You've done well, Drummond," he said with a knowing leer. "Amoreena Welles is yours."

11

FOR TWO days and nights Jean LeClair's private guards, men for whose loyalty he paid handsomely, scoured the Barbary Coast seeking Beau Ashton. They searched the ships anchored at the San Francisco docks, questioned both officers and crew, to learn nothing. Amoreena was worried and impatient, but followed Jean's instructions to await word from him and not leave the hotel. On the second day, Jean, acting on a hunch, decided to pay a personal visit to a Ranger saloon. Spider Joe had been cooperative once before in assisting Jean's men in the shanghai of Billy Hagan. For a price, Jean knew, Spider Joe would even sell his beloved spiders.

It was early evening when Jean walked into Spider Joe's, but the place was nearly empty. He spread out a hundred dollars in greenbacks on the bartop before the ugly proprietor, whose attention was focused on the web behind the bar, where one of his pets had trapped a helpless fly. "Information," Jean said.

Spider Joe was surprised when he half-turned to see LeClair. His shifty eyes darted about the room. When he was sure no one was within earshot he said, "It must be important for you to come after it yourself, so let's just up the ante another fifty."

Jean shrugged, then gathered up the bills and stuffed them into a side pocket of his jacket. Without a word he left the bar and started for the door. He walked slowly, for he knew Spider Joe would not let him leave.

"Hey!" Spider Joe called, "Come back here. I was just kiddin'."

Jean returned, but did not again put the money down on the bar. Instead he held it in his hand as he confronted Spider Joe. "Where's Beau Ashton?" he asked.

The bartender shook his head. "Never heard of the dude," he said. "Describe him."

Jean frowned, then described Beau as well as he could, adding that Beau had been picked up by Rangers outside the Pirates' Nest two nights before.

"Now I remember," Spider Joe said. "Drake Bocko's runners got him."

"Where did they take him, and where is he now?"

"Let me feel your money, LeClair," Joe said.

Jean peeled fifty dollars from the wad in his hand and gave it to Joe.

Spider Joe sniffed hungrily at it as if it were a prime cut of steak. "Bocko sold this fella for crew to the captain of the *Singapore Queen*," he declared, pocketing the money.

The *Singapore Queen*? That was the ship docked opposite the harbormaster's office! Ashton had been aboard it all the time! "Is the ship still in port?" Jean asked, suppressing the anger he felt at being so close to the object of his search, yet missing him.

"Gotta feel some more money," Spider Joe said.

"Dammit, man, I'm in a hurry. Did the ship sail?"

"Gimme ten dollars more and I'll tell you."

"Forget it! I'll find out myself."

Spider Joe sighed. "Okay," he said. "The ship sailed yesterday afternoon."

Jean cursed, left another ten dollar bill, then stalked out of the saloon. All the way to the Pacific Inn he swore, furious at himself for not checking the *Singapore Queen* while he had been down at the dock. Had his men questioned the captain and crew of the *Singapore Queen*? He could not be sure, but if they had, they had learned nothing. Perhaps if he himself had gone aboard, the captain might have been more candid.

Jean had been half-seriously considering talking to the captains of several of the ships at the docks when he was distracted by Reverend Cornelius Drummond. Jean neither liked nor trusted the minister, and his misgivings about Drummond were increased by the reverend's mysterious appearance at the waterfront. What business, he wondered, could he have at the docks? Fishy business, no doubt, Jean supposed. If Jean had been in better spirits, he would have laughed at his thought, but he did not.

How would Amoreena take the news that her fiancé was gone—out to sea—and might never return? She had been strong thus far and he admired strength in a woman, but he knew even strength had its limits. Although he wasn't personally sad over Ashton's disappearance, he wished he didn't have to deliver the news.

Amoreena had been sitting before a small writing desk in her room when Jean arrived. He saw the white sheet of paper on the desk and asked, "Are you writing a letter?"

She nodded, resuming her seat at the desk. "To my parents, back in Norfolk. I learned at dinner today that a month ago there was a horribly bloody battle in Antietam. My mother was originally from Antietam. We lost the battle. When I think of all those poor soldiers who died

and the women back home who'll never see them again . . .''
She sighed. "I guess I'm lucky in a way. There's every
chance Beau is alive and will come back to me." She
fidgeted with the pen. "Then, too, there's talk that the
Federals are going to try again for Richmond. This darn war!
I hope this letter gets to my parents, what with all the
fighting going on in Virginia and Maryland."

She was unusually garrulous tonight, he thought. Since
he had first walked into the room, she had only glanced at
him. And since resuming her seat, she had kept her eyes
pinned to the sheet of paper before her. He suspected it
was because she knew his presence meant he'd learned
something, and she was afraid of what he might say.

She *was* attractive, and he felt a strong compulsion to
take her into his arms, soothe her, tell her everything was
going to be all right. But was it? With Ashton gone, what
would become of her?

"Amoreena," he said gently, "I have some news."

She placed the quill pen in its holder and slowly met his
eyes. "Have you found him?" she asked.

He nodded. "You're not going to like this," he said,
"but . . ."

"Beau's dead," she finished, her eyes lifeless.

"No," Jean said, "he's not dead. But I've confirmed
that he's been shanghaied."

She bit her lip. "As we feared," she said. "Where is he
now? Is the ship still here?"

Jean shook his head. "It has sailed," he said. He did
not tell her that Beau had been on the *Singapore Queen*
while they stood talking to the reverend. There was no
need to upset her further.

"Then he *was* the man those runners carried off."

"I'm afraid it looks that way."

She lowered her eyes. A tear fell on the paper to blur
the ink of the neatly written letter. She quickly wiped her

eyes with the back of her fingers. "Is there anything we can do? Any way we can stop the ship?"

Jean shook his head and took her hand in his. "The best we can do is hope he can get off the ship when it docks in Washington—before it sails for Singapore."

She stood up and crossed to the room's one window. She wrung her hands as she stared sightlessly out at the city. The sun had set and a purplish glow made the streets and buildings seem haunted. So this was San Francisco— the city that was to give her and Beau a new beginning! It had ended everything she had and left her empty. "He was everything to me, Jean," she said. "My past, my present, and my future. I don't know what I'll do if . . ." She brought a tiny fist to her mouth.

Jean moved forward, taking her in his arms and holding her tightly. "Go ahead and weep," he said. "There's nothing shameful in crying. I cried once—when my mother died. She was the only one in my family who cared about me."

"I'm sorry," she said.

"It was years ago, Amoreena. At the time I was a child and it seemed my whole world was falling apart. My mother worried, even to the hour of her death, that my father and brother would treat me badly when she was gone. She made me promise not to provoke their anger. It was a promise I never should have made."

"Why?" she asked.

"They treated me as if I were weak, feeble-brained— they delighted in tormenting me. Then my brother killed a man and had me blamed for it. I went to prison for him in Australia. I broke out and came to the Barbary Coast."

"Would your brother's name be Armand?" she asked, startling him.

"How did you know that?" he asked.

"I came to your house alone about a week ago, hoping

to prepare you for when Beau approached you about the land. I hoped I might persuade you to go easy on him. Your brother was just leaving your house and I mistook him for you. He even answered to the LeClair name. Only after I told him my business did he inform me he was not the LeClair I wanted."

"Then he knows about Beau's claim?"

She nodded.

"It's just the kind of thing that would please him, Amoreena."

"I'm sorry, Jean. I should have been smarter and asked him if he was *Jean* LeClair."

He kissed the top of her head. "It's not your fault. How were you to know there were two LeClairs? Armand is to blame for deliberately being deceitful."

"I must say I didn't like him right off. I'm glad you're not like him. If you were, Beau and I would . . ." Suddenly her face clouded and she fought back a new torrent of tears. "Darn!" she said, "I'm such a baby!"

He held her at arms length. "I don't want you to stay here in this hotel, Amoreena. You must be a guest in my house until you decide what to do."

"Thank you, Jean, but not today. I have a lot of thinking to do, and I'd really like to be alone. I wish . . ."

"What do you wish?" he asked.

"If I had had any idea when Beau first learned of his land here that the Barbary Coast was such a hellhole, I'd have insisted we begin our life together somewhere else."

"Where?"

"I always wanted to see France," she confessed, "but I never mentioned it to anyone. Then Beau had—or thought he had—the property here, and so we came here. I've heard stories about Europe and how pretty it is, and I'd really like to live there."

"Perhaps one day you will," Jean said. "Who can tell what the future holds?"

Rose stared at her reflection in the cracked mirror over the washstand in her small Kearney Street apartment. Around her throat was the ruby and pearl necklace Jean had given her several weeks ago. She wore it when not at the Pirates' Nest, in the mornings and early afternoons. She did not wear it to work for fear someone might steal it.

Now as she looked from the smooth white neck the piece of jewelry adorned to the sad face above, she scowled. There were lines at the corners of her eyes and dark spots beneath them! Was the woman in the mirror only eighteen years old?

She felt a great wave of sadness sweeping over her. So much had happened since that awful night in London nearly three years ago. If not for that night she'd be an actress now—a star, and people would know and love her. Or she'd be married to an English nobleman, and have a child or two.

Instead she was just a pretty prostitute on the infamous Barbary Coast. A nameless whore who lived from day to day, from man to man, and had nothing but old age and loneliness to look forward to.

She couldn't even love a man. Jean had been good and kind, and at first she had tried to love him. But in some ways he reminded her of her father . . . and that had prevented a real love from developing.

Her father! She shuddered at the thought of him. She had loved him, but now she despised him! Hated him more than she could say!

She made a face and turned away from the mirror. In truth she hated herself, too, and what she'd become. She was a callous, uncaring woman who did despicable things without a second thought. Look at what she'd done to the lame southerner, Beau Ashton. Yet perhaps there was hope for her still, for she had lost sleep over what she had done to him and had thereafter refused to go to work. She was more than a little afraid of what Jean would do if he learned that she had lied to him the night he'd come inquiring about Ashton, for Jean was a man capable of great fury, though he concealed it well.

How was she supposed to know Ashton was a friend of Jean's? If he was. She was sure of one thing—she dared not tell Jean that she'd had the southerner dumped unconscious into an alley!

She supposed she'd have to go to work tomorrow, or Jean would really become suspicious. What *had* become of Beau Ashton, she wondered. Had he been killed for the fun of it by a drunken Ranger? She shivered. If he had, it was her fault.

How had she come to be so mean? So cruel? The Rowena Pendleton she had once been was a gentle girl—a good girl.

Beau had been snotty and brusque at first, but he had not hurt her. And later he had even become friendly. Not a bad sort at all. Yet, was his money so important to her that she had to do what she did?

Rose buried her face in her hands. Money. Her family had been wealthy and in England she'd always had everything she could want and more. Here she was a poor harlot with a great thirst for money and the luxury she had once enjoyed.

She sat back on a worn chair and looked around the one-room apartment. It was messy, uncomfortable, and ugly—a reflection of herself. But mostly it was lonely.

She was lonely.

Oh, papa! she sighed, remembering the horror she had tried to put out of her mind ever since it happened. "Why?"

she said aloud. "Why did you want me that way? If you hadn't touched me, I should not have had to go away!"

Feeling herself giving in to self-pity, she stood and angrily paced across the floor. "I won't," she said over and over, "I won't let you turn me into a monster!"

She opened the door for a breath of air and stood for a moment in the doorway looking outside. Nearby was Portsmouth Square and the Opera House. Pedestrians were scattered about, some arm-in-arm, others alone.

How long was it since she'd been to a respectable establishment? Too long, she thought. She was the daughter of a Member of Parliament—a lady. Neither time nor distance could change that. It was time she stopped feeling sorry for herself and started liking herself again.

She dressed in her best gown, a lacy maroon taffeta, and pinned up her hair. She applied only a touch of salve to her lips instead of the thick makeup that was part of her working attire.

Tomorrow she would be a whore again, but tonight she was going to be a lady! Rowena Pendleton was going to the Opera!

12

THE *Singapore Queen*, a five-hundred-ton, three-masted barque, was named for its usual destination—Singapore. It was a voyage that took anywhere from eight to thirteen months to complete. The *Singapore Queen* transported grain and produce to Washington, lumber to the Orient, then took on cargo of silk and rice to bring back to California. The crew included twenty-five regular seamen who had served on the ship for years, and fifteen new men, usually shanghaied on the Barbary Coast.

The unfortunates who'd been way-laid had one thing in common—they would have chosen to be anywhere but aboard the *Singapore Queen*. The treatment they could expect would be dreadful at best.

Each shanghaied crewman arrived on board with a doctored sheet of ship's articles—a document which signed over part of his rightful wages to the Barbary Coast crimp who had brought him to the ship. The rest of the wages went to the ship's master—to be dealt out to the new

seamen or not, as the captain saw fit. The majority of
them, however, saw little or no money, barely enough to
purchase second-hand clothes and necessary sundries from
the captain's "slop-chest."

Now, the *Queen* was riding low in the water, having
taken on its San Francisco cargo and set sail up the California coast. While a hot sun blazed overhead, Beau Ashton
stirred, blinked, then opened his eyes wide in confusion.
The first thing he saw was a blurred orange orb in the sky,
and he squinted against its glare. His eyes traveled slowly
downward, focusing as they came to rest on several heavy
iron bars which were fixed to the deck of the ship just
abaft the mainmast. Iron shackles secured Beau's ankles
and wrists. Although there were at least a dozen more sets
of shackles in a row besides him, he was the only prisoner
locked in them.

He frowned, searching his memory for an explanation of
how he had come to be on a ship. But right now, even
thinking hurt. He closed his eyes for a moment and con-
jured up a fuzzy image of a red-haired girl, a cot, then a
strong smelling cloth she had used. Rose—she had drugged
him! A cold fury swept over him.

But then a laugh startled him, and Beau half turned his
head to see a dirty-faced, dark-haired seaman wearing a
blue and white striped jersey. There was a grin on the
man's weathered face as he gently nudged Beau with the
toe of his boot.

"Thought you slipped your cable, I did, lying there like
a lump drinking up the sun. Me tally's Jimmy Oliver, but
you can call me Ollie. I'm the second greaser 'round
here." Beau's jacket had been stolen by the runners, and
the plaid shirt he wore was ripped and frayed at the seams
and wrists. "I see you're all decked out in Maltese lace,"
Ollie said, noticing the torn shirt. "We'll have to get you
some top gear."

"Where am I?" Beau broke in. "How did I get here?"

"This here's the good ship *Singapore Queen*. You were chosen, m'lad. The old man's in a fine trim 'cause we're gunnels under and you swab jockeys are floodin' the gunwales."

The older, experienced seamen engaged in a language of their own, Beau knew, and he understood some of it. What Ollie had said was that the captain of the ship was in good spirits because he had acquired the services of many sailors to work without pay. "How did it happen and where are the others?" Beau asked.

"Several Jack nastyfaces, poor as piss and twice as mean, brought you and the others aboard. Our mate Pequest—we's old ships, him and me—paid them Jacks in wads of greenbacks and they rowed off for the Coast. The old father bought some bodies this time that knowed the ropes and some who was wet as scrubbers. I don't give a fish's tit for most mates shanghaied, but there was one this time—a young fella who was by the wind. He ups and bolts, making like he's gonna swim back to shore! Well, 'ol Pequest, he got a purser's grin on his face and had the young fella flogged fifteen times! Stay clear of Pequest, matey, 'cause he ain't no doggie. Not any more. I knowed he was a bucko when I first laid eyes on his damned brothel creepers."

"Brothel creepers?" Beau said. The term was one he hadn't heard.

"Aye. White shoes with brown decoration."

Were it not for his unhappy predicament, Beau would have chuckled. Apparently he was one of many men shanghaied from the Coast. Some were experienced seamen, others were men who had never sailed. "I have to get out of these irons, Ollie," Beau said. "Every minute now this ship is sailing further away from land and my fiancée!"

"Pequest has been at swordspoint with the cap'n about

you. Everyone else is up and scrubbin' decks and you still sleep. Pequest wanted to throw you overboard 'cause you weren't contributin'. The captain, old salt that he is, wouldn't take no jaw, so's you're still alive. My advice is to work hard, keep out of Pequest's way, and watch out for white rats!'' White rats were spies who mingled with the sailors and listened for gossip to report back to the first mate.

"I can't sail with you, Ollie. You've got to help me escape!"

"You're on the wrong tack now, matey," Ollie said, as he took off the irons at Beau's wrists, than his feet. "The cap'n and me, we's old friends. It wouldn't be smart for me to help one of his prizes escape now, would it?"

Beau grunted, massaging his hands, then his ankles. He made an effort to stand, but dizziness swept over him and he collapsed. "Wha . . . what did they hit me with?" he asked with a groan. "A lead pipe?"

"The runners found you, said you was drugged. You came outa it fast enough, but before they was ready, so they clobbered you over the head to keep you quiet. Musta hit you too hard—you been out for almost three days."

Just then a big, barrel-chested man appeared next to Beau. His face was heavily whiskered and his pants were yellow stained and smelled like urine. "Well, lookee here," the first mate declared with a leer, "sleepin' beauty's awake! Get to your feet, scum, the bosun wants to see you."

Before Beau could protest, Pequest rolled him to his feet and was half-dragging him down the companionway to the bosun's cabin. The bosun was in his quarters when Pequest brought Beau in. "This here's the last of 'em," he said to the bosun, a greying man named Belko.

Belko was an incredibly ugly man in his mid-fifties. He had a medium frame, but his jowly face looked as if it belonged to a man three times his weight. Pockets of fat dangled beneath two chins, and the veins in his nose and ears were like a puzzle drawn with thick purple ink. When he spoke, his voice was a bark. Around his huge neck was a chain on which hung a whistle.

"Sit down," he barked, "and listen good, fellow. I tell new men this only once. You're now a deck hand on the *Singapore Queen,* and expected to follow orders. You'll work hard and stay out of trouble. The first sign of insubordination and you'll be flogged or worse. My mate will tell you what to do and where you'll bunk. You'll begin tonight by pullin' graveyard watch." Graveyard watch was so named because of the eerie quiet between midnight and four in the morning. "That's all, scum," the bosun concluded. "Get out."

"I won't take orders from you or anyone else," Beau now declared, "so you can throw me overboard if you like."

"We're a day and a half out of port," the bosun observed with a grin, "so you couldn't swim ashore if you were Jesus Christ himself!" Now Belko sat back in his chair and studied the sullen young man. "So you want to be punished, do you?" he said. "I can arrange that easy enough." He brought the whistle to his lips and a piercing screech followed. Immediately the bosun's mate and three guards rushed in. "Take the scum out and duck him!" Belko roared.

"Sir?" the young mate asked. Ducking was a form of punishment that had been phased out nearly two hundred years before.

"You heard me, Swaggert."

"Yessir."

The guards seized Beau and dragged him up onto the quarterdeck. He struggled to free himself, but several other seamen quickly joined the detail with rope. While two held Beau in a firm grip, the others coiled the rope around his body. When he was trussed up, they attached a grappling hook to the part of the rope that crossed his chest.

"All hands to witness punishment," Pequest shouted through a megaphone. The entire ship's crew soon gathered on the poop deck to watch as with a quick order, a stout rope was attached to the hook and Beau was hauled up to the yard arm of the mainmast.

Beau's heart hammered as he dangled precariously, high above the deck. At that moment his thoughts spun briefly back to his father's deathbed, when Monte Ashton told him about the San Francisco property—and Beau's chance for a new life.

Beau blinked. He had never seen a man punished this way, but knew it for what it was—a horror, and frequently fatal.

Down on the deck, Belko barked out a command and the deck pool feeding the rope began to turn as Beau's helpless body was lowered rapidly toward the cold Pacific.

Beau's eyes shut tightly as his feet parted the surface of the sea and he plunged into the frigid water. His body shook with the cold. He had sucked in a deep breath before going under and now held it as his head went underwater. He remained under for a half minute before the seamen were ordered to lift him back up.

Soaked to the skin, Beau's teeth chattered as he was hoisted out of the water and felt the icy wind clawing at him once more. Vaguely he was aware of the laughter of Belko and the other seamen, all of them standing by the rail as his ducking continued.

How much longer would his ordeal go on? How much longer could he take?

As Belko ordered the helpless captive ducked again and Beau disappeared from view into the waters of the Pacific, neither he nor his men noticed the appearance on deck of the man Belko had flogged a day earlier—another shanghaied sailor. His name was Georgie Ross, and he had just surprised the captain in his quarters and taken the man's six-shooter. His intentions were to fight his way off the ship when he had decided to make a try for the captain's guns—the only weapons carried by the ship's crewmen other than knives.

But now, as he saw what was happening, his heart sank at his recognition of Beau and the predicament his friend had gotten into. He stared at the trussed-up figure as Belko's men hoisted it out of the water. The shoreline of Oregon's Pacific coast could be seen on the ship's starboard side beyond the seamen clustered at the rail. It was no more, Georgie could see, than a mile away. If he could just get Beau freed and down into a lifeboat, they could easily row to shore.

But if they were to make it, he'd have to do something to prevent pursuit by the ship and its crew. A thought struck him then and he scanned the deck until he found what he was seeking—a barrel of kerosene used in the ship's lanterns. If he spilled it over the deck and set it afire, he could keep the ship's crew too busy to chase after them.

Quickly, keeping out of the view of Belko and the infamous first mate Pequest, he edged over to where the barrel was lashed firmly to the port side of the ship. A spigot was on the side of the barrel and he knelt beside it only long enough to open it up, then moved away as the kerosene began to flow in a thin stream to the planking of the deck. Hang on, Beau, he thought. Just a little longer. You saved my life—now I'm gonna save yours!

The ship held two life boats, one on each side, on davits. They would use one, Georgie decided, but cut the rope holding the other one as well to keep the crew from using it.

Now he scrambled up the rope ladder to a vantage point

on the crossbar of the mizzenmast. From it he could hit any of the seamen at the port side rail. He drew one of the two fully-loaded six-guns he'd stuck in his belt and cocked the hammer so he could get off a shot the moment he had to. Then he wrapped one arm around the mast to steady himself, drew in a deep breath, and took dead aim at Belko.

"Drop him in again, boys!" cried the bosun to the sailors manning the ropes. "This time, let him stay under a couple of minutes. If he survives, we'll bring him aboard for a lashing!"

"No, you won't, Belko!" roared Georgie. "Pull him in and cut him loose or you're a dead man."

Belko looked upward and found himself blinking into a blinding sun. "Who the hell are you?" he demanded. "Come down where I can see you."

"I will when I'm ready," Georgie said. "I said cut your prisoner loose, bosun."

"The hell I will," Belko said. "He's gonna feed the goddam sharks, he is, for his insubordination!"

Georgie pulled the trigger and the six-gun roared. His aim was perfect and Belko took a shot in his throat, made a gurgling sound, and fell to his knees, then died.

"Pequest!" yelled Georgie. "Give the order or die. Now!"

Pequest's mouth was open wide as he looked from the dead bosun toward his killer high up on the mast. He had no choice but to comply with Georgie's order, and a sodden Beau was soon deposited on the deck and freed by the others.

"All right, Pequest," Georgie shouted, "back off. Now, I want all you men who were shanghaied in San Francisco to stand over by the lifeboat. Any of you who want to stay aboard this bucket can do so if you want."

A dozen men jumped with alacrity toward the boat.

"Help him into the boat, then get ready to jump in yourselves and lower it into the water. But don't go until I give the word."

"Don't listen to him, buckos," Pequest roared. "You'll not get away!"

The group of shanghaied men ignored him as they picked up the shivering Beau and lifted him into the lifeboat.

"All right, Pequest. Take your men and move aft—in a hurry now if you don't want a hole in your chest."

Pequest grumbled, but moved and so did the others. As they moved, Georgie released the mast and descended from his position toward the deck. He was just about to set foot on it when one of Pequest's seamen whirled and hurled his knife. He had got a good look at Georgie as they moved away and was an expert with the throwing knife.

Georgie grunted as the knife hit him, imbedding itself in his left shoulder. He fired at the sailor, but missed, and Pequest's men scattered.

Blood spurted from his wound as Georgie hit the deck next to Mack Reynolds, one of the other shanghaied men. "Cut away the other boat," Georgie ordered in a low voice, "then light a match and throw it over by the barrel of kerosene. The kerosene is all over the deck by now. The whole ship'll be in flames in a minute."

The man hastened away as Georgie, the knife still imbedded in his shoulder, covered Pequest and the others thirty feet away and fought off a wave of dizziness and nausea fast enveloping him. He signalled the others to occupy the port side boat, and heard the second lifeboat fall into the water as the other shanghaied sailors scrambled into the one where the half-conscious Beau had been placed.

Reynolds rejoined Georgie before lighting the match.

"Can you get in the boat?" he asked. "I'll take the gun and cover them, then throw the match."

Georgie blinked, a cold sweat all over his body. Reynolds pulled the gun from his hand just as the wounded man fell unconscious to the deck. Pequest, seeing Georgie go down, rushed forward, followed by his men.

Reynolds squeezed the trigger and the gun barked in his hand. A look of surprise came to the first mate's face as the slug buried itself deep in his stomach and he tumbled over backward. The others retreated.

Reynolds dragged Georgie to the boat and hollered for help. Two of the other shanghaied men responded and lifted Georgie over the side and into the boat.

Immediately Reynolds struck a stick match and threw it on the kerosene-soaked deck. Fire erupted with a whoosh and he leaped into the boat. He fired wildly at the sailors as they rushed forward to try to stop the boat from being lowered.

Before the boat hit the water, the top deck of the ship was in flames and the sailors were trying desperately to fight the fire.

"Man the oars!" Reynolds ordered. Every man in the boat except Beau, who was unconscious from exposure, and a mortally wounded Georgie, pulled with oars as the lifeboat headed for shore.

Monique's new quarters upstairs at the Pirates' Nest were small and dingy and very much the opposite of Jean LeClair's palatial home. Though she regretted having left Jean's, she knew he had had no choice but to move out of the mansion after he'd humiliated her. Whenever she thought about him, she longed to get even with him, though she hadn't the slightest idea how to do so.

Monique's relations with Faye had been bearable since her arrival. If Faye had been displeased at her daughter's unexpected presence at the Nest, her actions didn't convey it. She had gone out of her way to accommodate the girl and seemed to be trying to gain her confidence by visiting Monique in her room for frequent talks.

Monique didn't appreciate the visits and put up with them with difficulty. She thought her mother much too inquisitive, and always asking about things that would get Monique in trouble. Still, Faye was showing outward signs of caring—it was only a couple of days ago that Monique overheard two of Faye's girls gossiping about Faye and how she had cancelled several dates with her current paramour, just to spend time with her daughter.

At first Monique was mildly touched by the gesture, then after thinking about it awhile, she decided it was due solely to desire to get her in trouble. Faye had not bothered with her in years, so why should she now show any great concern for her. Her mother couldn't possibly care about her! So Monique avoided her mother like the plague, spending more and more time with Luke and his tough friends down at the waterfront shack they used as headquarters.

Now it was late afternoon as she waited for Luke in a Pacific Street alley. It was beginning to grow dark, and she hoped he would show before night fell. He arrived moments later.

"Why didn't you want me to bring the guys?" he asked with a grin. "You wanna do some fast rollin' in the hay?" He tried to hug her, but she twisted away.

"We're going to make some fun, Luke," she said, "but not *that* kind."

"What've you got in mind?" he said, his disappointment evident.

"I want to do something about the laundries, Luke. They're all over Chinatown! Everywhere you turn there are funny looking little slant-eyed men washing and ironing and hanging out laundry. Only Celestials work in these laundries—and that means decent white folk like us with families to feed are out of jobs! The Chinese should never have come here in the first place, and we're going to make them see that.''

"And how we gonna do that?" Luke said.

Monique looked straight into his eyes. "We're going to burn a laundry or two," she said.

Luke's eyes grew wide, then he shook his head. "Christ!" he said, "you're crazy!"

"What's the matter, Luke? Scared?"

"Who me? Shit no! But what you got in mind is just plain. . . You gonna kill those chinks. You know that?"

"Don't be silly, Luke," she declared. "We won't kill anybody. They'll see the flames and smell the smoke and get out right away. You'll see." She moved up against him and took his hand and put it on her breast. "Are you with me?"

"I dunno," he said. "We start doin' things like that, first thing you know my old man'll see me hang over at old Fort Gunnybags, he will. He told me the vigilantes are mean sonsofbitches and don't like it much when people start gettin' killed all over the place."

"There aren't any vigilantes, Luke," she said. Suddenly two long shadows appeared at the entrance to the alleyway, blocking its only open end. Luke frowned and looked around, shushing her.

The alleyway ended in the stone wall of a building ten feet beyond where they stood. The two men moved into the alley. Quickly Monique dived behind a foul-smelling barrel containing refuse.

Luke followed and squatted beside her. "They saw us," Luke whispered. "We're in for it now. They must've overheard your crazy scheme."

"Shhh!" Monique said, exasperated at him.

The two big men moved closer and now Monique could see they were armed, one carrying a club, the other a knife. "Okay, you two," one man said in a nasty, nasal voice, "we heard you. Come on out or we'll come in after you."

"Who are those guys?" Luke whispered, staring at them.

"I don't know."

"What'll we do?"

"Will you shut up, Luke? I'm trying to think!"

Now the second man spoke. His voice was deeper and more menacing than the other's. "Come on out, Monique," he ordered. "We won't hurt you."

"They want *you*!" Luke said. "I thought you didn't know them!"

"I don't," she returned. But their knowing her gave her courage and she stood up and faced the men, still some twenty feet away from them. "Who are you?" she asked defiantly. "And what do you want with me?"

They didn't answer. Instead they rushed forward, grabbing Monique and twisting her hands up behind her back while one shut off her outcry with a fat, fishy-tasting hand. The other man crashed into Luke, who stood and tried to help Monique, his knife in hand. The knife clattered to the ground as the stranger clubbed Luke with a stout hickory club. Monique cried out at the bone-shattering crunch made by the club against Luke's skull.

"Let's go," Luke's assailant said to the thug holding Monique. "Armand won't like it that we're late."

Armand? Just before he passed out, Luke heard the name, but it meant nothing to him.

When his men brought Monique to him, Armand LeClair sat smoking a cigar on the narrow bed in the crib he used for his headquarters. Earlier he had sent home the Chinese prostitute who plied her wares there. If Jean's kid was as enticing as he had heard, he would soon need the bed for his own purposes.

Armand scowled at Blackjack and Lobo, a tough Ranger who often worked with Blackjack, as they shoved Monique into the room. "What took you so long?" Armand demanded.

"We looked all over the Coast for her," Lobo said. "We was lucky to catch up with her at all."

Now Lobo pulled his hand away from the girl's mouth. She turned and spat in his face, then glared at Armand. "Who are you?" she declared, "and why have these idiots abducted me and hurt my friend?"

Armand ignored her. "What did you do with her friend?" he asked Blackjack.

"Just clobbered him, boss," Blackjack replied. "He's the son of a Ranger."

"You should have drowned him in the bay!"

"Aw, he ain't gonna hurt us none, Armand. He don't even know who we are."

"Dummy!" LeClair roared. He struck Blackjack two stinging blows to the face. "Go back to where you left him and dispose of him."

"No!" Monique jumped to her feet and hurled herself at Armand, her hands balled into fists, and began beating on him. "You can't hurt him. Luke hasn't done anything to you!" she cried.

Armand slapped her viciously, then flung her across the room. She hit the wall and slid, stunned, to the floor. He went to her, then reached down and seized her by her long hair. He drew her to her feet.

"Tell me about Luke," Armand said. "Is he your lover? Does he please you, little one?"

"None of your business!" she muttered. "Just don't hurt him."

Armand looked at her reflectively, his eyes on her breasts

straining at the front of her blouse. She was enticing and there was no need to incur her enmity over the son of a Ranger. "Very well, Monique, I shall let the boy live. Blackjack, take Lobo and go. I won't need you again."

The two left and Armand locked the door behind them, and turned to Monique, who was staring at him with large eyes.

"Ah!" Armand said. "You have recognized me?"

"You look like . . . like Jean LeClair."

"I should. He is my brother, though we are enemies."

"Really?" Monique looked at him with new respect. "Then you might be my uncle, for I may have been fathered by Jean."

"I know." Armand cupped Monique's chin in his palm and kissed her mouth. "You've a tough mouth, but tasty," he said. He reached down inside her blouse to capture a heavy breast and stroke it.

Monique did not resist. "It doesn't bother you that I may be your niece?" she asked.

"Should it?" Armand withdrew his hand and calmly began unfastening her blouse.

"It bothers Jean. I offered myself to him, but he'd have nothing to do with me."

Armand smiled, but said nothing more as he proceeded to strip Monique naked.

"Would you like to undress your uncle?" he said, his hands exploring her hot flesh.

"How did you know I would let you do that?" she asked, as his hand reached her most intimate spot.

"If you're a LeClair, you've an adventurous side to you, and what better adventure is there than to be rendered vulnerable by your uncle?"

"If I let you have me, will you help me get even with your brother?"

He picked her up and carried her to the bed. "I will

have Jean's wealth,'' he murmured as his mouth took her breast and began kissing the hard nipple. "I'll have his power just as I will have his little girl. If you wish to hurt Jean, you may begin by becoming my concubine—and by telling everyone.''

"I want to do more than that!''

He kissed her and freed a rock-hard member, bringing it to bear on its youthful target. "And so you will, my dear. In good time.''

After making love to Monique, Armand got rid of her before the arrival of leaders of his Ranger strike force. They were a rag-tag lot, but tough—every manjack of them, Armand could see as he stood before them.

"Tomorrow we begin the process of bringing the Barons to their knees,'' he told them. "For a long time now, you, the Rangers, have done their work and they've made the profits. We're about to change that—but to do so, you must do your work well. Each of you has been assigned a company of twelve Rangers and given the names of your targets—the most profitable Baron businesses on the Barbary Coast. Though you are free to devise your own plan of attack, I want to stress that you are not to kill, or destroy property, for that is not our objective. Not, at least, this time. Murder would only demand action from the community and might even spark the formation of a new vigilance committee, and large scale destruction of property is contrary to our goals. We can become masters of the Barbary Coast and will, but only if you do what I've outlined.

"You will put the fear of God into them,'' Armand continued. "Sack their dives! Take their cash, and their liquor, too. We'll use it ourselves later. Scare their customers away. We must show the Baron owners that their days on the Coast are numbered.''

A roar of approval swept through the men, but they had questions. Armand answered a dozen before dismissing them. When they'd left, Armand relaxed with the second cigar of the evening. Everything was progressing as planned, he thought. He had taken control of Jean's daughter. Tomorrow war would break out on the Barbary Coast—a war Armand was going to win! He *had* to win! And he would, as he always had against Jean.

He took a long drag on his cigar and watched the smoke from a blue-grey curtain. As the curtain dissipated, it seemed to form a face—the face of a woman—the Welles woman Cornelius Drummond wanted so badly.

His thoughts turned to the lovely Amoreena. His night's work was just beginning. Before the sun again made its appearance on the horizon, he would deliver Amoreena to the none-to-tender mercies of the sadistic preacher.

13

AMOREENA LAY in bed tossing, turning, her body tired, but her mind too active for sleep. Two days had passed since Beau's disappearance—two thought-filled days for her. She was sure now what she had to do. For one thing, she could no longer remain in this hotel. It was full of shattered dreams and memories of futility and loneliness. She would accept Jean LeClair's invitation and stay with him in his mansion—for a while at least. She had packed her bags and would leave in the morning.

A wail from the adjoining room now assaulted her ears. She could have cried! The manager of the hotel had told her earlier that he could no longer keep Beau's room open, and now a young Eastern couple with two babies had taken Beau's room.

Yet it mattered little, she supposed, since Beau wouldn't be back from his involuntary ocean voyage for a year or more—if at all. Jean had tried his best to find Beau, to bring him back to her, and she was grateful. Now she needed to pick up the pieces of her life. Jean could help her do that.

Jean. In spite of her sadness over the loss of Beau, she smiled as she thought of the handsome Barbary Coast Baron. Though other Barons were said to be barbarous, ruthless, greedy lawbreakers, Jean was not. That was obvious from the start, and she had wanted to like him even though he had title to Beau's land. He had been kind in trying to help her track down Beau, then in offering her the comforts of his home. And, though he owned houses of ill repute, he had never once tried to seduce her. Lord knows he had opportunity! she thought, remembering. What would she have done had he tried to touch her when he stood naked beside his bed with her? She flushed at the certain knowledge that she would have let him. She had wanted him to! Her admission startled her and made her shiver. She would not let just any man touch her, she knew. She was a virgin and had always thought to remain that way until her wedding night. Yet . . . she flopped over on her stomach and buried her face in the pillow, ashamed of herself. What was happening to her?

She loved Beau. She had always loved Beau! But now her heart was pounding and she sat up in bed, to stare blankly in the darkness of her room. Of course she loved Beau! She *had* to love him! Or did she? Was it love? Really love? If it wasn't, then what was it?

And what was the feeling she had for Jean—that made her knees wobbly, her resolve weak?

Her reverie was suddenly shattered by a loud knocking at her door. "Who is it?" she called.

"Armand LeClair."

"Armand? Jean's brother? What did he want with her? She opened the door a crack, confirming Armand's identity. "Really, Mr. LeClair, it's late."

"I was sorry to learn of your fiancé's disappearance,"

he said, his expression sympathetic as he stood in the hotel hallway.

"I appreciate your sympathies," she said, "but I'm not dressed and must get some sleep. Please leave."

"But I have news, Amoreena! News of your fiancé! It appears that your young man is still on the Coast! He was robbed and beaten. A kindly old woman has taken him in and is nursing him. If you wish to see him, I can take you to him."

Beau! Still here in San Francisco! The good news was shocking—and a bit disturbing, too. She hesitated only a moment. "I'll get my coat," she said.

Armand was pleased with himself as, out of the corner of his eye, he watched the girl seated beside him in his carriage. They were headed toward Rincon Hill and Cornelius Drummond's house, though she believed he was taking her to her fiancé.

She had fallen for his lies easily and completely, yet at the moment seemed withdrawn and uncommunicative— almost unhappy. Armand wondered why she was not rejoicing over her chance to find her fiancé. He cared not a whit about her love life, but found her conduct curious.

His first impression of Amoreena Welles had been that she was beautiful and desirable. Now he found her something else as well—remote. He was almost glad she had not agreed to become his mistress. He had always been fortunate in finding bedsport—there was usually a pretty, available wench around whenever he felt the urge. And now there was Monique.

His smile widened at the memory of their furious session barely an hour ago. In spite of her tender age, she had proved better than whores he'd bedded, and far more inventive.

Now he looked directly at Amoreena. She smiled feebly, then turned to look out at the starry night as the rig bounced along the mud-scarred street. She was cold and lifeless, compared to Monique, he thought. Amoreena was like an exquisite ice carving adorning some fancy culinary delicacy, attractive to look at, but hardly as tasty as the main course.

At last the carriage pulled up before a dimly-lit house on Rincon Hill. "Is *this* where Beau is staying?" she asked doubtfully.

"That's right, my dear." He took her hand and helped her descend the carriage steps, then followed her up to the front door and knocked.

Drummond's manservant appeared. "This is Miss Welles," Armand said. "She's expected."

The servant nodded. Armand took Amoreena's hand and kissed it, then smiled. "Au revoir, my dear," he said.

"You're leaving?" Amoreena asked, confused.

"This way please, miss," the servant interrupted.

"You don't need me," Armand said. He turned and left.

A puzzled look was on her face as she stepped across the transom and into a large center hallway.

Armand was chuckling as he went back to the waiting carriage. How, he wondered, would the ice princess react to the whip of the fat, crazy reverend?

It was morning and Jean LeClair, wearing a red smoking jacket, sat in his breakfast room finishing the last of his breakfast. Between sips of a mug of hot coffee he re-read the note a courier had delivered to him last night:

DEAR JEAN:
   I've decided to accept your kind invitation to stay with you and will arrive early tomorrow morning.

                                        Yours truly,
                                        Amoreena

The note pleased Jean. He had a feeling he could enjoy Amoreena's presence in his home, for as well as beautiful, she seemed intelligent and warm and capable of deep feeling. He grinned at the thought that beneath her genteel exterior, he had a feeling there was a fiery passion waiting to be kindled.

Now he frowned, for she had just lost her fiancé, so Jean would have to be especially considerate of her. He would not try to seduce her—though he had a feeling she wanted him. For now, he would simply enjoy her company.

The coffee was cooling, so he drained the cup and went to his study to set about his morning business. He became so engrossed in his business paperwork, that several hours passed without notice. The growling of his stomach signalled that it was lunch time and he suddenly realized that Amoreena had not yet arrived.

Jean was concerned. Amoreena had specifically said in her note that she'd come "early" in the morning. Had she run into trouble checking out of the hotel, or was she unsuccessful in locating a means of transportation? He wished now that he had sent a carriage for her.

He summoned his butler and instructed him to have his carriage brought around. Soon the carriage was rolling down the steep incline leading downward from Telegraph Hill. He hoped Amoreena was all right, that she had merely overslept, or something. But a feeling of foreboding was in his mind.

When the carriage pulled up in front of the hotel, he rushed inside. "Has Miss Welles checked out yet?" he asked the desk clerk.

"No, sir. Come to think of it, I haven't seen her this morning. She usually comes down for breakfast."

Jean scowled, but wasted no time with unnecessary conversation. Amoreena, he knew, could be in bed too ill to cry out for help. He got a key from the clerk and rushed

up the stairs to her second floor room. When his knock
went unanswered, he used the key.

What he saw inside confused him completely—her bed
was empty, but on the floor alongside the washstand were
her two traveling bags. He picked one up and opened it. It
was full of neatly folded clothes.

He searched the room, looking for a note, but found
nothing to indicate where she was or why she'd left without her bags.

Her bed had been slept in, and left that way. There were
no signs of anyone having entered forcibly. As his eyes
settled on an empty coat hook, he realized that wherever
she had gone, she had taken her wrapper. If she had the
time to dress, she could have left a note for him, yet she
had not. Something was wrong, he thought, very wrong.
Despite the indications that she had simply left the room of
her own will, he had a strong feeling she was up to her
neck in trouble. He had no idea what kind, but was, he
thought, damned well going to find out.

While Jean was puzzling over Amoreena's disappearance,
Monique was summoned to see her mother in her quarters.
Jean had told Faye of his twin brother's appearance on the
Coast, and Armand's threat to overthrow Jean's empire.
She had been shocked and angered by Armand's gall, but
no less so by what she had just heard—that Monique had
slept with a man who was very possibly her blood uncle as
well as her father's enemy.

"I've heard some disgusting rumors, Monique," Faye
said, as Monique, a smirk on her face, walked in and sat
down on the chair across from her. "I feared your being
here at the Pirates' Nest would be damaging to your
reputation, and it appears I was right."

Monique stretched lazily in the chair. "They are not

rumors, Mother," she said. "And I don't like being here any more than you like having me."

Faye heard only the first part of the girl's statement. "You can't mean that!" she declared. "Are you saying the filth I heard about you and this Armand trash is true?"

"Every bit of it." Monique met her mother's eyes defiantly.

Faye was speechless. "Why?" she said simply.

"Why not? I'm not ashamed of what I did. Armand is a great lover—better than any man I've tried."

Faye grew red with rage. "Can't you see he's only using you, Monique? That he wants to flaunt you in Jean's face!"

"I don't care why he wants me, Mother. I'm damned glad that he does. I'll probably become his mistress—like you were Jean's."

"You're a tramp," Faye cried, standing up in front of the chair Monique occupied.

"No worse than you."

Faye slapped her hard. "I was never a tramp! Sure, I bedded Jean and other men, but I had to. I had no parents and no money. Sex was always business to me, Monique. *You* throw your favors around as if it's free for the asking. That's far lower and more vile than prostitution. The way you turned out, I might as well have raised you myself and not bothered with expensive eastern schools!"

Monique jumped angrily to her feet. "Did it ever occur to you, Miss Holier than Thou, that I hated those schools? That every holiday when the other girls went home, or their families came to visit, I wanted desperately to see you—to have a mother visiting at least? I never really knew who I was or where I belonged. Not until just before I left. I'll always hate you for that!"

Monique had struck a nerve. Every Christmas and Easter, Faye had thought about visiting her—but she couldn't bring herself to go. The simple truth was she had always hated the fact that she had whelped a baby in the first place. And preferred not remembering her at all.

For a time after bringing the child East, Faye couldn't visit the girl because she was struggling to stay alive financially, for she got no help from anyone in the Gold Rush town of San Francisco of the '50s. Afterward, the memory of the little baby she'd held in her arms was no more than that—a memory. Along with the bill, Faye had received regular correspondence from the headmistress of Monique's school, saying the child was healthy and happy and doing well in her studies. There was no reason for Faye to appear there to shake up Monique's well ordered little world.

Now she suddenly realized she'd been wrong. Dreadfully wrong. "I'm sorry, Monique," she said, meeting her daughter's stare. "I'll make no excuses, though I suppose I was a terrible mother. But I can change. Let's forget the past and begin again."

But Monique shook her head. "Save your breath, Mother, it's too late. I'm the way I am and there's no changing it. Armand wants me—more so at least than you or Jean. I need that and intend to have it. I won't stop seeing him."

"Go ahead. See him. I guess you have to learn by your own mistakes. But remember what I say . . . he'll use you, then discard you."

"He won't! I think he loves me!"

"Hah! That's a laugh. Such men don't know the meaning of the word."

"But *you* do, Mother?" Monique returned cruelly.

Faye frowned. Had she ever loved anyone? She closed her eyes and remembered the tiny tot suckling at her breast. Even though she hadn't wanted her, those were special, tender moments. That was love, Faye thought. She recalled how she had wept for days over her decision to give up the child. Those were tears of despair caused by love.

She had been capable of loving then, and she still was. The emotion had merely been buried over the years. Had some of the love she'd had for that suckling baby returned since Monique's arrival back on the Coast, she wondered. She had become protective of Monique and had even gone out of her way to please the girl.

"You're wrong about me, Monique. I may not have been a good mother, but I swear I always loved you. Always!"

"*Loved* me?" Monique echoed, her voice creaking with emotion. "You had a strange way of showing it, madam!"

Now Faye could see the beginnings of tears in her daughter's eyes and longed to hug her to her breast. She reached out a hand to touch Monique's cheek. "I love you, Monique," she said. "I did, and I do. I always will, for you're my daughter and nothing can change that."

Now the girl pushed Faye's hand away. "You can't make up for thirteen years of neglect with words of love! Good-bye! I'm going to stay with Armand. I'll . . . drop you a note sometime."

14

JEAN COULD think of but two possible explanations for Amoreena's absence. Finding herself unable to sleep, she might have gone for a walk and run into some young toughs or lowlife—or seized, as occasionally attractive women were, by thugs working for Lyle Benson. Jean disliked the Baron melodeon owner whose principal occupation was the procurement of white slaves for export to China.

Now Jean set several of his men to the streets to see what could be learned, while he paid Benson a personal visit at the white slaver's Skye Palace on Stockton Street.

The Skye Palace was a rectangular establishment half the size of Jean's Pirates' Nest. No women were allowed except for waitresses and performers and a standard admission of one bit was charged upon entrance at any of the Palace's doors.

It was early Sunday afternoon when Jean arrived there and business was just beginning to pick up. Jean could count the patrons at the bar on one hand. Several old timers sat quietly drinking at round tables near the center platform where racy theatrical diversions featuring half-dressed Celestials were sometimes staged. The performance to begin shortly was a vulgar play advertised by Benson as "freedom from constrained etiquette."

"Beer," Jean said to the bartender, a skeleton-like man named Clarence who had once worked for Jean before Benson hired him away. The bartender nodded, filled a smudged glass and placed it on the counter before Jean. Jean handed the man fifteen cents, but made no move to touch the beer. "Where's Lyle?" he asked.

"Don't know, Mr. LeClair. He had business north of here a ways. Left three days and he ain't been back since."

"Has he picked up any new girls lately?" Jean asked.

"Only one I know about is a real slaver's prize—a hot-blooded, red-haired Jewess," he said. "About a week ago. He brought her in to show her off before he tried her out. Gorgeous, she was."

"None today? Or yesterday?"

"Nope."

"Are you sure?" Jean said.

"Hell, yeah! Whatever the boss' business north of here, he took Howie and Rufus with him."

Howie and Rufus, Jean knew, were Benson's right hand men. With the two men away from the Coast, Benson couldn't have taken Amoreena, for he did nothing without his toughs.

Jean hoped his men on the streets would be able to learn something.

Just as he was considering his next move, a volley of six-gun fire broke the quiet of the place. Jean swiveled around on his barstool, while Clarence and the few patrons dove for cover. Jean scowled as he recognized some of the marauders who had just entered the place with guns blazing.

They were Rangers. He knew the leader—a Ranger called Tank because of his square frame.

"Well, hello, Tank," Jean said amicably. "Come for a drink?"

Tank, obviously angered by Jean's bravado, raised his gun and fired over LeClair's head, shattering a huge mirror which hung on the wall behind the bar. "Won't the others be green with envy when I tell 'em my group roughed you up, LeClair!" he bellowed.

Jean calmly picked up the beer he hadn't touched and brought it to his lips. "Well, Tank, if I'm to be roughed up, let's get on with it. I have things to do."

"Brave sonofabitch, aren't you?" Tank sneered. "We'll see how long you stay that way. Search 'em!' he ordered his men.

Two Rangers pulled Jean off the stool, grabbed his arms and held them behind his back while two others searched him for weapons. One of the thugs found the deringer he carried beneath his vest in a shoulder harness and tossed it to Tank.

"Very good, boys," Tank said. "Always wanted one of these here little guns. Okay . . . let him go."

The thugs backed away, and Jean watched Tank stash the deringer in his belt. "All right, break up the joint" Tank croaked, covering Clarence and Jean with his six-guns.

Several Rangers whooped and began shooting up a crystal chandelier. Then Jean had to duck as the Rangers used the scores of bottles lining the shelves behind the bar for target practice. Colored liquid poured in streams from broken bottles, filling the room with a heavy, sweet odor. Two Rangers robbed the cash box.

"Give my regards to Armand," Jean said. "Tell him I'll be seeing him real soon."

"That's enough outa you, LeClair!" Tank snapped,

bringing the gun to bear on Jean. "One more word and it'll be your last."

"Armand wouldn't like that," Jean said. "He wants me for himself."

Tank grinned evilly. "You may be right there, LeClair, but no reason why we can't soften you up a bit. Get him, men. Knock some of the cockiness outa him!"

With that, three of his men surrounded Jean, who still stood with his back against the bar. All three held billy clubs and knew how to use them.

But Jean had learned much from his stay in the Sydney, Australia, prison colony. Though he had a soft, luxurious life now, he remembered well how to defend himself, and was still in good physical condition.

He watched the Rangers' approach warily, awaiting the first blow. He was not worried about Tank's gun. The Ranger would not use it, Jean was certain of it. But a beating was another matter. He would not accept one, at least, without making his assailants pay. They were three and he was only one, but he was as though as they, and would soon prove it.

The big Ranger at his right lunged at him at the same moment that the one on Jean's left—a smaller, wiry man—tried to crush his skull with a blow from the club. Jean took the club across the shoulders as he threw his body into the smaller Ranger and buried his fist in the man's stomach, doubling him over.

Jean wrenched the club from the man's hand and swung it quickly at the other two Rangers, then launched a long-legged kick at the big Ranger's groin. The man howled in agony when the toe of the boot connected. But Jean's third assailant stunned him with his club and Jean went down.

"Now we've got you, LeClair," the Ranger roared, and rained a series of blows with the club to Jean's head as LeClair only half-protected himself with his arms.

The sound of Tank's laughter roused Jean from his half-conscious state and he sprang upward so suddenly, his head struck his assailant on the point of his chin. The Ranger dropped his club and crumpled to the floor.

"Now, Tank," Jean said, ignoring the stream of blood flowing from a cut over his eye and the pounding in his head from the beating he'd just taken, "it's your turn."

Tank leveled the gun at his stomach, backing away as he did so. "Stay away from me, Jean, or I swear I'll shoot."

"Get out of here, Tank, or I'll make you shoot. Then my brother will kill you instead of me."

Tank watched LeClair take two steps forward, then barked an order to his men and headed for the door. "Let's go, men!" he roared.

Jean collapsed in his tracks as the Rangers left. He awoke moments later with the taste of scotch in his mouth. The bartender was holding him up and pouring the amber fluid down his throat.

Jean gasped, swallowed and winced at the throbbing in his head.

An hour later he was back in the Pirates' Nest, which had not been sacked. He was in pain, but even more angry than hurt. After issuing crisp orders to his men to post armed guards at all his establishments, he dispatched runners to his fellow Barons, suggesting a meeting to discuss the situation and decide what to do.

He ordered the runners to make inquiries and try to find Armand's whereabouts. "He's probably hiding out right now, but I want him found," Jean declared.

Rose joined him in a small office he had recently taken in the Pirates' Nest, after being told that none of his people had been able to learn any news of Amoreena Welles. "You look like hell!" Rose observed, staring at him as she reached his desk. "What happened?"

LeClair made a face and gingerly touched the lumps on his head. "I've just had a run-in with my brother Armand's Rangers. They sacked Benson's place while I was there and Tank Brewster set three of them on me with clubs."

"Three of them could only do that?" she said. "As bad as you look, you ought to look a lot worse."

"Speaking of 'looks', Rose, you look different. Did you change your hair or something?"

She shrugged. "I cut it, and I'm making up different these days, that's all."

"I like what I see," he said. "You look great, and a lot younger. The younger and less experienced you appear, the higher a price you can earn."

Rose frowned. "I'm not doing it for the customers. I promised you I wouldn't bed any more of them, and I haven't."

He patted her hand. "That was a selfish thing I asked of you, Rose, and I'm sorry. You don't have to give up your profession. If you want to bed your customers, go right ahead. I want you to."

She glared at him. "So that's it," she declared. "That's why you haven't asked me to come to the 'Hill' in weeks. The truth is you don't want me any more. Isn't it?"

Jean was only a little surprised. Rose was bright and not easy to fool. Women were sometimes hard to judge, but he thought she seemed almost relieved that he no longer wanted her. The truth was that he *hadn't* wanted her recently—not since meeting Amoreena Welles. "You never wanted me all that much, I think," he said, "so by releasing you from your promise now, I'm only giving you what you want."

"Shrewdly put, Jean. It lets you off the hook without hurting my feelings. I'll be honest with you. I'm not going to be anyone's whore anymore. There are lots of other ways to get money without having to take men upstairs."

"Do I detect a new Rose surfacing?" he asked.

"I . . . don't know. But I think it's time I got involved in other things—things outside the Nest. Maybe I'll even go to church again."

At the mention of church, Jean's forehead furrowed as Cornelius Drummond came to mind. He scowled, then smashed a fist down hard on the table. "That's it!" he cried. "That's where she could be—the fat scoundrel! He wanted her to be his friend, he said. Told her whenever she needed to talk, to stop in and visit him! Maybe she did!"

"What are you talking about?" Rose said, baffled by Jean's odd conversation with himself.

"Nothing." He drained the last of his scotch and left, all but running out the door. It made sense now. Amoreena no doubt went to Drummond's church, needing someone to talk to. And if she did . . . The thought was not pleasing. Drummond was a lecherous fool, Jean knew. He didn't figure Cornelius would touch a white woman, but who could tell?

Jean hailed a cab and gave the driver directions to Rincon Hill.

The sound of footsteps outside the bedroom door startled Amoreena. She lifted her head from the pillow she had wept into when first the Reverend Drummond had locked her in the room late last night. She had been surprised to find herself in his house, but not worried until he had shoved her rudely into this room.

"Armand said Beau was here," she had cried, "so where is he? Why did Armand bring me here?"

Drummond laughed at her. "You're mine now," he had said. "I'll not let you out. You'll not need to worry about your fiancé again—only how to please me."

How to please him? What was he talking about? Was he mad? She shivered, remembering how Drummond had whipped the sailor who had tried to seduce her.

She had to get out of there. In a few hours it would be daylight and she was to meet Jean. He would wonder what had become of her. "There's been a mistake," she said, measuring the distance between her and the door with her eyes. "I'd better go." Then she bolted for the door, but he quickly blocked her retreat with his rotund body.

"I see you've come prepared to please me," he had said, a twinkle in his dark eyes as he looked down inside her partly open coat.

She had been in such a hurry when Armand brought her news of Beau, that she had not bothered to change. She wore only a thin cotton nightgown beneath her long coat. The top two buttons of her coat had come open, and the reverend was staring lasciviously at her white bedclothes beneath it.

"You're a man of God," she said, closing her coat. "How can you act so . . ."

He stopped her with a slap from one beefy hand. "You must learn obedience," he said. "Any questions you have will be answered tomorrow, when we will have plenty of time to get to know each other." He chuckled. "My Celestial, Lotus, has tired me out tonight or I'd indoctrinate you right now, my dear. Tomorrow morning will come quickly and, along with it, my Sunday services. I must be alert for my congregation, so I'll leave you now. Have a pleasant sleep."

"I won't stay here!" she declared, again trying to squeeze past him.

"You have no choice. The door locks from the outside."

"You mean to lock me in this room?"

"After you learn your place as my servant, you'll have free rein of my house."

"You're not a man of God, you're an animal!"

"God has given me my need, girl, and He sanctions all I do. My power comes from Him. Remember that." Then he left, slamming the door in her face. He slid the lock in place after him.

Amoreena had tried the door several times during the past twelve hours, but it remained locked. By seven o'clock in the morning she had worn herself out trying to think of something she could do, finally falling asleep. A maid left a tray of freshly baked muffins and a pot of hot coffee just inside the door while Amoreena slept, but when she awoke a little before noon, the breakfast was cold and the door was again locked.

The room had one window, a low one she might have jumped out of were it not so high off the ground. There was a forty-foot drop to a stone walkway below.

Now the footsteps she had heard stopped outside the room and she sat up in bed, listening. The knob turned and Amoreena grabbed the pillow, clutching it to her, as though it could shield her.

The door squeaked open and Amoreena breathed again. A slender Oriental girl with long blue-black hair and the saddest expression Amoreena had ever seen entered. The girl closed the door behind her, and Amoreena immediately heard someone lock it from behind. Folded over the girl's arms were clean white towels and a silken blue robe. She also carried a small tray laden with oils and perfumes.

"I am Lotus," the girl said, bowing. "I have come to prepare you for the master."

After his church service and return to Rincon Hill, while Lotus was with Amoreena, Cornelius Drummond had an unexpected visitor. He had only just got home when through the parlor window he saw Jean LeClair's carriage pull up. It frightened him and his first thought was to pretend he wasn't home; but then, before Jean could use the knocker on the front door, Cornelius changed his mind. It was best to admit LeClair and find out what he wanted. Drummond doubted Jean could have knowledge of Amoreena's presence, so Jean's visit must be on other business. The reverend had been edgy all morning as he thought about his new white servant and his hands had actually shaken as he delivered his sermon. Now he could feel his hands begin to shake again.

"I have no news for you about the Rangers' intentions, Jean," Cornelius said gruffly as LeClair came into the house.

"I don't need you for that," Jean said. "If I relied on you, the war would be over before I knew of it."

"Then why have you come?" Drummond asked nervously.

"I'm looking for a friend who seems to be missing. You know her, too—Miss Welles. Have you seen her recently?"

Cornelius' hands were shaking so badly he had to stuff them in his pockets as he met Jean's eyes. He took a deep breath to steady his nerves, telling himself LeClair could know nothing, and forcing his expression to remain impassive. "The last I saw her was the day at the wharf," he said. "You were there. Has anything happened to her?"

"That's what I'm trying to discover," Jean said. "She hasn't come to see you since that day? Not even to talk?"

"I would surely remember if she had. Miss Welles is a lovely young lady and I should relish a visit from her."

Jean frowned. "Don't relish it too much, Cornelius. She's not your type."

His type? What was his type? Celestials? Did the Baron bastard think Cornelius Drummond could enjoy only yellow flesh? For a moment, he wished he could flaunt Amoreena in LeClair's smug face, but knew that would be asinine, so he said nothing.

Jean stood to leave. He looked really disturbed. "If you should see her or hear from her, let me know immediately. There would, of course, be a reward for your troubles."

"I understand," Cornelius said. "Good luck. When you find Miss Welles—do give her my best."

"The master?" Amoreena said, standing before the Chinese girl who'd just entered, the towels and perfumes still in her hands. Amoreena had no idea Jean was at that moment in the parlor below talking with Drummond.

"Master Cornelius, miss."

"Cornelius Drummond is a minister. He's no one's master."

"He owns me and now he owns you," the girl said.

"That's ridiculous!"

The girl shrugged. "Please to lay on bed?"

"I'll do no such thing. Why am I here? And what time is it?"

Lotus placed the towels on the bed and her dark eyes met Amoreena's. "It is afternoon. We are here for master Cornelius' pleasure. I was given him as slave, just as you were."

"No! No man has the right to do that—to pass us around as if we were horses!"

"Lambs," Lotus corrected. "Lambs are used for sacrifice. So also are we. Now I must prepare you, or master Cornelius will be furious and beat me."

"He wouldn't!" Amoreena said, horrified.

Lotus turned her back to Amoreena, then gently lowered the top half of her silky robe. "Look," she said.

Amoreena shrieked at the purplish scars that striped the girl's slender back. Then Lotus re-covered herself and turned around. "He did that to you?" Amoreena asked, her voice sticking in her throat.

Lotus nodded. "The reverend like to whip me. It is best we do as he command."

"I'll never submit to such a monster!"

Lotus ignored her, intent upon carrying out what she

had come to do. She took a soft sponge, soaked it in warm water, then squeezed it out. She looked apologetic as she said, "Please to remove your gown, miss. Master Cornelius will hurt me much if I not bathe you."

There was terror in Lotus' eyes and Amoreena felt pity. She slipped the gown down to her waist, then lay across the bed as the Chinese girl began to sponge bathe her shoulders and arms. Amoreena had had only a glimpse at Lotus' back, but she recalled now that the wounds looked raw and ugly. They must be infected. "Stop, Lotus," she said, turning and taking the sponge from the Chinese girl's hand. "You lie down and take off your robe, please," Amoreena said.

Lotus looked puzzled, but complied.

The wounds were deep and festering. The girl needed medical attention. It must hurt terribly, Amoreena thought, yet Lotus gave no indication of the pain. She was brave.

Amoreena rinsed the sponge, then doused it in some of the herbal oils. "This will sting," she said, as she brought it to Lotus' back, "but it should help a bit."

The girl winced as the sponge touched the whip's gashes, but did not cry out. Amoreena could feel Lotus' muscles tensing. "You can cry out if you want, Lotus. Sometimes it helps. If I were you, I'd scream like a lunatic."

"No," she said. "Lotus does not cry. Master Cornelius like her to cry and beg for mercy. He has got everything else from Lotus, but I will not give him that."

"Good for you, Lotus!" Amoreena said, then sobered. "We've got to get you out of here and to a hospital."

Lotus jumped up. "No! No hospital! Please, miss!"

"Why not?"

"When Chinese girls are sick or old . . . their masters make them go to hospital." Her eyes widened and Amoreena saw pure panic within them. "The hospital is where they send us to die!"

THE BARBARY COASTERS 259

"Nonsense, Lotus. They are to cure sick people."

The girl shook her head vehemently. "Not hospital on Dupont Street, miss," she said. "You do not know what that hospital is like. I do. I hear many stories from the master and from other Chinese people who knew girls who never come back. The hospital, it is one small, dark room with no windows or heat. They leave sick girl there with one cup of water and boiled rice and little oil for lamp. They know when oil is to burn out, and when they unlock door, they find the girl has starved—or taken her own life. If she is somehow still alive, then they kill her."

Amoreena was appalled. "That can't be true," she said. "Surely it's only a tale to frighten you and keep you in line."

"I think it is true, miss. The master must not know of my wounds . . . or he'll send me there, too!"

Just then the door opened and Cornelius Drummond, carrying a brown canvas satchel, walked in. Lotus quickly pulled on the robe to hide her scars and Amoreena buttoned her nightgown.

"Don't hide your beauty from me," the minister said to Amoreena, a grin on his face. "It is a gift from the Lord, and you must be proud of it." Then he turned to Lotus. "Why have you not done as I ordered? Why is Miss Welles not prepared?"

"I am sorry, master."

"Sorry? You are inept, disgraceful . . . worthless." He slapped her so hard she stumbled backward and tripped against the side of the bed.

Amoreena bent to help her, but Drummond pulled her away. "Get up, slave," he ordered Lotus, "or I'll make you sorry you ever disobeyed me!"

"Leave her alone!" Amoreena cried. "She's done nothing to warrant your anger."

Drummond glared at her. "I planned to make your first

time with me as pleasant as possible, Miss Welles," he said, "but if you continue to interfere . . ."

"Do not quarrel over me," Lotus said weekly as she struggled to her feet. "May I go, master?"

"Stay . . . over there, in the corner. I may need you."

"Yes, master." She scurried into the corner like a chastened dog and stood, her eyes downcast, while Drummond turned his attention to Amoreena.

Amoreena shrank back in terror. He caressed a lock of her hair. It was soft and silky and smelled pleasantly of scented soap she had used on it yesterday. "Take off your gown, my dear," he said.

"I will not. You've no right to ask that of me!"

"We all have masters to serve, Amoreena. The Lord is my master, I am yours."

"You're crazy."

"I'm divine!" he roared, his voice almost a shriek. "Don't ever call me crazy!" He pulled a leather whip out of the satchel and before Amoreena could blink an eye, slashed at her. "Off with the gown and on the bed . . . quickly!"

Amoreena backed away. He laughed. "There's no avoiding me, Miss Welles."

"You're a vile, demented pig!"

He wielded the whip again and it caught Amoreena around the waist. He dragged her to him. As his face twisted in rage above hers, she stifled a cry. "Do as I say and I'll go easy on you the first time," he declared.

Amoreena saw the look in his eyes—it was wild and distant. He *was* insane. There was no reasoning with a madman. She nodded and backed slowly toward the bed, taking her time, trying to form a plan of escape. The girl Lotus . . . why did she stand in the corner as if she were a . . . puppet? Was she that fearful of Drummond?

"Take off the gown, girl!" the reverend ordered again. With shaking hands she began to unbutton her gown.

"Hurry," he barked. "I'm impatient to see you."

She took a deep breath and turned away as she slipped it down around her waist, her hips, then let it slide the length of her legs to her ankles. She stepped out of it. The air in the room was chilly as it kissed her flesh. It was the first time a man had laid eyes on her nakedness, and she covered herself with her arms and hands.

"Good," he said. "You may hide yourself now, but when I wish it, you will display yourself for me. Now lie on the bed."

She tasted vomit in her throat. If she could only get Lotus to help! she thought. The two of them could subdue him.

"Lotus," she cried, "help me! Don't let this monstrous beast rule you any more!"

The girl did not stir, her eyes lowered. Drummond shook his head, clucking his tongue, as if displeased with a naughty child. "Lotus will not bite the hand that feeds her, Amoreena. In time you will become quiescent like her."

"Never!"

His wrist came up and he slashed the whip again, this time drawing the leather downward from the peaks of her breasts to her stomach. She gasped, horrified.

"Lie on the bed or I'll whip you senseless!"

Blood was rushing to her head, making her dizzy with fear. She swayed as she sat on the edge of the bed.

"Down!" he demanded, standing before her now, the whip in his hand. "And spread your thighs.!"

She lay on her back, but continued to cover her intimate spots with her hands. She could not bring herself to open her legs for him, whip or not. He dug into his satchel again, this time removing a knife and a long length of rope. Amoreena gasped at the sight of the knife and her fear pleased him. He chuckled as he took the knife and cut the rope into four even pieces. Then he laid the knife on the table beside the bed and forced her wrists away from her body. In spite of her efforts to pull away, he bound them together, then raised them over her head and tied them to the bedposts. When they were secure, he forced her legs apart, tying each flailing ankle to a bottom post. Then he stood back and inspected her. All of her. Drummond's look of triumph changed suddenly.

He licked his lips, his eyes on the most intimate part of her body beneath her abdomen. Amoreena watched in horror as he began to tremble, his hand actually shaking as he reached down and touched himself through his pants, then opened the buttons. A rock-hard member appeared and Amoreena, almost hypnotized, stared as he stroked it, fondled it, then fell on top of her.

She screamed. And screamed, until he peeled off his ascot and shoved it between her teeth to quiet her. "Never have I taken a white woman," he murmured, almost to himself, "but I will now." He stroked himself once more, then with a roar that sounded only half human, he plunged his organ up against her, trying clumsily to penetrate her.

Amoreena continued to scream, but with the cloth in her mouth, little sound came out as the fat minister entered her. A wave of pain accompanied his first thrusts and she closed her eyes against the sight of the bloated face above her. She almost fainted when one violent push impaled him in her.

Lotus, standing quietly in the corner, kept her eyes averted—as though removed from reality. Then she looked up and her eyes fell upon the body of the reverend atop

Amoreena. She, too, had been chaste until the disgusting minister had done that to her! Anger and hatred overcame her at this latest outrage, and with a lithe grace, she seized the whip from the floor beside the bed and began to flog Drummond with it.

It happened so fast, Drummond was too stunned to do more than cower for a moment from the blows being rained upon his back. Then, furious, he jumped to his feet, grabbed the end of one of the whip's leather thongs and pulled. Lotus could not match his strength and had to let go.

"Judas!" he screamed. "You would betray your master?" Without giving her time to answer, he seized her by her thin neck and squeezed, forcing her down to her knees. His fingers tightened around her neck. "Sinner! Beg me for mercy, you female Judas!" he snarled. "Beg me to forgive you for your treachery. Let the Lord Himself hear your confession!"

Lotus whimpered, but refused to cry out, choking to get her breath.

Drummond spat out his order again. He had lost all control now and kept his fat thumb in her windpipe, shaking Lotus as he cursed her, intent only on punishing the traitor before him. "Cry out," he raged, "cry out for mercy!" He tightened his grip and shook her harder.

She tried feebly to pull his hands away, but his fingers were like steel and she could not budge them. Her eyes grew wide with the reality that death was near.

Drummond, almost in a trance, didn't seem to realize he was strangling her, nor did he hear the frenzied cries from the gagged Amoreena. "Say it!" he shouted at Lotus, whose mouth was wide open, gasping for air. Even if she wanted to cry out now, she couldn't, for his thumb pressure on her windpipe had cut off all air. Suddenly her eyes all but popped out of her head and she went limp. He continued to choke her for a moment, then realized something was wrong and looked stupidly at the dead girl in his hands.

As reality dawned on him, he gasped, opened his hands, and the girl dropped limply to the carpet. "My God!" he cried. "What've I done?" He whirled around and saw Amoreena tied to the bed. "It's you!" he declared. "It's all your fault! You're a witch! You must be the very same serpent who tempted the Lord! I knew white flesh was a curse! The devil sent you up from the flames of hell to get me!"

Amoreena thrashed her head from side to side, denying the reverend's crazed allegation, but Drummond ignored her, his eyes focused squarely on the beam of sunlight that had come in through the window. It was a beacon that lit up the table near the bed and glinted against the metal of the knife he had put there, telling him what he must do.

Yes, he thought, the serpent must die. He must kill it and send it back to the fires of hell. His would be a blaze of glory! Glory—the final retribution for what his mother had done to him—what the Welles devil had done to him—what the evil influences of the Barbary Coasters had done to him. He would slay the female serpent called Amoreena Welles and achieve glory from the deed.

He picked up the knife and held it high in the air, madness in his eyes, and on his face. A low laugh issued from his throat as he turned toward the bound and gagged figure.

Amoreena gulped at the sight of the gleaming knife. Was this how it all would end—with Beau gone God-knew-where and she the victim of the mad Reverend Drummond?

As if he had read her mind, Drummond brought the knife to Amoreena's breast and toyed with her nipples.

"No, Miss Serpent, I will please you before I dispose of you. It is the least I can do before I send you back to hell."

With that he mounted his helpless victim again and began pounding at her like a maddened bull.

But Amoreena knew it not, for she had fainted.

15

SHAKING WITH feverish chills, Beau Ashton made his way on foot across town to the Pacific Inn. A kindly farmer had found him asleep in a southern Oregon field, huddled with one of the other shanghaied survivors of the *Singapore Queen* to keep warm against the frosty air two nights ago, and offered him and the other man a ride in the back of his wagon. The farmer was heading to a small town south of San Francisco, and Beau had accepted the man's offer with alacrity, though the other man had not, having had enough of the Barbary Coast.

The farmer had given Beau the old woolen blanket he now wore wrapped around his shoulders. Even with the blanket around him, Beau still felt cold, though his forehead was beaded with sweat. The dunking in the icy Pacific, the ensuing flight by boat to shore, the cold days and nights, and a gnawing hunger had taken its toll on his health. No longer did he desire food, only water to cool his parched and sore throat. He knew he was sick, but there was no time to waste on doctors even if he had money to pay for one. He had to see Amoreena again, to let her know he was alive.

During the ride down from the Oregon territory, he had had a lot of time for thought. He now knew he had been wrong to bring Amoreena to this diabolical land. His motives had been pure enough—to build a home for them far from war-torn Virginia. But he had been foolish and his naivete in not realizing how really dangerous San Francisco was, may have cost them any future they might have had together.

Could they be happy again after all that had happened? He doubted it. They had both gone through a sort of hell. He, physically; she, no doubt emotionally, thinking he had deserted her. His scars would heal with time, but her emotional ones were another matter. Even with Amoreena's spunk and optimism, she could only be miserable living in a land that nurtured the Barbary Coast.

Yet what had happened to Beau affected him strangely. A huge feeling of need had engulfed him—the need to show the Barbary Coasters that they could hurt him but not beat him—that Beau Ashton's spirit was alive and well. The land on Montgomery and Washington was his, and he'd be damned if he'd let anyone tell him different! He'd take the matter to the Supreme Court if he had to, and if the judges ruled against him, he'd find another way to get his land back—even if he had to resort to violence to do so!

He coughed now as his thoughts turned sadly to Georgie, his dearest friend. Georgie's last words on the lifeboat before he died in Beau's arms were forever burned upon Beau's memory.

"I was always afraid, Beau, but I'm not anymore. You helped me a lot. I was glad I could pay you back. I hope you'll remember me as I am and not as I was. And go back and fight them. Regain what they've stolen from you." He had reached for a pewter pendant which hung on a thin chain around his neck, freed it, and held it out to Beau. "It's my good luck charm." He managed a feeble smile. "Maybe it'll be luckier for you than it was for me!"

Now, a lump in his throat, Beau fingered the pendant. "I'm back, Georgie," he said aloud, "and this time they'll not get rid of me!"

By the time Beau reached the hotel, his strength was sapped and he had begun to feel faint. He rang for the desk clerk, who was napping in a small office behind the registration desk. The clerk blinked as he recognized him.

"Mr. Ashton!" the clerk exclaimed. "Where . . . how . . . we'd thought . . ."

"Is Miss Welles in her room?" Beau said immediately.

The desk clerk shook his head. "She's . . . gone," he stammered.

"Gone?" Beau repeated, his heart in his throat. "Where?"

"I don't know. Only yesterday Mr. LeClair came and asked for her. I couldn't tell him either."

"LeClair?" Beau said. "What did he want with Amoreena?"

The clerk gathered his wits now and shrugged. "Ask Mr. LeClair," he said. "You understand since she disappeared and hasn't returned, we had to give her room . . . yours, too, to someone else and . . ."

"You said she *disappeared*?" Beau broke in incredulously.

"Her bags were packed and then left behind. She never came back for them."

His vision was blurry and his head began to buzz, so he grabbed the edge of the desk for support. "Where are her things?" he demanded.

"In the backroom with yours. I'll get them." The clerk

suddenly realized Beau was sick and asked, "Is there anything I can do for you, Mr. Ashton?"

"I'm all right. Just get Amoreena's and my things?"

The clerk watched Beau open Amoreena's bag, then turned away. By the time the search of the bags was finished, Beau was perspiring profusely from the exertion. But he had found nothing that gave a clue to where she'd gone. He did find some bank notes he had given her to hold—the last of their funds—and they were important. "What did you tell LeClair when he asked for Amoreena?" Beau now asked the clerk.

"Nothing more than I told you," he said.

"Can I leave this stuff here? I'll be back later and will take a room."

"Of course. Would you like to use my office to change clothes?"

Suddenly Beau realized what a mess he was. He still wore the salt and dirt-stained clothes he had worn when he was shanghaied. "Yes, thank you," he said gratefully, and took his bag into the clerk's office. Undressing and getting into fresh clothes took him twice as long as it normally did, for he was feverish, dizzy, and weak and had to stop to rest from his efforts. But finally he was dressed and ready to go.

He decided to start his search for Amoreena by questioning Jean LeClair. Whatever energy he'd had was now nearly gone and he could barely walk, so he hailed a cab for the trip to LeClair's mansion. There, he had the cab wait for him.

At the door, LeClair's butler regarded him cooly and told him LeClair was not in.

"The hell he isn't," Beau said, stepping past Hays and into the hall. "LeClair!" he yelled, "come on out. I know you're here!"

A few servants peeked their heads out of rooms to see

what the commotion was about, but Jean LeClair did not materialize.

"He's not here, Mr. Ashton," Hays said. "If you wish, you may search the house."

"Then where is he?" Beau demanded.

"I am not his keeper," Hays said stiffly. "He does not report to me."

Beau hesitated, then whirled and stormed out into the sunny street. The bright sunlight hurt his eyes and brought back his dizziness, and he had to stop for a minute to clear his head. Where could Amoreena have gone without her bags? he wondered. And what did LeClair want with her? Anger welled within him. He ignored the pounding in his temples and had his cab take him to the Pirates' Nest. There he dismissed the cab and staggered inside.

"Jean?" the bartender said, in answer to Beau's question. "Sure, he was here, but he left a couple of hours ago."

"Where was he heading?" Beau asked.

"Anywhere he damned well pleased. How should I know?"

Beau glared at the man and was about to accuse him of lying when he saw in the mirror behind the bar the reflection of Rose—the whore who had drugged him and was responsible for everything bad that had followed! Amoreena and LeClair were both forgotten in his rage as he turned to face her.

Rose spotted him even before he saw her. She had a moment to bolt and run, but chose not to. The old Rose might have, but not the new one. She had no idea what the unshaven, weak-looking man at the bar had been through since the night she had drugged him. But there was pain in his expression, and she knew that whatever tormented him now was her fault. She was sorry for what she'd done to him and wanted to beg his forgiveness, yet as he stared at her, the fury in his eyes terrified her.

She backed slowly toward the stairway behind her, but he summoned his strength and ran across the room to seize her wrists, twist them up behind her back, and force her up against him.

"Cry out, whore," he said through clenched teeth, and "I'll kill you." There was so much laughter, noise and song in the room that no one heard him or paid attention. She knew it was best she do whatever he wanted. He was not a killer, so she was sure if she didn't provoke him, he wouldn't harm her.

"Upstairs . . . to your room," he ordered. He was weak, but managed to follow her up the stairs.

When they were alone in her room, he leaned exhausted against the door and stared at her. "Why?" he growled. "Why did you drug me? What did I do to deserve that?"

"Nothing," she said. "I'm sorry. I have no excuses, Beau. I only wanted your money."

The room was spinning now as he swayed. "My money?" he said. "All I had was about thirty dollars!"

"I'd have done it for ten," she said.

Beau shook his head sadly. "How much did you get when you had me shanghaied?"

Shanghaied? She gasped. "I didn't . . . I had nothing to do with that," she declared.

"Come on, Rose, you can lie better than that!"

"Honestly, Beau. I had nothing to do with it. When Jean asked me if I'd seen you, I had no idea you'd been shanghaied!"

His face twisted. "LeClair!" he snarled. "His name keeps popping up in my life. Why was he asking about me?"

"He and the girl—your fiancée, I guess—came here looking for you."

"*He* was with Amoreena?"

"They both seemed geniunely concerned about you. I thought he was your friend."

"He's no friend of mine," Beau snapped. "Why was LeClair with Amoreena?"

"I suppose he was helping her look for you."

"A likely story, Rose! Don't try to fool me. You know what's going on. Has he been bedding Amoreena? Is that where she is right now?"

"No!" she said defensively. "I don't know where she is, but I do know that Jean and I are lovers, so he couldn't be bedding her." Yet even as she said it, she knew it was not true. Not any longer. Only a short time ago Jean had told her she could bed anyone she chose. Could it be because he *was* bedding Beau's fiancée?

Now she saw that he was ill—probably burning up with fever, judging by his sweat-soaked hair and face. Her fear of him vanished. She had to do something for him, if only to make up for the troubles she'd caused him. "You look sick, Beau," she said. "You'd better lie down." She took a step toward him and offered him her hand.

But if she no longer feared him, he feared her. He pushed her away weakly. "Don't touch me," he said, his voice little more than a whisper. Then he collapsed.

After Jean left Reverend Drummond's house and Rincon Hill he rode to the docks—the place he'd always go when he needed to be alone to think. The air was cool and refreshing no matter what time of year, and he found that staring out at the seemingly endless sea made his problems less awesome.

Now as he stood along the pier, leaning against the wooden rail, he felt that Amoreena was near—not necessarily at the harbor, but somewhere on the Coast. He could sense, too, that she was calling for help. He felt humbled and frustrated by his lack of power.

Then his thoughts turned to Armand. With his mind preoccupied with Amoreena's disappearance, could Jean exert the strength necessary to deal with his treacherous brother? He had to, if he was to keep the empire he had built these last thirteen years.

He turned around and stared at the crooked, hilly streets of the city. Over the last decade San Francisco had been a source of endless fascination for him with its changing landscape and declining morals. It had been a challenge to begin with nothing and end with an empire—a real empire which had fulfilled his goals. Now he had everything.

Or almost everything.

Suddenly he sensed a hostile presence. He reached for the knife he wore in a scabbard on his belt beneath his coat and swiveled, the gleaming knife in his hand.

Spider Joe's eyes bugged. "Hey, Jean," he said, holding up his arms, "I'm not out to get you. Put the shiv away."

Jean stuffed the knife in its sheath. "Then what are you doing here?"

"I gotta talk to you, LeClair, and I didn't want nobody to know, not even my own kind. There's an empty shack my kid usta use for a clubhouse nearby. Let's go. O.K.?

As the Ranger saloon-owner led him to a small, one-room shack, Jean wondered if this might be a trap engineered by Armand to take him prisoner. He thought it highly unlikely. Armand's Ranger thugs had no orders to take him prisoner or they would have tried during the raid that afternoon. Nevertheless, he kept his hand on his knife as he followed Joe inside.

"Listen, LeClair," Joe said in a low voice after he'd made sure they were alone, "I got some information—and this one's on the house. I hear you been askin' around after some blonde lady. Well, my sister goes with a straight kid, you know, the kind who don't mess with street gangs or smoke opium. He's all for makin' an honest living, so he drives a cab nights. Today he told my sister about a fare he had last night—after midnight it was—the new leader of us Rangers and a blonde lady. He dropped them off at that preacher man's place—Drummond.''

Jean could barely believe his ears. Armand and Amoreena— together at Drummond's? It was fantastic. And yet . . . he had been so busy associating Armand with the Ranger feud that he had forgotten Amoreena had met Armand once.

Was Armand using her somehow? To throw Jean off guard while he went after Jean's Nests? Was Amoreena right now a prisoner—in Drummond's care? The news was indeed important, but its source was suspect. ''Why are you telling me this?'' he asked Spider Joe. ''What's in it for you?''

Spider Joe met Jean's eyes. ''Armand had my kid Luke roughed up,'' he said. ''He's hurt real bad and Doc says there's no tellin' if Luke'll ever be okay again.''

''I see,'' Jean said. ''I'm sorry, Joe.'' Even a shrewd, ugly old codger like Spider Joe had a soft spot—his son.

After they parted, Jean wasted no time getting back to Drummond's house. The minister's manservant told Jean the reverend was ''resting'' and could not be disturbed.

''We'll see about that,'' Jean snarled, and shoved the servant aside, then took the steps of the main staircase three at a time.

''Sir!'' the servant called after him. ''Please don't go up there!''

Jean ignored him. When he reached the top of the stairs, he stopped and looked around. There were three bedrooms on the floor. One had to be Drummond's, the other Lotus', and the last a guest room.

He tried the knob on the first room and it opened to reveal an empty suite. The second was empty, too. The room at the end of the hall had to be the one he wanted.

Jean tried the door and found it locked. He stepped back and threw his shoulder into the door. It flew open and his momentum carried him inside.

What he saw now froze the very blood in his veins. Drummond, naked from the waist down, was thrusting furiously against a naked Amoreena, who was spread-eagled beneath him on a wide bed! On the floor barely six feet away lay Lotus, her dead features contorted in a grotesque expression.

Jean's stomach churned and a black rage welled up in him. With a roar summoned from the depths of him, he seized the shirt collar of the huge preacher and yanked him off Amoreena, then hit Drummond with both fists. Every ounce of strength Jean had went into the two blows—one to the reverend's stomach, the second to his fat chin.

Drummond collapsed in a heap.

Then Jean turned to Amoreena. She was unconscious and said nothing as he took the scarf from her mouth and began untying her arms and legs. He noticed streaks of blood staining the sheet between her legs and cursed Drummond for the pig he was.

She opened her eyes as he raised her to a sitting position. "Jean!" she said. "How did you find me? The reverend—he's crazy! I . . ."

"It's all right, Amoreena. He can't hurt you now. I'm going to get you out of here." He held her face tenderly between his hands and kissed her.

Suddenly she pulled out of his embrace, her eyes wild with terror. "Look out!" she screamed.

Jean turned and saw Drummond moving toward the bed with the knife he had used earlier to cut the rope into pieces. The minister's eyes were big and wild, the knife in both hands as he advanced.

"Die, Satan!" the reverend screamed as he hurled himself at Jean, who jumped off the bed and reached for his own knife.

Drummond was thrown off balance by Jean's maneuver and fell to the floor. Jean launched a kick at the man's head, but missed as Drummond rolled away and sprang to his feet, still waving the knife.

Jean had his knife out now, but had to retreat toward the window. Suddenly the minister rushed him, howling like a banshee, the knife held in his hand as if it were a sword. Jean nimbly side-stepped and Drummond was carried forward into the window by his own momentum. The glass shattered as Drummond's great weight crashed into it. The minister released a final screech as his half-naked body sailed through the window and flew forty feet to the ground. At that height he might have survived the fall but for his own knife, which had turned in his hand as he hit the ground and imbedded itself in his groin.

16

AWARE THAT the first thing Jean would do upon learning of the Ranger attacks would be to try to capture him, Armand moved his headquarters to a small warehouse on the waterfront at the Clay Street Wharf. It was a one-story wooden building housing textiles brought in from China by one of Jean's Baron friends and would probably be one of the last places the Barons would look for Armand. At least that was what he hoped. In the rear was a large empty room where Armand's fifteen top Ranger aides now gathered.

From here Armand would order his next attack on the Barons. The first series of sackings had been only partly successful, for Jean had been in the first place raided and sent warnings to some of the other Barons to alert them. They were thus armed and ready for Armand's thugs. The sackings had, however, been profitable—and proved to the Barons that Armand meant business and that other attacks, more effective than the first, would surely follow.

Armand had purchased explosives from an ammunition ship in the harbor and had hidden it along with barrels of highly flammable kerosene in the cellar of a crumbling old Spanish church not far away. Now he began to outline to the Rangers his plans for a second attack.

It was dark when Beau again awoke, feeling hot and thirsty. He was lying on a cot, and on his forehead was a cool, wet cloth. Two woolen blankets covered him.

He looked to his right in the candle-lit cubicle and saw Rose sleeping in a rickety old chair. What had happened to him now? he wondered. Had Rose drugged him again?

He pushed the covers back and threw his legs over the side of the cot, but found to his dismay that he was weak as a kitten. He summoned all his strength to lift himself and managed to stand. Before he could take a step, however, his bad leg gave out and he fell backward on the cot.

Rose opened her eyes. "No, Beau! You have to rest!" she declared, jumping to her feet. She pulled the covers back over him.

"Did you drug me again?" he asked.

"I'm not a monster, Beau," she said. "I'm trying to help you now . . . to be your friend."

What was that old saying, he thought—with friends like her, who needs enemies? Yet she looked sincere, and he sensed something different about her in the way she spoke, even the way she looked. She was softer, somehow. But why should she care about him? "Is this a new tactic to get my money?" he asked, looking away. "If so, don't bother. You're welcome to what I have—if you haven't grabbed it already."

She looked hurt. "I suppose I deserved that," she said, "but I don't want your money. Not any more. In fact, if giving you back the thirty dollars I took could reverse everything bad that I've caused, I'd certainly do it."

The candle's flame hurt Beau's eyes, so he closed. them. "Have you reformed?" he asked wryly.

She re-soaked the cloth, dropped to her knees beside him and placed the cloth back across his hot forehead. "You may not believe this, Beau, but I *am* a different person. I've done a lot of thinking, and I have to admit I don't like the old Rose very much, though I'm not a bad person, really. At least the *real* me isn't."

"What are you talking about?" he asked. "What real you?"

"Well . . ." She hesitated, looking down at him reflectively. "I never told anybody this, but my name's not really Rose. I'm English and my real name is Rowena Pendleton. My . . . father is a member of the British Parliament. Back in England my family once had enough money to buy the whole Barbary Coast!"

But most of her words were lost on Beau, whose head was pounding. There was a loud ringing in his ears as well. "Water," he said.

She poured a glass and held it to his lips. "I'm going to get you a doctor," she said.

"There's no time. I have to find out what happened to Amoreena."

"How do you intend to do that if you can't even stand?"

He was afraid she was right. He knew, too, that if he weren't treated medically, he might never be able to stand again. The pain in his bad leg was terrible and he bit his lip to keep from crying out. He did need a doctor—and quickly. "You win," he said. "Get me a doctor."

Her face lit up. "Now you're making sense. I'll leave right now." She stood up and started for the door.

"Rose," he called. "What's a lady from England doing in a Barbary Coast brothel?"

She turned and looked at him sadly. "My father, Beau, . . . he desired me. My mother was cold and denied

him, so he came to me and . . . took me. I grew to hate him
and myself. When I couldn't stand it any more, I threatened to tell and he had me taken away and placed on a
ship bound for America. He left me with three hundred
dollars and a note telling me that he had disinherited me. I
learned later that he told everyone I had been sleeping
around and had been gotten with child. He lied, Beau, but
I wasn't there to defend myself and I suppose everyone I
knew and cared about believed him.''

"You never went back?''

"I no longer wanted to. I was hurt and determined to
make it on my own without them.''

"So . . . you ended up a whore.''

"I had little choice,'' she said, "for I knew no other
way to support myself.''

"I'm sorry.''

"So am I,'' she said, as she left.

Her encounter with the maniacal Reverend Drummond
left Amoreena in a state of shock. Jean brought her to
Telegraph Hill and made her drink several glasses of brandy
to stop her shaking, then had the maid tuck her into a
warm bed in the upstairs guest chamber.

While she slept, Jean turned his attention to business
and he soon learned that a number of other Baron establishments had been attacked while he was freeing Amoreena
from Drummond's clutches. In early evening he found out
that the other Barons had met and were plotting a crushing
counter-attack against Armand and the Rangers.

Jean still awaited word from his own men who had been
trying to locate Armand. It was close to ten o'clock now
and the black sky was starless. San Francisco, he thought,
was quiet tonight—almost as if it sensed that something
dreadful was about to happen.

Whatever the other Barons did in retaliation, Jean had a

feeling it would spark further attacks from the Rangers and lead to much bloodshed. To truly end the Ranger uprising, Armand had to be dealt with and no one was better equipped to do that than himself. But he would not give Armand his empire, nor would he allow him to become a czar of the Coast. What Jean would do, he decided now, was bring Armand the violence his brother seemed to savor. Jean would kill him!

"Mr. LeClair," Maude the maid said, interrupting Jean's thoughts, "Miss Welles is awake now. She seems better. She said she'd like a bath, so I've had water drawn for her. Do you want me to do anything else?"

"No. You can go to bed now."

Jean went upstairs. There were many things he had to attend to tonight, but Amoreena was the first—as important to him as any. He had to make sure she was all right, but more than that, he wanted to see her again. Amoreena brought out a side of Jean LeClair he didn't know existed. He wanted to protect her, cuddle her, reassure her, not merely love her physically. They were new emotions for him. As he walked in her room, he wondered if what he was feeling was love.

She had just finished her bath and was wrapped in a fluffy white towel when he knocked. Busy drying her hair, she didn't hear his knock, so he pushed open the door and walked in. With her head down, she didn't see him and so he used the moment to study the long, slender legs beneath the towel, the firm derriere partly exposed as she bent over to let her long hair hang forward as she dried it.

She was enticing, and he wanted to seize her and touch her everywhere. He waited until she had stopped toweling her hair and straightened before saying, "You smell fresh as a spring flower and look even more delightful. I trust you're feeling better."

If she were startled or upset to find him there, she gave

no indication of it, perhaps still numb from her earlier shock at Drummond's. She sat on the edge of the bed.

"Much better now, thank you," she said. "If it weren't for you, Jean, that horrible man would have killed me. As it is, he . . ." She saddened and shook her head. "I was saving myself for Beau," she said. "Now I have nothing to offer him or any man."

He sat beside her. "Wrong," he said. "Any man would be lucky to have you just as you are. I know I would."

She stared at him, and blushed. At that moment their eyes spoke what neither could say. Jean moved slowly to kiss her. She closed her eyes and raised her face to meet his lips. Their kiss was tender, exploring, then their mutual needs turned it deep. Jean traced the contours of her lips with his tongue, and she opened her mouth. Her tongue met his with fiery abandon, and Jean pulled her gently down on the bed and lay beside her.

They kissed long and passionately. With any other woman, Jean would have had her naked by now, but with Amoreena he wanted simply to savor the moment. Kissing her gave him more pleasure than the physical act of bedding some of the others he'd had. He could tell by her response that she felt the same way.

Now as his lips feasted upon hers, he eased her towel loose. Her breasts were firm and full, though not large. The hot bath water had left her skin a glistening pink, and she smelled delightfully of lavender soap. He tore his mouth away from hers to seize and tongue a rosy peak. He flicked it back and forth, then took it into his mouth and sucked her as if he were a hungry child. She closed her eyes, enjoying his nearness and the pleasant sensations he evoked within her.

He fondled her breasts with his hands as he moved lower, his lips leaving a searing trail of desire across her chest to her lower abdomen. When his mouth found her most intimate place, she opened her eyes wide. A cry of alarm sounded from her lips.

"I love you, Amoreena," he said, startling himself as well as her.

She smiled happily and stretched as he did things to her she had never dreamed of. "I love you, too," she said. She sighed, but didn't relax until later. Much later.

The doctor Rose had brought up to her room in the Nest diagnosed Beau's ailment as fever caused by exposure. He prescribed medication and told Beau to get plenty of bedrest.

Several hours after he had gone, Rose continued to apply cool towels to Beau's forehead. Later he felt stronger and not as hot. The fever, he guessed, must have broken. He even felt well enough to eat, and Rose got him some freshly made chicken broth and rolls from a corner cafe.

"I wish we were at my apartment instead of here," she said. "It isn't much, but the bed's more comfortable."

"This is fine, Rose," Beau said, sipping the piping hot soup. "I won't be staying that long. I already feel better."

"You'll stay until you're completely well," she corrected, "and I'll stay with you."

"You don't have to pamper me, Rose." He smiled. "I guess I forgive you. You have other things to do, so . . ."

"I'm glad you forgive me, Beau, but I'm staying anyway. Because I . . . want to." She looked at him strangely, the way Amoreena used to look at him once.

Beau frowned. "Do you know what you're saying?"

"I . . . I think so."

"I'm betrothed to Amoreena," he reminded her.

"You don't love her."

"How can you know that?"

"It's written all over you. I believe you *think* you love her. I believe, too, that you care about her. But eyes have a language all their own, Beau, and yours are telling me that Amoreena is not the girl you want to spend the rest of your life with.''

"You're a pretty astute reader of eyes,'' he said, finishing the soup and lying back on the cot. "Amoreena and I grew up together. Our parents expected we'd marry one day. We were always good friends.''

"Friendship is hardly a good recommendation for a marriage partner.''

"It's better than marrying someone you have nothing in common with.''

"What have you in common with her?'' Rose asked. "Besides having grown up in the same environment?''

"We . . . There's . . .'' He groaned.

"Have you ever made love to her?''

He shook his head.

"Then you have nothing in common. A man cannot truly love a woman until he's made love to her, and the same applies for the woman.''

"How do you know so much about love, Rose . . . or should I say Rowena?''

She smiled at his use of her real name. "I'm a pretty astute observer, as well as a reader of eyes,'' she said.

"But you know nothing of love from personal experience?''

"If you mean have I ever been in love, then the answer is no. After my father took me, I could never enjoy sex. In fact, I hated it.''

"You speak in the past tense,'' he pointed out.

"I think I've found a man who can make me enjoy it as a woman should.'' She went to him and lay down alongside him on the cot.

"I hope you're right,'' Beau murmured. He kissed her gently.

"Mmmmm,'' she said, and nuzzled up against him. "The doctor said you need plenty of bedrest,'' she said, "so let's find out the rest in bed.''

* * *

"We have to be very careful," Armand LeClair warned the Rangers who sat around the table before him in the warehouse at the Clay Street wharf. "Jean will have his saloons and parlor houses heavily guarded, and the other Barons will, too. My idea is to strike where they'll least expect it."

Blackjack spoke up. "Where's that?"

Armand grinned widely. He was enjoying himself matching wits with his brother again. "We'll hit them where they live! Their homes, their mistress' homes, even their churches!"

Cheers rang throughout the room.

While Armand went over the details of what he proposed, eight burly armed Rangers were posted as guards. They worked in pairs. Two watched the front of the warehouse, two were up on the roof, the others in the narrow alleys at each side. The rear wall of the warehouse was flush against the end of the pier with a twenty foot drop to the bay right behind. There was a rear window, but the door—no longer used—had been boarded up years ago.

Flanking the warehouse on either side were a seafood restaurant and a gambling house. The restaurant closed at dusk, and the moored ship that had been converted to a gambling saloon was ablaze with light and sound.

None of the four guards at the sides of the warehouse or the two on the roof saw or heard their silent attackers. All, however, felt the cold kiss of razor-sharp steel across their windpipes. They died quietly, without alerting the others.

Now two giant Baron toughs jumped down on the two front guards, their knives slitting two more Ranger throats. After dragging them behind bushes, they produced cans of kerosene and poured the volatile fluid around the foundation of the building.

Then the leader backed away and motioned for his men

to do the same. He lit a torch and threw it at the warehouse. They all dove for cover beside the other Baronmen, who were armed with rifles and six-shooters and positioned behind two parked carriages at the front of the warehouse.

Immediately the building ignited with a mighty rush, and curtains of orange flame sprang up before their eyes. The sky lit brighter than daylight.

Armand was about to adjourn the meeting when he smelled smoke. "Better get out fast," he yelled. "If the building's on fire, it'll go up like a tinderbox."

The Rangers wasted no time. The smoke was pouring into the building as they fled through the front door. All but two of Armand's aides were outside when the Baron sharp-shooters opened fire.

Armand did not follow his own advice, however. He lagged behind with BlackJack and Fisheye, the last of his lieutenants, a nagging suspicion in his brain. When the sound of rifle fire exploded in his ears, he was ready. "Quickly," he said to the two Rangers, "we'll have to go out the window at the back!"

The shooting continued as Armand and the last of his men raced through the smoke and flames to open the back window and dive into the icy bay. Wary that the attackers might be guarding the nearby wharves, Armand swam well north before wading ashore.

Then, keeping to the alleys and deserted fringe streets of the Barbary Coast, he reached his boarding house, changed clothes and shoved a six-gun in his belt, a knife in his boot and headed for the Pirates' Nest.

So, he thought, his brother had tried to ambush him! To pick him off like a duck on a pond. Well, if Jean and his fellow Barons wanted fire, Armand would give it to them! A fire they'd never forget!

Armand's rage continued to grow all during his trip to the Pirates' Nest, where he'd see Monique if she was there. He'd use her—Jean's own daughter—to destroy him. If not, he'd kill her and leave her to burn up with the Pirates' Nest.

The smell of smoke from the fire at the wharf was in the air as he reached the building where the Pirates' Nest was located and climbed up the flight of outside stairs leading to a door to the second floor dens and living quarters occupied by Monique and her mother, Faye Langlois. Monique had given him her key, and now it came in handy.

He unlocked the outside door and rapped on the door to Monique's room. A moment later she opened it.

"Armand!" she cried, surprised but pleased to see him.

He moved past her, then frowned when he saw that sitting on Monique's bed was Faye Langlois—Jean's chief madame and one-time mistress.

The woman stared at him. The resemblance to Jean was more obvious to her than to most. She jumped to her feet. "Go away!" she cried. "You're not wanted here!"

Armand smiled, but his eyes were cold. Langlois, he decided, would die before he left the Pirates' Nest. Not only was she a part of Jean's property, but she was a sharp-tongued bitch!

"I'll handle her, Armand," Monique said. She turned to face her mother. "We've said enough, Mother. Leave us alone now."

"No, Monique. Don't have anything to do with him. He's filth, trash! Can't you see that?"

"Shut your mouth, whore!" Armand growled. "Monique, I've just taken an icy swim in the bay and I don't have time to play games with her. Get some rope."

"Rope?" she repeated, a puzzled look on her face. "Where?"

"The sash cords of the curtain," he said. "Cut them." He tossed her his knife, then grabbed Faye.

"Take your hands off me," Faye declared, trying to pull away.

Armand, far bigger and stronger, flung her down into a small arm chair as Monique handed him the cord.

"What are you going to do?" she asked as she realized that Armand meant to use the cord on her mother.

"Stop him, Monique!" Faye cried, and suddenly twisted out of Armand's grip. She tried to get to the door, but Armand caught her and knocked her unconscious with a big fist to her jaw.

As Faye slumped to the floor, Monique gasped. "Why did you do that?" she cried. "She's done nothing to you."

"I thought you were free of her, Monique," he said, dragging Faye back to the chair. "Don't tell me you care about the old slut."

"I . . . I don't know," she said, geniunely confused. "We were having an argument over my leaving before you came. I'd just finished packing my things so I could move in with you."

"Forget it, kid. I've no place for you. There's a war going on in the Barbary Coast between my brother and me, and I don't intend to lose it because of you or your mother."

Armand had been binding Faye to the chair as he spoke, now he took Monique by the shoulders and looked into her eyes, forcing an earnest look on his face. "Here's your chance to get even with Jean," he said. "You can pass through the streets freely and get to Jean's house without anyone stopping you. He'll be out with the rest of the Barons, looking for me. I want you to burn his bloody mansion, Monique—to the ground! This is the chance you were looking for to really hurt Jean. You still want to, don't you?"

"Yes," she said, her eyes moving to her mother's

unconscious and bound body on the chair. "But why did you hit Faye? And tie her like that?"

"To keep her out of my hair. Now, listen, kid, you liked what we had, didn't you? If you want us to have it again, you're going to have to do what I say. And do it right—understand?"

"I . . . suppose so," she said slowly, "but I don't want you to leave my mother here like that. She doesn't know what we're going to do, so she can't hurt us."

"She'll send a messenger to my brother to tell him where I am, if I let her loose. So trust me—she'll be okay. Now get out of here."

She hesitated, then turned and left. He waited until the sound of her footsteps on the back staircase had faded away, then pulled out his six-gun. He held it to Faye's temple just as she groaned and opened her eyes. She screamed when she saw the pistol, but Armand silenced her with a hand over her mouth.

"I guess I didn't hit you hard enough," he said. "You heard everything I told Monique, didn't you?"

"I heard nothing," she mumbled, her eyes on the weapon.

"It doesn't matter," he said, waving the gun in her face. "If I win this war and become king of the Barbary Coast, there'll be no place in it for you or your promiscuous little brat. If I lose, I'll be dead, but so will a few of Jean's closest friends like you—and so will his kid, Monique."

Terror filled Faye's eyes now and she began to sob. "No," she pleaded, "please don't kill me!"

Armand pulled the hammer back and fired point blank into her temple, then jumped away as her head exploded. He scowled at the bloody mess she'd made, then struck a match. He walked over to the white cotton drapes, held the flame to the hem and watched the material catch fire and the flame curl upward. It would take a few minutes for the fire to take hold of the ceiling and walls, he knew, and during those moments he'd be on his way down the outside stairs.

"Goodbye Pirates' Nest," he said as he left the blazing room and Faye Langlois' lifeless body and closed the door behind him.

Although Monique was excited at the prospect of finally getting back at Jean for his neglect, she was also troubled as the hansome cab she took from the Pirates' Nest headed toward Telegraph Hill—troubled by Armand's brutality to her mother. Was it really necessary? And did she have to be tied? By the time Faye regained consciousness from the blow he had laid upon her, Monique would have already set Jean's house ablaze and Armand would be far away.

She was struck by a sudden strong wave of sympathy for Faye. But before she could react to it, a fire bell sounded in the distance, then another. Fire? She was on her way to start one, she thought, and the coincidence sent shivers up and down her spine. She wondered if it were a sign of some sort. Monique's conscience suddenly bothered her—a rare occurrence indeed. Was she right, whether or not she loved Armand, to set fire to her own father's home?

Her father? For the first time she thought of Jean as her father. In the mess that was her life she had found a family. A mother, father, and even an uncle. Tears swelled in her eyes. She had always longed for a family and now she was about to destroy it! For Jean would surely have no more to do with her after she had burned his fine mansion. And Faye . . .

Her mother. She hated what Armand had done to her. And she shouldn't have gone without first making sure her mother was untied. Even if she had to wait around until after Armand left, then sneaked back to free her, Monique should have done so.

She sat back in the leather seat and chewed on her fingernails as the carriage mounted the first of the Hill's steep inclines. Should she go back?

"Turn around," she yelled to the driver, "and take me back to the Pirates' Nest." She felt better immediately, but her heart was in her throat at the sight she saw when the cab pulled up at the Pirates' Nest. Heavy black smoke was pouring out of several rear windows of the second floor. She stared with horror as flames licked at the second floor doorway she had so recently come through.

"No!" she shrieked, jumping out of the cab. "My mother's in there!" She raced up the staircase, wrenched open the door and ran inside. The hall was smoky and the bitter taste of it scratched her throat and made her cough as she ran into the room.

The walls and ceilings were in flames, but she ignored the fire, trying to see through the thick, acrid smoke, a choking courier of death. Her eyes burned as they focused on Faye. Her mother was slumped to the side, still tied to the chair where Armand had left her. "Mother!" Monique screamed, "I'm back! I'll save you!"

But Faye made no sound as Monique raced to her side. Immediately Monique froze with horror. Her mother was dead! But not from the fire or smoke. She had been shot in the head! There was a hole in her temple and blood and tissue were on her dress.

Monique dropped to her knees, a scream frozen in her throat. The only sounds which came out were pitiful, animal-like whimpers. Armand had killed her mother! He had sent Monique away, then killed Faye in cold blood. While she was unconscious and helpless!

"Why?" she said aloud, hot tears suddenly pouring down her cheeks. "Why did you have to kill my mother?"

Then she was a child again, alone and afraid. "Mommy!" she wailed, hugging her mother's bloody head to her breast, "Mommy, please wake up! I need you!"

Flames crept along the floorboards barely inches from her, but she was oblivious to it and the danger as she cried and cried and cried. At last a finger of fire touched the bottom of her gingham gown and crept upward.

Monique squealed and scrambled to her feet, beating at the flames with her hands, burning her palms. Then she pulled a blanket off the bed and wrapped it around her, rolling over and over across the floor until the flames went out. She jumped to her feet and raced out the door.

17

WHILE ARMAND was killing Faye Langlois in Monique's room, Rowena Pendleton and Beau rested, contented but exhausted in each other's arms on a cot in a room at the other end of the narrow hall. They had just finished making love, and found now that speaking of what they'd shared brought them closer emotionally and prolonged their pleasure.

"I've had sex before," Rose said with a sigh, as she nestled in the crook of Beau's arm, "but this is the first time I've made love."

He kissed the tip of her nose but did not admit to her that this was his first time ever. "Me, too," he said.

"I don't even feel dirty," she declared. "I always had to scrub myself after having a man, but not now. I'm just going to lie here and enjoy you until you push me out."

"Then you might just lie here forever," he said.

Their lips met in a light kiss; but Rose broke away, a

look of concern on her pretty face. "What about your fiancée?" she asked.

"I still have to find her. If she's left the Coast, and gone back to Virginia . . . well, I have to know."

"What if you discover she's with Jean?" she said cautiously, herself wondering about the very real possibility. "Could you accept that?"

"An hour ago I might have said no."

"You *will* be staying in San Francisco?" she declared, suddenly worried that he would not.

Recognizing her urgency, Beau hastily reassured her. "Yes," he said. "This cot, this room, this whole property belongs to me." He told her about his father, the two deeds, and how before he was shanghaied he had planned to sue LeClair.

At the reminder of his ordeal, Rose stiffened. "I hate myself for what I did to you, Beau . . ."

He hugged her, than kissed her again. "Let's forget it, Rowena. It's over. I'm fine now. That's all that counts."

She moved on top of him, reached a hand down, and was surprised and pleased to find him rock hard again. She was about to wriggle in position against him when she stopped and sniffed at the air. "Beau?" she said. "Do you smell anything?"

He sniffed too, and his eyes widened. "It's smoke!" he declared. "But . . ."

Just then they heard footsteps in the corridor and a voice screaming, "Help! Fire in my room!"

Beau, still fully clothed, got up and as Rose slipped into her gown, he flung open the door.

Monique was running down the hall, screaming. She saw Beau and Rose and ran to them. "Help me," she pleaded. "My room is on fire! My mother . . . she's dead! Armand . . . Armand LeClair killed her!"

"Oh!" Rose screeched, recognizing Monique. Faye—

dead? Then she saw the girl's charred gown and a gasp escaped her throat. "Are *you* all right, she said.

"Yes . . . but . . . the fire!"

"Rowena," Beau said, forcing himself to be calm, "go downstairs and warn everyone. I'll see if I can stop the fire from spreading."

"Beau . . . be careful," she said, hesitating only a second.

He touched her cheek gently, then gave her a little push toward the stairway and limped away down the now smoke-filled hallway. A couple of other prostitutes engaging their customers in the upstairs dens smelled the smoke and heard Monique's cry and were now rushing out of the rooms and down the stairway after Rose.

Monique didn't go with Rose. Instead she raced back down the hall after Beau. "There's no water up here," she declared, "but we'll surely need some."

By the time they reached the room, however, Beau could see that it was already too late for a bucket brigade. The door knob was hot to the touch and tongues of flames were curling out of the crack beneath the door. Smoke was pouring out as well, and Beau knew the whole building was in jeopardy, for the Nest was made of wood and would burn quickly.

"My God!" Monique cried.

"It's out of our hands. We've got to get help. Or at least get out of here before the smoke gets to us." He gagged and began to choke. Grabbing Monique, he dragged her back down the hall to the stairs. Within minutes the entire top floor was ablaze and flames were licking at the frame of the first floor and spreading to the saloon below.

Beau and Rose stood outside, a safe distance away, watching, their faces stained with smoke and sweat from the intense heat. Monique had disappeared after Beau and she had reached the street. Employees and patrons of the

Nest were pouring out of the place; others were standing around wide-eyed and stunned.

Now Rose had a thought. She half-turned to Beau. "Jean!" she said. "He should know! I have to tell him."

Beau nodded. It seemed he and LeClair now had something in common—they'd both lost their property. "I'll go with you," he said.

It was near midnight and most of the carriages for hire and been liveried for the night. Only a handful operated on the Barbary Coast at this late hour, driven by young men who had to brave robbery or murder to do so. These carriages were in great demand and hard to find.

After leaving the burning Pirates' Nest, Monique tried to locate transportation to Telegraph Hill but this time could not find a cab. Out of desperation she stole a horse—a dirty, trail-weary gray mare tied to the hitching post outside a Montgomery Street bordello. But dirty and trail-weary or not, the horse moved fast and quickly carried Monique up the steep streets to Jean's house.

She left the mare tied to a tree alongside the house, then fished out the key Jean had given her when she first moved into his house. She was glad he had not asked for it back. The house was dark and quiet, and Monique knew the servants would be asleep at this hour. She didn't know if Jean was home and she didn't care, for her business here had nothing to do with him.

As she let herself in the front door and padded soundlessly up the carpeted marble staircase, she hoped Jean had not moved the gun he kept in a desk drawer in his second-floor study. She had stumbled upon the gun by accident one day while looking for a pair of scissors. Obtaining the gun would give her the means to kill Armand LeClair.

Armand. She gritted her teeth at the thought of him. She had believed she loved him, but now she hated him. She

had been duped! Her mother had warned her about
Armand—how he was using her—and she had been right.
Monique longed to tell her so—and to beg forgiveness.
But now Faye would never know, thanks to Armand.

Her mother had been right in another respect. Armand
didn't know the meaning of love. He had needed Monique
for his dirty work and nothing more. If, Monique thought,
he could murder Faye without provocation, he could just
as easily kill Faye's daughter as well!

Well, soon Armand would be through hurting people.
Monique would see to that!

She approached the door to the study, and quietly let
herself in. The room was dark, so she lit a candle and
placed the candleholder on the desk top. Her fingers shook
as she pulled out the middle drawer on the right—the one
she hoped would contain the gun.

She held her breath. The weapon was there! Nestled up
against the rear panel of the drawer was a Colt .44.

She pulled it out and turned it over in her palm. It felt
heavy, cold and deadly. Luke had taught her how to fire a
gun once. Could she use it to kill a man? If the man was
Armand, she decided, she certainly could!

She checked to see if all six chambers were loaded, then
seeing that they were, stuffed the gun into her skirt pocket.
She pushed the drawer back in and stood. No sooner had
she done so than the door to the study flew open and she
faced Jean LeClair.

He glared at her from the open doorway. "What are *you*
doing here?" he said.

"I . . . left a . . . book on your shelves somewhere. I
came back for it."

"At midnight?"

"I just remembered it," she said lamely. She could not,
of course, tell him her true purpose—that she had come to
steal his gun.

"What's the title of your book," Jean said, seeing through her subterfuge. "I'll help you find it."

"I . . . don't recall . . . but I'd know it by its cover!"

"You're lying, Monique," he said. He walked into the room and shut the door behind him. "Suppose you tell me the truth now."

She sat back down on the chair behind his desk and thought about it, quickly deciding she could tell part of the truth, but not the part about the gun. "I wanted to warn you about your brother. He's out to get you. He killed my mother tonight. Shot her through the head! Then he set fire to your Pirates' Nest. It's burning right now."

"He what!" Jean roared. "Faye? Dead? Armand . . . If this is some monstrous joke on your part, Monique, I'll . . ."

"It's the truth," she said. "Look outside and see for yourself."

He did just that. Through the window overlooking the front of the house he stared down the hill. A bright orange light was flickering ominously against the black sky over Montgomery and Washington Streets. "I'll kill him!" Jean declared, banging his fist against the wooden window sill.

Jean would have to stand in line, Monique thought.

Then Jean saw a carriage approaching the house on the drive below. He watched as two people got out of the vehicle and headed up the stone path. In the light cast by gaslights flanking his walkway, Jean recognized the faces of Rose and Beau Ashton.

Beau Ashton? Where had *he* come from? He'd supposedly been shanghaied. Was there to be still more trouble tonight? His face was livid as he turned back to Monique. "How bad is the fire?" he asked.

"Real bad. Beau Ashton was going to try to put it out, but it was already out of hand."

"Ashton was at the Nest? And was going to help me?"

She nodded, watching him as the truth became clear.

Jean walked past her to the safe he kept inside a wall cabinet. He opened it and took out a rolled sheet of paper, returning with it to his desk. In the light of the candle he scribbled something on the paper and re-rolled it. Monique had no idea what it was, or what he'd written.

"With your mother dead and the Nest gone, I want you to live here with me, Monique. I trust you'll agree. I must go now. You stay here. I don't want you out on the streets anymore tonight. It's too dangerous. I have matters to attend to—one of them my murdering brother."

Monique hurried to the window after Jean left and looked down. She saw Rose and the lame southerner approaching the front porch, no doubt to tell Jean of the fire. She had to leave and quickly, before Jean returned and discovered the gun missing. He would never understand her need to take care of Armand herself and probably try to lock her up.

How could she get out of the house now—with Jean and the others downstairs? Suddenly she remembered the mare she'd tied to a tree alongside the house. The other window in the study faced that side, so she went to it and saw that the tree her horse was tied to was close enough that she could use it to climb down to the animal.

Without further thought she raised her skirts and tied them up around her waist to make it easier to descend. Then she raised the window and went out onto the ledge, caught a thick elm branch, and clambered down, jumping the last four feet to the ground. She led her horse cautiously through the trees to the gate then mounted up and headed the horse down the street toward the Barbary Coast.

Here I come, Armand, she thought. Beware or be dead! "Let him be dead soon," she prayed, "at my hands!"

*   *   *

As he left Monique in the study Jean could hardly believe what he'd just learned. Just a short while ago, when he had been with Amoreena, his world had seemed perfect. And now . . . How could it change so quickly?

It was obvious why Armand had burned the Nest, but why had he killed Faye? Had Armand finally lost his mind? Or was he so evil that he cared not who he killed? There was no reason for Faye to die—unless it was because Jean cared about her as he did. Faye had been special—a good worker, a trusted employee, a friend as well. Although he loved his Pirates' Nest, the loss of it meant little compared to losing Faye! Armand was a blood-thirsty devil, and had to be stopped!

Jean's thoughts turned to Ashton. How had he managed to get back to the Coast? Shanghaied victims didn't usually return for months, sometimes even years—if at all. Yet, if what Monique had said was true, he owed a debt to Ashton.

Jean descended the main staircase, the deed to the Pirates' Nest in his overcoat pocket. Ashton had wanted the land on Washington and Montgomery, claimed it was his, and perhaps it really was. If it weren't for Jean's feelings for Ashton's fiancée, Jean would have fought Ashton tooth and nail for the property. But Jean realized now that he wanted to marry Amoreena, so he decided to let Ashton have the Pirates' Nest—or what was left of it. Ashton had come to claim a piece of ground, and that was what he'd be getting.

His last thought before he answered the pounding on his front door was of Amoreena. He truly loved her and was now sure she loved him, but he wondered how she would react when she found out Beau was alive and had returned. Was her love for Jean strong enough to cause her to break her betrothal to Beau? Jean would soon find out.

"Jean," Rose said breathlessly as she and Beau stepped inside. "I have terrible news."

"I already know," Jean said. "My brother has killed Faye and set the Nest on fire. Monique told me."

Rose clutched Jean's arm. "I'm sorry," she said. "I know how you must feel."

Jean felt a huge lump in his throat and he forced his thoughts away from Faye and the Nest. His eyes were on Ashton as he said, "I see you made it back. Where were you?"

"Far enough, LeClair, but nothing—not even a shang-haiing—could keep me from coming back for my property!"

"And Amoreena?" Jean said.

Beau's face reddened. "Of course."

Jean dug into his coat pocket, pulled out the deed and handed it to Beau. "Take it," he said. "It's the deed to the Pirates' Nest. The Nest may be gone, but the ground isn't. It's yours."

"But . . ." Beau was speechless.

"But why?" Jean finished for him. "As a wise man once said, fair exchange is no robbery. And besides, tomorrow I may be dead if I fail in my mission tonight."

"I don't understand you, LeClair," Beau said puzzled.

Jean turned to Rose. "Take Beau upstairs to the guest bedroom. There's something I think he should see." He started for the front door.

"Aren't you coming, Jean?" Rose asked.

"I've some unfinished business. His name's Armand LeClair—and he's going to die!"

18

"JEAN? Is that you?" Amoreena said worriedly as the door knob turned. She was wearing one of Jean's robes and sitting up in bed as she awaited Jean's return. He had heard a noise downstairs and gone to investigate, but it had been at least fifteen minutes now since he'd left and she'd been just about to go looking for him.

Now she blinked as two people entered the room—one, the red-haired girl Rose, the other Beau Ashton. *Beau!*

"Beau!!" For a moment she just sat there in a state of shock.

He seemed just as shocked to see her. "Amoreena!" his mouth said, but no sound emerged.

Finally, she jumped off the bed and ran to him. He opened his arms and hugged her. He held her loosely, though, and had she not been so excited she might have noticed. Rose made a face but neither Beau nor Amoreena were watching her.

"I'm so glad you're safe!" Amoreena said. "I was

worried about you. I looked everywhere for you. Where were you?'' How frail he looked, she thought. As if he'd been ill. A strong sense of guilt touched her at the thought.

He fidgeted as he said, ''I was shanghaied and had to fight my way off the ship to get back here. I'm okay now. Rowena—Rose—has been taking care of me.''

For the first time Amoreena really noticed Beau's companion. Rose's expression was not hard to read. The girl didn't like her very much, and judging by the look of her when she was watching Beau, Amoreena could guess why. She was in love with Beau! How that had come to pass Amoreena couldn't imagine, for she had been sure of nothing in her life more than Beau's love for her. Until now.

''Rowena, would you please leave us alone for a few minutes?'' Beau said.

Rose looked for a moment as if she were about to object, but then nodded and left.

''That's an interesting robe you have on,'' Beau said casually. ''A bit too big, isn't it?''

''It's Jean's,'' Amoreena admitted. ''He's been awfully kind to me. He tried to help me find you. Then . . .''

''So you repaid him by giving him your body?'' Beau interrupted.

''What a horrible thing to say, Beau!'' She had, she knew, lain with Jean out of love not gratitude! But how could she explain that to him?

''Horrible or not, it's obviously true. How could you do it, Amoreena? How could you give that Barbary Coaster what you denied me?''

''Perhaps I wouldn't have denied you—if you'd made an effort. There were many times I wanted you, but you were aloof.''

''Aloof!'' he cried. ''You were the perfect virginal ice princess!''

"I'm hardly a statue," she declared angrily. "And what about you, Mr. Perfect? How has Rose or Rowena or whatever her name is been taking care of you?"

"I've been feverish. She nursed me and gave me medicine."

"And bedded you?" Amoreena's voice showed her fury, though it was not caused by her jealousy, but Beau's.

"No!"

Amoreena shook her head. "You're lying, Beau. I know you well enough to know that."

"I guess you do," Beau said, his face reddening. "Yes, I made love to Rowena, but . . . what does LeClair mean to you?"

Amoreena forced herself to keep her eyes on him as she replied, "Everything, Beau. I love him."

"I knew it!" Beau declared. "That's it! That's why LeClair signed over his deed! The deed is payment for taking you away from me."

"Jean *gave* you the deed? Where is he?"

"He all but threw it at me! He said he was going after his brother tonight and tomorrow he might be dead."

"Oh, Beau, he *will* be killed! Armand's a killer. We've got to do something!"

"Count me out."

"You won't help?"

"Why should I help the skunk who stole my fiancée?"

"While Rose was stealing you," Amoreena pointed out.

"Rose is a sensitive, wonderful girl."

"And you love her?"

"I think so."

"Then it's settled," she said. "Our engagement is off. I'm sorry, Beau. Really."

"No need to be. I guess it wasn't right from the start. It's best we found out now."

"I'd like to stay friends," she said. "I *do* care about you."

Beau's facade melted and he pulled her into his arms. "I care about you, too," he said. "Friends. Always."

There were tears in her eyes as she said, "Will you help Jean?"

"I don't even know his brother, so how can I help him?"

Amoreena quickly told him what Jean had told her about Armand. When Beau told her what Armand had done to Faye Langlois and the Pirates' Nest, she was shocked.

"I guess I have a reason to get Armand LeClair, too," Beau said, since I now officially own the property he burned."

Rose, who had been listening at the door, now burst in. "I'm going with you," she said. "Jean's always been good to me."

"I'm going, too," Amoreena said. "We'll get a carriage and . . ."

"Hold it, girls," Beau interrupted. "Neither of you is going anywhere. It's too dangerous. I'll go, but alone or not at all!" Beau laughed nervously. "If I'm not back by daybreak, check all the ships out of here. I might be on one again . . . bound for China!"

After Armand killed Faye Langlois and set the Pirates' Nest ablaze, he secured the beer wagon of one of his dead lieutenants and drove to the ruins of the old Spanish church on Clay Street where he had concealed kerosene and explosives. There he loaded gallon bottles of kerosene along with kegs of black powder explosives into the wagon.

As he worked, there was a ferocious, half-crazed gleam in his eye. As he was finishing, the two Rangers who had escaped with him from the meeting at the warehouse arrived on horseback.

"We just seen your brother Jean on his way to the Pirates' Nest, Armand," said Blackjack.

"He didn't look too happy," said the other, a cadaverous young man with bulging eyes, appropriately named Fisheye. "Did you start the fire there?"

"I did, and Jean'll be a damn sight less happy when I get through with him." Armand put the last jars of kerosene into a corner of the wagon. The wagon had three-foot high planked sides all around to keep barrels from rolling off, but to make sure his deadly stores couldn't be detected, Armand covered the kegs and bottles with a heavy, black tarpaulin.

"What are you going to do with all that kerosene?" Blackjack asked. "Burn down San Francisco?"

Armand cackled. "Only the Barons' part of the Coast," he declared. "If *we* can't have it, nobody can."

"Say," said Fisheye, "you told us we shouldn't destroy the Baron joints. If we burn 'em down, there ain't gonna be nothin' left to take over!"

"Let me worry about that," barked Armand. "We'll rebuild them, we will."

But Armand had no plan to rebuild anything. Right now he just wanted to destroy—destroy everything that his brother and the other Barons held of value. When he had touched a match to the mostly wooden buildings of the tinderbox Barbary Coast, he would find Jean and kill him as he had Jean's madam and one-time mistress Faye Langlois.

Now Armand ordered his Rangers to follow along as he headed the two-horse team pulling the wagon into the heart of the Barbary Coast at Pacific Street. His immediate objective was the two largest Baron-owned gambling emporiums—both of them three stories high—which stood side by side near the corner of Pacific and Kearney Streets.

There were guards in the area all around the buildings

on watch for Ranger troublemakers, so Armand parked the wagon in an alley nearby and handed each of his men a bottle of kerosene with a rolled paper wick protruding from the top of the bottle.

"Light them just before you throw them," Armand instructed, "then get back here. I'll cover you." He picked up his gun and moved through the shadows to a vantage point across Kearney Street from the buildings.

Blackjack and Fisheye looked anything but dangerous as they wandered up in front of the guards standing before the front of one of the two buildings. They sang off key and stumbled into each other's paths as if drunk, each carrying a jug which looked like corn liquor. The Coast was always crawling with drunks, so the two Baron guards paid little attention to them.

They stopped before the swinging doors of the Pink Elephant and concealed the bottles with their bodies as they lit the paper fuses. They waited only long enough to make sure the fuses were burning brightly before stepping inside and hurling them. Immediately there was an explosive whoosh as flaming fluid emerged from the bottles and spread everywhere. Panic seized the occupants of the bar just inside the door as well as the gamblers and whores in the gambling rooms. There was a general rush for the door.

Armand's men were first out, hollering "Fire, fire! The damned place is on fire!"

Pleased at the ease with which they had set their first blaze, Armand gathered his men and drove the wagon down Kearney Street between Jackson and Washington to his next destination—Jean's Rat's Nest dancehall.

The building was not as large as the Pirates' Nest. Raw, jolly strains of a trombone hung on the slight breeze and Armand wished the wind would pick up to spread his fires more rapidly.

He halted the wagon at a closed livery stable just down the street from the Rat's Nest. Four pistol-toting guards looked over anyone who approached the Nest's front doors. "The drunk act won't work here," Armand said, his eyes on the guards. "Jean has too many guards posted. Walk up to them and strike up a conversation. Keep them busy while I circle around back. I've some black powder specials for this place. When they hit, they'll explode and spray flaming kerosene all over the place. I'm going to heave them up on the porch around back. When you hear them go off, get back here."

The two Rangers made their way across the street and nodded to the guards. "Just came from the Pink Elephant," Blackjack said. "There's a fire broke out there."

"Yeah?" the guard said. "I wondered what I was smellin'."

"Somebody's settin' fires all over the Coast," Fisheye declared. ":You better watch out."

"Why the hell you think we're here!" the guard said contemptuously. "Ain't nobody gonna mess with this here place." Now the guard looked at Blackjack. "You goin' in, or what?"

Blackjack saw in the bright gaslight surrounding the entrance to the dancehall that five minutes had elapsed since Armand left. He nodded to Fisheye. "We're moving along now," he said. "Cheers."

He and Fisheye reached the street just as they heard three explosive booms. A quick glance back told them Armand had achieved his purpose. The glow of flames was already lighting the sky at the back of the building.

Off in the distance they could hear fire bells and the sound of teams of horses dragging water wagons. Behind them, as they reached the wagon, there were screams of terror as the dancehall began to empty. The guards had disappeared.

"Where's the boss?" Blackjack said. "I hope they didn't catch his ass."

"They'll never do that," Fisheye declared. "He's a slippery sumbitch! Even his brother Jean's no match for him, I'd say."

"And you're sure as hell right, Fisheye!" came the booming voice of Armand out of the shadowed street to the right. "Nobody's a match for me and don't you forget it. Now let's get out of here. Blackjack, you take the reins while I fix up some more of those black powder and kerosene cocktails."

As they pulled away from the curb, several wagonloads of haggard-looking San Francisco policemen passed them and stopped in front of the burning building. "Christ!" Armand heard one of the men say. "Another one? Pretty soon the whole damn city'll be in flames."

Pleased, Armand cackled his pleasure as Blackjack drove the wagon up the hill and away from the fires throwing light high in the sky, illuminating the bay itself and the hundreds of tall ships swaying at anchor.

At the top of the hill near Chinatown, Blackjack stopped the wagon so they could survey the pure chaos they had created. He, Fisheye, and Armand all sang out their pleasure at the realization that they had awakened the whole Barbary Coast. Or so it seemed, for the streets below them were filled with people and cabs and wagons, all of them fleeing the flames.

No one paid much attention to Armand's wagon as Blackjack drove it past the Chinese Theaters on Jackson Street and turned back onto Pacific near Stockton. There Jean owned a large, fancy, blue and white painted parlor house, next to it several other bagnios operated by various Barons.

Blackjack stopped the horses a good distance away, noting that there were a dozen or more guards posted before the parlor houses. Armand frowned. "Jean's guards'll do him no good," he declared. "We're going to bomb him from the street. See the porch off the second floor? Aim for it. Blackjack, go slow until I give you the word, then whip those horses."

He and Fisheye picked up two of the explosive jugs and prepared to light them as Blackjack urged the horses forward at a slow gait.

Jean, his emotions jumbled and confused, took his fastest horse, a purebred Arabian and rode straight to the Pirates' Nest. There wasn't a thing he could do for the blazing building. The street was crowded with onlookers, some employees, some not, all of them standing about shaking their heads as the proud Nest was devoured by the crackling flames.

"Ain't that a bitch?" the bartender said when he saw Jean. "They say your brother killed Faye. You know that?"

Jean said nothing for a moment, his eyes cold as he watched the fire. The air was smoky and stifling, burning his cheeks and making his eyes water, but he ignored his discomfort. "Where's her body?" he asked.

"Didn't they tell you, Jean? He left her in there!"

Jean was not surprised at this infamous act, but he found it hard to swallow thinking of the charred corpse which had only an hour or so ago been his friend and ally. Suddenly several explosions sounded and Jean looked up in the sky to see a burst of orange to the north. Had Armand struck again? The fire was in the direction of Pacific and Kearney and Jean without hesitation mounted his horse and headed there.

He arrived just as a bucket brigade was forming to haul in water. The Pink Elephant and Patsy Malone's place, the two largest gambling houses on the Coast, were on fire. Armand. Of course, Armand!

Where would he strike next? Where he would get the most satisfaction, Jean thought. But which of Jean's places would he attack first?

Just then still another brace of explosions rocked the Coast. Several women screamed, pointing down Kearney street. "The Rat's Nest!" someone shouted.

The Rat's Nest—Jean's dancehall! He turned his horse and raced it down the street to the Nest. The building was already a pyre, its fingers of flame reaching skyward, when he got there. He pushed his way through the crowd and learned from his guards that a number of patrons and employees had died in the fearful fire explosions.

Jean's fingers tightened around one of a pair of matched Remington six-shooters in his belt, a new rage filling his mind. Since Armand had arrived on the Coast, Amoreena Welles had been raped and nearly killed because of him, Faye was dead, and two of his Nests were ablaze. Lives of innocent people had been lost, and Armand seemed intent on destroying the Coast. He had to be stopped, and now!!

Jean tried to guess where Armand would head next. Already he had burned two gambling houses, a saloon and dancehall. There were plenty of other such establishments in the Barbary Coast and Chinatown he could strike at.

Yet . . . a thought now struck him—Armand had not yet set fire to a bordello. There were over a hundred cribs and cowyards stretching from Chinatown to the waterfront. And then there were the plush parlor houses, some of them Jean's.

That was it! Armand would next strike the parlor houses, for they were larger and more profitable to Jean and the Barons than the cribs, therefore more important. But which parlor house?

His brother would hit Jean's, of course. Jean owned

one, Birdie's place, about four blocks west on Pacific Street. Also, there were other, smaller bagnios, owned by other Barons, bordering his. An ideal objective for Armand.

Jean rode as fast as he could through the crowded streets up Dupont to Pacific. Birdie's, he now discovered, was untouched. Had he guessed wrong? Along the sidewalk in front of the four-story building stood a dozen guards. The adjacent bagnios were also well guarded and seemed safe enough.

Jean dismounted and went to talk to his guards. One pointed a rifle at Jean, but another said, "Hey, Mick, that's the boss—Jean LeClair!" The guard reddened, lowered his rifle, then apologized.

"Good work," Jean said. "Keep your rifle ready and we may yet ward off trouble."

"You think there's going to be some, Mr. LeClair?" another guard asked. "You think they'll hit here?"

"I don't know, but I believe they'll try. Keep your eyes and ears open and shoot to kill."

"Even if it's your brother?"

"Especially if it's Armand!"

As Jean finished speaking, a beer wagon turned the corner and headed up the street at a slow pace. There was no other vehicular traffic, yet it was an odd time to be delivering beer, Jean thought. He frowned, then gaped as the wagon's driver snapped the reins at his horses and they leaped ahead at a furious clip.

Then two figures stood up in the back of the wagon, in their hands what looked like flaming torches. "Hit the ground!" Jean yelled, just as the two men flung several jugs high in the air toward the porch on the second floor. But Jean did not follow his own order. Instead he pulled out his guns and began firing at the driver of the careening wagon. Behind him black powder explosives rocked the building and the screams of Birdie's girls filled the air.

The wagon raced away, as none of Jean's hurried shots struck home. But Jean ran after the wagon and got a clear shot at one of the two men in its back as he hurled an explosive jug at the neighboring bagnio. The shot burrowed into the man's chest and the jug fell to the street and exploded, sending fiery kerosene everywhere. The man toppled backward off the speeding wagon and dropped unmoving to the street.

Jean avoided the fire and raced to the man's side. He cursed to see it was not Armand. Jean had never seen the cadaverous-looking Ranger before. He ran back to get his horse, mounted and raced the animal after the fleeing wagon.

Soon he realized Armand was heading toward the last of Jean's Nests—the Crow's Nest, a melodeon on Dupont Street. Jean could see the wagon several blocks ahead, and he spurred his horse faster.

The driver halted the wagon a hundred yards up the street from the apparently unguarded Crow's Nest. The manager there, learning what had happened elsewhere, had his guards concealed, awaiting an attack.

Armand had no idea Jean was following him, but it was too dark for Jean to see what Armand was up to. Jean now approached the wagon on foot, tying his horse to a hitching post. There seemed to be no one on the wagon. Carefully, he edged his way around it until he was opposite the driver's seat. He raised his gun. A bearded figure sat upon the seat, his eyes on the Crow's Nest.

Armand had sent Blackjack across the road to see why there were no guards evident. A hundred yards farther the road was blocked by crowds of people, police, and firefighters, at one of the fires Armand had started earlier. It had spread and consumed almost an entire block. It could, Armand thought, pose a problem in getting out of there.

As Armand waited quietly on the driver's seat for

Blackjack's return, Jean surprised him—suddenly appearing alongside the wagon, his loaded six-gun pointed at his brother's belly.

"At last, brother!" Jean declared. "Your life is in my hands!"

Armand reached for his own gun, but Jean cocked the hammer, stopping him cold. Then a slow smile spread across Armand's face. "The game is not yet over, Jean," he said. "*I* still hold all the cards. Your Nests are burning; and before I'm through, the whole Coast will be only a memory."

"You're out of your bloody mind," Jean said.

"Perhaps, but what a glorious feeling!"

"It ends here, Armand," Jean said, "even if I have to kill you. I suppose I should have done that when you first came to the Coast."

"Ah, but you didn't, and that was your mistake, brother. You always were lily-livered!" Armand's smile widened and his eyes darted to a point behind Jean. "And now, Jean, you are my prisoner."

Before Jean could turn around, the barrel of Blackjack's gun came down hard on his head. He grunted, then crumpled to the ground beside the wagon.

"Good work, Blackjack. Tie him up and put him in the wagon," Armand ordered. "Later I'll have the pleasure of snuffing out his life, but first he'll witness the end of his empire."

Blackjack nodded, removing Jean's two six-shooters and stuffing them in his own belt before tying Jean's wrists and ankles.

19

MONIQUE SOON saw the patterns of Armand's attacks and spurred her horse toward the Crow's Nest on Dupont Street when it appeared to her that it would be next on Armand's hit list.

She forced herself to go on chasing her erstwhile lover in spite of a mounting fear which was invading her every fiber—a fear which had begun to shake her thirteen-year-old world when she saw Armand knock her mother unconscious, a fear that in the end she would not catch Armand, but he would catch her.

She turned her head and spat at the thought of Jean's brother, then dug her heels into the flanks of the horse.

Armand was burning the Coast, Monique thought, watching scores of people fleeing fires which were engulfing entire blocks of wooden structures, fanned by a freshening breeze from the sea to the west. He was mad—she could see that now. How had she ever been able to love such a monster? Surely Armand had never done anything he could take pride in. Unless he took pride in killing.

Yet Monique had herself been not a great deal better than Armand, she now realized. In the past her greatest joy was hurting people—her teachers, her classmates, her mother, her father. Jean? Jean's only crime had been to refuse to make love to a little girl who was his own daughter. And she had hated him for it!

How, she wondered, could she have been so evil and not realized it? Evil and unfair, too. Unfair to Jean and unfair to her mother.

She could have cried and only a great effort of will forced back the tears. She would avenge her mother in spite of her fears. In spite of the fact that she was but a thirteen year old pitted against a monster. She would do it, somehow.

And then . . . then what? Did she have a future? With her mother gone and . . . She bit her lip. Of course she had a future. She still had her father, and she was damned if she was going to let his brother get the drop on Jean!

Now she reached Dupont Street and saw a beer wagon parked along the dark side of the road not far from the Crow's Nest. If Armand were here, she thought, he might well have a wagon like that, with high sides to conceal his killers. She must be careful.

She left her horse tied to a hitching post near a small general store on the corner and made her way on foot toward the wagon. Then she stopped, hearing voices. A familiar laugh. She strained her eyes and saw two men near the rear of the wagon. They were talking. She edged up closer, staying in the shadows of buildings to the right. Then she saw him! Armand! The other man was the one called Blackjack, who had captured her and slugged Luke.

She felt in her pocket for Jean's Cold .44 and smiled as her fingers closed around the cold metal. What was it Luke called a gun? An equalizer? Well, at least it gave her a chance against Armand. But could she shoot them both? Blackjack, too?

She had her doubts. Luke had showed her how to fan a six-gun, but she wasn't at all sure she could do it. Not now. So what to do? She had to surprise them. But how? As she wondered how, the two men left the wagon and disappeared. She caught sight of them running toward the Crow's Nest a moment later. No doubt they were going to attack it. Could she wait in the wagon and surprise them when they returned? She could try, and she would!

She climbed in the rear of the twenty-foot wagon and peered into the blackness. She saw nothing but canvas-covered barrels and bottles, so she moved toward the front behind the driver's seat. Muffled sounds immediately caught her attention. She crept closer, then saw the helpless figure of a man, bound and gagged, lying in the back. She gaped, for the man was her father—Jean LeClair. Armand had captured him!

Suddenly the Crow's Nest erupted in two fierce explosions, then yells and gun shots. Monique knelt by her father's side. "Jean!" she said, "it's me. I'm going to free you. Armand and his friend just attacked the Crow's Nest." She pulled the gag from his mouth and began working on the rope binding his wrists together.

"Monique!" he said. "How in hell did you get here? I told you to stay home."

"Be glad I'm here," she said, working desperately on knots as she spoke. "Armand killed my mother and now, it seems, he wants to kill my father! Well, I'll not let him."

But she heard more shouts and shots outside and the sound of running feet. "They're coming back," she said softly. "I'll crouch behind you. It's dark in here and they'll be in a hurry to get going, so they won't look too closely."

"Get out of here, Monique. Armand will kill you."

"Shhh," she said, holding her hand gently to his mouth. "I'm staying with you." She went back to work on his knots, but kept her eyes on the open end of the wagon, her body concealed from view by Jean's.

Now they heard Armand cursing, then: "Get this rig moving!" Armand instructed Blackjack.

Monique felt the shock as Blackjack climbed up on the driver's seat behind her. Then Armand jumped into the back of the wagon and peered into the darkness at his brother's trussed up body. The wagon began to roll a split second later, as Blackjack took the reins, released the brake, and whipped the horses. Armand turned away from his brother to deal with one of the Crow's Nest guards, who stood in the middle of the street, firing a six-gun wildly at the swerving wagon. Armand's first, carefully-aimed shot dropped the man in his tracks.

Monique had little experience with knots and was having problems freeing Jean's hands. She had partially freed them, however, and Jean could now complete the task himself. As she tried to loosen the rope on Jean's ankles, she could see the black figure of Armand standing in the back of the swaying wagon and hear his laughter as the vehicle left the newest scene of destruction he'd caused.

She shrank back in terror when Armand suddenly wheeled around and stalked toward the dark front of the enclosed part of the beer wagon where his prisoner lay. His eyes had become accustomed to the darkness by now and he stopped short as he saw her.

"Well I'll be damned!" he said. "And what have we here?"

Monique ceased her attempt to free Jean's ankles, pulled the gun from her skirt pocket and aimed it at Armand. "It's me, you bastard," she declared.

"Monique? Where did you get a gun? And why are you . . ."

"You killed my mother, Armand! I found her the way you left her—with her head blown off!"

Jean worked frantically to wrest his hands free so he could help Monique.

Armand's gun had been in his belt, but now he pulled it out and waved it at Monique, ignoring the girl's weapon. "I'll kill you, Armand," she said.

"Not now you won't, you nasty little child," he replied, and reached across Jean's body to grab her gun. She tried to fire it before he took it away, but the gun remained silent. She had forgotten to cock it!

But now Armand was taken by surprise by Jean, who leaped off the floor and threw his weight into his brother, knocking him off balance and the guns clattering to the wagon floor.

"What the hell's going on back there?" yelled Blackjack from the driver's seat. He half-turned to see Armand go down under Jean's onslaught. They were a long way from the Crow's Nest by now and Blackjack pulled the horses to a stop, set the brake. Then he yanked out his own gun and brought it to bear on Jean, who had jumped on Armand and was rolling around on the wagon floor with him. Each brother had his hands on the other's throat, but neither was able to exert enough strength to put the other out.

"That's enough, Jean!" ordered Blackjack, his finger on the trigger. "Get your hands off him or you're dead."

But now Monique grabbed at the gun and wrested it out of the Ranger's hand. It went off, but the shot flew wild as the gun fell to the floor. Monique scrambled in the darkness after it—and was immediately leaped upon by Blackjack.

"Oh, no, you don't, you little minx," he bellowed, recognizing her. He pinned her to the floor with his weight and groped around them for his weapon.

But Monique had accomplished her purpose, for she could feel the full length of the long gun beneath her, pressing into her back, but out of Blackjack's reach as well.

Jean and Armand were evenly matched. They fought furiously, but neither could gain a clear advantage until Armand surprised Jean by butting him with his head, then following by standing and kicking Jean in the jaw with a heavy boot. Then he picked up his unconscious brother and hurled him out of the wagon.

Monique screamed when she saw Armand best his brother and start to throw him out of the wagon. ''No! No!'' she cried, ''you can't do that!''

''The hell he can't,'' replied Blackjack, who had given up looking for the gun and was pawing at Monique's breasts as he kept her pinned.

''Get your hands off her, Blackjack,'' Armand now commanded. ''She's my property. I'll deal with her.''

''Aw, shit, Armand. She don't mean nothin' to you. Anyway, I was just havin' a little fun. She's nice and soft and . . .''

''Get off! Now!!''

Monique had been working her right arm beneath her while Blackjack was having his ''fun'' and finally got her fingers on the gun as Blackjack's weight came off her. She thumbed back the hammer, yanked the gun out and fired at the Ranger. Her bullet struck Blackjack squarely in the chest and he was dead before he crumbled to the floor.

Still on the floor, Monique re-cocked the pistol and aimed it at Armand, who was about to rush her. He stopped in his tracks. She staggered to her feet and stood, swaying a little, in front of him.

''It looks as if Blackjack paid dearly to fondle you,'' Armand said, his eyes on the blouse his man had torn open and the plump white flesh revealed by it.

"I'll kill you!" Monique sputtered angrily.

Armand shrugged. "When you pull the trigger, little one, you had better be accurate, for with my dying breath I will choke you senseless."

She ordered him to move to the end of the wagon and followed him there. Lying motionless in the roadway behind the wagon was Jean, his ankles still partly tied. "Jump down, Armand, and pick up your brother. Bring him back here."

"And if I will not?"

"Then die right now!" she snapped.

"Very well," he said, and jumped nimbly to the ground.

She followed, knowing if she did not, her chances of hitting him with a shot were slim. At Jean's side, he bent and picked his brother up, throwing him over his shoulder like a sack of potatoes.

She backed toward the wagon, motioning Armand to follow. A long, low groan came from Jean as Armand carried him toward the wagon. As they reached it, Armand surprised Monique by throwing Jean at her. She tried to dodge, but could not. The gun exploded in her hand as she fell to the ground beneath Jean's weight.

Before she could extricate herself from Jean's dead weight, Armand had raced around to the front of the wagon, jumped up in the driver's seat, and started the horses moving.

Monique stared at the departing wagon, then at Jean, a huge bruise on his temple, another discoloring his jaw. Then she gasped, for there was blood soaking his shirt from a bullet wound in the fleshy part of his left arm. Her bullet must have creased him! She tore a piece of cloth from the remains of her blouse, wadded it up and held it against his wound. Then, hugging his face to her breast she began to cry softly.

*   *   *

Beau Ashton spent more than an hour on the burning Barbary Coast seeking Jean and his brother Armand. He never found them. Instead, he found trouble.

Riding one of the horses from Jean's stable, he went from fire to fire, like Jean and Monique before him, figuring that it was Armand who was torching the Baron places. But his knowledge of the Coast was limited and there were Ranger looters everywhere—and men with rifles defending the Barons' establishments, not to mention the milling throngs which surrounded the burning Coast dives.

When bullets began whizzing past his head near a place called the Crow's Nest, Beau wheeled his horse around and began retreating from the Coast to ride back toward Telegraph Hill. He could do nothing for Jean LeClair if he couldn't find the man, he thought. Amoreena would have to be satisfied with that, for Beau had tried hard to fulfill his promise to her.

As he rode up a hilly street east of the waterfront, he heard a shot coming from the area ahead of him, then saw a large beer wagon drawn by two horses go racing away.

He stopped and debated whether to skirt the area. There was no more shooting, however, and he was on the most direct route to Telegraph Hill, so he resumed his ride up the street.

The road was wider hereabouts and there were a row of Mexican fandango houses at his left, a cluster of high-class brothels to his right—the northern limits of the Barbary Coast. The fandango houses had shut down early because of the trouble generated by Armand LeClair, but at least one of the bagnios was busy, for two small rigs were parked out front, each with a brace of handsome roans nibbling at a hopper containing feed.

Beau paid them little attention, his eyes on the spot where the wagon had been. There was someone sitting on the side of the road, he saw as he came closer. He slowed his horse, then stopped when he saw who it was. It was Monique—and someone was with her. It was LeClair—Jean, not Armand.

Before he could question her, Monique told him what had happened, then added, "I've an idea Armand's headed for Telegraph Hill to blow up Jean's house. He's got enough explosives on the wagon to blow up all of San Francisco!"

Beau swore. "Rose and Amoreena are there. I can't let him do it!"

"What about us? You can't just leave us here like this."

Beau hesitated only a moment. "There are a bunch of bagnios over there," he said, pointing. "I saw a couple of rigs tied up in front of one. If you hurry, you can borrow one."

Then he dug his heels in the horse's flanks and spurred him away at a gallop.

Monique encountered no difficulty in stealing the rig from the bagnio. When she returned Jean was sitting up, trying to regain his wits. Monique had stopped the bleeding from his flesh wound with the gauze from her gown, but Armand's butt and kick had given him a huge ache in his head. Swiftly she told him that Blackjack was dead, but Armand was probably headed for Telegraph Hill.

In spite of the pain he was in, Jean regained his feet without help and climbed onto the driver's seat of the rig. Monique sat beside him as he moved the horses out.

Beau cut across several estates to get to Jean's mansion ahead of Armand and did—arriving just as the beer wagon reached the lower drive.

Beau dismounted, picked up the Remington rifle he had taken from Jean's stable before he left and was limping toward the front of the house when the wagon rounded a bend in the drive and sped up toward the house. Beau raised the rifle and aimed hurriedly at the driver. "Stop right there, LeClair!" he roared.

In answer Armand dove for the floorboard but wheeled the horses out of the driveway and headed them straight for Beau.

Beau fired, then dove for the safety of a tree beside the drive. He was unsuccessful in both actions, his shot missing Armand, his lame-legged dive just too slow. The last, however, was almost fatal as one of Armand's horses stepped on his bad leg. He doubled over in agony and left the rifle where it lay as he dragged himself out of the path of the wheels.

Rose and Amoreena appeared at the front door and both screamed when they saw what was happening.

Now Armand pulled up the team of horses in front of the mansion. He stood, bowed deeply, then laughed uproariously. "I'd run for my life, ladies, if I were you," he declared, "for my brother's mansion is about to join the rest of the Barbary Coast—in flames."

Armand reached into the back of the wagon and secured one of his explosive jugs. He held the jug up high, and was about to strike a match when Jean and Monique arrived in the borrowed rig.

Jean had the reins in his left hand and the colt .44 in the other as the rig raced up the drive. He pulled at the reins to stop the horses just as Armand lit the fuse of his deadly explosive cocktail and hurled it toward them.

"Jump!" Jean yelled at Monique.

Then they were both sprawling in the hedges at the side of the driveway as the bottle exploded and sent glass and flame in every direction. The horses attached to the now-flaming rig bolted and tried to get past the big beer wagon blocking their path, but succeeded only in wedging the front of the rig against the rear of the wagon.

Jean stared at the wagon, which was already catching

fire. He untangled himself from the hedges, ignoring the ache in his head, the soreness of his left arm, and refocused on Armand, who was reaching for another deadly jug.

"That's enough, Armand," he yelled. "Better get off that wagon in a hurry before it blows up."

"Your concern touches me, brother," Armand said.

"Don't mistake my meaning, Armand," Jean replied. "I intend to see you dead. You sent me to jail once, now I'm going to personally send you to hell!"

Armand scowled, looked at the back of the wagon, where the flames were getting near a barrel of black powder. He picked up his last jug and jumped down from the driver's seat. "I'm unarmed," Armand said as Jean cocked the hammer of his pistol. "You won't shoot a man who can't defend himself. I know you."

"You *knew* me," Jean corrected. "Thanks to you, I'm just as immoral as you."

Armand didn't believe it. "Go ahead, Jean," he taunted, "shoot me."

Jean's fingers tightened on the trigger, but he didn't pull it. He wanted to. Oh, did he want to! This was a cold-hearted vermin who had murdered Faye Langlois in cold blood. It should be easy for him to put an end to Armand's life. But it wasn't. He cursed and lowered the gun.

And that's when Armand made his try. He produced a gun he had reclaimed from the back of his wagon on his way to Telegraph Hill, cocked it and fired at Jean, just as Beau roared a warning from where he still lay, writhing in pain.

Jean dodged to his left, leveled his gun at Armand and put a shot straight through his brother's heart. There was a look of disbelief on Armand's face as he pitched face forward on the ground clutching at his chest.

Then they all ran, as the beer wagon became a sea of

flame. Rose helped Beau hobble behind the stable and Amoreena and Monique ran with Jean behind the house.

When the black powder exploded, the boom could be heard in the middle of the Barbary Coast, where the war that Armand LeClair had waged against his brother and the Barons continued.

20

THE FIRES raged for nearly twelve hours and by the next afternoon more than half the Barbary Coast had become a steaming rubble of smouldering embers. The Barons and Rangers had fought it out well into the daylight hours. Many lives had been lost on both sides, but the battles changed little—the Barons were still masters of the Coast.

Some things had changed, however. A radical change had taken place in Monique, who had clung to her father after he'd killed Armand, telling him, "You're all I have now. I'm going to be a different girl from now on. You'll see. I'll stay out of trouble . . . and if you don't mind, I'd like to call you father."

From his home Jean watched the beginnings of the cleanup of the Coast. He sat in a cushioned velvet chair in front of the floor-to-ceiling windows looking down at the smoking city. It would take months, perhaps even years, to rebuild the businesses, saloons, bordellos, even schools and churches which had burned to the ground. Nothing

could, of course, be done about the lives lost in the
flames.

Another who had changed was Jean. It was a greed and
vengeance borne of captivity that had led him to build his
Barbary Coast empire. He had thought wealth was all-
important—that the more he made the better a man he'd
become. Now he realized that though he had made his
money—enough to last two lifetimes—something was
lacking. Always he had despised himself in a way, knowing it had been his own immorality and lack of ideals
which had carried him to the top and kept him there in an
immoral world where ideals ran second to just about
everything.

Now Jean wanted only to start again, in a new land far
from the Barbary Coast. And with the woman he loved.

Sensing his thoughts, Amoreena came up to stand alongside him. He stood and took her into his arms. He pointed
out a tall, majestic clipper ship rocking at anchor at a pier
far below. "That's the first ship I bought when I came to
the Coast—we called it Sydney-town then," he told her.
"It's my wedding gift to you. After our wedding tomorrow,
it'll take the three of us—you, me, and Monique—anywhere
you want to go."

Amoreena's eyes lit with pleasure. "All the way to
Europe?" she asked.

"Even to France—if you still want to go there."

With all the love in her heart, she kissed him. But as she
pulled away, her eyes fell upon his bandaged arm. "Does
it still hurt?" she asked.

He shook his head. "I'll be all right. It's Beau's leg I'm
worried about. He got quite a gash from those horses'
hooves."

"I know, Jean, and you're a darling to care. But the
doctor says he'll be fine in a week or so. Rose is taking
good care of him upstairs. She missed her calling, Jean,

she should have been a nurse! Or perhaps it's just that she loves him.''

"Does it bother you that Beau has her?''

She met his eyes. "For many years I was sure I loved Beau, but I know now that what I felt was just a deep friendship. Since Beau's my friend, can a friend deny him his happiness?''

"You're quite a lady, Amoreena.''

She nestled deeper into his arms, comfortable as never before. "I just hope Beau can handle the job he's agreed to take on for you in the new Barbary Coast. Rebuilding your establishments and managing them will be taxing.''

"He'll do fine,'' Jean declared.

"What makes you so sure?''

Outside the sun was setting, leaving in its wake a breathtaking kaleidoscope of color, and Jean, in answer, pointed to the city below. "In the years I've lived here, I've seen the Coast conceived, grow, prosper, and now wither. But the adventurous spirit of the Barbary Coasters will never die. Soon the Coast will be reborn and with it the dreams of a new generation of ambitious young men like Beau Ashton.''

"Let's hope,'' Amoreena said, "that the new breed will have learned something from the old and engage in no more wars.''

Jean poured each of them an early glass of wedding champagne. "A toast,'' he said, clinking glasses with hers, "to the new Barbary Coasters!''

. . . AND MORE!

Twenty-second in the series:
THE GUNFIGHTERS
The saga of the men who lived and died by the gun—
of a legendary lawman, his young sidekick and
the woman who loves them, on a rendezvous with fate

Twenty-fourth in the series:
THE DONNER PEOPLE
Death, degradation—and worse—lay in wait for the
people of the accursed Donner-Reed wagon train at a
storm-battered pass in the high Sierras

Twenty-sixth in the series:
THE NIGHTRIDERS
Two gallant men and one fiery woman are caught up in the
agony of the fallen South, as crosses burned and
the masked "nights" of the KKK rode in vengeance

Twenty-eighth in the series:
THE EXPRESS RIDERS
Two headstrong brothers, one riding with the Pony Express,
find themselves threatened by a scheming beauty's web of
intrigue and passion

Thirtieth in the series:
THE SOLDIERS OF FORTUNE
Two gentleman adventurers from Tennessee find action,
passion and treachery with the mysterious
"Liberator of Nicaragua"

DON'T MISS A SINGLE EXCITING TITLE
IN THIS BESTSELLING SERIES
—ON SALE AT BOOKSTANDS EVERYWHERE
FROM DELL/BRYANS